"I am so sure that  **gasp with desire, s... you explode with p... am wrong, Laney, ... million dollars."**

Ten million dollars.

The amount staggered her. She thought of what it would mean. She could go back to New Orleans and hire full-time caregivers for her father. Her grandmother, who'd worked her fingers to the bone for fifty years, could finally relax and enjoy her life. Laney could be with the family she loved.

"But the amount I'll pay if I lose doesn't matter." Kassius looked down at her, his eyes glinting wickedly in the moonlight. "Because I intend to win."

Laney licked her lips. "Just for the sake of argument, if you do make me…um…if you prove I'm not frigid, then what would you want in return?"

"Beyond the sweet prize of your body?"

He moved suddenly, leaning over the bed, running his wide hand in a sensual stroke down her body. His expression was deadly serious.

"If I cannot give you pleasure, Laney, I will give you ten million dollars and you will walk out of here a wealthy woman. But if I make you explode with joy you will surrender everything. You will allow me to take possession of your body and fill you with my child. You will be mine—forever."

Wedlocked!

Conveniently wedded, passionately bedded!

Whether there's a debt to be paid,
a will to be obeyed or a business to be saved…

She's got no choice but to say, 'I do!'

But these billionaire bridegrooms have got another
think coming if they think marriage will be easy…

Soon their convenient brides become the object
of an inconvenient desire!

Find out what happens after the vows in

Trapped by Vialli's Vows
by Chantelle Shaw

The Billionaire's Defiant Acquisition
by Sharon Kendrick

One Night to Wedding Vows
by Kim Lawrence

Wedded, Bedded, Betrayed
by Michelle Smart

Expecting a Royal Scandal
by Caitlin Crews

Look out for more *Wedlocked!* stories
coming soon!

BABY OF
HIS REVENGE

BY
JENNIE LUCAS

MILLS & BOON

First Published in Great Britain 2016
By Mills & Boon, an imprint of HarperCollins*Publishers*
1 London Bridge Street, London, SE1 9GF

© 2016 Jennie Lucas

ISBN: 978-0-263-92133-5

Our policy is to use papers that are natural, renewable and recyclable
products and made from wood grown in sustainable forests. The logging
and manufacturing processes conform to the legal environmental
regulations of the country of origin.

Printed and bound in Spain
by CPI, Barcelona

USA TODAY bestselling author **Jennie Lucas**'s parents owned a bookshop and she grew up surrounded by books, dreaming about faraway lands. A fourth-generation Westerner, she went east at sixteen to boarding school on scholarship, wandered the world, got married, then finally worked her way through college before happily returning to her home town. A 2010 RITA® Award finalist and 2005 Golden Heart® winner, she lives in Idaho with her husband and children.

Books by Jennie Lucas

Mills & Boon Modern Romance

A Ring for Vincenzo's Heir
Nine Months to Redeem Him
Uncovering Her Nine-Month Secret
The Sheikh's Last Seduction
To Love, Honour and Betray
A Night of Living Dangerously
The Virgin's Choice
Bought: The Greek's Baby

One Night With Consequences

A Ring for Vincenzo's Heir

At His Service

The Consequences of That Night

Princes Untamed

Dealing Her Final Card
A Reputation for Revenge

One Night In...

Reckless Night in Rio

Unexpected Babies

Sensible Housekeeper, Scandalously Pregnant

Visit the Author Profile page at millsandboon.co.uk for more titles.

To Pete, who inspires me every day.

CHAPTER ONE

"I SHOULD FIRE you right now, Laney." Her boss glared at her. "Anyone would love to have your job. All of them less stupid than you!"

"I'm sorry!" Laney May Henry had tears in her eyes as she saw the hot coffee she'd just spilled on her boss's prized white fur coat, which had been hanging on the back of a chair. Leaning forward, she desperately tried to clean the stain with the hem of her faded cotton shirt. "It wasn't..."

"Wasn't what?" Her boss, a coldly beautiful American-born countess who had been married and divorced four times, narrowed her carefully made-up eyes. "What are you trying to imply?"

It wasn't my fault. But Laney took a deep breath. She knew there was no point in telling her boss that her friend had deliberately tripped her as she'd brought them coffee. No point, because her boss had seen the whole thing and had laughed along with her friend as Laney tripped with a noisy *oof*, sprawling helter-skelter across the carpet of the lavish Monaco flat. For her boss, it had all been a good joke—until she saw the coffee hit her full-length fur coat.

"Well?" Mimi du Plessis, the Comtesse de Fourcil, demanded. "I'm waiting."

Laney dropped her gaze. "I'm sorry, Madame la Comtesse."

Her boss turned to her friend, dressed in head-to-toe Dolce and Gabbana on the other side of the white leather sofa, smoking. "She's stupid, isn't she?"

"Very stupid," the friend agreed, daintily puffing out a smoke ring.

"So hard to get good help these days."

Biting her lip hard, Laney stared down at the white rug. Two years ago, she'd been hired to organize Mimi du Plessis's wardrobe, keep track of her social engagements and run errands. But Laney had quickly discovered why the salary was so good. She was on call day and night, often needing to work twenty-hour days and endure her boss's continual taunts. Every day of the last two years, Laney had fantasized about quitting and going back to New Orleans. But she couldn't. Her family desperately needed the money, and she loved her family.

"Take the fur and get out of here. I can't stand to look at your pathetic little face another moment. Get the coat to the cleaners and heaven help you if it's not back before the New Year's Eve gala tonight." Dismissing her, the comtesse turned back to her friend, resuming their earlier conversation. "I think tonight Kassius Black will finally make his move."

"You think so?" her friend said eagerly.

The comtesse smiled, like a smug Persian cat with a golden bowl of overpriced cream. "He's already wasted millions of euros giving anonymous loans to my boss. But the way things are going, my boss's company will be bankrupt within the year. I finally told Kassius that if he wants my attention, he should stop throwing money down the drain and just ask me out."

"What did he say?"

"He didn't deny it."

"So he's taking you to the ball tonight?"

"Not exactly…" She shrugged. "But I was tired of waiting for him to make his move. It's obvious he must be wildly in love with me. And I'm ready to get married again."

"Married?"

"Why not?"

Her friend pursed her lips. "Darling, yes, Kassius Black

is rich as sin and dangerously handsome, but who *is* he? Where does he come from? Who are his people? No one knows."

"Who cares?" Mimi du Plessis, who liked to brag about how she could trace her family history back not only to the Mayflower, but to Charlemagne, now shrugged it off. "I'm fed up with aristocrats without a single dollar to their name. My last husband, the comte, bled me dry. Sure, I got his title—but after the divorce I had to get a job. Me! *A job!*" She shuddered at the indignity, then brightened. "But once I'm Kassius Black's wife, I'll never have to worry about working again. He's the tenth-richest man in the world!"

Her friend elegantly blew out another smoke ring. "Ninth. His real estate investments have exploded."

"Even better. I know he'll try to kiss me at midnight. I can't wait. You can just tell any wife of his would be well satisfied in bed..." Her sharp face narrowed when she saw Laney still hesitating unhappily by the sofa, heavy coat in her arms. "Well? What are you still doing here?"

"I'm sorry, madame, but I need your credit card."

"Give you my card? That's a joke. Pay for it yourself. And get us more coffee. Hurry up, you idiot!"

Beneath the weight of the white fur coat, Laney took the elevator downstairs and trudged through the lobby of the elegant Hôtel de Carillon onto the most expensive street in Monaco, filled with designer shops, overlooking the famous Casino de Monte Carlo and the Mediterranean Sea. As she walked out of the exclusive residential hotel, the doorman gave her an encouraging smile. "Ça va, Laney?"

"Ça va, Jacques," she replied, mustering up a smile. But the heavy gray clouds seemed as leaden as her heart.

It had just stopped raining. The street was wet and so were the expensive sports cars revving by, along with the sodden-looking tourists crowded together in packs on the sidewalk. In late December, the winter afternoons were short and the nights were long. But that only added to the delight of New Year's Eve. It was a popular time for people, especially wealthy yacht owners, to visit Monaco and enjoy exclusive parties, designer shops and world-class restaurants.

Laney comforted herself with the thought that at least the rain had stopped. Aside from her worries about the coat getting wet, she'd run out of the building too fast to grab her coat and just wore a plain white shirt, loose khakis and sensible clogs with her dark hair pulled up in a ponytail—the uniform of the servant class. But even without rain, the air was damp and chilly, and the sun was weak. Shivering, she held the fur coat tightly in her arms, both to protect it from being splashed by a passing car and to keep herself warm.

She didn't like her boss's fur coats much. They reminded her too much of the pets she'd loved growing up at her grandmother's house outside New Orleans, the sweet, dopey old hound dogs and proudly independent cats. They'd comforted her through some heartbreaking days as a teenager. Thinking of them reminded Laney of everything else she missed about home. A lump rose in her throat. It had been two years since she'd last seen her family.

Don't think about it. She took a deep breath. The fur in her arms was bulky and big, and Laney was on the petite side, so she shifted the coat over her shoulder to look down at her smartphone.

But as she scouted out the nearest fur cleaner, she was suddenly jostled by a large group of tourists stampeding by, blindly following their guide's flag up ahead. Stumbling forward, Laney tripped off the curb and fell forward into the street. Turning with a gasp, as if in slow motion, she saw a red sports car barreling down on her!

There was a loud squeal of tires, and Laney felt a surge of regret that she was going to die, at twenty-five, far from home and everyone she loved, holding her boss's dirty fur coat, run over by a car. She just wished she could tell her grandmother and her father one last time that she loved them...

She closed her eyes and held her breath as she felt the impact. The car knocked her over the hood and she flew, then fell hard on something soft.

The air was knocked out of her lungs, and she wheezed for breath as everything went dark.

"Damn you, what were you thinking!"

It was a man's voice. It didn't sound like the voice of God, either, so she couldn't be dead. Laney's eyes fluttered open.

A man was standing over her, looking down. His face and body were hidden in shadow, but he was tall, broadshouldered. And, it seemed, angry.

A crowd gathered around them as the man knelt beside her.

"Why did you run out in the street like that?" The man was dark-haired, dark-eyed, handsome. "I could have killed you!"

Laney suddenly recognized him. Coughing, she sat up abruptly. A wave of dizziness went through her, and she put her hand on her head, feeling sick.

"Be careful, damn you!"

"Kassius—Black," she croaked.

"Do I know you?" he said tersely.

Why would he? She was nobody. "No..."

"Are you injured?"

"No," she whispered, then realized to her shock that it was true. Looking down, she saw the fur had blocked her impact against the street like a soft pillow. Incredulously, she touched the nose of the wildly sleek and expensive sports car pressing into her shoulder. He must have stopped on a dime.

"You're in shock." Without asking permission, he ran his hands over her. He was no doubt searching for broken bones, but having him touch her—stroking her arms, her legs, her shoulders—caused heat to flood through Laney. Her cheeks burned, and she pushed him away.

"I'm fine."

He looked at her skeptically.

She look a shuddering breath and tried to smile. "Really."

Of all the billionaires in Monaco—and there were tons—she'd just inconvenienced the one her boss wanted, this mysterious and dangerous man. If the comtesse found out Laney had caused *him* problems, on top of everything else…

Laney tried to stand up.

"Wait," he barked. "Take a breath. This is serious."

"Why?" She glanced back at the glossy fender of the car. "Did I hurt your Lamborghini?"

"Funny." His voice was dry. He was looking at her narrowly. "What were you thinking, jumping in front of me?"

"I tripped."

"You should have been more careful."

"Thanks." Rubbing her elbow, she winced. On the two occasions she'd seen the man before, while he was having lunch meetings with the comtesse, Laney had vaguely thought Kassius Black must be an American raised in Europe, or possibly a European raised in America. But there was a strange inflection in his voice that didn't suit either theory. In fact, it was an accent she recognized well. But it obviously wasn't possible. She rubbed her forehead. She must have hit it harder than she thought. "I'll try to take your advice in the future."

Rising to his feet, he looked around at the crowd that

had formed a semicircle around them in the street. "Is there a doctor?" No one moved, even when he repeated the request in rapid succession in three other languages. He pulled his phone from his pocket. "I'm calling an ambulance."

"Um…" She bit her lip. "That's nice and all, but I'm afraid I don't have time for that."

He looked incredulous. "You *don't have time* for an ambulance?"

She gave herself a quick look for gushing blood or maybe a broken leg she hadn't noticed. But the worst that seemed to have happened was that she'd had the wind knocked out of her and had gotten a little lump on her forehead. She touched it. "I'm on an urgent errand for my boss."

Wincing a little, she pushed herself off the street and rose to her feet. He reached out his hand to help her. When their hands touched, she felt electricity course through her body, making her shake all over. She looked up at him. He was nearly an entire foot taller than she was, handsome and powerful and sleek in his dark suit. She could only imagine what a pathetic mess she looked like right now. Talk about *noblesse oblige*.

She dropped his hand.

"Well, thanks for stopping your car," she muttered. "I'd better get going…"

"Who's your boss?"

"Mimi du Plessis, the Comtesse de Fourcil."

"Mimi?" Abruptly, the man stepped closer, searching her face. Recognition dawned. "Wait. I know you now. The little mouse who scampers around Mimi's flat, fetching her slippers and finding her phone."

Laney blushed. "I'm her assistant."

"What was her errand, so important that you nearly died for it?"

"But I didn't die."

"Lucky for you."

"Lucky," she breathed as she tilted her head back. Her mind felt oddly blank as she looked up at him. Up close, he was even more handsome. And his face had character, with an interesting scar across one of his high cheekbones. His aquiline nose was slightly uneven at the top, as if it had been broken when he was young and not properly re-aligned. This man hadn't been born rich—that much was for sure. He was nothing like the wealthy playboys Mimi had gone through like tissue paper since her divorce. This man was a fighter. A thug, even. And for some reason, as he looked down at her, he made Laney feel dizzy—as if the world had just moved beneath her sensible shoes.

His gaze sharpened. "So what was the errand, little mouse," he repeated, "so important you were willing to die for it?"

"Her coat—" That reminded her. Looking around for it, she gave an anguished cry.

The expensive white fur was now soaked in a muddy puddle on the street, ripped to shreds where one of his tires had gone through it.

Laney took a deep breath.

"I'm so fired," she whispered. Her head was starting to clang with headache as she knelt and picked it up. "She told me to get it cleaned before the ball tonight. Now it's ruined."

"It's not your fault."

"But it is," she said miserably. "First I spilled coffee on it. Then I wasn't paying attention where I was walking. I was too busy looking at my phone to get directions to a cleaner... My phone!"

Looking around wildly, she saw it had been crushed beneath the back wheel of his car. Going to it, she lifted its crumpled form into her hands. Tears rose in her eyes as she looked at its shattered face, now crushed into un-recognizable metal.

She wouldn't let herself cry. She couldn't.

Then just when she thought things couldn't get worse, the gray clouds burst above them, and it started to rain.

It was too much. She felt cold raindrops pummeling her messed-up hair and chilled, bruised body. It was the final straw. Against her will, she started to laugh.

Kassius Black looked at her like she was crazy. "What's so funny?"

"I'll definitely lose my job for this," she gasped, hardly able to breathe for laughing.

"And you're happy about it?"

"No," she said, wiping her eyes. "Without my job, my family won't be able to pay rent next month or my dad pay for his medications. It's not funny at all."

Kassius's eyes turned cool. "I'm sorry."

"Me, too," she replied, thinking what a strange conversation this was to have with the ninth-richest man in the world. Or was it the tenth?

A car honked, and she jumped. They both turned to look. The crowds of people around them had already started to disperse now it was clear she wasn't going to bleed out and die on the street. But his car was still holding up traffic. The drivers of the similarly expensive cars lined up behind it were starting to get annoyed.

Kassius's jaw clenched as he made a rude gesture to them then turned back to her. "If you're not hurt and don't want to see a doctor—" he watched her carefully "—then I guess I will be on my way."

"'Bye," Laney said, still mourning her broken phone. "Thanks for not killing me."

Turning away from him, she dropped the fragments of metal in a corner trash can. Slinging the ruined fur over her shoulder, Laney started to walk desolately down the sidewalk in the pouring rain. She'd go back to the Hôtel de Carillon and ask Jacques if he knew a fur cleaner that could perform magic. Oh, who was she kidding? Magic? He'd need to turn back time.

She felt someone grab her arm. Looking up in surprise, she saw Kassius, his handsome face grim. He said through gritted teeth, "All right, how much do you want?"

"How much of what?"

"Just get in my car."

"I don't need a ride—I'm just going back to the Hôtel de Carillon."

"To do what?"

"Give my boss her fur back and let her yell at me and then fire me."

"Sounds like fun." Lifting a dark eyebrow, he ground out, "Look. It's obvious you threw yourself in front of my car for a reason. I don't know why you're not doing the obvious thing and immediately asking for money, but whatever your game is—"

"There's no game!"

"I can solve your problem. About the coat."

Laney sucked in her breath. "You know how to get it fixed? In time for the ball tonight?"

"Yes."

"I would be so grateful!"

His voice was curt. "Get in."

By this time, the cars behind them weren't just honking, but the drivers were yelling impolite suggestions.

Kassius held open the passenger door, and she climbed in, still clinging to the ruined, muddy, ripped fur coat. He climbed into the driver's seat beside her, and without bothering to respond to the furious drivers behind them, he drove off with a low roar of his sleek car's powerful engine.

She glanced at him as they drove. "Where are we going?"

"It's not far."

"My grandma would yell at me if she knew I'd gotten in a car with a stranger," she said lightly. But part of her was already wondering if she should have refused his offer. The fact that he drove an expensive car didn't mean he could be trusted—in fact, in her admittedly limited experience, it generally meant the opposite.

"We're not strangers. You know my name."

"Mr. Black—"

"Call me Kassius." He gave her a dark sideways glance. "Though I don't think Mimi ever introduced us."

"All right. Kassius." The name moved deliciously on her tongue. She licked her lips. "I'm Laney. Laney May Henry."

"American?"

"From New Orleans."

His sudden look was so sharp and searching that it bewildered her. She wasn't accustomed to being noticed by men, and especially not a man like him. She felt Kassius Black's attention all the way to her toes.

Her boss had said the man was inscrutable, that he had ice water in his veins. Why was he bothering to help her?

But she needed his help too badly to ask questions right now. "Thank you for helping me. You're being very kind."

"I'm not kind," he said in a low voice. He looked at her. "But don't worry. You won't lose your job."

Her heart lifted to her throat. She couldn't remember the last time anyone had helped her. Generally she was the one who was responsible for everyone and everything.

"Thank you," she repeated, her voice cracking slightly as she looked out the window, blinking rapidly.

Monaco was a small principality, only two square kilometers, pressed against the Mediterranean Sea on one side, surrounded by France on the other. But as the country had no income tax, wealthy people from all over the world had flocked to become citizens, so it was said that a third of the population were now millionaires. It was famous for its nineteenth-century grand casino, its elegant society and the Grand Prix held every year on the notoriously winding streets.

"I don't see how this can possibly be made perfect again," she said sadly, looking at the ragtag coat in her arms. She looked at him. "Maybe you could come back with me to her suite and explain what happened? If you put in a good word, then the comtesse wouldn't fire me."

His voice was cool as he focused on the road. "Mimi and I are business acquaintances, nothing more. What makes you so sure I'd have influence on her?"

"Aren't you in love with her?" Laney blurted out.

"In love!" His hands clenched on the steering wheel, causing the car to sway slightly on the road. Then he looked at her. "What gave you that idea?"

Laney realized she'd gotten it by eavesdropping, and her cheeks went hot. She didn't want to be indiscreet or spread rumors about her boss. Embarrassed, she shrugged, looking out at the pouring rain. "Most men seem to fall in love with her. I just assumed..."

"You assumed wrong." He pulled the car abruptly into a spot on the street and parked. "In fact, I've been accused of having no heart."

"That's not true." She smiled at him shyly. "You must have one. Why else would you be helping me?"

He gave her a darkly inscrutable glance. Without answer, he turned off the engine and got out of the car.

Laney's heart pounded as he swiftly strode around the front of the car. He was very tall, at least a foot taller than her, and probably a hundred pounds heavier—a hundred pounds of pure lean muscle. But in spite of his muscle, he moved with almost feline grace beneath his sleek dark suit. Opening her door, he held out his hand.

She stared at it in consternation, wondering if she dared to put her hand in his when it had caused such a powerful reaction in her before.

"Fur?" He said impatiently.

Oh. Blushing, she handed it out to him. He threw the coat casually over his shoulder. It seemed small compared to him. He reached out his hand again. "You."

For a moment Laney hesitated. She was afraid to make a fool of herself, and the chance seemed high. When she was nervous, she always blurted out stupid things, and Kassius Black made her very nervous.

She timidly placed her hand in his and let him help her out. The warmth and strength of his larger hand against hers did all kinds of strange things to her insides. Dropping his hand quickly, she looked up at the Beaux Arts–style building with a frown. "This doesn't look like a dry cleaner's."

"It's not. Follow me."

She followed him through the doors of a very elegant designer boutique. He handed the old fur to the first sales-girl he saw standing inside. "Here. Get rid of this."

"Of course, sir," she replied serenely.

"Get rid of it? What are you doing?" Laney cried. "We can't throw it away!"

But he was looking at the beautiful, well-dressed sales-girl. "Get us a new coat just like it."

"What?" said Laney.

"Of course, sir," the girl repeated calmly, and Laney had the sense that her courteous response would have been the same to the request of any wealthy customer, whether it involved tossing a candy wrapper or disposing of a dead body. "We do have one very similar from the same line. The cost is fifty thousand euros."

Laney nearly staggered to her knees, but Kassius didn't blink.

"We'll take it to go."

Ten minutes later, he was driving her back to the Hôtel de Carillon with the elegantly wrapped new ermine tucked in the trunk, which was confusingly in the front of the car, not the back. Rich people always did some things a little differently, she thought.

But there were some things they did the same.

"There's only one reason you'd blow all that money on a coat," Laney informed him as he drove. "Admit it. You're wildly in love with the comtesse."

Kassius glanced at her out of the corner of his eye. "I didn't do it for her." He gave her a sudden grin. "I did it for you."

"Me?"

"You know who I am and the resources I have. And yet you haven't tried to take advantage of the fact that I hit you with my car. You should be claiming whiplash, spinal injury, threatening to sue. That's what I assumed you were after when you flung yourself in front of my car."

"I didn't fling myself anywhere," she protested.

His dark eyes seemed to trace over her petite, curvaceous body, as if imagining her without her button-up white shirt and khakis. As she blushed, his eyes met hers coolly. "You could be lawyered up, demanding millions."

Millions? That thought hadn't even occurred to Laney. That kind of fortune could have completely changed her life—and more importantly, her family's.

But...

"That wouldn't be right," she said slowly. "I mean, it wasn't your fault I fell into the street. You did everything you could not to hit me. Your quick reflexes saved my life."

"So if I offered you a million euros right now to sign some kind of legal release attesting to that, you would sign it?"

"No," she said, sadly, cursing her own morals.

His cruelly sensual mouth curved up cynically. "I see—"

"I would sign it for free."

He looked startled. "What?"

"My grandma raised me to tell the truth and not take advantage. Just because you're rich doesn't make me a thief."

Kassius gave a low laugh as he took a tight left turn. "Your grandmother sounds like a remarkable woman."

"She is." She smiled. "A true Southern lady."

Kassius stared at her for a moment, and his dark eyes glimmered in the fading gray twilight.

His car pulled up in front of the grand entrance of the Hôtel de Carillon. But as he turned off the car engine, she saw something in his face that twisted her heart.

Without thinking, she timidly touched his shoulder. She immediately regretted it as she felt the hard muscle beneath his sleek black jacket. Her hand fell away, but she couldn't stop herself from saying, "Why do you look like that?"

His dark eyes met hers. "Like what?"

She wondered if he'd felt the same sizzle of energy she had when they touched. No. Of course not, that was ridiculous. He was interested only in her employer, who was beautiful, aristocratic and glamorous—everything that she, Laney, was not.

She took a deep breath. "You look...sad."

Kassius stared at her for a long moment. Then he gave her an abrupt, hard smile. "Billionaires don't get sad. We get even." He turned away. "Come on. I'll save you from Mimi."

Her own car door suddenly opened. Jacques, the doorman, looked completely and utterly astonished to find her returning to the building in a sports car. He said, "Mademoiselle Laney?"

"Oh, hello," she said with an awkward laugh and—she

feared—a guilty expression. "Um. Monsieur Black was kind enough to offer me a ride in the rain."

Jacques looked even more shocked when he saw Kassius, who handed him keys and what looked like a very large tip with a murmured, "*Merci,*" before he retrieved the carefully wrapped brand-new fur from the front of the car, then walked with her into the lavish lobby.

"Tell me," Kassius said casually as they walked, "What do you think of Mimi? Is she a good employer?"

Laney bit her lip, struggling for words. "I'm grateful for the job," she said finally, with complete honesty. "She pays a generous salary, and I'm supporting family back home. Thank you for helping me keep it."

But she felt a little less happy about that prospect from the moment she got back into the comtesse's suite.

"Laney! You lazy girl! What took you so long? You wouldn't even answer your phone," her boss said accusingly the moment she walked in. "You took so long that I was actually forced to get my own coffee. I had to call room service myself. *Myself!*"

"I'm sorry," Laney stammered. "I was in an accident, and my phone was—"

"Why do I even bother to pay you, you useless—"

Then Mimi saw Kassius enter the suite behind Laney, and her jaw dropped. Her friend Araminta, lounging on the sofa by the windows, smoking and thumbing idly through a *Paris Match*, was so shocked her cigarette fell from her mouth.

Both women instantly rose to their feet, tossing their long hair and tilting their hips.

"Kassius!" Mimi cooed, smiling as if butter wouldn't melt in her mouth. "I didn't realize you were coming for a visit."

"I wasn't. I ran into your assistant on the street."

He winked at Laney, who blushed.

"What do you mean?" The comtesse looked between them, clearly unwilling to be left out of any private joke. Kassius looked irritated.

"I ran into her with my car," he said bluntly.

She whirled on Laney.

"Stupid girl, why did you run out in front of Mr. Black's car?"

Kassius choked out a cough. "It was my fault entirely." He placed the black zipper bag from the expensive furrier into her arms. "Here. To replace your coat that was ruined in the accident."

Zipping it open, Mimi gasped. "A new fur! I take it back, Laney," she said sweetly. "You can let Mr. Black hit you with his car any time he wants."

And Laney didn't think her boss was joking, either.

Mimi's red lips lifted in a flirtatious smile as she stepped closer to Kassius. "Buying me a new fur coat before we've even gone on our first date? You really know how to please a woman."

"Do you think so?" Kassius glanced sideways at Laney. "It's been a long time since I've been inspired to pursue anyone."

Laney's heart pounded strangely. He couldn't be talking about her—could he? No, of course not. It was her boss he wanted, with all her blonde, slender, wickedly fashionable glory. Not Laney, dumpy, plain, ordinary. And clumsy—so clumsy!

"Just wait until you see me at the ball tonight." Mimi preened. "You'll be inspired to try a few other things to get my attention, maybe like..." Leaning up on her tiptoes, she whispered something in his ear. His expression was unreadable as he drew back from her.

"What an...intriguing thought." He looked around at the three women. "So I will see you tonight?" His gaze paused on Laney. "All of you?"

"Of course Laney's going," the comtesse said. "I need her there holding my handbag with my lipstick and safety pins in case my dress breaks…it's tight and mini and held together by tiny straps." She giggled. "You'll die."

Kassius turned to Laney gravely. "Are you, also, planning to wear such a dress?"

Laney blushed in confusion. "I…that is…"

"Laney?" Her boss laughed. "She'll be wearing a uniform, like the other servants. That's right and proper. Isn't it, Araminta?"

"Right and proper," her friend agreed, lighting a fresh cigarette.

"You should go, Kassius." Mimi waved her hand airily. "Let us get ready for the ball. Laney has a lot to do…"

Kassius turned the full force of his dark gaze on her. "I wondered if you would do me a small favor."

"Anything," she breathed.

Kassius glanced back at Laney. "Laney wouldn't go to a hospital, but she should at least rest. She hit her head. I'm concerned about her. She's seemed a little…out of it."

"Laney's always out of it," Mimi replied irritably, and in this case, Laney privately agreed, though it hadn't been the car accident that had made her brain freeze and her body extra clumsy with sensual awareness. It was Kassius. She'd never had any man affect her like this. Or look at her the way he'd looked at her.

"Do me a favor. Give her the next hour or two off to recuperate."

"But I need her to—" But beneath the force of his gaze, her boss sighed grumpily. "All right. Fine."

"Thank you." His gaze went over all of them but seemed to linger on Laney. Then he tipped his head. "Ladies."

The comtesse and Araminta beamed at him as he turned and left through the door. Then her boss's smile dropped.

"All right, Laney. I don't know what you did to get his

attention—his pity—but you truly embarrassed yourself, pushing yourself forward! So tacky!"

"So tacky," Araminta agreed.

"Now go steam my dress."

Without the electric distraction of Kassius beside her, with his powerful body towering over her and his dark sensual gaze, Laney suddenly realized she did have a seriously pounding headache. "But you said I could rest a bit—"

"You can rest while you steam my dress."

"And mine."

"Consider it a gift." The comtesse gave her a hard smile. "Pretend you're at the sauna. The day spa. Enjoy yourself."

And oddly, as Laney stood in front of the tiny, fancy gowns—which seemed to be made solely of hooked ribbons—and steamed the wrinkles out, she did enjoy herself. She kept picturing Kassius's dark eyes searching hers, the resonant timbre of his voice, the touch of his hand as he'd helped her out of the car.

Laney stopped, then shook her head. "You're being ridiculous," she told herself out loud. "At midnight, he'll be kissing her—not me!"

She heard the doorbell of the suite ring. Setting down the garment steamer, Laney hurried to answer the door.

A young man was holding a large box. "Delivery."

"*Merci.*" Giving him a tip from her own wallet—her employer was notoriously cheap where tips were concerned—Laney took the big white box, accompanied by an envelope. "Madame la Comtesse, you have—"

Then Laney looked at the name written on the envelope and nearly staggered in shock.

Mademoiselle Laney Henry.

"What is it?" Her boss was suddenly standing beside her. "A delivery for me?"

"Actually..." Laney breathed. "It's for me."

"What?" Her boss snatched up the envelope. "Who

would send you a gift?" She ripped it open and read the message, then staggered back. She glared at Laney with shock in her thin, lovely face. "What did you do?"

"What do you mean?"

She thrust the note at Laney. She looked down at it.

I'm sure you'd look good in any uniform, but consider this instead. Be there before midnight.
Kassius

A hot glow like fire suddenly filled her heart, somewhere between triumph and joy. "He sent me a gift?"

"Open it," Mimi ordered.

Laney wished Mimi and Araminta weren't there so that she could just open his present alone and savor it without their glares. But setting the large white box on the table, she lifted the lid.

All three women gasped.

Inside the white box was a sparkling golden gown. It glistened in the light of the suite, strapless, with a sweetheart neckline and wide, voluminous skirts of glittery tulle. Laney lifted a long white glove from the box and suddenly felt like crying. It was a gift fit for a princess. No one had ever given her anything like this in her whole life.

She lifted the gown completely out of the box, holding it up against her body. She barely recognized her own reflection in the gilded mirror, the laughing brown eyes, the way the golden gown set off her creamy skin and dark hair.

"What did you do, throw yourself in front of his car on purpose?" Her boss glared at her. "You sneaky little gold digger, dazzling him with some poor-helpless-little-woman routine? I *invented* that routine! You think I'll just let you steal him away from right under my nose?"

She stared at Mimi in shock. "No—"

Her boss looked her over sneeringly, from her plain

white shirt to baggy khakis to her sensible clogs. Her lip curled. "What could any man possibly see in you?"

"I'm sure he was just trying to be nice," she stammered.

"Trying to make you jealous, Mimi," Araminta said.

"Maybe." She turned back to Laney. "Fine. Wear that dress. Go to the New Year's Eve gala tonight. And if he asks you to dance—" her eyes narrowed "—I want you to accept."

Her? Dance with Kassius Black? In this dress? In spite of herself, Laney swayed deliriously at the thought, nearly hugging herself with happiness.

"Then—" Mimi looked down at her with her red lips curving "—you will tell him you are sick of his attentions and want him to leave you alone. You will insult him until he believes you."

Laney's sweet candy-pink dreams all fled. "No!"

"If you don't, you'll be out of a job." The comtesse tossed her long blond hair, putting her hand on a tight white-jeans-clad hip. "Not only that, but I'll personally make sure no one ever, ever hires you again. So what's your choice?" Looking at Laney's miserable face, her smile widened as she added sweetly, "I thought so."

CHAPTER TWO

Kassius grabbed a crystal flute of champagne from the tray of a passing waiter, sipped it and wrinkled his nose. Too bubbly. Too sweet. He would have preferred a martini, but then, he would have also preferred to spend the evening driving fast on a curvy road, or getting naked in bed with a beautiful woman, rather than being stuck here at some gala, wearing a tuxedo and surrounded by society revelers, many of whom were already tipsy in spite of the fact it was barely ten o'clock.

The party was hosted by royalty, and guests allowed only by exclusive invitation, so it was well attended. The ballroom was in a grand Belle Époque building off the Avenue Princesse Grace, on a peninsula overlooking the bay. Inside, enormous crystal chandeliers hung from high, painted ceilings, sparkling against gilded walls. An orchestra played music that was ponderous and classical and entirely appropriate, and he didn't much like that, either. He would have preferred rock and roll, or pop, or rap, or even the music that had once been his mother's favorite, the blues. But then, his mother had been originally from New Orleans, where the blues were born.

Just like Laney.

Kassius pictured her sweet, pretty face. Her big brown eyes, so straightforward and honest and kind. Strange that he'd barely noticed her before today, or maybe not so strange, the little helpful servant fading invisibly into the wallpaper behind her employer.

But now, that had all changed.

Now she had his full attention.

Since he'd left Mimi's apartment, he'd already had an

investigator run a background check on Laney. Born Elaine May Henry, age twenty-five, from a little town outside New Orleans, graduated high school with top honors but skipped college to go straight to work. Her ailing grandmother and disabled father had needed her income, especially since Laney's mother had abandoned them years before.

The thought of that abandonment made prickles tighten down Kassius's neck. He'd been abandoned by a parent, too. His father. And his own sweetly fragile mother, once the sheltered darling of a wealthy family from a far different New Orleans neighborhood than Laney's, had never recovered.

He pushed the memory away, focusing back on the far more pleasant thought of Laney.

After high school, she'd gone to work as a nanny for a professional football player's family. Two years later, she'd become personal assistant to a famous chef who specialized in Cajun cooking, with a chain of restaurants, including one in Paris. It was there that, two years ago, Mimi had offered her a job at a large increase in pay, then brought her to Monaco. Through it all, one thing remained constant: Laney worked constantly and sent everything home to her family.

She was kind. Loyal. She hadn't complained about her boss, even when Kassius had deliberately given her the opportunity. Nor had she lied and given Mimi nonexistent good qualities. When pressed for her opinion, Laney had simply expressed honest gratitude for the generous salary.

And yet, even needing money so badly, she hadn't asked him for a cent after he'd nearly run her over with his car. She'd barely allowed him to replace the fur coat he'd destroyed, and…he suddenly realized he still owed her a phone. She hadn't brought it up, even when she needed money so desperately, while he had so much now he never even thought about it anymore.

Oh, yes. Laney Henry interested him. After just a single afternoon in her company, he'd seen old-fashioned values he'd heard about, values that were truly rare: self-sacrifice. Kindness. Honesty. Generosity. Loyalty.

And more than that.

Her warm nature attracted him, like bright sunshine after a dark frozen winter. Was it something in the gentle lilt of her voice? Her accent, which reminded him of the all too brief happiness of his early childhood?

Or was it something far more earthy than that? Was he roused by the novelty of Laney's petite body and outrageous curves, so different from the tall, stick-thin, cool-to-the-touch mistresses he'd taken over the years, who had left him sexually sated but never quite satisfied?

Whatever it was, he found himself unable to think of anything but her. He found himself hungering for her sunlight and heat and fire. Craving an old-fashioned woman that he could trust—and even control—because of her own good, kindhearted nature. But also desire. Oh, yes.

Interesting.

For so long, he'd planned his revenge. He was so close now, but there was one part of his plan that hadn't yet fallen into place. When he finally destroyed the old man, revealed his true identity and took everything the man cared about—his failing company, his gaudy pink mansion on Cap Ferrat—Kassius had thought he would already have his own snug home, wife, children. How else could he give the widowed, childless old man one last taunt, by showing him the family he would never see again and the grandchildren who would never have the chance to love him?

Kassius allowed himself a cold smile. Across the ballroom, he could see the old Russian's gray hair as he spoke with friends. Kassius kept his distance, like a shark observing his prey before he went in for the kill.

He suddenly remembered Laney's quiet voice. *You look sad.*

And his own grim reply. *Billionaires don't get sad. We get even.*

Strange that Laney knew what it was like to be abandoned by a parent, too. Kassius had been astonished to read that in the report. But it had affected her very differently. Rather than creating impenetrable armor to protect herself, rather than growing hard and defensive, she'd somehow stayed soft, like a flower. Laney gave the world everything she had and held nothing in reserve.

He wondered what it would be like to kiss her. To do more than kiss her.

He wondered what it would be like to have her petite, curvaceous body in his arms. To have her look up at him with shining brown eyes and tell him, with a sweet tremble in her husky voice, that she wanted him to take her. That she never wanted to leave him. That she was pregnant with his baby.

The image shouldn't have turned him on, but it did. A lot.

In the past, he'd never let himself be vulnerable. Becoming too intimate with any woman might allow her to discover the truth of his past, and his real identity, potentially jeopardizing his plans.

Plus, all the women of his acquaintance were like Mimi du Plessis—beautiful, venal, hard as nails. Mimi would betray anyone for the slightest advantage. Or even, he thought, for her own amusement on a cloudy day.

But then, that was exactly why he'd sought her out.

For nearly twenty years, Kassius had plotted his revenge, rising from poverty on the streets of Istanbul, working night and day with one ruthless goal: to destroy Boris Kuznetsov.

But even Mimi, dim-witted and self-centered as she was, had started to grow suspicious about Kassius gathering up the man's loans and anonymously offering more. They were loans the Russian couldn't hope to repay. The man was desperate to save his flailing energy company and keep providing for his employees. Even useless ones like Mimi, who was supposedly Kuznetsov Oil's director of public relations and corporate outreach, but rarely roused herself to do more than attend cocktail parties.

So Kassius had deliberately let her believe he might be pursuing her. He didn't feel guilty. Mimi du Plessis was well versed in this game, and usually the victor, leaving a trail of broken hearts. She risked only her vanity, not her heart.

But sooner or later, the deception would end. That afternoon, when Mimi had whispered in his ear that she wanted him to handcuff her to a bed and cover her in whipped cream, he'd barely managed to control his revulsion. He wasn't attracted to Mimi at all. If he handcuffed her to a bed, it would be only so he could leave her more swiftly.

But where was she? Why hadn't she arrived yet with Laney?

He wanted to see Laney in the gold dress. Coming out of the elevator, he'd seen the gown in the window of the designer boutique on the first floor of the hotel and impulsively bought it for her. Would it fit? Would she wear it? Would it show off those curves barely hinted at in her shapeless white shirt and oversize khaki pants?

Finishing his champagne, Kassius dropped the flute on a passing silver tray and, giving a wide berth to Boris Kuznetsov, he went in search of a martini—and Laney Henry.

He pushed through the well-heeled crowds on the edge

of the enormous dance floor, ignoring the inviting smiles of the women and annoyed glares of lesser men. Walking toward the bar, he looked right and left for the glitter of a gold dress.

Then he saw her.

He stopped. Her big brown eyes widened when she saw him. She stopped, too, and as her delectable lips formed his name, all thought of a martini fled his mind.

He'd known Laney would be beautiful.

He'd never imagined this.

The exquisite golden ball gown showed off her hourglass shape, her full breasts and tiny waist. Her skin looked like creamy caramel, with her long dark hair pulled back in a classic chignon. Her long white gloves reached up past her elbows, so the only bare skin revealed was her upper arms, her shoulders and clavicle, with just an enticing hint of cleavage. She was beautiful to him, as fantastical as a princess from a fairy tale.

And so much more alluring than the skinny, hard-eyed blonde now stepping between them, in a tight, short dress made of strategically placed straps that left almost nothing to the imagination.

"Kassius! Darling! I'm so happy to see you." Mimi du Plessis fluttered her fake eyelashes, then, glancing behind her dismissively, gave a fake, tinkly laugh. "You were so kind to send a dress to my assistant. She might have worn overalls otherwise—no fashion sense whatsoever. Laney." Wrapping her arm around Kassius's shoulder, Mimi squashed her cheek to his as she turned around to face Laney. "Take a picture of us," she demanded, "so we can show everyone what a good time we're having."

But as Laney obligingly lifted her boss's crystal-encrusted phone, Kassius detangled himself before she could take a photo. "Thank you, Mimi, but I prefer my privacy."

She narrowed her eyes. "It's strange, Kassius. You have

no online presence. Searching for you on the internet, one comes up with almost nothing."

"Tragic, but then, I'm in real estate development, not the entertainment business," he drawled. His expression changed as he turned to face Laney. "You look beautiful."

"Thank you," she breathed, tilting back her head to meet his gaze. Her dark eyes were wide, her cheeks rosy. "You were so nice to send this dress—what possessed you?"

"You," he said, taking the phone from her and dropping it into Mimi's hands. "Dance with me."

"Dance?" With a troubled glance at her employer, Laney licked her full, pink, delectable lips. Just at that, his body tightened with instantaneous reaction. He nearly groaned aloud. "I don't know if that's a good idea…"

"It's a very good idea," Mimi said smugly. He was almost surprised she was being so reasonable.

"Come now," he said firmly. Taking Laney's gloved hand, he pulled her out onto the marble dance floor, and with a twirl of her skirts, tugged her back hard against his body.

He felt her petite form cradled against him, all soft, lush curves beneath the sparkling gold bodice and wide sweep of skirts. Her skin was bare above her gloves. He had to fight the desire to caress her shoulders, to see if her skin was smooth and satiny as it looked.

"I don't know how to waltz," she confessed, trembling as she lifted her gloved hands to his shoulders.

"It's easy." He gave her a sensual smile. "I will show you what to do."

He adjusted one of her hands on his shoulder, and took the other in his own.

"See?" he murmured. "You're a natural."

Her lips parted as she looked up at him, so pretty, so gentle, so everything he hadn't realized he desperately desired until this exact moment.

Yes, his body said. *Yes. Yes.*

Holding her at the prescribed distance as he led her in a waltz, dancing in time with all the other couples on the ballroom floor, his body hungered. He wanted to get her alone, rip off her clothes and feel her naked body against his. He wanted to be above her. Beneath her. Inside her.

He wanted her in his bed. Tonight. Within the hour. If not sooner.

"Mr. Black…" Laney said falteringly.

"I told you. Kassius."

"Kassius." Her lips trembled as she whispered his name. Looking up at him, she tried to smile politely, but as her fingers tightened, he knew that she felt the same overwhelming current between them.

"You've done so much for me already," she said shyly. "Replacing the fur coat. Defending me to the comtesse." She looked down at her gold ball gown. "But this takes the cake. I've never owned anything half so beautiful as this."

"It made me think of you." He slowly looked her over. "But seeing you in it now, the gown barely does you justice. You are the star."

As they continued to swirl around the dance floor, he saw Mimi glowering at them. She'd already grown suspicious about his loans. One word to her employer and she could make it much harder for Kassius to achieve his goal. If he were smart, he knew he wouldn't pursue Laney like this, flaunting his desire before the other woman's eyes, injuring her pride.

But he couldn't stop himself. After twenty years of obsessive focus on one goal, he found he could no more pull away from this intoxicatingly beautiful, warmhearted woman than he could voluntarily stop breathing.

A blush burned Laney's cheeks as her dark eyelashes swept against her skin. "No one has ever said such…" Then she followed his gaze to Mimi, and her expression shuttered. "Oh," she said, and the sound was like a wistful sigh. "You really are just trying to make her jealous, aren't you?" She shook her head and tried to smile, but her eyes seemed to glimmer. "The games rich people play. You should just try being honest." She abruptly stopped dancing. "Go ask her to dance. And leave me out of it—"

But as she tried to pull away, he held her fast.

"I do not play those kinds of games. I do not need to play them."

"Then why—"

His eyes flicked toward Mimi du Plessis, in her ridiculously tight bandage minidress, whispering to her friend Araminta. "If I wanted her in my bed, she'd already be flat on her back."

"That's a crude thing to say."

"You said you wanted honesty."

"It's not nice."

"I could have her." He slowly looked around the dance floor. "I could have most of these women. I know, because I have already had some of them, and the rest have made the invitation clear."

"Is this your idea of bragging? Telling me you've slept around? I'm not impressed that you've had so many lovers."

"No?" His hands tightened on her. "But I am impressed you've had so few."

He heard her intake of breath as her eyes widened. "How can you—"

She cut herself off.

"How can I tell?" He ran one hand down her back. "I can tell in the way you shiver when I touch you." He cupped her cheek with the other. "I can tell in the way you hold your breath when I look at you." He twirled her on the dance floor, then pulled her tight against his body. "I can feel it," he said roughly, "in the way your body trembles against mine."

Kassius looked down at her. She was so tiny in his arms, he thought, so feminine and vulnerable. And yet it was her vulnerability that most impressed him. He marveled that anyone could be so fearless.

"It's part of what makes you different," he said in a low voice. "Your warmth. Your kindness. You're not just beautiful. You give so much of yourself and ask for so little."

"I'm…just…ordinary," she said softly, her dark eyes pleading.

"No." He shook his head with a slow-rising smile. "You're far from that."

"You're wrong—"

"You refused to take my money, even when I offered it. Refused to speak badly of Mimi, even though she cannot be a considerate employer. You give up your whole life to work, to take care of your family." He ran his hands gently over the nape of her neck. He yearned to pull her hair out of the prim fastenings of her chignon and let it tumble down her shoulders. Abruptly the fantasy came into his mind of her sitting naked on him, her thighs wide, leaning over to kiss him, long dark hair brushing against his skin as her full breasts pressed against his chest.

Soon. Soon.

With a deep breath, he took hold of himself and continued frankly, "Tonight you look like a princess. But I'm starting to believe it only reflects the way you are inside. There's something about you I can't resist…" Leaning forward, allowing his lips to brush against the sensitive flesh of her ear, he whispered, "I want you."

But as he drew back and looked down at her, a shadow crossed her lovely face. With a small glance back toward her boss, she pulled away from him, her expression sorrowful.

"I'm sorry, but I'm just not interested."

Kassius hadn't expected that at all, not with the way

he'd felt her trembling in his arms. Had he misjudged her desire?

Then he looked more closely at her beautiful face, at how she'd turned pale beneath the blush on her cheeks, her eyes haunted and black. She was lying. But why?

"Really," he said evenly.

She nodded furiously, but as the couples around them continued to waltz around where they stood stock-still on the dance floor, she refused to meet his gaze.

"Tell me why."

"Because..." She licked her lips uncertainly then lifted her chin. "Because you're a playboy who sleeps around in such a disgusting way."

"Try harder."

"You're not even slightly attractive to me."

"Explain."

She looked him over desperately. "You're too—um—tall."

He snorted. "Too tall?"

"Fine. I'll give you a reason," she snapped. "It's not you, it's me. I'm just a frigid virgin, all right?"

"The virgin I might believe. But frigid?" Shaking his head, Kassius gave a low laugh. Pulling her closer, he ran his hands over her soft, bare shoulders. He felt her tremble as she looked up at him breathlessly. He could see the shape of her taut nipples through her silky bodice. Running his hands slowly, sensuously, down her arms, he said, "You are far from that."

She looked at him with big eyes. "Please...please don't."

"Why?"

"Because—" She swallowed, then said in a voice so low he had to strain to hear, "If I don't make you stop pursuing me, my boss says I'm fired. And she'll make sure I never get another job."

He was so shocked he almost laughed. "She said what?"

But it was obvious Laney didn't see it as a joke but a real threat. Her face was anguished. "If I can't work, how will I support my family? So you have to go away and leave me alone." Her pleading brown gaze fell to his lips as she whispered, "Just go..."

Her words might be saying one thing, but her body was saying another. She didn't even know what she was really asking him for. But he did.

Laney was a virgin? He could hardly believe it. He'd never made love to a virgin before. It was almost cruel. It made him desire her even more, when he was already nearly exploding with need, and would also force him to seduce her more slowly. He didn't know how much more self-restraint he could endure. Where women were concerned, he wasn't accustomed to it.

The orchestra's music stopped, and as the other couples left the dance floor, he felt their curious glances as they passed, felt Mimi's glower from the crowd.

He knew he was making a mistake. He'd always been private to the point of mania, but here, in the literal spotlight, he suddenly didn't care who might be watching.

Pulling Laney roughly against his body, he tangled his hands in her hair, tilting her chin upward. "Get one thing straight," he said, searching her gaze ruthlessly. "I don't give a damn about Mimi or anyone else. I only care about one thing."

She looked at him defiantly. "And what might that be?"

"Taking what I want," he said ruthlessly. "And I want you."

And cupping her face with his hands, he lowered his head and kissed her, right there on the dance floor of the New Year's Eve ball.

His lips were soft against hers at first. Laney felt the roughness of his chin, the sweet taste of his mouth.

She had no idea what to do. The one time she'd been kissed before, it had been a total disaster.

But this was different. *He* was different. As Kassius's mouth began to move more forcefully against hers, taking rather than asking, she realized she didn't have to do anything but surrender. Her eyes squeezed shut.

As she relaxed against him, his kiss deepened, and he pushed her lips apart, plundering her mouth. She nearly gasped at the pleasure that went through her, a *whoosh* of sensation that electrified her from her lips to her earlobes to her breasts and lower still. Her nipples tightened. Low in her belly, she felt a new sensation coil deep inside her.

Pleasure seemed to be exploding from her body like light. She'd never experienced anything like this—never—

"You're mine," he whispered roughly against her lips. "Mine."

She realized she'd tightened her hands against his shoulders, bringing him down hard against her in the kiss. Then he abruptly pulled away, leaving her bereft.

Her eyes flew open, and she saw the orchestra had taken a break—they were alone on the dance floor and the entire ballroom had fallen silent, staring at them. Mimi's eyes were beaming such lasers of fury Laney feared she might burst into flame. Then she remembered.

"Oh, no," Laney choked out. Her hands went to her face in dismay. What had she done, letting him kiss her? How could she have been so selfish as to give in to the moment when her family was counting on her? "What have I done?"

"Nothing. Yet." He sounded almost amused as his larger hand took hers. His dark eyes seared her. "But you will. You're coming home with me. Now."

Laney looked up at him, feeling like her whole future was hanging in the balance.

She looked at Kassius in his sleek bespoke tuxedo, so

tall and broad shouldered. Power and wealth clung to him as ineffably as his faint scent of cypress and musk.

There was no way a handsome billionaire could actually want Laney. She was just a regular girl. She liked fried chicken and po' boy sandwiches, not foie gras and caviar. She drank sweet tea, not Dom Pérignon. She bought her clothes from discount warehouses, not based on prestige or even appearance, but comfort and practicality.

She had nothing in common with the typical girlfriends of billionaires—nothing!

"You can't want me. You can't possibly want me."

"Why?" he demanded.

"Why? Because you're—you. And I'm me." She could still hardly believe that she was even here, in this illustrious gilded ballroom in Monaco, with its soaring crystal chandeliers, full orchestra and a thousand members of the international jet set. Her only other dance experience had been at senior prom, in a school gymnasium with paper decorations and balloons, a punch bowl and a DJ. She'd been hopeful and excited, wondering if the high school quarterback would kiss her. And look how *that* night had turned out. "Please just let me go."

Kassius's dark eyes glittered. "Is that really what you want?"

No. No. Of course it wasn't. She felt intoxicated and alive for the first time in her life. She wanted to be beautiful and desired by the most handsome, powerful man on earth, one of the richest men in the world. The thought was like a dream to her. A deliriously impossible dream.

She felt everyone staring at them, the only ones left on the dance floor. The center of attention.

She whispered, "Everyone is staring at us."

"Staring at *you*. They're wondering who you are."

She gave a low laugh. "I've lived here almost two years!"

"As a servant. Invisible." He stroked her bare shoulder, looking down at her in the shimmering gold gown. "You're not invisible anymore."

Because of you, she thought. Her heart was pounding in her throat.

"Come with me. Now. Tonight." His handsome face was hungry and hard as he took her hand.

She did not—could not—resist. He led her through the ballroom, and a path magically cleared for him—all six foot four, two hundred pounds of muscle—through the crowd.

Out of the corner of her eye, she saw Mimi and Araminta's thin, shocked faces as they passed by. But she couldn't think about that now, or her future. All she could do was follow where Kassius led, out of the ballroom and the vast building to the street outside, where a sleek dark car swiftly pulled up to the curb and a uniformed driver hastened to open her door.

Outside, the moon was pearlescent in the dark sky. A ghostlike glow frosted the palm trees swaying in the abrupt hard wind. Winter in Monaco was generally sunny and mild, but sometimes after a rain, the strange rare wind of the mistral would rise, a legendarily violent wind capable of driving men and women mad.

The mistral. It was her only excuse...

Without a word, Kassius pushed her into the backseat of his limo. The door was barely closed behind them, the vehicle just starting to pull out into the street, before Kassius's mouth was on hers. He pushed her back against the smooth leather, and she closed her eyes, feeling his hands everywhere, over the sparkling layers of her golden gown. His hands ran over her naked shoulders, cupping her face as he kissed her roughly, his mouth searing hers, taking possession without permission or apology. She felt the strength and weight of his body pressing against her.

As he kissed her, he peeled off her long gloves one by one, and as she felt the soft whisper of fabric move slowly down her skin, she shivered from sensation. Her breasts felt heavy beneath the fabric of her strapless bodice, her nipples agonizingly tight and so sensitive as he brushed against her, pushing her beneath him, caressing her, mastering her. She felt bewildered, dizzy.

The passenger door of the limousine suddenly fell open.

She opened her eyes in shock to see that the car was now parked in front of the Hôtel de Carillon. In the heat of their embrace, she hadn't noticed the drive, the route, even Kassius's driver and bodyguard sitting at the front. Both of those men were now standing on the sidewalk beside the open door, carefully not looking in their direction.

The doorman, Jacques, had no such discretion. When he came forward, his mouth fell open.

"Mademoiselle Laney?"

Her cheeks went hot with shame as she sat up hurriedly, making sure her breasts weren't falling out of the bodice of her dress. She could only imagine what she looked like...

"Thank you," Kassius said coolly, "but I'll help her out." Getting out of the limo, he turned and held out his hand. With a deep breath, feeling overwhelmed with embarrassment and humiliation, she tried to keep her face expressionless as he led her past the doorman into the lobby of the residential hotel.

"You're bringing me home," she whispered over the lump in her throat. She wasn't even surprised. She could still hear that harsh voice from long ago. *Frigid little virgin*...

"Yes," Kassius said.

"You brought me home before midnight." She gave him a weak smile. "Like Cinderella."

They reached the elevator, and the doors opened. He drew her inside and pushed the button.

"That's the wrong floor. Mimi doesn't live in the penthouse."

"But I do."

Her heart twisted in her chest.

"You do?" she whispered.

He came closer to her in the elevator, looking down at her. He cupped her cheek. "I just bought it."

"You did?" She looked up at him, feeling dizzy and strange. "Why?"

"I needed a place in Monaco." His voice was husky. Sexy. "Until I am able to buy a special villa I want on Cap Ferrat."

"You—you want me to come upstairs with you?" she breathed, hardly knowing what she was saying.

"I do," he whispered, running his hand down the side of her neck. The edges of his lips curved upward. "And you will…"

Roughly, he pushed her back against the mirrored elevator wall. Her head fell back as she closed her eyes, lost in sensation as he kissed down her neck, her cheek, sucking her earlobe as his hands ran over her bare arms, her shoulders, cupping her breasts through the fabric.

The elevator door opened to the top floor, and for a minute she didn't, *couldn't*, move, just leaned back against the mirror, her knees feeling weak.

So he picked her up as if she weighed nothing. Her sparkly tulle skirts fluttered behind them as he carried her swiftly down the hall.

Held against his powerful chest, Laney looked up at him in a daze as he brought her into the luxurious penthouse suite of the Hôtel de Carillon.

The suite was dark, but she could see the ceilings were two stories high. The furniture was stark and modern, but she barely saw it amid the shadows before her gaze was transfixed by the wall of floor-to-ceiling windows with views of the sparkling lights of nighttime Monaco, and beyond that, the vast dark Mediterranean.

Kassius set her down slowly, letting her body drag against his, falling in a cascade of tulle. For a moment, he looked down at her, then with a low growl, he whirled her around so he was looking at her back. She blinked at the view. She saw a few lights of ships floating through the dark sea, like stars in the sky.

She shouldn't be here. She should go. But she felt like time and reality had fled, as if she were someone else entirely. Someone reckless...

He slowly unzipped her dress, dropping it to the floor. The cool air licked at her skin as he turned her back around to face him. She was almost naked, wearing only a strapless white bra and plain white lace panties. He slowly looked her over. "You are so beautiful."

And even in the shadows of the penthouse suite, she saw in the hard lines of his face, of his body, that he did desire her. Fiercely.

She should leave. Her brain and heart were begging her to leave—leave now. Because there was only one way this could end. Badly.

But for some reason, her body refused to budge as he pulled off her shoes, one by one.

Rising to his feet, Kassius slipped off his black tuxedo jacket. Taking her hand, he drew her into the bedroom.

Translucent gauze curtains covered the windows and sliding glass door to the balcony. He opened the balcony door, and she took a deep breath of the cool, hard wind, scented of salt sea and golden mimosa flowers in bloom.

Laney stood nearly naked in front of Kassius Black— this handsome, dangerous billionaire who was so much larger than she, in every possible way. She lifted her face to his.

His dark eyes were hungry as he came back toward her,

and, nervously, she backed away from him, falling back softly onto his enormous king-size bed, against the large white pillows on the white comforter. Standing over her, he deliberately pulled off his black tie.

Wearing only his white shirt and black tuxedo trousers, he kicked off his shoes and reached toward her on the bed. Slowly, he ran his fingertips down her cheek, then her throat, then the hollow between her breasts. She could not move as his fingertips lightly stroked downward, past her silky strapless white bra to her rib cage and the bare skin of her belly. His hand traced downward, ever downward, to the top edge of her lacy white panties.

She suddenly stopped him with her hand.

"Don't," she choked out.

His forehead furrowed. "Why?"

"I'll only disappoint you."

"You're a virgin. How do you know?"

"I know."

Silvery moonlight streaked through the windows, frosting the gauzy curtains and the hard lines of his cheekbones and jaw as he leaned back, staring down at her incredulously. "You actually think you're frigid, don't you?"

"I know I am."

"Why?"

"The boy who took me to prom…he told me."

"And you believed him?"

"He would know. He kissed a lot of girls." A lump rose in Laney's throat. "Look, it's almost midnight. You should go back to the party. Find someone who knows how to kiss—"

"I have the one I want." His fingertips changed course, skimming over the curve of her hips to her bare thighs.

"Look—" she swallowed "—I don't know why you chose me, whether you're just slumming or—"

He abruptly dropped his hand.

"You spoke earlier about games, Laney. Let's play a game now, you and I."

"What game?"

His gaze locked with hers. "I will prove to you that you are not frigid. That you are a warm, desirable woman. A woman made for pleasure."

"What if you can't?"

He gave a low laugh. "I will. All I have to do is touch you—even look at you—to know I am right."

"And if you're wrong?" she said desperately, remembering the humiliating night of prom when she was eighteen.

"Then I will pay a forfeit." He smiled. "Shall we say— one million dollars?"

She gaped at him. "Is that a joke?"

"No."

"That's the second time you've offered me a million!"

"Is it not enough?" he said lazily, looking at her beneath heavily lidded eyes. "Two million, then. Ten. I am so sure that I can make you gasp with desire, so sure I can make you explode with pleasure, that if I am wrong, Laney, I will pay you ten million dollars."

A noisy burst of wind flew through the open balcony door.

Ten million dollars.

The amount staggered her. She thought of what it would mean. No more abuse from her horrible boss. She could go back to New Orleans and hire full-time caregivers for her father. Her grandmother, who'd worked her fingers to the bone for fifty years, could finally relax and enjoy her life. Laney could be with the family she loved.

"But the amount I'll pay if I lose doesn't matter." Kassius looked down at her, his eyes glinting wickedly in the moonlight. "Because I will win."

Laney licked her lips. "Just for the sake of argument,

if you do make me, um…if you prove I'm not frigid, then what would you want in return?"

"Beyond the sweet prize of your body?" He moved suddenly, leaning over the bed, running his wide hand in a sensual stroke down her body. His expression was deadly serious. "You would be completely mine."

Her mouth went dry. "What do you mean?"

He ran his hand softly against her cheek. "I am tired of the bachelor life. I want a family. I want a wife. Children."

Now she really did feel dizzy. Could the half a glass of champagne she'd drunk at the party be affecting her brain? "You can't possibly mean—"

"If I cannot give you pleasure, Laney, I will give you ten million dollars and you will walk out of here a wealthy woman. But if I make you explode with joy, you will surrender everything. You will allow me to take possession of your body and fill you with my child. You will be mine—forever."

CHAPTER THREE

LANEY SAT UP straight on the king-size bed, her eyes wide. Before, she'd thought she was dreaming, or possibly drunk.

Now she wondered if she'd lost her mind.

"Let me see if I understand," she said faintly. "If you make me come, I must marry you and have your baby?"

Kassius's expression was unreadable. "What is your answer?"

"It's either a ridiculous joke, or else you're crazy!"

"I'm perfectly sane, and I've never been more serious."

"But risking marriage—children—based on sex? That is insane!" Her eyes went wide as he pulled off his shirt, dropping it to the floor. She stared at his hard, muscular chest, laced with dark hair. She licked her lips and tried to remember what she'd been saying. She stammered, "We'd need to be in love. We'd need to be compatible partners. You have to be sensible—"

Leaning over the bed, he stopped her with a kiss. His lips were hard and hot, his muscled chest pressing against her. She was suddenly very aware she was wearing only a strapless bra and panties.

He drew back, searching her gaze. "Your answer."

No would be the sensible response.

Hell, no would be even smarter, while running out of here like her hair was on fire.

But...

Ten million dollars.

Though inexperienced, Laney knew quite a bit about sex, of course. She'd seen her share of R-rated movies, so it wasn't like she was a total innocent. When Bobby Joe Branford, the football hero of her high school, had asked her to prom, she'd been excited at the thought of her first kiss.

But the night had been a disaster. Halfway through the dance, he'd pushed her out into a dark school hallway and kissed her against the lockers. His lips had been rubbery and cold, and she'd nearly choked when she'd tasted sour whiskey on his breath as his tongue shoved down her throat. It was so horrible she knew she must be doing it wrong. She'd tried to remain perfectly still, until finally she could take no more and she tried to push him away. He wouldn't let her, so she'd given him a hard shove with all her strength. He'd fallen to the floor in drunken surprise just as some of his friends walked by. They'd laughed, and Bobby Joe had glared at her.

"Frigid little virgin." He'd wiped his mouth. "I should have known I'd be wasting my time with you."

Bobby Joe had caught up with his friends and found another girl to dance with, leaving Laney in her wrinkled secondhand prom dress and wilting corsage to find her own way home.

But it had gotten even worse. She'd returned to school Monday to find herself a laughingstock. She'd already been unpopular, the short, chubby girl who lived in that ratty house near the bayou, who wore outdated clothes from the thrift shop, whose blind father was in a wheelchair and whose mother had abandoned her family, to run off to California with her lover.

But now the high school quarterback had rendered final, fatal judgment, and the entire school thought of her in his terms: *frigid little virgin*. The other students didn't just think it, either. They called her that. To her face.

Remembering the bewildering pain and humiliation, Laney still felt hot all over, then deadly cold.

All that pain had to be for something.

What was the risk? She would take that ten million dollars and walk out of here like a queen, able to take care of her family for the rest of her life.

Lifting her chin, she looked at Kassius Black with glittering eyes. "I accept."

A flash of triumph crossed his handsome face. Leaning forward, he loosened the pins of her chignon, causing her long dark hair to tumble down her shoulders.

"At last," he said huskily and pressed her back against the bed, kissing her, hard and deep.

She felt nothing. That ten million dollars was as good as in her pocket.

He ran his hands slowly, softly down her body. His kiss gentled. Where a moment before his lips had demanded and possessed, now they caressed like a whisper. Luring her.

She felt a strange shiver in her breasts and low in her belly. She pushed it away. *Frigid little virgin.*

Moving his hands behind her, he unlatched her strapless white bra. She nearly gasped as her full breasts spilled naked into his hands.

With a soft hiss of appreciation, he pushed her back against the bed, running his hands down her body. He cupped a heavy breast, squeezing it lightly, until the full, ripe pink of her nipple presented itself between his fingers like a rose-colored pearl.

She felt *nothing*, she told herself. Her heart was pounding. She was *like stone.*

He lowered his head. She felt the warmth of his breath, then he pulled her virgin nipple fully into his mouth. As he suckled her, electricity sizzled up and down the length of her body. She stiffened, gripping his shoulders tightly.

Like stone, she told herself desperately. *Stone!*

He cupped her other breast, suckling the taut, red, aching nipple. She sucked in her breath.

Suddenly, he gripped both her wrists, pushing them up

against the headboard. Leaning forward, he growled in her ear, "You are going to lose."

"I won't," she panted, but a trickle of fear went down her spine. She couldn't lose. Not only would she lose her family's security, but her own. It would mean possibly getting pregnant by a man she barely knew. Becoming his wife. It would mean a loveless marriage. She wouldn't do that just for one moment of pleasure! She couldn't, wouldn't, let herself do that.

Could she…?

His heavily muscled body pressed hers deeper into the mattress. His hard grip held down her wrists as he kissed her, then licked and nibbled down her throat, her earlobes, her clavicle. She felt the hardness of him, straining between her legs. She whimpered.

Releasing her wrists, he kissed her more gently now, stroking her with his hands, caressing her cheek, her throat, her aching breasts. He explored her belly, the curve of her hips. He ran his fingertips along the top edge of her white cotton panties, teasing her. His touch was like a whisper.

No. Her hands gripped the white comforter beneath her. She couldn't let herself feel pleasure!

She had to resist!

He paused, then deliberately stroked over the thin cotton panties, over the mound between her legs. She choked back a gasp, biting down hard on her lip. He kept moving downward, running his palms over her thighs, causing prickles of heat to spread across her body.

Pushing her legs apart, he lowered his head in little kisses down her belly, all the way down to where his hands recently had touched. He paused at the top of her panties, then deliberately teased her with the warmth of his breath, kissing the edges of the fabric, stoking her desire.

Desire. Was that what she felt? She desired him. But she couldn't. This couldn't happen.

Getting pregnant would change her life forever. And not just hers. She'd always known when she became a mother, she would do it properly. She'd find a nice, kind, trustworthy man whom she loved. They would date for a year, pay for their own simple wedding with the income from their sensible, stable jobs, then save up for the deposit for a house with a white picket fence. Only then, when they both were ready, would they deliberately choose to bring a child into the world. Because a baby deserved security and love and stability. Laney knew this better than anyone.

So even if the chance was small that she could get pregnant tonight, she couldn't take that risk. Not for some ridiculous challenge!

She had to tell him to stop. To call off this game. Tell him he could keep his stupid money.

She had to get out of here, before it was too late!

Just be stone! Her brain shrieked.

The trouble was she no longer felt like stone.

Her breaths came in little gasps as he knelt at the foot of the bed, between her legs. Noises suddenly thundered outside, in explosions. They both turned to face the windows of the balcony. Through the translucent curtains, they saw brilliant fireworks bursting across the dark sky. Kassius looked down at her.

"It's midnight," he said huskily. "Happy New Year."

Cupping her cheek, he kissed her. His mouth was searing, demanding. She felt the roughness of his chin, felt the lure of his tongue against hers. She was lost in his sensual warmth, held beneath the weight of his powerfully muscled body, and worse—the weight of her own desire.

Just one more minute, and I'll tell him to stop, she promised herself. *Just one more minute...*

A burst of wind swirled the gauzy curtains, filling the room, twisting around their entwined, half-naked bodies and cooling their overheated skin. She clutched at his shoulders.

Holding her down, he pushed her lips firmly apart, stroking her tongue with his own. He lured her, enticed her, until suddenly she realized she was kissing him back. Moments later—or maybe hours—he lifted his head. But she didn't have time to catch her breath as he moved down her body. His soft, wet mouth wrapped around her hard, aching nipple, and pleasure ripped through her.

She swallowed, squeezing her eyes shut, gasping beneath the sensual wet swirl of his mouth. His hands slowly stroked her hips. Her thighs. The tender skin between them.

He straightened from the bed and slowly slid her panties over her thighs, down her legs, before tossing them to the floor.

She was completely naked now, spread-eagle across his enormous bed.

"You—frigid!" he muttered almost angrily. "What fool convinced you of that!"

He dropped his trousers and silk boxers to the floor. He sprang out, thick and hard and unrestrained.

She looked at Kassius's naked, powerful body in the moonlight and couldn't look away.

His chest was muscled like warm marble, and the trail of dark hair went down his body to his flat, taut belly. Beneath that… She swallowed. It was the first time she'd seen a fully naked, erect man. He was huge, both in girth and length, and so hard.

Her hand tentatively reached out. He grabbed it.

"Please, can I?" She took a deep breath. "I've never…" She blushed. "Never touched…"

He stared at her. Then released her hand.

She shyly reached out to touch him lightly with her fingertips, stroking the edges of his shaft. He felt like velvet over steel. He bucked beneath her stroke.

She looked up at him in shock. "You...want me...so badly?"

"Let me show you," he said huskily.

Placing his hands on her shoulders, he pushed her back against the mattress and kissed her hungrily, covering her with his naked body. She felt the heaviness of his muscled legs, rough with hair, against her own, felt his stubbled jawline like sandpaper against her soft skin. Most of all, she felt the thick hardness of him against her belly.

She was tight and aching all over. She nearly cried out from the friction of his hard chest against her sensitive nipples as he slid down her body. She felt him between her legs, demanding entry, and it was all she could do not to spread her legs wider, like a wanton desperate to have him inside her. But he kept moving down, down, all the way to her feet.

Kneeling between her legs, he kissed the hollow of a foot, and the sensitive back of her knee. He stroked slowly up to his thighs, pushing her thighs farther apart.

"What are you—"

"Shh," he whispered. "You'll like it."

He lowered his head. She felt his hot breath on the tender skin of her inner thighs, and a rush of desperate need coursed through her. She knew she was running out of time. She had to push him away, to tell him no, to jump up and run screaming from the bed.

But she couldn't. She gripped the white comforter, her body shaking, unable to stop him as he lowered his head between her legs.

Reaching his hands around her backside, he held her tight, and she felt the warmth of his breath on her most secret core. For a moment, he paused. As if giving her one last chance to refuse.

Then he ruthlessly lowered his head. Spreading her

wide, he took a long, languorous taste with the full roughness of his tongue. As she gasped, he sighed in pleasure.

"You taste like caramel," he whispered huskily. "Salty
and sweet."

She felt his hot breath on her thighs as he nuzzled her.
Felt the roughness of his bristly chin against her thighs, the
silky swirl of his mouth against her aching wet core. In-
voluntarily, her hips rose to meet the thrust of his mouth...

This was madness. She had to stop now. Now!

Just one more minute, she thought desperately. *Just
one.* She would die if she didn't have one more minute...

Her hips twisted beneath his mouth as he worked her
with his tongue, swirling around her. He eased a finger
just barely inside her. She gasped, gripping the bed. She
started to shake.

Pushing the finger inside her, then another, he stretched
her even as his satin-steel lips and slick wet tongue worked
her, making her hold her breath, giving her pleasure until
her toes started to curl and she saw stars behind her eyes.

She couldn't...

Oh, this was so good!

She mustn't...

Don't stop!

As he lapped her with his wide tongue, his thick fingers inside her, her shaking intensified. Pushing her
thighs more roughly apart, he suckled her, twirling her
with the tip of his tongue, then lapping her. Her hips
twisted beneath him, but he held her tight against his
mouth, forcing her to surrender, to accept the pleasure.
She gripped his shoulders, and her back started to arch.
Her hips rose from the bed as she started to writhe beneath him. Her lips parted as she held her breath...held it
and held it and...

Pleasure exploded in patterns of light and color. She
cried out, gripping into his shoulders, deep, deep, deep

with her fingernails, her dark hair flying in a cloud as she shuddered and shook and gasped for air.

Lifting his mouth off her, he positioned his hips between her legs. He filled her with a single thrust.

She cried out as he ripped ruthlessly through her barrier, impaling her to the hilt, hard and deep. In the middle of blinding pleasure, she felt searing pain.

He didn't move, just held himself still inside her. He took a deep breath, as if steadying himself. Then he lowered his head to her ear. She could hear the masculine smugness, the triumph in his cruel, sensual whisper.

"You're mine now."

Kassius nearly passed out with the sensation of burying himself inside her hot, tight sheath.

She felt so good. Even better than he'd dreamed. Her body was soft and slick with sweat and the loud cry of her pleasure was still ringing in his ears. For a moment, his hard thick length pulsed wildly inside her, and he had to fight to keep himself from exploding right there and then, on the first thrust.

For the last hour, he'd held himself back. He liked to believe he had amazing self-control, but a man could only stand so much.

Kissing Laney, suckling her, feeling her naked body against his own, tasting her—it had been sweet torture. All he'd been able to think about was how desperately he wanted to plunge himself inside her tight body, to fill her with a single thrust. She'd sorely tested his self-restraint as he proved she was a woman made for loving, built for pleasure.

Laney—frigid! He still marveled at the ridiculous idea. He could hardly believe that any man had convinced her of that. But he was almost glad. Now she was his, and his alone. She'd been trembling and warm, a goddess of desire.

He'd never wanted any woman more.

And he wasn't interested in a one-night stand. He didn't want a simple love affair. He didn't want to spend weeks, months, years pursuing her, convincing her of his love.

Kassius was ready to settle down. He wanted a real home, with the pride of a wife and family in addition to the success of his business empire.

But not just any woman would do. He needed a wife he could trust. An old-fashioned woman who would be devoted to their family and home—and obey his every command. All that, and she had to be so delicious in bed that he'd want no other.

He'd found her.

He could have just seduced her, without playing the game or extracting her promise. But he'd wanted Laney Henry to know exactly what he intended to take from her—and what he intended to give. He wanted their relationship sealed without question, starting as he meant to go on. With her full and complete surrender.

She would be his wife. He'd get her pregnant as soon as possible.

A low groan came from him at the thought of Laney, heavily pregnant, buxom and round. As he'd first pushed inside her, filling her deeply with one rough thrust, it was lucky he hadn't immediately exploded inside her like a damned volcano.

Now, so deeply inside her, he held himself very still, holding his breath until he could regain control. Then he looked down at her beautiful face, glorying in the moment of his possession as he said huskily, "You're mine now."

She opened her big brown eyes, and he saw her pain. The ecstasy had disappeared. Instead, her teeth were clenched. *Virgin.* Damn it. He cursed himself silently. He'd been so focused on his previous goal of giving her pleasure, then his desperation to satisfy his own pent-up desire, that he'd forgotten it would be painful for her.

He lowered his head. "I'm sorry," he said in a low voice. "I forgot it can hurt the first time. I've never been with a virgin before."

"Me neither," she whispered and tried to smile.

Cupping her cheek, he lowered his head and kissed her lips gently. He tasted the salt of her tears. He kissed them away. At first, she didn't respond. For long moments, he did not move his hips, just giving her body time to adjust to the feel of him, hard and deep inside her.

Then he heard a sound from her like a sigh, and in his soft, slow embrace, her shoulders started to relax. Tentatively, she reached up and stroked his chest, which was heavily muscled from his years training as a boxer and martial arts fighter.

He shuddered beneath her soft touch. Pressing his body against hers, he gloried in the sensation of her bare skin against his, the fullness of her breasts crushed against his chest.

She was soft, so soft. He couldn't remember the last time he'd had a woman with a shape like this, so petite and sensual. Had he ever? He doubted it. His taste in lovers had always been conformist—he'd chosen the same tall, super-slender supermodels as every other billionaire, just as he chose the same type of sports car and expensive yacht and palatial ski lodge. In his business empire, he was an innovator. In his personal life, he'd been depressingly unoriginal.

Until now.

Until *her*.

He didn't know how much longer he could keep still. Even after all this time without moving inside her, he was so hard and aching he thought he might burst. Feeling her softly curved body beneath his, so pliable and desirable in every way, he wanted to ride her, hard and fast, until he exploded with joy.

But even that wasn't enough. Part of what had made him so crazy was watching her face as he gave her pleasure for the first time. Ten million dollars had been hanging in the balance, truly an immense fortune to someone with her background, and yet Laney still hadn't been able to hide her own passionate nature, or resist her desire.

Kassius wanted more of that. He wanted to make her writhe and gasp all over again. To make her reach a level of ecstasy greater than the one before. To hear her cry out his name. Only that would satisfy him now.

He deepened the kiss, and when she kissed him back, wrapping her arms around his shoulders, only then did he start to move inside her, inch by inch, with agonizing slowness that tortured him, when all he wanted to do was slam himself into her.

Instead, he swayed his hips back and forth, gritting his teeth as he held himself on the razor's edge of self-control. Again. Slower. He stroked her.

She gave a soft gasp. He looked down at her beautiful face. Her eyes were squeezed shut with new rapture; her cheeks were rosy and flushed with heat. Her red, bruised lips parted, and he couldn't resist the invitation. Lowering his mouth to hers, he nibbled her lower lip, flicking her with his tongue. As he kissed her, he finally started to increase the pace he thrust inside her, riding her harder, faster.

He felt the quick rise and fall of her breath beneath him, her lusciously full breasts moving against his chest. She writhed and swayed, and her fingernails dug into the flesh of his shoulders. Her whole body clenched beneath him as she held her breath, then suddenly she started to shake; suddenly she was screaming his name. His name…

It was too much. With a low cry, he thrust inside her

one last time, so deep, deep, deep, he lost track of where he ended and she began, filling her to the core, and he felt such mind-blowing pleasure that his own low, hoarse shout joined hers as he exploded.

When he opened his eyes again, the moonlight had shifted slightly across the bed. He looked down, and saw that he was holding Laney's petite body tightly in his arms. Odd. He'd never fallen asleep in a lover's arms.

But he'd never had a night like this. Or a woman like this.

Laney's long dark eyelashes fluttered across her creamy skin, her cheeks still flushed pink from the intensity of their lovemaking as she slept. Kassius felt a strange sense of tenderness as looked down at her, this woman who had fallen in front of his car, the employee of his father's employee, who somehow already wielded such power over him. She didn't realize how much.

And he'd make sure she never would.

She smiled in her dreams, her small body naked and warm in his arms, her long dark hair tumbling over the pillow they shared.

Marveling, Kassius took a deep breath. He was the only man who'd ever had her, and the only one who ever would. He would get her pregnant as soon as possible and make her his bride.

She'd be in his bed every night. The thought made him shiver inside. He intended to take long, hard use of her. She almost made him feel like he, too, was a virgin. As if, even with all his sexual experience, he'd never had the full measure of pleasure. Until her.

He had her now. And he never intended to let her go.

CHAPTER FOUR

THE NEXT MORNING, Laney sighed in satisfaction as she rinsed shampoo from her hair. She yawned, stretching in the hot, steamy shower. She felt like she'd barely slept, but her whole body ached with happiness, every muscle, every sinew, especially the secret places Kassius had explored last night. She'd woken up glowing with happiness after a night in his bed, sleeping in his arms. She'd only woken when he'd stirred beside her when his phone rang. Some business call from a distant place. She'd felt grimy, so as he took the call, she'd stumbled into the shower.

Now, standing in the enormous white marble bathroom of the penthouse, it was hard not to linger over the memory of the lovemaking that had caused all that sweat on her skin. As she washed away the traces of his many kisses, the sweet ache of her well-used body remained. She shivered, no longer just warmed by the steamy water but by the memory of how ruthlessly he'd taken her virginity.

Then she straightened beneath the hot water, as *everything* she'd done last night reasserted itself in her memory. Including the fact that they'd made love with no protection whatsoever.

What the hell had she been thinking?

"Oh, no," Laney whispered. Closing her eyes, she leaned her forehead against the cool tile.

She was a good girl who'd always followed the rules. She knew the potential ramifications of getting pregnant—how could she not? Her parents, high school sweethearts, had already broken up before her mother discovered she was pregnant. Her father had done the dutiful thing and married her, only to discover that they couldn't live together without loud arguments. He'd promptly found work on an oil rig that required long months away in the Gulf of Mexico—it paid well, plus he got time away from his wife. The marriage had bumbled along until Laney was ten, when her father was in a horrific accident on the rig, which caused him to lose his sight and the ability to walk. When his broken body was returned to New Orleans, it was the last straw for her mother.

Rhonda Henry had announced she'd had enough of sacrificing herself for other people. Dumping her husband and child on her mother-in-law's doorstep, Rhonda had hitched a ride with her musician boyfriend, heading west for love, fame and fortune in California. But love swiftly disappeared, and fame and fortune never came. Her mother had comforted her disappointment at first with alcohol, then worse things, until years later she'd died of an overdose on a beach near the Santa Monica Pier.

It had all started with Rhonda accidentally getting pregnant. If not for that, maybe her mother would be alive now, and her father strong and unhurt. If not for Laney being born.

Now she'd taken such a risk!

Stupid. So stupid. She covered her face with her hands. How could she have done it?

Especially knowing that she was certainly going to get fired today?

Turning off the water abruptly, Laney got out of the shower and wrapped herself in a towel.

She wiped the steam off the mirror. Her chin lifted as she looked at the reflection of her own dark, haunted eyes, at her wet hair that looked black cascading down her shoulders.

Whatever Kassius had said last night in the heat of the moment, fairy tales didn't come true. Princes didn't marry housemaids. Handsome billionaires didn't marry ordinary-looking personal assistants.

She would just have to go home and figure it out.

Home. A lump rose in Laney's throat as she thought of her father and grandmother. It had been two years since she'd seen them. She'd been away for too long, trying to earn enough money to support them all. But without her job here in Monaco, how would they all survive?

Taking a deep breath, she started to comb her wet hair. She'd just have to be strong, that was all. Maybe she'd get lucky. Maybe she could talk to Mimi. Convince her to forgive.

Yeah, right.

She reached for the oversize white robe on the back of the door. Kassius's robe? It hung huge on her, dragging on the floor, making her feel like a child dressed up in grown-up clothes. The sleeves hung well over her hands. She rolled them up, then pulled the belt as tightly around her as she could before she went to the kitchen.

"Good morning." Kassius looked at her appreciatively. "I like you in that."

Her cheeks colored. "Thanks. Is that coffee?"

He gave her a sudden grin. "Made it myself."

"Really?" she said, musing how the comtesse wouldn't have known how to pour water from the tap. "Yourself?"

"It's New Year's. My housekeeper has the day off. I'm not totally incompetent. I can make coffee, eggs and toast."

"Wow."

"No sarcasm, please. Not until you taste this." Pouring her a cup, he said, "Cream or sugar?"

"Both, please."

He added two lumps of sugar and a good amount of cream then watched her as she drank it.

"Good?"

Her whole body relaxed with a sigh. She said honestly, "The best coffee I've ever had."

"I thought so," he said smugly. "Now go sit down."

A moment later, he brought out two plates with buttered toast and scrambled eggs. Sliding a plate in front of her, placed his own across from her at the dining table.

She took a bite of the food and was astonished.

"This is delicious."

"Of course it is. I'm good at everything."

"Modest, too."

He took a bite of toast. "You're pretty good yourself." Their eyes met across the table. "I've never met a sexier woman in my life."

That reminded her. She bit her lip unhappily. "Last night, we had sex…without protection."

"Yes," he agreed, taking a bite of scrambled eggs. He didn't look at all sorry about it.

"Was I drunk? Were you?" She put down her fork. "To risk getting pregnant by someone I barely know…"

"If you feel you'd like to know me a little better—" his gaze fell to her breasts, then he gave her a smoldering smile "—we could go back to bed."

Her cheeks went hot as she looked down and saw the top of the oversize robe was gaping widely, showing far more of her chest than was decent. She yanked the robe up higher. "How can you joke?"

His expression changed. "Joke?"

"I can't believe I risked getting pregnant when I'm about to be unemployed!" She clawed back her wet dark hair, blinking back tears as she raged, "How could I have been so stupid!"

He looked at her skeptically. "Are you seriously worried about losing your job? You can't tell me you'll miss Mimi."

"No, but—"

"You have nothing to worry about." His voice was distinctly chilly as he abruptly rose from the table. "I'll go with you to Mimi's."

"You will?" Hope suddenly rose in her. "You'll talk to her? Try to convince her to keep me on?"

"No. It's better to end this quickly."

Better to end this quickly. Her hope faded, and she felt a little sick inside. Bad enough that she'd slept with him without protection. But would she now discover he'd just been slumming with a one-night stand and had taken her virginity as a momentary amusement? Had all his talk about marriage and children been a lie, or a whim, already forgotten?

Kassius being who he was, and Laney being—well, who she was—how could it be otherwise?

Hiding her deep hurt and regret, she looked down at the white robe. "What should I wear? This?" She lifted her arm, with the oversize sleeve hanging past her hand, to point at the gold ball gown still crumpled on the floor from the night before. "Or that?"

His sensual lips quirked. "You pick."

She sighed, then grumbled, "Robe, I guess." Finishing the coffee and food, she said sullenly, "Thanks for breakfast."

"My pleasure."

As she rose to leave, he followed her. She turned to him, desperate for the awkwardness to end. "You don't need to walk me down. There's really no need."

"Oh, but there is." He shrugged. "Anyway, I need to talk to Mimi."

Now he was done taking her virginity, did he want to make romantic plans with her soon-to-be-former boss? Laney's scowl deepened. "Fine."

Silence fell as they got in the elevator and pressed the button for her boss's floor. She couldn't help comparing this ghastly morning-after situation to last night, when they'd steamed up the mirrors, unable to keep their hands off each other.

She glanced at him out of the corner of her eye. Even now, when she was horrified and furious at herself, she could understand why, after being sensible and quiet her whole life, she hadn't been able to resist him. Kassius had made her feel beautiful. Desired. She'd been swallowed up by ecstasy, devoured by the pleasure of the moment.

But now the moment was over. As soon as she was fired and had packed her things, she'd return to New Orleans. Soon, this night—the most amazing night of her life—would be nothing more than a distant memory.

Unless she was pregnant.

The elevator doors opened with a ding.

"After you," Kassius said, holding the door.

As she walked down the hall toward the comtesse's suite, she heard his cell phone ring, and his footsteps slowed behind her. She kept walking.

Could she be pregnant?

What if she was?

Her lips curved softly at the idea of having a baby of her own to love, to hold in her arms…a child with Kassius's dark eyes…

No. She couldn't let herself think that way. She was unlikely to be pregnant, and that was a good thing. It would be a disaster right now. A baby was a serious responsibility, and she had nothing to offer. She didn't have money, a proper career, a husband. She didn't even have a real relationship with the baby's father.

All she really knew about Kassius Black was that he was a dangerously sexy billionaire who, for one magical night, had turned her from a servant into a fairy-tale princess in a golden gown. Remembering the way he'd made her feel last night, when she'd nearly wept with ecstasy in his arms, she couldn't even regret losing her chance at ten million dollars. Because in an important way, he'd changed her life. By seducing her, he'd proven she was desirable, and could feel desire. He'd opened her eyes.

For years, she'd felt invisible, unworthy of love. Now she'd never think of herself as a frigid little virgin again.

But would she soon be a single mother?

Laney could still hear the husky echo of his voice: *I am tired of the bachelor life. I want a family. I want a wife.*

But whatever fantasy he'd been indulging in last night, he'd obviously come to his senses this morning. *It's better to end this quickly.* When Kassius actually took a bride, she would be a beautiful, elegant, sophisticated woman of his own class. A woman like Mimi du Plessis.

Opening the door of the suite, Laney took a deep breath, bracing herself, and walked inside.

Her boss rose from the dining table with a tranquil smile. She murmured, "Have a good time last night?"

Was that a trick question? Was there a chance she wasn't about to be sacked? "Um, yes?"

Then Laney looked across the elegant suite, with all its feminine decor of Louis XVI furniture and wall-to-wall white shag carpeting, and saw her suitcases and a big box of her things sitting on the floor. And she knew she wasn't going to get lucky here.

Desperately, she said, "Madame, please forgive me. I owe you an apology—"

"Too late for that." Coming forward, the comtesse shoved a fifty-euro bill into Laney's hands. "Here."

"What's this?" she said, confused.

"Your last paycheck."

"But my next paycheck is due tomorrow, for two full weeks. And then there's also eight weeks of paid vacation time you always postponed—"

"Too bad. That's all you get."

"That's illegal!"

"Who's going to fight me? You?" Mimi's expression was hard. "You think you're my equal now, just because Kassius Black took you to bed? You're nothing, Laney. No one. Common street trash." She tossed her blond hair. "Now he's used you, he'll toss you out like garbage—"

"Ah. Mimi. So nice to see you this morning."

Kassius's husky voice made Mimi whirl around with a gasp. "Oh! I didn't expect—"

"Happy New Year." Tucking his phone back into his pocket, he gave her a smile. "I came to help Laney get her things. But also to talk to you."

"To me?" Mimi said.

His dark eyes were warm. "We have a few things to discuss."

Laney felt a stab of wild jealousy that made her sick inside, and no amount of reason could argue her out of it.

"Sir?"

A large man had suddenly appeared in the doorway behind Kassius.

"Ah. Benito." Kassius looked at Laney. "Are those your suitcases?" She nodded. "Is that everything?"

"Of course it's everything," Mimi snapped. "Do you think I want her trash left behind?"

He gave her a hard smile, then turned back to the man. "Please take Miss Henry's suitcases up to the penthouse."

"*Tout de suite*, monsieur."

"Thank you." He looked pointedly at Laney. "Can you manage the box?"

"Of course I can, but I don't see why—"

"I'll see you upstairs later," he interrupted.

She scowled. She didn't understand why he'd apparently asked his bodyguard to take her suitcases up to his penthouse. But she'd clearly been dismissed. And so coldly. Kassius couldn't wait to be alone with Mimi—probably to whisper sweet nothings in her ear and make a date for tonight. While Laney felt exactly like the harlot her ex-boss had implied—standing here like a fool in his oversize robe!

"Sure," Laney said coldly. "Later."

As Benito got her suitcases, she tightened the belt of the robe and lifted up the box that held old books, a plant and her grandmother's quilt. Turning, she left Mimi's suite with as much dignity as she could muster, without looking back.

Once in the hall, she turned to the bodyguard, or whoever he was. "I'll take those suitcases. There's no reason for you to take them upstairs. I'm just going to the airport."

The man shook his head. "Sorry, mademoiselle. Monsieur Black said to take you and the baggage upstairs, so upstairs you will go."

He insisted on taking her up in the elevator to the penthouse—her and the rest of the baggage. Once there, Laney stomped to the bedroom, fuming.

"I'm not going to wait for him!" she yelled back grumpily, but the man had already left. Fine. She'd just change her clothes and leave.

She dug through her suitcases for comfy cotton panties and a bra and started to reach for a white shirt and khaki pants. She stopped, remembering she wasn't anyone's employee. Not anymore.

Instead, she grabbed a brightly colored vintage T-shirt she'd bought at a flea market, advertising a rock concert in Paris in 1976. She put on red jeans that fit her like a glove, skimming tightly over her small waist, curvy hips and butt. Finally, she zipped up a fuzzy purple hoodie and pulled her hair back in a tight, French ponytail, tumbling straight down her back. Then she reached far into her suitcase for a tube of shocking red lipstick. There. Looking at herself in the bedroom's mirror, she smacked her lips with satisfaction.

She was done being anyone's servant.

She was now a woman with prospects.

On second thought, maybe her prospects weren't so great. But she was at least a woman of ambition.

Let's face it—she'd always known that working for the spoiled Mimi du Plessis was not exactly a lifetime occupation. It was time she figured out what she really wanted to do with her life, rather than squandering it by fits and starts.

There were other ways to make money. She could go to community college and train for something useful, like nursing or teaching. At twenty-five years old, she was no longer a kid. She could, and should, start acting like it. She would find a way to have a decent career that didn't leave her depressed and ashamed, one that would let her be close to her family and home. It wouldn't be easy. She'd likely have to work full-time while she attended night classes. But the sacrifice would be worth it.

She missed her family. Her home. Right now she would have killed for her grandmother's famous jambalaya with dirty rice, or her fried chicken and collard greens. Cheesy fried grits. A little crawfish étouffée or a muffuletta sandwich. She licked her lips at the thought of the tangy olive salad. Or the perfect breakfast—chicory coffee and hot buttery beignets, laced with powdered sugar, from the Café du Monde.

It was time to face the real world, of work and bills, but also, she thought hopefully, of chicory coffee and fried chicken. The real world, with both its hardships and joys.

But she'd always remember the New Year's Eve ball and the night she'd been Cinderella.

Her eyes fell on the exquisite golden ball gown on the floor. Slowly, she picked it up and folded it neatly across the back of a chair. Her fingers traced the sparkles of gold over the netting and tulle.

She would never forget the night. Or the man. Ever.

For the next ten years, when she was working two jobs

to pay her way through school and studying all night and eating ramen noodles and beans, she'd remember the one night she'd gone to a ball in Monte Carlo, like Grace Kelly.

Laney stuffed her grandmother's quilt into one of the suitcases and the empty box in the trash. She looked regretfully at the potted geranium. She'd have to leave that behind. She started digging in her small tattered handbag for her phone to order a ride to the airport, then stopped. She had no phone. It had been crushed by Kassius's car.

But it could have been so much worse. After giving him her virginity, after feeling such unbelievable pleasure and sleeping in the protective comfort of his arms all night, she felt how easily she could have fallen for him. A few more such nights, and he could have really broken her heart.

A phone? That could be replaced.

Snapping the suitcase shut, she stood, and looked around one last time at his lavish penthouse suite, with its expensive modern furniture and floor-to-ceiling views. The sun was shining across the bright blue sea.

With a deep breath, she squared her shoulders and turned away. Dragging the two suitcases, she started for the door. Then stopped when it opened and Kassius came in. He looked at the suitcases, and his expression turned dark.

"What do you think you're doing?" he growled.

"What does it look like?" She returned his gaze steadily. "Leaving."

"Leaving?" He gave a low laugh, then closed the door behind him. "Laney, we're just getting started."

She swallowed and hated how her heart fluttered. The expansive suite suddenly felt small with him stretching the walls inside it. All she could see was him. "I assumed when you wanted to be alone with Mimi…"

"That meeting was not personal." His dark eyes glittered. "Just business."

She blinked. "You're offering another loan to her boss? I've met Boris Kuznetsov, by the way. He's nice. Takes good care of his employees. Is that why you keep offering him loans?" she said curiously. "Just to help him out?"

"Something like that." His eyes were hard and veiled as he came closer, holding out a wad of bills. "Here."

Oh, dear heaven, he surely wasn't trying to pay her for what they did in bed last night? She said coldly, "What's that?"

"The money Mimi owes you. Two weeks' salary. Plus all the vacation she owed you for the past two years."

"How did you get it from her?"

The edges of his cruel, sensual lips lifted. "I asked nicely."

Hmm. Truly he had magical powers. She started to reach for the pile of euros, then stopped suspiciously. "What do you want from me in exchange?"

"You think I am trying to buy you?" He sounded amused. "I cannot buy what I already own."

"What are you talking about? You don't own me."

"We made a deal last night." He ran his hand lightly along her shoulder, over her thin vintage T-shirt. "Or did you forget?"

She had sudden memory of his words, huskily spoken in the dark. *If I make you explode with joy, you will surrender everything. You will allow me to take possession of your body and fill you with my child. You will be mine— forever.* She blushed.

"But that was ridiculous. A joke," she stammered. "Verbal foreplay. You don't actually expect me to—"

"I never joke about deals. Or go back on my word." He looked at her in the slanted light of morning. "Are you saying you do?"

The morning light of the Mediterranean caressed the hard edge of his cheekbones, with that lightly etched scar, the dark bristle of his sharp jawline, the boyishly mussed-up dark hair that looked so soft that even now, she longed to run her hands through it again. She forced her hands to remain still and lifted her chin. "In my experience, the wealthy have many whims that quickly change."

"It's not a whim. My proposal was straightforward. I want a family. I want a wife I can trust. You seemed to indicate you might be such a woman, but your only fear was that you would be inadequate in bed. That fear was proven false." He leaned forward. "You surrendered yourself to me, Laney," he whispered, his lips inches from hers. "Everything."

Her mouth went dry. "What kind of choice did you give me? I had no experience. No chance to resist your expert seduction."

Towering over her, he narrowed his eyes. "Are you saying I took you against your will?"

"Of course not," she said helplessly. She spread her hands. "It's just…women are interchangeable for you. An amusement. You switch them out like dirty socks, never committing to any of them."

"I'm willing to commit to you."

She swallowed, shivering with desire. "But it was just fantasy," she said helplessly. "Don't men always say things they don't mean to get women into bed?"

"You feel like home to me." Reaching down, he cupped her cheek. "I intend to marry you, Laney. Soon. Even now, you might be carrying my child."

The idea of marrying Kassius…of having his baby…it was a dream, a silly romantic dream. It couldn't be real! Girls like her didn't marry billionaires!

"You're just toying with me," she whispered.

For an answer, he pulled her into his arms, and kissed her.

His lips were rough and sweet, and as he kissed her,

slowly and tantalizingly, her fears and doubts disappeared. She felt lost in the hungry demand of his embrace, the warmth and power of his body against hers. She clung to him, reaching on tiptoe to wrap her arms around his neck, kissing him back with all the long-dormant passion inside her.

He drew away. "You are mine now," he whispered against her lips. "Accept what your body already knows."

She was shaking all over. "Why choose me? We barely know each other!"

"For the same reason I sometimes buy land the moment I see it. Sometimes it's not about the data or growth numbers or years of study." Looking down at her, he stroked her long dark hair. "Sometimes you see something, and you just know."

Was it truly possible? Laney thought of her own parents, who'd known each other their whole childhoods, growing up on the same street, dating all through high school. And look how that turned out.

Was marrying someone you'd known your whole life any less risky than taking a chance on love at first sight?

Love?

Could she love him?

Was she half in love with him already?

She shivered. Infatuation, she told herself. But how would she even know the difference? Maybe love was nothing more than infatuation that lasted.

"But I am going back home to New Orleans," she said numbly. "To get a job."

"No." Kassius ran his hand slowly down her back. "You're going to stay here and marry me, Laney. You know it. I know it."

She stared up at him, her whole body shaking, feeling wildly alive, her heart in her throat. Oh, this was insane.

"But strangers don't just decide to marry," she breathed.

"Don't they?" Lifting her hand to his lips, he kissed it. She felt the warmth of his breath, the gentle seduction of his lips. She thought how wonderful it was to have someone beside her. Someone watching over her.

"Would it help if I got down on one knee?" His lips curved humorously as he did just that. Pressing his hand to his heart, he said a little mockingly, "Elaine May Henry, will you do me the honor, the incredible glory, of becoming my—"

"Stop, stop!" she cried, her cheeks burning as she pulled him to his feet. "Don't tease!"

He looked down at her, his dark eyes serious.

"You are the one doing the teasing, Laney," he said. "For once and all, what is your answer?"

Her answer?

No.

No, of course.

Except...

Except it was yes.

After a lifetime of being sensible and good, of working all hours and being invisible, she felt the pull of being reckless. Of feeling *alive*. She yearned to be brave enough to do it—to love him—to jump headlong into the unknown. Right or wrong. She wanted to *live*.

She exhaled. "All right."

"You will?"

"Yes."

"There will be no going back," he warned.

"I won't go back." She offered him a trembling smile. "As you said. The deal was made. I honor my promises."

"And I honor mine." Pulling her tight into his arms, he tilted up her chin gently. "From now on, I'll always take care of you, Laney, and everyone you love. You'll never have to worry about anything, now you have my ring on your finger..."

She looked down at her bare left hand.

"Which ring is that?" she teased. She looked around the lavish penthouse suite. "Maybe we can find a ribbon or string or something that we can tie around my finger. A plastic ring from a Cracker Jack box?"

Smiling, he started to pull her toward the door. "I can do better than that."

"Where are we going?"

"The jeweler's."

"I was joking," she protested, then shook her head. "Besides, it's New Year's Day. Won't all the shops be closed?"

His smile widened. "They'll open for me."

CHAPTER FIVE

MONEY, KASSIUS OFTEN REFLECTED, was magic.

He'd built his business empire from nothing, fueled not by any desire for luxury, but his need for power. From the age of sixteen, he'd been grimly determined to make sure he'd never be desperate and helpless again. Never be ignored or left behind. He'd known he'd someday be so powerful and rich that he could get his revenge on the man who'd left him and his beloved mother behind, like garbage.

At eleven, Kassius's relatively happy childhood had ended when his father had abruptly stopped visiting or even sending money. No father. No money. No power. No name. News rushed through their neighborhood that Kassius's parents had never even been married, and just like that, the comfort of their little apartment in a quiet Istanbul street had ended.

He and his mother had suddenly found themselves outcasts. The wives of their neighborhood, distrustful of Emmaline's beauty, immediately froze her out, while their menfolk suddenly believed she would welcome their advances. Kids who'd once been Kassius's friends turned on him at school, repeating cruel taunts they'd heard from their parents. "Your own father doesn't want you—why don't you just curl up and die?"

But in the end it had been Kassius's fragile mother who had died—first her dreams, then her soul, finally her body. She'd been poisoned by waiting.

"Why don't we just sell the apartment and leave, Mama?" Kassius had asked her, stricken and bewildered. She'd shaken her head.

"We can't leave. Your daddy will be back soon…"

But he'd never come back. His Russian father had loved his company and his fortune and his dreams of a Cap Ferrat villa more than he'd loved them.

So that was what Kassius would take from him.

After his mother's death, when he was still a teenager, he'd sold everything he owned and left Istanbul. He'd borrowed as much money as he could get—some from banks, some from less legal, more dangerous loan sharks—to buy a single run-down tenement in an up-and-coming neighborhood in Athens. He'd rebuilt it himself, brick by brick, risking everything, holding back nothing, sleeping on the floor just four hours a night.

He'd put his foot on the throat of success and forced it to cough up what he wanted.

Over two decades, his small real estate holdings had grown into an international conglomerate. He'd bought up beachfront properties in Croatia, factories in Eastern Europe, spreading to Western Europe, then the Americas, Asia and, most recently, Africa.

In the last few years, as Boris Kuznetsov's oil company had run into trouble, he'd pounced, quietly buying up his loans and distressed assets, vacation homes around the world, his jet, the yacht. Kuznetsov still did not realize whom he'd lost them to, and why. But all the man had left now were the two things he cared about most: control of his flailing company, and the gaudy pink villa on Cap Ferrat, a luxurious enclave thirty minutes outside Monaco.

No, Kassius hadn't built his empire because he wanted luxury. He'd wanted power. He'd wanted revenge.

Occasionally, however, the luxury that could be purchased with unlimited money did bring unexpected pleasures. Such as right now.

"Are you sure?" Standing in front of the designer boutique's three-way mirror, Laney looked anxiously back at her deliciously ample backside in the tight, short red dress.

Sitting on a nearby sofa, holding a flute of expensive champagne brought to him by a salesgirl, Kassius stared at her. "You are exquisite."

And she was. The clingy red dress revealed the shape of her hourglass figure to perfection. Kassius couldn't look away from the glory of her wide hips, tiny waist and—he took a quick, shallow breath—those full breasts—

Frowning, Laney turned back to look at herself in the mirror, her lovely heart-shaped face uncertain, her long dark hair tumbling down her shoulders. She bit her full pink lip. "My grandmother would chew me out if she ever saw me walk out of the house in this." Her cheeks turned pink as she looked at the short hem. "I'm embarrassed just to let *you* see me in it!"

Kassius set down the barely tasted champagne. Rising to his feet, he walked a half circle around her. And he smiled.

Money was magic. It had made this all possible.

Designer boutiques and salons had opened just for them, eager for the patronage of the ultrawealthy, mysterious Kassius Black.

Laney had been reluctant to let him buy her anything. So he'd persuaded her with military precision, using logic. First, he'd bought her a replacement phone. That had been relatively easy, because after all, he owed her one. But he'd replaced her old, cheap phone with a top-of-the-line smartphone at ten times the price.

Next, he'd taken her to the most famously exclusive jeweler in Monaco to buy her an engagement ring. As she'd browsed the plain gold bands, he'd quietly purchased in her size a twenty-carat diamond engagement ring set in platinum. He'd overridden her protests that she didn't need anything so expensive. Of course she needed it. She was going to be his bride.

He'd made sure she didn't know how much it cost, however. If she'd known, she would have certainly rebelled at the thought of wearing a sparkling rock on her finger that cost approximately the same as three average houses.

After buying the ring, they'd gone for an elegant lunch near the harbor overlooking the yachts, a slight respite before he'd taken Laney to a salon, where a world-famous hairstylist had left his own New Year's Day house party in Nice to trim and style Laney's dark, lustrous mane. As a manicurist and pedicurist buffed her nails, a makeup artist shaped her brows, adding just the right shade of lipstick, eye shadow and creamy blush.

Laney had never been pampered in quite this way before. As far as he could tell, she'd never been pampered at all. Obviously. She'd been a virgin who'd—incredibly— believed herself to be frigid until he'd seduced her. She'd been unnoticed by men till now and spent all her time working, providing for her family.

After the salon, she no longer put up a fight. He took her to expensive designer boutiques, buying her clothes, shoes, handbags, an entirely new wardrobe, replacing her thrift store bargains with the chic, sophisticated outfits her new life would require. He'd particularly enjoyed selecting her lingerie. But this—

He lost his breath looking at his bride-to-be.

"Leave us," he said hoarsely.

The two salesgirls and boutique manager hovering in the background glanced at each other uncertainly. Kassius turned to the manager with a cold glare.

"Now."

The manager gave a swift nod and clapped his hands at the two salesgirls, who fled before he followed them out.

A second later, they heard the bell of the door as they went out into the cold twilight.

Yes, Kassius thought. Money was magic.

As he turned back smugly to Laney, she was staring at him in disbelief.

"Does everyone always do what you say?"

He came closer to her, his eyes intent. He kissed her bare shoulder, brushing back soft dark tendrils of her hair. "Yes."

He felt her tremble beneath his touch.

"You can't be…thinking that we…" Laney sounded breathless as she looked up at him with big brown eyes. He saw the quick rise and fall of her breasts. But Kassius was past thinking anything.

Pushing her back against the three-way mirror, he roughly kissed her, cupping her magnificent breasts through the tight red dress.

"Not here," she breathed, struggling. "They might walk in…"

"They won't," he whispered huskily, his lips brushing against her ear. "Benito is no doubt entertaining them outside in his lamentable French."

"It's rude kicking them out of their own store, out into the cold after we dragged them here on New Year's Day…"

"They're well paid to wait and not to see or hear anything."

"But if they do—"

"Then let them hear," he said coldly. "Let the whole world hear, and see, and wish you were theirs. Let them be jealous you are mine."

He kissed her roughly, and with a sigh of surrender, she fell back against the mirrored wall. He was rock hard for her, his body straining, as he ran his hands along her hips in the red dress, her bare thighs, the cleavage of her full breasts pressing against the tight fabric.

He needed her. Now.

Roughly, he yanked her short red dress up to her hips, revealing her lace panties.

Kissing her passionately, he lifted her bare legs to wrap around his hips, her back against the mirror. Unzipping his trousers, he roughly yanked her panties aside and without asking permission, he thrust himself inside her with a groan, sheathing himself to the hilt.

She gasped, clinging to him, the tight red dress now pushed up to her waist. Her eyes were closed, her head tossed back with pleasure. She swayed her hips as he pushed inside her, thrusting hard and fast until he heard her cry out, until he felt her shake. Hearing that, feeling it, he exploded inside her.

For a moment, he just held her tight against the wall, her thighs still wrapped around his hips, and she held him. Then, slowly, the world intruded. He released her, and she slid back down to stand in front of him. He zipped up his trousers, smoothed her lace panties and pulled her dress back modestly over her thighs.

"I guess we'll have to buy the dress now." Reaching out, he rubbed smeared lipstick off her chin.

Self-consciously, she touched her skin, then looked up at him accusingly. "Whose fault is that?"

"Yours."

"Mine?"

"For being too desirable." He looked down at her seriously. "I can hardly wait to marry you."

"When did you have in mind?" she said tartly. "You've taken charge of everything today. Are you planning to drag me from here straight to a justice of the peace?" She looked down at the expensive red dress, which hadn't even been paid for yet but was already wrinkled. "Is this my wedding dress?"

He gave a low laugh. "We have dinner reservations at Le Coq d'Or. We can talk about wedding plans over wine."

"Le Coq d'Or?" Her lips parted. "How on earth did you get reservations there? I heard the comtesse complain about how impossible it is to get in."

He shrugged. "I called them today and gave them my name. They suddenly had space."

"You always get everything you want, don't you?" She sounded grumpy. "You never even have to wait."

"I do sometimes," he said grimly, thinking of the plans for revenge he'd first formulated twenty years before. At her searching glance, he gave her a bland smile. "Shall we tell the boutique staff it's safe to come back?"

Ten minutes later, Benito and their sedan's driver were stacking yet more of their shopping bags into the trunk. Kassius held the car door open for Laney, who was now wearing a long, expensive, belted black coat over her red dress, which he'd insisted she should wear, to keep off the cool air.

"You want to drive?" She looked surprised. "But it's a lovely evening. Le Coq d'Or is just up the hill. Why not walk?"

"*Just up the hill?*" He snorted. "It's a half-hour walk."

"So?"

He looked pointedly at her feet, now shod in wickedly expensive stilettos. "In those?"

Her ankle turned slightly on the sidewalk, proving his point. She regained her balance and glared at him. "So?"

"Most women I know complain if they have to walk more than a hundred meters in shoes like that. And they're more accustomed to wearing them."

Laney tossed her head, looking offended as she retorted, "Most of your other women were probably not accustomed to working sixteen to twenty hours a day on their feet."

What was she trying to prove? He looked at her, amused. "True."

"So." Her chin lifted, and her eyes glittered. "We're walking."

Kassius shrugged. "As you wish." He gave his bodyguard and driver a nod, and they got into the sedan and drove on. Tossing her head, she started walking with a determined stride. Ten steps later, she wobbled in her stiletto heels and had to grab his arm.

"You sure you're up for this?" he inquired.

"It's your fault if I have trouble."

"Because I bought you the shoes?"

"Because you bought me such an obscenely huge engagement ring." She looked down at it. "It weighs five pounds. No wonder my balance is off."

Kassius gave a low laugh. Laney fascinated him. She seemed to be so many women, all at once. At the ball, she'd looked like an enchanted princess from a fairy tale. That morning when he'd proposed to her, she'd looked like a bohemian college student in her vintage rock T-shirt and red jeans—vibrant, chaotic, alive.

Now...in the sleek belted black coat and stilettos...with the red dress beneath...

He shuddered with desire, already wanting her again. He took her hand, looking down at her. "We could skip dinner," he said huskily. "And go back to the penthouse."

She stared up at him. "Seriously?"

"Why not?"

"Are you trying to starve me?"

"Can't have that." He looked appreciatively at her curves and sighed with regret. "All right. Dinner first."

Her triumphant expression lasted only about ten minutes, which was when the road started to go sharply uphill. Soon, she was wincing with every step.

"I'll call my driver."

"Why?" she said through gritted teeth. "Are you tired?"

She was determined, he had to give her that. But he didn't understand why she was being so stubborn about this. "Just kick your shoes off and walk barefoot."

"I'm fine," she panted, forcing her lips into a bright, fake smile. "Six-inch stiletto heels are comfortable to me. Just like fuzzy bunny slippers!"

When they were two blocks away from the restaurant on the Boulevard du Jardin Exotique, she really started to stumble. The edges of her skin, where they were crammed into the shoes, looked red and swollen. The back of her ankle had started to bleed. It was too much. With a low growl, Kassius swept her up into his arms.

"What are you doing?" she demanded.

"I'm not letting you kill yourself for the sake of your pride, you little fool." Ignoring her weak struggles, he carried her the rest of the way down the block to the expensive, exclusive restaurant with vast windows overlooking the Monte Carlo district of Monaco and all of the bay.

"*Bonsoir,*" he said pleasantly to the valets and doorman, who were goggling at them. The staff at Le Coq d'Or had no doubt seen a great deal of peculiar behavior they were paid to overlook from their wealthy, spoiled clientele, but apparently this was a new one, even for them.

"Put me down!" Laney hollered, then proceeded to curse Kassius roundly and colorfully until the other men's eyes widened farther still. She cursed him until he set her down and her feet actually touched the ground, when she visibly winced and her cheeks turned pale with pain.

Now Kassius was the one to curse. Getting down on one knee before her, he yanked off her stiletto heels, one after the other. "Laney, what are you trying to prove?"

"Nothing!"

"These aren't hiking boots, you little fool."

"I know, but—"

"But what?"

Her cheeks burned, and she looked away.

And he suddenly knew.

"You're tougher than any of them, Laney. Better than any woman I've ever been with. Is that what you're trying to prove? Well, you are." He handed the shoes to her. "And for the record, a million times sexier, too."

"I wasn't trying to prove anything." But her pale cheeks turned red, and he knew he'd guessed correctly. She mumbled, "And I am not sexier."

Looking down, he said softly, "Want me to prove how much I want you? Right here and now?"

"You wouldn't," she breathed, her eyes big and incredibly appealing. But by the nervous look in her face, she was remembering their earlier encounter at the designer boutique. And probably wondering if he intended to take savage possession of her body right in front of the restaurant, with the doorman and valets looking on.

"But I can't have you faint from hunger." He gave her a wicked grin. Leaning forward, he whispered, "Not with what I've got planned for later."

Her eyes went big, and she licked her lips, which just made him want to kiss her more.

It was amazing to Kassius how even though he'd just made love to her an hour ago, he already wanted her again. He wondered if his desire for her would ever be sated, and doubted it. But that would just have to wait until they got back to the penthouse. Tucking her stilettos into her expensive new handbag, he led Laney into the expensive restaurant.

The maître d' spotted him, and his expression became obsequious. "Monsieur Black, welcome. We have your table ready." The man's glance fell to Laney's bare feet, and for a moment his mien faltered, but then his smile reasserted itself. "May I take your coats? This way, if you please, monsieur, mademoiselle."

Laney held Kassius's hand tightly as they walked through the crowded restaurant, past the elegant diners and buzz of polyglot conversation in French, German, Russian, Italian, English, Japanese and others. Le Coq d'Or was internationally famous, and well-heeled patrons often flew here on their private jets for a hard-to-get dinner reservation. But conversation seemed to stop as they passed by.

She clung to his hand, and whispered, "They're looking at me."

He glanced back at her indulgently. "Because you're beautiful."

"Because I'm barefoot. They think I'm a hick."

"You are with me. You can be whatever you want to be."

You can be whatever you want to be.

His own words brought him up short. For a moment, Kassius was distracted by a flash of light through the wide windows, of the lowering twilight sun sparkling across the silver sea. A memory floated back to him of his mother's raspy words as she lay dying.

"You can be whatever you want to be, darlin'." He could still hear her low laugh. She'd never lost her lilt, the drawl of the American South. "Believe it or not, my own parents wanted me to stay home and be a political wife in a big mansion."

"So why didn't you?" he'd asked her then in a low voice, heartsick over her illness and nearly overwhelmed by grief and rage at what he'd just discovered about his long-absent father.

"I wanted adventure," Emmaline Cash had whispered. "And I got it." Smiling through her tears, his mother squeezed his arm weakly. "It's the secret of life. You can be whatever you want to be, darlin'. As long as you're willing to pay the price..." Her words ended in fierce coughing. From her bed, she'd motioned around the tiny, sagging apartment on the edges of Istanbul. "You don't have to settle for what others want for you or for the life you're born in. You can decide."

He'd looked down at his mother's tiny, fragile form beneath the blankets, feeling like he'd been kicked between the ribs. She was too young to die. She'd barely lived.

"Do you have any regrets, Mama?" he'd choked out.

She gave him a trembling smile. "I wish I could live long enough to see the man you'll be, the family you'll have someday." Her smile abruptly faded. When she spoke again, her voice was a low rasp he'd never heard before. "And I wish the first time your father came up with excuses why he couldn't marry me I'd let myself see him for the liar he was, rather than make excuses. If I'd only been brave enough to leave him right then and there, our lives could have been so different! Maybe I could have found another man who would have loved us. Cherished us. But I was so sure—" Her dark eyes shone with sudden anguish as she put her hand over his. "If someone ever shows you the truth of who they are, if they lie or cheat or betray you, promise me you'll believe them the first time!" Her voice broke on a sob. "Don't destroy your life, or your child's, wishing and hoping and pretending they'll change—"

"Kassius?" Laney said.

He abruptly focused on her, coming back to the present as they were seated at a prime table by the windows. Numbly, he helped her with her chair then took his own seat as the waiter handed them menus and poured their water.

She looked at him thoughtfully. "So I can be anything I want to be, huh? How about prima ballerina, or a circus lion tamer?"

Kassius gave a small smile. "Why not?"

He wondered what she would say if he told her about his

past, told her what had driven him to become the man he was today. She was dying to know. She, like every woman. Like every business competitor or shareholder. They all claimed they needed to know the particulars of his past, as if that could be beneficial, as if that would inspire trust and cooperation.

The truth was, if they knew what had driven him since he was sixteen years old, if they knew his real name, they would only find a way to use that information against him. They would use his old grief as a wedge in his soul to devour him, to destroy him.

Reveal weakness to no one. It had been a hard lesson to learn, when his first business partner, someone he'd trusted, had run off with his money, setting Kassius back an entire year of backbreaking work. Showing your throat even to the meekest sheep would only reveal weakness and give the sheep the sharp greedy teeth of a wolf. He wouldn't give anyone the opportunity to go for his jugular.

But the most important lesson in success was from the example of his own father. He'd learned to be selfish and pursue his own desires. No matter how it might hurt others. He'd learned to only care about himself.

He'd chosen Laney not just because of her deep sexual appeal, but also her sweetness, her innocence. Her kind heart. He'd thought perhaps he could let himself be vulnerable with her, after they were wed.

But now he suddenly realized he couldn't take that risk. If even Laney knew his weaknesses, she could use it against him. She could leave him, or betray him.

He would never give her that power. She would get no ammunition from him—no bullets from his past she could use against him.

"I think you'd make an excellent lion tamer," he said mildly and opened the menu. "What looks good?"

She looked at her own menu, filled with very elegant

and precious delicacies such as foamy quail eggs, and sighed. "What I wouldn't give for some good Southern cooking right now." She brightened. "Maybe we could stop at the supermarket on the way back to your penthouse."

"Southern?" He looked up sharply. "You know how to cook Southern cuisine?"

"Sure," she said with a shrug. "Fried chicken, grits, collard greens. Gumbo, dirty rice, muffuletta sandwiches. All that stuff. My grandma taught me."

The waiter came to take their order. By this time Kassius's mind was so full of Louisiana cooking that he barely cared about some impossibly exclusive three-star French restaurant. He impatiently ordered them both the tasting menu and a fine red Bordeaux, a 2005 Château Lafite Rothschild. As the waiter departed with a bow, Kassius leaned forward. "I've been trying to hire a Louisiana chef for my ski chalet in Gstaad, but it's hopeless."

"You must not be looking in the right places." Laney smiled at a different waiter, who brought a bread bowl to their table. She immediately helped herself to a piece of the plump, fresh bread and slathered it with butter. "Where I'm from, everyone knows how to cook."

"Didn't you once work as assistant to that world-famous Louisiana chef?"

She frowned. "How did you know that?"

Oh. Right. She didn't know about the investigator. Shrugging, he gave her a charming smile. "I heard it somewhere."

"Huh." She looked a little confused, then continued, "Sure, I learned some stuff from him. But if you ask me, my grandmother is the best cook in New Orleans."

"That's quite a statement."

"It's true, and she taught me everything she knows."

A shiver went through Kassius. Sitting at this exclusive restaurant on the Côte d'Azur for a meal that might easily cost fifteen hundred euros a plate, his mouth was suddenly watering for something more simple. The home cooking of long ago. When he'd had a home. And when someone had cooked for him, not for money, but for love.

The waiter brought the wine and poured a bit in a large wineglass. Kassius swirled it, sipped, then nodded. The waiter poured for them both.

"I haven't been home for over two years. I miss it."

"What do you miss?" he asked curiously.

"My family. The city. The food. The smell of cypress and magnolias. Everything." She sighed as she sipped her wine and settled back in her chair. "Even Mardi Gras. What a party. The whole city goes crazy." Crossing her leg, she bounced her bare leg. Her toenails were a wicked, glossy red. He had a hard time not staring at her crossed leg, bouncing. She continued dreamily, "Nothing but parades and music and food, and the whole city out of their mind with joy."

"Sounds…nice." His mother used to speak wistfully about Mardi Gras, too. But he'd never been to New Orleans, not once, or seen the house where she'd been born on St. Charles Avenue. Her wealthy, disapproving parents had disinherited her at nineteen, when Emmaline had run off to be a stewardess rather than accepting the decorous marriage they'd arranged for her. Sixteen years later, after Emmaline had been abandoned by the father of her son, when she was desperate and grievously sick, she'd humbled her pride and written her parents to ask for their help. She'd asked them to promise to take her teenage son, whom they'd never met, if she died from her illness.

Their answer had been scathing.

You made your bed, Emmaline, they'd told her. *Now lie in it.*

His mother had never told Kassius about this, of course. But after her death, he'd found the letter from her parents,

Eugene and Thelma Cash, tucked next to his own birth certificate.

Kassius's grandparents wrote him after her death, to try to take back their cruel words, to make him part of their lives. "We thought she just wanted money. We didn't realize she was actually dying." He threw their letter in the trash and left for Athens.

Later, after he'd made his fortune, after his grandparents had both died, he'd bought their old house in New Orleans. He'd had it destroyed. He'd never wanted to see it.

But suddenly, Kassius wanted to see New Orleans through Laney's eyes.

"Sounds like a good place for a honeymoon."

At this, she abruptly stopped bouncing her leg. "What are you saying?"

"We could even get married there. Isn't Mardi Gras next month?"

She stared at him, her eyes joyful. "You mean it? My family could be there?"

She seemed far more thrilled by the prospect of having a party with her family than she'd been by the over half a million euros he'd spent on her today. He found he liked being the object of her gratitude, the person who gave her joy. He liked it very much. He wanted more of it.

"Sure, if that's what you want. By the way—" he took a sip of the red wine "—since you were so concerned about your family's financial situation, I have instructed my business manager to call them and make sure they have any money they need, without limit or question."

Her brown eyes were huge. "Seriously?"

"Of course."

"Oh, Kassius—" Then she bit her lip as her expression faded. "But they can be proud, especially my father. I'm not sure they will accept money from you."

"Of course they will," he said firmly. "It is my responsibility now to provide for all of you. And money doesn't matter. It's not what I care about."

"What do you care about?"

He looked at her.

"Finishing this damn dinner," he said frankly, "so I can take you to bed."

"Oh, just you wait." Ignoring all the high-powered tycoons and socialites at surrounding tables, Laney rose from her chair. Her beautiful face was suffused with joy as she went to him and climbed in his lap. He could feel the entire restaurant goggling at the sight of Laney in the red dress as, wrapping her arms around him, she bent her head and whispered in his ear, "I intend to thank you tonight. Very thoroughly."

Kassius felt fire whip through his blood, from his brain to his groin. And though they hadn't even been served their dinner yet, it was all he could do not to immediately raise his hand and call for the check.

"Oh, no," Laney whispered aloud. She stared down at the bathroom scale, which was giving her news she didn't like at all. She looked at herself in the mirror. Her face was green.

But was it any wonder she felt so ill and run-down? For the last eight weeks, since they'd left Monaco, she'd had too much of everything.

Too much travel, for a start. Too many days with Kassius on his private jet, accompanying him on business trips around the world, from London to Berlin to Tokyo to Johannesburg to Sydney to Nairobi to Santiago and back to their home base in London. She felt exhausted just thinking about it.

Too much shopping. In each new city, Kassius had insisted on showering her with expensive gifts of clothes, handbags, shoes and jewelry, when she already had so much, her big walk-in closet at the town house in London was threatening to explode. She hadn't yet had time to wear half of what he'd bought her.

Too much time spent planning their upcoming wedding in New Orleans. Laney would have been fine with a simple ceremony she planned herself, with a few friends and maybe some rum punch and her grandmother's homemade Cajun dinner, but Kassius had insisted she hire a wedding planner in New Orleans to manage everything. Which meant Laney was constantly on the phone with her, and spending far too many hours over ridiculous decisions, like what candy color the iPads in the guest gift bags should be.

And worst of all—Laney had suffered through far too many of Kassius's business dinners in expensive restaurants, where the red-faced, oversize men all seemed to have stomachs of iron, and ate huge dinners of steak, foie gras and baked potatoes covered in butter and sour cream, then smoked cigars as they washed it all down with scotch and drank oceans of expensive wine. Their girlfriends and wives, skeletal as fashion decreed, seemed to meekly subsist on lettuce leaves and an occasional gin and diet tonic.

Kassius thought that was ludicrous and had threatened to end their engagement if Laney ever followed their example. "I like every single pound of you," he'd told her firmly. "Don't lose a single one."

Laney had liked it when Kassius said it, but now she was in a panic. Because just this last week, without trying, she'd lost five pounds.

All the fault of this exhausting lifestyle, she thought grumpily. And since they had sex at all hours, she hadn't had nearly enough sleep. No wonder her body was breaking down. She'd felt so nauseated that four days ago, she'd actually sent Kassius off alone on his business trip to Hong Kong. He'd been none too pleased about it.

She hadn't been, either. She hated having him so far away from her, even just for a few days. Though she didn't always love the forced luxury of their overscheduled, shallow lifestyle, she did love living with Kassius, being in his arms, in his bed. She loved that he was the first person she saw in the morning, and the last person she saw at night. It was starting to feel like…a relationship.

She shivered at the thought.

All the plans she'd once had for her life seemed like pale shadows compared to her daily joy of being with him. All thoughts of going to college or getting a job had flown out the window. The thought horrified her. Here she was, a twenty-first-century woman, but all she wanted to do, all she wanted to be, was the lover—the *wife*—of this intoxicating, infuriating, sexually electrifying man.

And soon, the mother of his child? They were going to be a family. As someone who'd always had to work for a paycheck, just being able to spend her days with him, *for* him, made her deliriously happy. Even if the activities that filled their days weren't ones she would have necessarily chosen, somehow having Kassius beside her made it endurable. Even magical. Suddenly, all the fairy tales were making sense.

Did Kassius feel the same? she wondered. He hadn't liked leaving her in London. He wanted her with him constantly. It was the reason why, after eight weeks together, he still hadn't let her visit her family in New Orleans.

"You'll see them soon enough, at the wedding," he'd growled. "Until then, I need you with me. You're my woman."

Words that made her toes curl in happiness.

He was due to return from Hong Kong tonight. But it worried her. After four days spent alone in Kassius's huge London town house, barely getting out of bed, she'd thought she'd be feeling better by now. She'd thought she would be back to her old self, and able to welcome him home properly—and by properly, she meant in bed.

Since they'd left Monaco, London had been their new home base. She'd liked the city from the moment they'd arrived at a private airport and a car had arrived to whisk them to a fancy neighborhood that Kassius told her was called Knightsbridge.

At the four-story town house, Laney had met additional house staff, besides the bodyguards and driver carrying their luggage. Four people were waiting to formally greet them as they walked in.

"Welcome home, sir," a thin, elderly woman said.

"Thank you, Mrs. Beresford. I'd like you to meet my fiancée, Miss Laney Henry."

Mrs. Beresford had shaken her hand politely.

But later, as Kassius led Laney up the sweeping stairs of the elegant mansion, she whispered to him, "I don't think your housekeeper likes me."

He'd looked at her, surprised, then shook his head in amusement. "She's just nervous."

That thought surprised Laney so much she stopped on the stairs. "Her, nervous?"

"You're her new boss."

"Me?"

He smiled. "As my wife, you'll rule the home, and I have five of them—houses, I mean—with a paid staff at each. You're now their boss."

The thought astonished Laney. Her, the boss?

"Really?" she squeaked.

"Why? Are you afraid?"

Terrified. "Um…and they all live here?"

"Only Mrs. Beresford. But they all exist to serve our desires." His eyes darkened, turned hungry. "As you, Laney, exist to serve mine."

Then he'd taken her to bed.

But Laney's whole life hadn't been spent in bed, unfortunately. Or even on his very comfortable private jet, zipping to exotic locales.

Sadly, she was also expected to be his hostess, and his companion at social events and those awful business dinners. Those were the worst. She always feared she wasn't interesting enough and they were laughing behind her back. When it all got too stressful, the only good cure was calling her family for a nice long chat. But even those weren't the same as they used to be.

When she'd first phoned her grandmother and father to tell them she was engaged to Kassius, they hadn't exactly been overjoyed. Her grandmother had been shocked and dubious. Her father had been downright mad.

And now, eight weeks later, not much had changed. Each time she called them, it was the same.

"You sure about this wedding, Laney May?" her grandmother kept repeating. "You just met the man, and marriage lasts a long time. It ain't just about great sex."

"Gran!" she cried, embarrassed. But talking to her father was even worse.

"What kind of man is he, to propose marriage after two days' acquaintance?" her father growled into the phone.

"We just met, and we knew…" She blushed. "Kassius is amazing, Dad."

"So amazing he won't let you come home for a visit? So amazing he can't be bothered to come meet your family and ask your father for your hand in marriage?"

"Of course he's dying to meet you and Gran. He's just such an important man, Dad, and so very busy…"

It had sounded pretty lame, even to her own ears.

"Busy?" he'd said scornfully. "Doing what—counting his money? Flying you all over the world on that private jet of his, traveling everywhere *but* your home? Face it,

Laney May. The man doesn't respect you. And he sure doesn't respect us."

No, talking to her family wasn't nearly as comforting as it used to be. But at least she had assurances from Kassius's business manager that her family had been informed they now had access to any and all financial resources they might desire. She'd been a little surprised they'd consider his offer, given their opinions about him, but since they hadn't said no, she tried to take it as a good sign.

Her wedding day was almost here. She and Kassius were supposed to leave for New Orleans tomorrow, and their wedding would be held the day after. It was a tight schedule, but he'd been busy wrapping up a deal in Asia.

At least her wedding dress was finished—her grandmother had sent Laney her wedding gown, used fifty years earlier when she'd begun her own long, happy marriage to her grandfather. The elegant 1960s gown had been recut and tailored to Laney's size, and lengthened for her extra two inches of height. Last week, when she'd first seen herself in it, she'd cried.

"Everything is set. Your wedding will be perfect, Miss Henry," the wedding planner had told her that morning over the phone.

But it wouldn't be such a perfect wedding, Laney thought unhappily now, if she was violently ill into her wedding flowers.

Maybe she should call a doctor. Because she was really starting to worry. In the four days since Kassius left, she'd existed on saltine crackers and lemon-lime soda. It seemed strange she wasn't feeling better. She felt so tired all the time. And her breasts still felt so sensitive, when Kassius hadn't made love to her for days. It was almost as if…

She sucked in her breath.

"Is there anything else you require, madam?" Mrs. Beresford peeked in at the door of the front sitting room.

"I'm going to retire for the night." She frowned, coming closer. "Are you quite all right, Miss Henry?"

Laney sat up straight on the sofa. "Can you help me find a doctor who does house calls?"

Two hours later, after Dr. Khan congratulated her and left the house, Laney walked back to the sofa in a daze.

She wasn't sick. She hadn't been feeling ill because she'd eaten too many fattening meals or traveled too much or had too much sex…or actually—she blushed—her situation was the result of precisely that last one.

She was pregnant.

"Oh, my dear," Mrs. Beresford said gently, patting her on the shoulder, "I'm so happy for you. I did wonder all week if that might be the cause…"

"You did?" Of course Mrs. Beresford knew. Household servants were always the first to know. Often even before their employers did.

After the kindly older woman left for her own suite, Laney hunkered down on the sofa to wait for Kassius to come home from the airport. She cuddled beneath her grandmother's homemade quilt, feeling dazed as she put her hands over her belly.

A baby. She'd soon be holding a sweet baby in her arms. Kassius's and hers.

She felt overwhelmed by emotion, caught between joy and anxiety. Her family's words came back to haunt her.

Face it, Laney May. The man doesn't respect you.

But Kassius did respect her. She knew he did. He always told her she was beautiful and how much he desired her. He told her he couldn't wait to marry her and start a family. He thanked her for accompanying him to business dinners—"You're a natural, you charm everyone"—and as for her cooking skills—well, his enthusiasm for that knew no bounds.

On Valentine's Day, she'd made him a romantic dinner in the house's enormous kitchen, with all of his favorite dishes.

"I'm in love," Kassius had moaned, his expression one of pure ecstasy. Unfortunately, he was looking at the fried chicken as he said it.

And maybe that was the problem.

Laney shivered under her grandma's quilt.

She didn't just want him to love her fried chicken, or her jambalaya, or her gumbo. She wanted him to love *her*.

Because she was in love with him.

She couldn't deny it anymore. Couldn't tell herself it was just a crush. Honestly, she'd been in love with him from the day he'd hit her with his car.

For her, it had been love at first sight.

But for him...?

Kassius never mentioned love. And though she tried to convince herself that he, too, must have also loved her at first sight—otherwise, why would he have proposed marriage?—she feared she was deluding herself. He had such hard edges. He rarely spoke of his feelings, or desires beyond sex or food or the next business deal. He sometimes spent hours working out at the gym, coming back bruised from sparring at the dojo. What drove him so hard?

She wished she knew. But when she asked him personal questions, he changed the subject. He didn't ask her about her feelings or her past, either.

If only he would trust her enough to let her in. If only he could love her. If only the news of their coming baby could be the crack that would let light, and love, into his heart!

The bodyguard peeked in an hour later.

"I just heard Mr. Black's plane isn't expected till later. Do you need anything, Miss Laney?"

She smiled up at him from the sofa, grabbing a magazine. Winter twilight was starting to fade through the windows, but she felt too exhausted to bother turning on a light. "No, thank you, Benito. I'm good."

And he, too, departed for his own suite of rooms in the basement, where he was always available in case of trouble, as a backup to the security alarm in their very safe neighborhood.

Laney's eyes soon grew heavy. She must have fallen asleep, because she woke in darkness when she heard the front door slam. Hearing Kassius's voice, she sat up on the sofa, ready to call out his name.

Then she heard a woman's low, throaty laugh in the foyer. "You're taking a risk, bringing me here."

Heart pounding, Laney sank down lower on the sofa, lifting the quilt back up to her forehead so they wouldn't see her as they walked by the open doorway.

"What will you do if your sweet little Laney finds out?" The woman continued. Her voice was familiar. Very familiar.

"She won't. She's a deep sleeper, especially lately." Kassius's voice was low and cool. "Better to do it here, where no one can see us."

"Ah, so the little angel sleeping peacefully upstairs has no idea what you're up to? I thought you two were so close. I heard you were engaged."

"We are."

"Funny sort of engagement. Seems she went from being my servant to yours."

Hardly breathing, Laney peeked over the back of the sofa to see Kassius, looking devastatingly handsome as ever in his suit covered by a long black coat. And the woman with him—her old boss, Mimi du Plessis!

"Here," Kassius said to her, grabbing a black velvet box from a drawer. "As promised."

She opened it and smiled. "You're a man of your word."

Lifting her blond hair off her neck, she glanced back at him flirtatiously. "Put it on me."

Setting down the box on the entryway table, he lifted out an exquisite diamond necklace and wrapped it around her throat. "There. Good?"

"Good." Turning back, she looked up at him and observed, "You know, it might have been cheaper for you to just marry me instead of paying me in gifts."

"Or not."

"Or not," she agreed. She gave him a mock salute. "Until next time."

Mimi du Plessis walked out of the foyer, her sharp little heels clacking against the marble floor. When the front door closed behind her, Kassius exhaled, pulling off his long black coat. His shoulders looked weary.

Trembling, Laney rose from the sofa and rushed into the brightly lit foyer. When Kassius saw her, his tired face lit up. But she was way past caring about that now.

"What the hell is going on?" she demanded.

It was so unlike her to curse, he stared at her in shock. "Laney—"

"What was *she* doing here? Why did you give her jewelry? Why?"

His expression shuttered. Turning back to his laptop bag, he pulled out his computer, then glanced back at the dark sitting room. "Eavesdropping, were you? Waiting in the dark to see what you could discover?"

"I fell asleep on the sofa, waiting to tell you—" She bit off her words. "It doesn't matter! I heard you!"

"And just what do you think you heard?"

"Are you having an affair?" she choked out, feeling wretched.

"Are you serious?"

A wave of nausea hit her, and she was suddenly afraid she might throw up into the potted palm at the bottom of the stairs. "Is she the one you actually love? Is that it? Was that why you proposed to me—just to make her jealous?"

Kassius's jaw clenched. "If you're going to talk crazy, I'm going to bed."

But as he turned away from her, Laney's knees sagged back toward the wall. Suddenly he was there, catching her. He searched her face fiercely.

"What's wrong?"

"I'm fine." Her teeth were chattering. "Just furious, and…" *Terrified.* That's what she was. Terrified.

"You're not fine," he said, and without asking for permission, he lifted her up into his arms.

She felt too weak to fight as he carried her upstairs. Setting her down softly on their bed, he poured her a glass of water from the en suite bathroom. "Why didn't you tell me you were ill?"

"It's—nothing," she said weakly.

He stood by the bed. His lips curved downward. "I'm calling a doctor."

"I already saw one…"

"You did?"

"Just tell me the truth," she pleaded. She grabbed his arm, looking up at him. The nausea was starting to abate, but her heart was filled with pain. "Do you love her?"

He looked down at her in the shadowy bedroom. "Of course I don't."

"Because if you do—"

"I'll never love her. Or anyone."

His answer, far from being reassuring, made everything even worse.

"Anyone?" she said through dry lips. She took a deep breath, looking up at him with anguish. "You'll never love me?"

He sat down on the bed beside her. "No," he said quietly. "Sorry."

Her face was hot, her eyes burning with shame. "Won't—or can't?"

"What's the difference?"

"Then why did you propose to me?" she said hoarsely.

"For the reasons I told you." Reaching out, he stroked a tendril of her hair. "Sex. Home. A family. Children."

"But all that is supposed to spring from love." She licked her dry lips, tried to be hopeful. "Maybe in time…"

His expression hardened. "No, Laney." He pulled away. "I thought you understood. I'm not a sentimental man. It's not in my nature."

"What happened to you?" she choked out. "To turn you like this?"

Kassius stared at her for a moment. Then, rising from the bed, he went to the window. He pushed it open and took a breath of the cold February air.

Winter in London had a hard chill, different from Monaco or New Orleans. Or maybe it was Laney's soul that felt so suddenly frozen. Maybe it was her heart.

She watched a curl of cold winter wind blow against the curtains as, for a long moment, he looked out blankly at the iced-over city. Then he looked at her. "Love was never part of the deal. You knew that."

"I didn't, I never knew that!" she cried.

He exhaled. "Well, you know now." He looked at her. "Do you want out of our engagement?"

Laney might have said yes, she wanted out. If she had known from the beginning that he would never love her… that he would only give his money and his body but never his soul, not even the tiniest bit.

But it was too late now. She couldn't leave. Not when she was pregnant with his child. After growing up with the heartbreak of having her mother put her own selfish, ultimately futile pursuit of happiness ahead of her family's needs, Laney had sworn she'd never do the same.

Nothing mattered more to her than family. Nothing. Her unborn baby deserved a father, especially a loving one, like she believed Kassius would be. And as long as he loved their baby, she told herself she could live without him loving her.

But oh, the thought hurt. She wanted him to love her. She wanted it desperately.

If only she could believe there was some chance, no matter how small...

"If you can't accept what I offer you," Kassius said quietly, "perhaps it would be better if I just let you go."

Biting her lip, she looked up at him. "Perhaps we could just get to know each other better. I know you don't like to talk about yourself," she added hastily, "but I could start by telling you about me. How I grew up, and—"

"I already know everything," he interrupted, sounding bored. "I had a private investigator pull up a dossier. I know absolutely everything about you."

She froze. "You do?"

He nodded.

"About—my father's injury? And how my mother left us?"

"Everything."

"Since when?"

"Since before the New Year's Eve ball."

So before their first kiss, Kassius had already known about her private griefs—her father's injury, her mother's abandonment and death. While she knew almost nothing about him at all.

Laney felt sick. Violated. "If you wanted to know about my past, you could have just asked me."

"More efficient just to buy the information."

A chill went through her. "What made you this way?"

"What way?" he said.

"So cold," she whispered. "Sometimes you're so warm,

and other times…so cold. Like you don't care about anyone and you prefer it that way."

"That's about right."

"Yes, it is, isn't it?" She gave a low, strangled laugh. "I should have known, just from your wealth."

"What's that supposed to mean?"

Laney looked at him steadily. "Normal people do not become billionaires. The relentless pursuit of money requires cold sacrifice and single-mindedness that few people have."

His sensual lips curved. "You're just now figuring that out?"

"The only ones who can do it have a hole in their hearts," she whispered. She looked at him in the shadowy bedroom. "What caused the hole in your heart, Kassius, that's made you willing to sacrifice your own happiness in pursuit of money and power?"

He stared at her, his jaw tight. "I was poor and made myself rich. You think that proves me heartless?"

"That's not what I said—"

"What do you want from me, Laney?" he demanded.

"I want you to…" *To let me love you. And I want you to love me.* But she couldn't say those things, because she already knew what his answer would be—dismissive, cold, sarcastic. So licking her lips, she said, "I want to know a little more about you. As your future wife, I surely have that right. The obligation!"

He rolled his eyes. "Fine. What exactly do you want to know?"

"For starters—where are you from?"

"Lots of places." He gave her a cynical smile. "I'm a citizen of the world."

"Sure," she said impatiently. "But where were you born?"

"Why does that matter?"

"Your first language—"

"I speak six of them. They all hold an equal importance to me."

"You must have a passport."

"I have a few." She wondered if he was joking, but he bared his teeth in a smile. "All perfectly legal, of course. I make large investments in many countries. You heard about the building project in Malaysia that will be the tallest skyscraper in the world? That's mine. Governments are grateful. I bring high-paying jobs for their citizens."

"And profit for yourself."

"Of course. Why else would I do it?"

She pounced. "So why do you keep lending money to Boris Kuznetsov? His company is on life support. You have to know you'll never get that money back. Even Mimi said so. In what way is that profitable?"

His expression turned hard. "It's not your concern."

"What does it have to do with Mimi? Why did you bring her here and give her diamonds? If you're not having an affair—"

"You want to know me? You won't learn this way. Talking isn't how people reveal themselves. It's how they hide." His jaw tightened. "I'm not having an affair with Mimi du Plessis, believe me. I'll never betray you, Laney. If you don't want me to lie to you, don't ask me questions I can't answer."

"Can't or won't?"

"I told you. It's the same thing."

"I'm to just stay out of your life—is that it? Just be sweet and grateful and warm your bed, without ever challenging you? Mimi was right." She lifted her chin. "You want a servant. Not a wife."

"I am who I am. If you don't like it, leave."

His voice was cold. As if he didn't care either way. As if he could go out and get himself a new fiancée tomorrow. Which, she thought miserably, he probably could.

While Laney was utterly trapped, both by duty and devotion.

She'd let herself fall in love him, based on the exhilarating way he'd made her feel. She hadn't bothered to ask serious questions or properly know him. She'd just let herself fall for him like a stone.

Laney's fingertips traced the huge diamond on her left hand. She yearned to give in to the demands of her pride, to rip the ring off her finger and throw it back in his face. She yearned to tell him exactly where he could take the ring and his cold heart.

But she couldn't. Not now. She was pregnant with his baby.

Laney thought longingly of her grandmother, and her father, and home, and the smell of magnolia blossoms, the bright red bougainvillea and weeping cypress trees. Her family had been right about everything. Romantic dreams had blinded her to reality.

Feeling heartsick, she whispered, "What about a baby?"

His expression changed. "What about it?"

"If we…had a child. You couldn't love our baby, either?"

"That's different. I'd always protect my children, and make sure they felt secure and loved."

She exhaled, closing her eyes. That decided her.

Her unborn baby hadn't been the one to make such a foolish mistake, getting engaged and pregnant and falling in love with a man before she ever thought to ask if he could someday love her. Laney was the one who'd made the mistake. She'd be the one to suffer for it.

Laney swallowed, feeling dizzy. She forced herself to say, "I have something to tell you."

Kassius looked irritated, as if he assumed she was going to say something he didn't want to deal with. Like *I love you*.

"Look, Laney." He clawed back his dark hair. "It's been

a long day. We're leaving for New Orleans tomorrow, and then we have the wedding the day after. I've had enough. I'm going to bed."

I'm going to bed. They hadn't seen each other for four days, and he wanted to go to bed alone. It was the first time he hadn't tried to touch her or lure her into bed with his wickedly seductive smile. Lure her to bed? He hadn't even bothered to kiss her hello!

Why? *Why?* Did it have something to do with Mimi du Plessis? Ugly suspicion choked her, and sick brittle fear. But whatever secret he held from her, it was too late to turn back now. She'd been innocent and stupid and naive. She'd jumped into bed, into love. And it had all led to this.

But she had to do the right thing. Just because he was unable to love her didn't give her the right to take away the one person he *could* love—their child.

"Wait," she said hoarsely.

"Fine." He looked at her wearily. "What do you want to tell me?"

She had tears in her eyes as she choked out the words that, just a few hours ago, had made her so happy. When she'd thought they had a future. When she hoped they were in love.

Looking at him with despair, she whispered, "I'm pregnant."

CHAPTER SIX

THE PILOT'S VOICE came respectfully over the intercom. "We've begun our descent into New Orleans, sir."

Finally. Rising to his feet, Kassius glanced across the plane's cabin, where his bride-to-be was huddled on a white leather sofa, as far away from him as possible. If Laney could have climbed out onto the edge of the wing to get a little farther away, he thought drily, she would have.

At least her nausea seemed to have improved. She'd only spent maybe an hour in the jet's bathroom. Other than that, in the hours since they'd left London, she'd been hunkered beneath that quilt, refusing to acknowledge his existence, though she managed to be friendly and polite to the flight attendant who brought her fresh water and saltine crackers.

Kassius ground his teeth.

Well, what had he expected? He'd chosen Laney because of her kind heart, her honesty and good nature. Of course, for her, love would be an expected part of marriage. She wasn't like Mimi du Plessis, who was coin-operated, motivated primarily by greed. Now that Mimi knew he wasn't pursuing her, she'd been frankly suspicious about his motives for quietly buying up all the loans and assets of her employer, Boris Kuznetsov. So he'd bought off those suspicions with an arrangement—she would be paid with gifts. The one she'd received yesterday had been particularly rich, a five-carat diamond necklace she'd seen advertised in an auction brochure that had supposedly once belonged to the Empress Josephine. He'd had it delivered to his house by a private courier earlier this week so he could give it to her.

But gifts, even expensive ones, wouldn't hold Mimi for

long. Sooner or later, the woman would realize that there was more money to be made from blackmailing him and threatening to go to her boss. Mimi didn't know his true identity—no one did—but she could put Kuznetsov on his guard.

Kassius just needed a little more time. Boris Kuznetsov was overextended, overmortgaged and nearly out of assets. In a few months, he estimated, he'd be a broken man. All he had left was a shell of a company, now nearly stripped of assets, and the pink mansion on the Cap Ferrat. The one he'd promised to buy for Kassius's mother someday.

When he was a child, on all the nights he'd cried for his father when he was away, Emmaline had soothed Kassius to sleep with stories about the pink palace on the sea where someday they'd all live together. "We'll get that puppy you keep asking for, Cash, and eat your favorite meals. Every day will be like Christmas!" she'd said, and he'd believed her. He'd been comforted and had fallen asleep in the warmth of his mother's dreams.

But later, as a teenager, he stopped believing. By then, he hadn't seen or heard a word from his father for years, and he was getting into fights almost daily: with loud-mouthed kids who sneered at him as a bastard or—far worse—called his sweet, softhearted, helpless mother a whore; and also with drunken neighbors who pounded their door at midnight, believing because they were poor and Emmaline "obviously slept around" that she was fair game, available either by payment or by force.

After his fights, his mother's face would be sad as she quietly washed his bloody knuckles, his ravaged cheek-bones and, once, his broken nose. She tried to hug him and tell him the same stories about the future, when his daddy came back, how they'd all live together in that pink palace in the South of France. But he no longer believed in fairy tales, even if she did. His mother never quite gave up hope.

Not until the end.

Kassius's hands clenched, just thinking about it. Kuznetsov had indeed bought that pink palace by the sea, but only for himself, after Emmaline was long dead. And the man had held onto it, treasuring it over his other possessions. So that fanciful pink mansion would be the last thing Kassius would take. An ironic smile lifted his lips.

Funny to think that his child would be born around September, too. All his plans were working out with eerie precision.

Laney. Pregnant with his baby. He still couldn't quite believe it.

And tomorrow, they'd be wed. The thought made him feel strange and jittery inside. Why? Because he'd nearly succeeded? Because he'd gotten everything he wanted? The fortune. The power. The wife. The child.

An empire. A family.

Everything that had once been denied him. Everything...

Kassius looked at Laney. Everything but a bride who was willing to even look him in the face. Gritting his teeth, he walked over to her. "We're landing soon."

She peeked over the quilt, her expression cold. "I heard."

"You should buckle your seat belt."

"I did."

And she went back under the quilt.

So much for olive branches. Irritated, Kassius returned to his white leather swivel chair and buckled his seat belt.

Should he have lied to her last night? When she'd all but accused him of cheating on her with Mimi du Plessis, should he have looked into her stricken face and said those three little words that would have magically fixed everything? If he had, she'd have smiled at him in joy, and kissed him, and taken him with her to bed.

As it was, she'd slept in the guest room last night.

He folded his arms, feeling disgruntled and unfairly judged. He'd told her the truth. You'd think she would have sense enough to be grateful for that rather than being angry he hadn't tried to deceive her with pretty lies! But no.

She'd slept in the guest room, then given him the silent treatment. He didn't like it. But it fueled him with the one emotion he did feel comfortable with.

Anger.

When the plane landed at the small private airport outside New Orleans, Laney slipped into one of the designer outfits he'd bought her, still not meeting his gaze.

They came down the steps onto the tarmac, and he instantly felt hit by humidity and heat. "Where are we? The jungle?" he gasped, taking off his jacket, rolling up the sleeves of his button-down shirt.

"It's nearly March. Warmer than usual for Mardi Gras," Laney agreed, then looked at him coolly. "You're the one who needs to buckle in now."

She walked right past him, proud as a queen, to where their driver held open the door of the waiting Bentley.

Kassius stared after her. She looked magnificent in her sleek black day dress. She had no problem walking in stiletto heels now, and the expensive designer purse hung carelessly from her arm, as if she'd had expensive bags all her life, as if they were expendable. He suddenly missed the old Laney. This new one seemed hardened on the edges. He watched her climb into the back of the sedan without even a backward glance at him, much less a smile.

Once the driver and bodyguard transferred their luggage from the jet into the back of the sedan, they drove from the airport toward the outskirts of New Orleans, where her grandmother lived.

Kassius looked out the window. Laney was right. Even the air here smelled different. He rolled down his window, taking a deep breath. Even in late February, the air was swampy, humid and warm. But it was more than that. He took another breath, closing his eyes.

Exotic flowers overlaid the distant salt of the Gulf of Mexico and the muddy Mississippi. Beneath that, the faint scent of the bayou, of Spanish moss, of cypress and oak and a sweet, musky rot.

He'd never been to the American South. His visits to the United States had been limited to California and the Acela corridor between New York City and Washington, DC.

But his mother had been born here. He wondered what his life would have been like if she'd left Istanbul when Boris had first refused to marry her. What would have happened if she'd come back here, pregnant, to plead her case to her parents? If she'd given birth in New Orleans, if his grandparents had actually held him as a baby—would even they have truly been cold enough to refuse to let them stay?

He doubted it.

What would Kassius's life have been like if he'd grown up in a comfortable home, surrounded by family, always knowing he belonged?

If Emmaline had given up her romantic dreams of Boris and freed herself to find a man worthy of her love?

She might be alive now. Happy.

He could still hear the anguished echo of her voice. *If someone ever shows you the truth of who they are, if they lie or cheat or betray you, promise me you'll believe them the first time! Don't destroy your life, or your child's, wishing and hoping and pretending they'll change—*

Who would Kassius have become here?

Someone else. Someone different. Someone who knew how to love, maybe, he thought cynically. Everyone seemed to think giving one's heart away was a good thing. He didn't understand why—they only ended up broken.

Better to remain tough. The poverty and misery of his childhood hadn't destroyed him. To the contrary. The struggle had made him stronger. Able to risk anything. *Endure* anything.

He glanced at Laney sitting beside him.

He'd told her he knew everything about her from the private investigator, but that wasn't precisely true. He knew the basic facts of her life: birth, schooling, father's injury, mother's abandonment and later death. Those had been collated for him like bullet points on a résumé. But he was suddenly curious to know more than just plain facts.

"What was it like, growing up here?" he asked.

"It was fine." Laney's voice was cold, giving nothing away as she continued to stare out the opposite window.

She was blocking him out. He recognized the strategy. He did it all the time, and turnabout was fair play. He should shrug it off, let it go. But the fact that she'd been treating him so coldly for so many hours, in spite of her warm, generous nature, made him feel uneasy. Made him worry that makeup sex might not be enough to melt the ice.

Plus, he had something else to do first. Something he dreaded.

Meet her family.

The driver pulled up to a tiny, narrow house on a sagging street on the outskirts of the city. Not even the carefully tended flower beds could distract from the falling-down roof, the peeling screen door. There was pride here. But no money.

He saw Laney brace herself, take a deep breath, and put a big smile on her face before she climbed out of the car.

"Gran!" she cried, and a wizened, stout, gray-haired woman on the porch beamed and held open her arms.

She was much shorter than Laney and had to reach up to hug her granddaughter tight, patting her shoulders fiercely. She drew back, mystified. "What are you wearing, child?"

"Do you like it?" Laney twirled, showing the sleekly expensive black dress.

"Like it?" The older woman's mouth lifted humorously. "It's pretty enough, but honey, seeing all that black, all I can ask is, who died?"

Her grandmother turned her sharp gaze on Kassius, who'd followed Laney up the five steps to the porch. Craning back her neck, she looked him over critically, from his freshly shaven jawline—he'd shaved on the plane—to the rolled-up sleeves of his white shirt, his tailored vest and Italian shoes. Her gaze shifted to the luxury sedan at the curb, with the driver waiting inside it. Her black eyes clearly weighed his good sense and found it lacking. She sniffed. "You must be Kassius Black."

Kassius suddenly realized how ridiculous his car and driver were here. He glanced at Laney, hoping for some hint of how to proceed, but all he got was a similarly cold stare. Apparently both Henry women had a similar opinion of him at the moment.

Giving the elderly lady his best smile, he stuck out his hand. "You must be Yvonne Henry," he said smoothly. "I can see where Laney gets her good looks."

Mrs. Henry snorted, rolling her eyes. But she seemed to thaw out slightly. She started to reach out her hand. Then he made the mistake of adding, as he looked over the shabby house, "Didn't my business manager contact you? You were supposed to have access to all the money you need."

He heard Laney's intake of breath, saw Yvonne Henry narrow her eyes, drawing herself up to her full four feet eleven inches.

"Laney," she said coldly. "Please inform your boyfriend that we are not in habit of taking charity. Especially from strangers."

Had he been rude to offer them unlimited money? For a moment he was bewildered, then he realized Yvonne had taken his words as a slight on their home's appearance. Which he supposed it had been.

Yvonne Henry began watering the flowerpots on the porch. "Lunch is almost ready, but you'd best go introduce the man to your father first."

"I can't wait to taste your cooking," Kassius said, trying to dig himself out of the hole. "Laney said you're the best chef in the city. I haven't been able to think of anything else!"

"My cooking is what you're looking forward to? Not meeting us? Bless your heart." She turned to her granddaughter. "Laney May?"

"Let's go in," she said quickly, tugging on his arm.

"Nice to meet you, ma'am," he said politely and followed Laney into the house. When the screen door slammed behind him, he exhaled.

Laney was staring at him in disbelief. "You really aren't good at this."

"I think she likes me," he said.

Her expression changed. She glanced around them, drawing closer. "Just be respectful, okay?"

"What are you talking about?"

"My dad didn't like how you proposed to me, without asking his permission."

"Are you kidding? Who actually does that anymore?"

"Look around you," she bit out. "We're not rich jet-setters who are too full of our own importance to bother with the old values. We still believe in family. In love and respect."

Hmm. Kassius sensed criticism.

"So whatever you might think of me and my family," she continued, "can you please keep it to yourself and just pretend to be a decent person?"

Pretend?

"Fine," he bit out.

As Kassius followed her through the dark, shotgun-style one-story house, he noticed the damp walls and peeling wallpaper. He knew her father was in a wheelchair. Had there even been a ramp from the porch to the street? He wondered how her father managed to leave the house. If he did.

Kassius was going to be a father soon. He suddenly wondered how he'd feel if someone proposed marriage to his son or daughter on the other side of the world, without making the gesture of at least meeting the family first. Not good.

Pushing open a door, she led him into a dark bedroom. "Dad, I'm here!"

"Laney!"

She clicked on a light, and Kassius realized the man had been sitting in the dark. The bedroom was tidy and scrupulously clean. But the furniture was old, and the walls covered with photos of Laney at every age, often with a pretty, laughing woman he took to be her mother. The woman who'd abandoned them when they needed her most. Pictures Clark Henry could no longer even see.

"What are you doing in here, Dad, in the dark?" Laney said affectionately. She looked down at open book in his lap. In Braille. "Good book?"

Clark's unfocused gaze lit up in a smile. "Just waiting for you to get home! Come here, girl!"

Her face was tender as she went to him in the wheelchair and hugged him tight. "I missed you, Dad."

"Oh, sweetheart, it's been so long," Clark Henry said, blinking fast as he hugged her tight. When she pulled away, he cleared his throat. "And you're not alone."

"Did you hear me?" Kassius said awkwardly, feeling like an intruder.

The man smiled, but his expression was tight. "I could smell you at ten paces. Cologne and car leather."

Kassius gave himself a surreptitious sniff.

"Yes, Dad," Laney said. "This is my fiancé. Kassius."

"Pleased to meet you, sir." Taking the older man's hand, he shook it. He noticed Clark still wore his wedding ring.

"Nice firm grip," her father said and abruptly withdrew his hand. "But as for the fiancé business, we'll have to wait and see. I haven't decided if I'm willing to give you away."

"Dad, the wedding is tomorrow night!"

"If I don't give you away, there will be no wedding. So let me ask your fella a few questions." He glared in Kassius's direction. "What makes you worthy of my daughter?"

"Dad!"

"I'll take good care of her, sir."

"How?"

Kassius hid a smile. "I own many houses around the world, two jets, with a personal net worth of—"

"I get it. You're rich." Her father snorted, waving an impatient hand. "My daughter already told me, and so did that guy who kept calling, wanting to shove your money down our throats. That's not what I asked."

"Sir?" Kassius said, feeling bewildered again.

"What I *asked*," Clark Henry said, as if speaking to a not-so-bright child, "was how you are *worthy* of my *daughter*."

That brought Kassius up short.

He looked down at the man who'd lost everything in an oil rig explosion, trying to provide for his family. Working as a roughneck was hard, dangerous, isolating work—which was why it was well paid. But after the accident, the drilling company had found a legal loophole to deny compensation. Clark Henry had lost his sight, his mobility, his wife. Now he had no ability to work or even leave the house. He'd literally lost the power to look out for his family.

Kassius took a deep breath. And gave the only answer he could.

"I'm not," he said humbly. "But I intend to spend the

rest of my life trying to make her happy. If you will please give me permission to marry your daughter."

The man's expression changed. He hadn't expected that. Nor, by the dumbfounded look on her face, had Laney.

Then with a cough, Clark frowned again. "Fine. You'll take care of her. But will you love her with all your heart? As my only child deserves to be loved?"

"Dad!"

"Let the man answer me, Laney May."

Kassius tried to think of what to say. Somehow he didn't think that his usual speech about "I'm just not a sentimental man" would satisfy Clark Henry. But he also had too much respect for the man to lie to him. He began, "The thing is…"

"Guess what?" Laney broke in, giving Kassius a warning glance. "I have news, Dad. Big news! The hugest! You need to come out into the kitchen so I can tell you and Gran at once."

"Good news?" her father said gruffly. "Or bad?"

"Definitely good." Laney kissed the top of her father's head. "But Gran will kill me if I don't tell you both. You go first, Dad."

Setting his jaw, her father pushed his wheelchair out of the bedroom, using his powerful arms to roll himself back down the long dark hallway. She started to follow him.

Kassius blocked her with his arm, putting his hand against the wall. He said in a low voice, "Thank you."

She stared at him for a moment, her deep brown eyes sad. "I didn't do it for you. I did it for them. They want so badly for me to be happy. They can never know you…"

She didn't finish the sentence. She didn't have to.

You don't love me.

Pushing his arm away, she left the bedroom. He followed her to the kitchen, where her grandmother was stirring a big pot on the stove.

Kassius took an appreciative sniff. "That smells fantastic."

"Oh, are you still here?" her grandmother replied, not bothering to look in his direction. Lifting her eyebrows, she glanced down at her son.

"I've decided to give the man a chance," Clark said gruffly.

"Really." She sounded skeptical. "Even after the way you were calling him a no-good—"

Clark coughed. "Laney said she has news."

Her grandmother paused in stirring the pot. "News? What news?"

Kassius looked at Laney. Now she was on the spot, her cheeks were pink. Clearing her throat, she said in an overly cheerful voice, "Kassius and I got a wedding present a few days early. We found out we're going to have a baby!"

Her grandmother's spoon dropped. "A baby!"

Clark turned toward Kassius with a blind scowl. "Baby?"

Kassius came behind Laney, putting his arms around her. He felt her trembling, though she gave her family a big smile. "Yes, a baby. And we couldn't be more delighted."

"A great-grandchild!" Yvonne breathed with delight. Then a shadow crossed her face. "But we'll never see the baby. You'll be living so far from us. We'll never see any of you."

"Just another member of the family he's taking from us," said Clark sourly.

Standing on the worn linoleum of the tiny, dimly lit, spotlessly clean kitchen, Kassius heard himself say, "Laney and I would be happy to have you stay with us. My jets are at your disposal. We have plenty of extra rooms. Please come and stay as often as you like."

Laney's jaw dropped.

Yvonne gasped, turning towards Clark, who had a stunned expression.

"I take it back." The elderly woman sniffed joyfully, wiping her eyes with her brightly colored apron. Coming up to Kassius, she stood on her tiptoes and enveloped both him and Laney in a hug. "Every bad thing I ever said. Because you're not just good people, Kassius—you're family!"

Later that night, Laney crept out of her childhood bedroom, with its pink ruffled comforter on her twin bed, foreign maps on the walls and overflowing bookshelves. Fresh from the shower, she was dressed in an old T-shirt and pajama pants as she sneaked down the hallway.

Engaged or not, pregnant or not, there were some rules that had to be followed in the Henry household, one of which was that an unmarried couple would never, ever be permitted to sleep in the same room. Even on the night before their wedding.

Too nervous to sleep, Laney had waited until her grandmother and father had gone to bed. Silently, she tiptoed down the long, dark hallway to the front room, where Kassius had been assigned to sleep on the sagging sofa.

Earlier that night, when her grandmother had handed him the pillow and blanket, Laney had half expected him to refuse and announce that he was off to a hotel. Instead, he'd just meekly said, "Thank you very much, ma'am."

Laney bit her lip. It wasn't the first time he'd surprised her today. She hadn't expected him to treat her family so well. As if he respected them. As if he really cared about their opinion. She was grateful but bewildered. Where was the arrogant man who claimed to have no feelings?

The front room was dark and empty, the pillow and blanket left in a pile on the sofa. Hearing a creak on the porch, she pushed open the peeling screen door.

Kassius was sitting on the old porch swing, his handsome face distant as he looked out into the dark night.

"What are you doing out here?"

He blinked, as if coming back to himself, and she wondered what he'd been thinking about. For answer, he just moved over, giving her a spot on the wooden swing.

She took a deep breath of the fragrant, cooling night air. She could hear the wind against the trees, the distant hum of city traffic. She could smell his expensive, woodsy cologne, the scent of cypress trees and musk.

"Not able to sleep, either?" she said.

"No."

She didn't want to ask if he was having wedding jitters like she was. "Is it the sofa?"

Kassius gave a wry smile. "It does have a hard spot right in the middle."

"I used to jump on it as a kid," she said apologetically. She bit her lip. "I feel guilty having a bed…"

"Don't," he cut her off. "I want you to have it. You need to be comfortable. How are you feeling?"

"Better. No nausea." She gave him a shy smile. "It might be because I'm home. Eating my grandma's cooking. I feel good. I feel…grateful." She looked at him in the shadowy night. A breeze blew the branches of trees across the nearest streetlight, moving light and shadow across his handsome, angular face. "Thank you for what you did today."

"I didn't do anything."

"You made my family love you."

He gave a low, cynical laugh. "By offering to give them use of my private jet? Or by not telling them the truth about my loveless heart?"

"You opened up your home to them. Home means family."

Kassius looked at her. In the dark, lowering sky, the crescent moon was haunted by a swirl of frosted cloud.

"How do you do it, Laney?" His voice was low and intense. "After everything that happened to you, how do you keep your heart open?"

"What do you mean?" she said with an awkward laugh. "Is there any other way?"

"Your mother abandoned you." His dark eyes seemed to burn through her. "She left your injured father and you and ran away with some boyfriend. It was monstrous…"

Laney sucked in her breath. "Don't say that! She made some mistakes, yes, bad ones, but—"

"Mistakes?" he said incredulously. "Abandoning a sick partner and a young, innocent child? It's beyond selfish. It was evil." His hands had tightened into fists, and his jaw seemed tight enough to snap. "She deserved to be punished…"

"She *was* punished," Laney said quietly. "She died. Of an overdose. Alone on a California beach, without my father or me around to help her and protect her from herself when she needed us most."

Kassius stared at her, then blinked, as if recollecting himself. He took a deep breath.

"How do you do it?" he repeated. He gestured toward the house. "All of you. After everything you've gone through, how can you still have such hope, such belief in love? Your father has clearly never gotten over her. He still has her pictures on his wall, pictures he can no longer see. He still wears his wedding ring!"

"You can't turn love on and off like a light when it's convenient," she said quietly. She stared down at the peeling finish on the wood porch. "I wish you could."

"You mean, you wish *you* could," Kassius said flatly. "Because you think you're in love with me."

Laney looked at him, astonished.

"But you're wrong." He shook his head. "You're not in love with me. You don't even know me."

For a moment, she didn't—couldn't—answer. Then

something about being here, in her own home in her own city, made her brave.

"There's a lot I don't know about you yet, that's true," she said quietly. "I don't know where you were born. I don't know your first language. I don't know why you gave Mimi those diamonds in secret, or why, for a man who worked so hard to create his fortune, you're willing to toss so much of it away on bad loans to her boss."

Folding his arms, Kassius set his jaw, looking away.

"But there are some things I do know." Laney tilted her head, looking at his silhouette in the moonlight. "I know you'll always be honest with me, even if that means saying things I don't want to hear. You're willing to commit your life to me, if not your heart. You have somehow already made my family love you. You're going to marry me tomorrow, and I know you will keep your vows to honor and cherish me. And I know above all that you will love our baby."

His eyes widened, and he turned toward her. For a long moment, they stared at each other in the moonlit Louisiana night, the only sound the creak of the chains on the porch swing and the soft whisper of the night breeze through the cypress and palm trees.

"Let me in, Kassius." Reaching out, she took his hand in her own. "Tell me your secret."

He stared at her for a long moment. Then, pulling back his hand, he abruptly rose to his feet.

"It's a busy day tomorrow. Get some rest."

And he left her on the dark porch.

CHAPTER SEVEN

STANDING AT THE altar of the two-hundred-year-old Gothic church, lit by candlelight on a dark February night in the heart of New Orleans, Kassius looked at Laney, radiant in her white dress.

"I now pronounce you man and wife," the minister intoned.

She looked like an angel, he thought. Her brown eyes glowed as she looked up at him. Her lips were full and pink, her dark hair pulled back beneath the long white veil. The wedding dress was vintage, with white lace sleeves and sweeping skirts.

The minister grinned. "You may now kiss the bride."

At last. Cupping Laney's cheek, Kassius lowered his head. He forgot about the hundred people watching from the pews and just kissed her. He felt her small body tremble. But her lips did not. She barely touched him before she pulled away. She was distant. Unreachable. Nothing like he'd expected from the warm, emotional woman he'd just married.

As Kassius drew back, suddenly he was the one who was trembling.

Around them, people were applauding and cheering from the pews, and a few threw rose petals as Kassius took Laney's hand and led her back down the aisle, past her openly weeping grandmother in the fancy hat, and her father, who was still blinking back tears from the experience of escorting his daughter down the aisle.

The nave of the tiny, Gothic-style church was lavishly decorated with expensive flowers and candles. But the real heart of the ceremony had been the joy of the wedding guests, mostly Laney's family and friends. He'd only invited one real friend, his best man, Spanish billionaire Ángel Velazquez. But that was the difference between them, wasn't it? Kassius had acquaintances, people he met for business dinners or a hedonistic week of skiing in Gstaad. He had business allies and rivals, suck-ups and hangers-on, all of whom he hadn't bothered to tell the wedding planner to invite.

While Laney had family. She had friends.

Newly wed, the two of them walked out of the stone church, and the wedding guests followed them out into the warm, dark, moist Louisiana night, a noisy, happy crowd, chattering, laughing, even bursting into song as they walked the short distance to the reception, being held at an antebellum mansion in the Garden District. The wedding planner, an accomplished woman, followed them with her headset, making sure everything was ready for their arrival.

When Kassius saw the location of their reception, he sucked in his breath. It was like seeing a ghost.

The mansion, set back from the street, looked exactly like his mother's childhood home. It had the same type of old Spanish architecture, with covered wrought-iron balconies. His mother's house had been built a hundred years later, two miles farther west, on St. Charles Avenue. He'd only seen it in photographs, before he'd had it destroyed.

A cold sweat broke out on his forehead, and his skin felt clammy beneath his tuxedo. He didn't know why this mansion, and the thought of a different house, was affecting him. The Cash house was in the past. Dead and gone. He'd never even gone to see the empty lot—that was how little it meant to him. So why did he suddenly feel dizzy?

He felt his bride's cool gaze on him as they walked past the wrought-iron gate, over a pretty path created by white rose petals and lit by white Chinese lanterns. He looked at her, and she instantly turned away to talk to a friend who'd come up beside her to squeal over her wedding dress, the beautiful ceremony, their future happiness.

And once they got inside the mansion, that was how the reception went, too. All night long, Laney offered bright smiles—fake! So fake!—to all of the people who loved her. For him alone—the one person on earth, it seemed, who did not love her—she offered coldness and a consistently averted gaze. As if she couldn't even bear to look at him.

And the ink was barely dry on their wedding certificate. Not a good sign.

To Kassius, the evening stretched on like torture, with an elegant sit-down dinner in the colorful high-ceilinged ballroom shimmering with lights. Gritting his teeth, he ate his dinner, barely tasting the blackened catfish or jambalaya. A tearfully happy wedding toast was offered by Laney's maid of honor, a childhood friend called Danielle Berly, now a married kindergarten teacher with two children. A much shorter, far less emotional toast was offered by his own best man, Ángel Velazquez.

He'd just held up his champagne flute and cried with a flourish, *"Buena suerte!"* Good luck. Which he obviously thought his old friend would need.

Kassius gritted his teeth and got through it. He smiled at all the right places and acted pleased when he and Laney cut the gorgeous six-tier wedding cake with its raspberry filling and white buttercream frosting with sugared flowers. He smiled for the photographer, leaning in toward his bride when she was refusing to touch him or look in his direction. When he took her out on the dance floor for their first dance together as a married couple, beneath the beaming smiles and oohs and aahs of her family and friends, he tried not to notice how she'd flinched when he'd touched her.

It didn't promise a very good honeymoon.

All he could think about was how different this night was from the New Year's Eve ball, when they'd first kissed and hadn't been able to keep their hands off each other. This wedding night should have been beautiful, and it had been, but coldly so, like a distant star. But why? What had changed?

With a sick feeling in his gut, he knew exactly why. Because she'd reached out to him last night, and he'd pushed her away.

He was tired of being alone. And weary, so weary, of having no one completely on his side.

Finally, at midnight, he'd had enough. She'd been visibly reluctant to depart, but he'd insisted. He'd finally taken her hand and led her out of the elegant old mansion to the circular driveway where a vintage Cadillac now waited, bedecked with sashes and white flowers.

Laney's footsteps slowed. "Where's the limo?"

"I decided it was too much."

"Really?" she drawled as the driver held open the back door. "Too much?"

Then she turned with a bright smile to wave at her family and friends who'd poured out of the mansion to bid them farewell. Kassius looked for Velazquez, but his friend was nowhere to be seen. He'd been such a hermit lately, Kassius was almost surprised the Spaniard had been willing to leave his half-million-acre Texas ranch to be his best man. Kassius certainly wasn't going to give him a hard time about ducking out early, but it meant only his bride's friends and family shouted and cheered after them as they departed, throwing white streamers at their car as they drove away.

Sitting beside his bride in the backseat, Kassius almost jumped when he heard loud bangs behind the car. Looking back, he saw rusty metal cans attached to the glossy bumper. He gave an incredulous snort. "I can't believe Ms. Dumaine—"

"The wedding planner didn't do those," Laney informed him. "I heard Gran giggling about it with the ladies of her bridge club."

The drive to the elegant hotel in the French Quarter where they were to have their honeymoon wasn't supposed to take long. Normally it would take fifteen minutes, the wedding planner had told him. But with the huge influx of tourists celebrating the weekend before Mardi Gras, traffic was heavy. The drive took forever.

Or maybe it just felt that way to Kassius, with the awkward silence in the backseat, the two of them not touching. Laney still wouldn't look at him and seemed more likely to strike up a conversation with the driver than the man she'd just pledged to honor and cherish.

Suddenly, he could stand it no longer. He leaned forward and spoke quietly to the driver, who nodded and changed the car's route.

"Why are we turning around?" Laney asked in confusion. The first words she'd spoken to him in ten minutes.

"You'll see," he said grimly.

The car turned back onto the wide, well-tended avenue, divided by tracks, for the historic St. Charles streetcar line. On both sides of the avenue were oak trees and gracious mansions, many at least a hundred years old.

"Here," he told the driver, and the man parked. Kassius abruptly got out.

It was past midnight now, and the street was quiet. This was a residential area, with a variety of architectural styles, from old Spanish to Greek Revival, Italianate to Colonial. Each mansion was evenly spaced with a large garden.

Except one house was missing, like a gap between teeth. He stood in front of the empty lot, stuffing his hands in his jacket pockets. Looking at a house he'd never seen.

Laney came up behind him. He heard the soft whisper of her skirts. "What are we doing here, Kassius?"

"You wanted to see the place I'm from?"

"So?"

Wordlessly, he pointed at the barren plot of land, lit up by a pale trickle of moonlight, ghostly and empty between the other elegant homes.

She stood beside him, looking at the lonely plot of land, nothing but overgrown grass and a single cypress tree. "You were born here?"

He shook his head. "My mother was." He looked at the empty lot. "This was her childhood home. She was the only child of the wealthy Cash family and ran off at nineteen to see the world rather than stay and marry the man they'd chosen for her."

A car drove past them on the quiet road, its lights illuminating Laney's big dark eyes.

"She fell in love with a Russian she met in Istanbul. She thought my father would marry her, but all he gave her was excuses. He floated in and out of our lives, promising he'd marry her soon, bringing us money and gifts. Until I turned eleven, and he disappeared completely." His jaw set as he looked out at the sad cypress in the moonlight, hearing the plaintive cry of night birds soaring invisibly above. "Later that year, my mother got sick. If we'd had money for proper medical care, she might have survived. As it was…it took her five years to die. Alone."

A lump rose in his throat. He didn't like the rawness of telling this story. He'd never told it to anyone before.

"But she wasn't alone," Laney whispered. Her hand reached for his. "She had you."

Kassius exhaled, almost shuddering with emotion. "When I was sixteen, as my mother lay dying, she wrote her parents and asked for help. She asked them to come see her, or at least to take me if she died. And they refused. *They refused.*"

He heard her gasp. He felt the warmth and softness of her hand as her fingers tightened protectively around his.

Turning away, he ground out, "This precious house meant everything to them. After they died, I bought it. Had it demolished." He gave her a crooked smile. "You know this is the first time I've seen this street?"

She stared at him. Reaching up, she stroked his cheek. Her dark eyes were luminous with unshed tears. "Oh, Kassius."

"That's why I changed my name. I didn't want my father's name. Or my grandparents'. So I chose my own. I bought a new birth certificate, new papers. I started a new life."

Standing on her tiptoes, Laney hugged him fiercely, and for a moment, he closed his eyes, accepting the comfort. He wasn't accustomed to it.

She drew back, looking up at him in her wedding dress, moonlight frosting her dark hair beneath the long white veil. "I know what it feels like," she said in a low voice. "To feel abandoned by family who is supposed to love you. That's what left the hole in your heart."

His voice was low and fierce. "Why don't you have one, Laney? Why? How can you still love like you do?"

"Because…" She blinked fast, then shook her head. "Because I still love my mother. I miss her. I try to remember the good times. Doing otherwise would bring me only misery."

Kassius stared at her, then shook his head.

"I feel differently," he said slowly. He looked at the bare plot of land. "Destroying this house was very satisfying. Looking at it now, I'm almost tempted to spit on the ashes."

"It won't bring you joy," she said in a small voice. "And it won't bring her back."

He looked at her sharply. For a moment, his heart was troubled. Then he steadied himself. Whatever Laney thought, he knew his plan for revenge against his father would make him happy. Very happy.

Crushing Boris Kuznetsov, taking his bankrupt business and the villa on the Cap Ferrat, would be the glory of Kassius's life.

"I'm sorry," Laney suddenly blurted out. Tears spilled over her lashes, and she wiped her eyes, trying to smile. "I was so angry with you. I ruined the most magical day of our lives."

With a low laugh, he took her in his arms.

"You didn't ruin it," he said softly. He gently wiped a tear off her cheek. "And a wedding is just one day. We'll have many magical days. A lifetime of them."

She gave him a grateful, watery smile, then a weak laugh escaped her. "This explains why you love Southern food. And why I felt like home to you." Her forehead furrowed. "So what was your name before? And how did you choose Kassius Black?"

He loved having her in his arms. He loved the way she was looking at him now. As if he were her hero again.

"When I was a child," he said slowly, "I liked hearing stories of ancient Rome. Kassius was the name of a Roman senator who raised an army to fight tyranny." He was also one of the conspirators who'd assassinated Julius Caesar, but he didn't elaborate. "And Black was how I vowed my heart would be."

Her eyes were shining. "Thank you for telling me."

"And now I need something from you." He looked down at her in his arms. "You know more about me now than anyone in the world. Promise you won't ask for more."

"But—"

His gaze held her. "Promise."

She sighed, looking sad. "All right. I promise."

He exhaled. He hadn't realized until then how tense he was. He felt horribly vulnerable. Exposed. But he also hadn't felt so close to anyone in a long time.

Laney was the one person he could trust. He suddenly knew she was the one person who would never betray him.

And he would always protect her, just as he would protect his child now growing inside her.

His child. The thought filled him with awe. He rested his hand against her gently curved belly. He would never make the mistakes of his father. He would be a good husband, a good father. Once his revenge was finished, he would leave the pain of his past in the rearview mirror. He'd spend the rest of his life focused on the future, on the present, always making sure that his wife and children were comfortable and warm and safe. They'd never have a single worry or fear. Those would be his jobs alone.

He looked down at Laney, pushing back a dark tendril of her hair. "You're my wife now. The mother of my coming child. The past is past. It's as your grandmother said. We are family. The future is what matters now."

"You're right," she whispered, and as he held her in the cooling night, she in her white dress, he in his tuxedo, their eyes met, and the air between them electrified.

"Mrs. Black," he said huskily. Lowering his head, he kissed her, tenderly at first, then with building need. In response, she wrapped her arms around him, drawing him down tighter against her.

Suddenly, all he could think about was ripping off her wedding dress. He wanted to forget. To be reborn in her. Inside her.

"Honeymoon," he growled, and pulled her toward the gleaming black Cadillac.

Laney felt the heat and weight of her husband's hard muscular body, barely restrained by the civilized tuxedo, as he pushed her into the car's backseat. The skirts of her white wedding dress plumped out like pillows as he savagely kissed her, pushing her against the smooth leather.

His fingers stroked through her chignon, causing long dark tendrils of hair to fall beneath her veil. His lips pressed against hers, causing her body to sizzle and ache from her fingertips to her toes and everywhere in between.

This was their true wedding, she thought as she kissed him. *This.* Where body met soul…

They barely made it to their luxury hotel, deep in the French Quarter, on famous Bourbon Street. It was lucky it wasn't far, and traffic had abated, or they might not have made it. They might have had their wedding night in the back of the vintage car with their driver in the front seat, fiddling with the radio and pretending not to notice.

When the car stopped, Kassius pulled her through the elegant lobby of the hotel, barely responding to the cheerful greetings of the employees and manager.

She breathed, "Don't we need to check in—"

"Everything is done."

Not everything, she thought hungrily.

As soon as they were in the elevator, he pressed the button for the third floor then pushed her back against the mirror and kissed her hard and hot. She barely heard the *ding* of the elevator door. He pulled her down the elegant, dimly lit hallway, then stopped in front of the door at the end. Pulling the key from his pocket, he opened the door and turned to her. Laney gasped as he lifted her up into his arms, her full white skirts and long white veil trailing behind them.

"You're mine now," he whispered. "Legally mine."

"Then you're mine," she murmured, twining her hands in his hair. "And I intend to use you exactly as I choose…"

Never taking his eyes from her, he carried her over the threshold. Kicking the door closed behind them, he set her down. She had only a brief glimpse of the large, elegant hotel suite and the gleaming neon lights of Bourbon Street visible through the French doors, which led to a covered wrought-iron balcony. He walked around her, staring at her wedding gown.

She blushed under his scrutiny. "Do you like it?" she said shyly. "It took forty-five minutes to get dressed, with all the buttons in back."

"If you think I'm going to wait forty-five minutes..." Reaching out, he ripped the back of her gown apart in a single violent movement, popping all the delicate buttons that held together the lace at the back.

She whirled around. "What are you—"

He spread the lace neckline wide, causing the seams to part, and pulled the dress straight down her body, leaving her standing in front of him wearing only a strapless white bra, a tiny lace G-string, a white garter belt holding up white fishnet stockings—and her long white veil.

"It was my grandmother's dress!" Laney cried indignantly.

"It was hers. Now it's yours. And what's yours—" Kassius's eyes were dark and smoldering as he roughly pulled her closer "—is mine."

A deep shiver went through her. Staring at his lips, she breathed, "You shouldn't have done it..."

"Like you said. The past is past. She had a long, happy marriage. And, starting tonight, so will we." He ran his fingers along the edge of her long white lace veil. "But you can keep this on," he said huskily. "I like it."

Picking her up, he tossed her onto the enormous bed, as if she were some kind of harem girl created exclusively for his pleasure. Two could play that game, she thought. Propping herself up on one arm, she reached out and grabbed the sleeve of his jacket.

"Take it off," she ordered.

He looked down at her in the shadowy bedroom of the hotel suite. Then he did as she bade.

"Now the tie," she said.

He undid the tie, dropping it the floor.

"Shirt."

He slowly unbuttoned his white shirt, then undid the cuffs. She had a vision of his hard-muscled chest, laced with dark hair, and the taut six-pack beneath. Her gaze lowered, her heart beating fast. She licked her lips.

"Trousers."

A sensual smile traced his lips as he looked at her with heavy-lidded eyes, then pulled off his black trousers and his boxers and socks in the bargain.

Her husband stood naked before her.

A deep shiver went through her as she saw his hard, naked body. His chest and shoulders were huge and muscular, tracing down to his trim, taut waist, and below that...

Holding her breath, mesmerized, she started to reach for him, wanting to wrap her hand around his huge, hard length, to cup and stroke and maybe even, if she dared, taste...

"Oh, no, you don't." His voice was low. "I followed your orders. Now you will follow mine." Leaning forward on the bed, he ran his fingertips up her leg, from the pale fishnet stocking to the garter on her bare thigh. "Take this off," he said huskily. "Take it all off."

Laney gave him a sensual smile. "As you wish."

Pulling the pins out of her chignon, she leaned back on her elbows and shook out her long, dark hair beneath the white bridal veil. She propped up one knee, exposing her bare inner thigh and the white garter, above the stocking.

His dark eyes widened as he looked her over. Her head was tilted back, her dark hair curling over her shoulders, her breasts—swollen from pregnancy—thrust forward, barely contained beneath the sliver of strapless white silk bra.

He licked his lips. His gaze slowly traveled down her body, to the soft curve of her belly, to the spread of her hips. Her leg was propped up, revealing an expanse of bare thigh. His eyes traced down the white garters and tiny lace G-string to the see-through fishnets that started halfway down her thigh, all the way to her scarlet-painted toenails.

"Take it off," he repeated hoarsely.

She saw the hunger in his dark eyes, the way he took shallow breaths through parted lips. A thrill went through her.

"That's what I'm doing," she said innocently. "Taking it off."

And she was. Very, very slowly. Like a striptease to torture him. She wasn't sure what made her do it. Maybe it was the sudden realization of her power. Maybe she liked feeling his desire for her. Or maybe, just maybe, the fact of their marriage, of being his legal wife, gave her a confidence she'd never had before.

Still propped on her elbow on the bed, she stretched up her arm, fluffing up her long dark hair beneath the long white veil. She moved her hand slowly down, brushing her cheek, her neck, her clavicle. She moved it slowly over her full breasts, overflowing the flimsy white strapless bra, cupping one breast, pressing it against the other.

His eyes were nearly popping out of his head as he leaned against the bed, naked, not touching her. He said hoarsely, "What are you doing?"

"Oh." She looked up at him with big eyes, feigning surprise. "I guess I need to roll over to reach the clasp..."

And she did so, turning over on the bed, rolling on her tummy. Reaching back, she slowly undid her bra, causing it to fall off. Her full, swollen breasts spilled out in all their naked glory.

Tilting her head, she pretended to consider, placing one fingertip against her wet lips. "Hmm..." Kicking up her heels behind her, she twisted her head and looked back at her own backside, completely naked except for the straps of the white garter and the slender ribbon of the G-string. "Now what should I take off next?"

It was too much for her husband. With a low growl, he fell on her, turning her over so she was on her back. Without a word, he ripped off the white garter belt with two violent hands and did the same with the flimsy G-string. All she wore now was her veil, twisted behind her on the mattress, and her fishnet stockings, which now hung loosely on her legs, sliding down her thighs.

He pushed her back against the soft pillows and stroked his hand possessively down her body, between her breasts. "Tease me, will you?"

She fluttered her eyelashes coyly. "Must you keep ripping my clothes?"

"Not if you stay naked," he whispered, stroking her hair. Cupping her face, he kissed her.

His lips were rough at first, then gentled, became tender. The bristles of his chin were like sandpaper against her skin, but even that felt good to her. His hardness and roughness made her feel soft and feminine. His tongue teased hers as he deepened the kiss. Her naked breasts were crushed against his hard chest, and as her sensitive nipples rubbed against his muscled body, she nearly gasped with the sensation.

Moving, he slowly kissed down her body. Cupping her breasts, he lifted them in amazement. He could no longer fit a breast in his hand. He said in wonder, "You're so big."

"That's what you get for knocking me up."

He looked at her huge breasts and her belly, now with just the slightest hint of a curve, and his expression changed. A low hiss escaped through his teeth. He gently squeezed a nipple, lowering his head to the other. She felt the heat of his wet mouth on her, the stroke of his tongue, the nibble of his teeth, and this time she did gasp.

As he suckled her, he slowly moved his other hand down her body, to the gentle curve of her belly and farther still. He reached between her legs and she shuddered beneath him, swaying her hips. She could feel his hard shaft against her thigh. She wanted him inside her. Her nails tightened against his shoulder as she whispered, "Take me."

Pulling back, he looked down at her, and smiled. She realized he intended to refuse, to tease her and torture her with wanting, as she'd done to him. No way. Reaching between them, she stroked his length, and felt how rigid he was, straining hard against her. She felt him pulse in her hand. His dark eyes widened, then narrowed as he looked down at her.

"Now," she breathed, challenging him with her eyes.

A low growl from deep in his throat. Pulling back, he positioned himself between her legs. He pushed himself inside her with a single thrust, rough and deep.

Her lips parted in a joyful gasp as she felt him inside her, so hard and thick, filling her. Gripping her hips, he pulled back and thrust again. Her legs curled around his muscular backside, pulling him tighter into her. She moaned softly, and he increased the pace, riding her hard and fast, until the headboard was banging against the wall, increasing desperately in noise and rhythm. Beneath the impact and shake, the wedding veil that had been on the pillow suddenly flew up in the air, lifting on a puff of breeze. She felt pleasure build inside her, and she held her breath as it went higher…and higher…and higher still… She started to explode and heard herself scream. His low, triumphant shout joined with hers, and as he exploded inside her, the last thing she saw before she closed her eyes was the white lace veil, falling softly onto his back.

Moments passed before he opened his eyes. Rolling off

her, he pulled her back against his chest, cuddling her into his arms. She nestled her cheek against his shoulder. He kissed the top of her head. "Wife."

"Husband," she whispered shyly. Her cheeks burned a little at the memory of how brazen she'd been. But he seemed to approve. He looked at her lazily beneath heavy-lidded eyes.

"It's just the start."

And so it was. If the wedding had been disappointing, because she'd been too mad at him to enjoy it, then their honeymoon, she would reflect later, was the most perfect, most romantic week of her life.

After they slept in each other's arms, they made love again, then slept some more. When morning light came through the windows, they ordered breakfast in bed from room service, trays of waffles with powdered sugar and maple syrup, grits, fresh fruit, fried eggs with eye-watering red-hot pepper sauce, fresh-squeezed orange juice, and smooth chicory coffee with cream and sugar.

When Kassius accidentally got some powdered sugar on his cheek, she reached out and traced it lightly with her fingertips. "How did you get this scar, Kassius?"

His eyes darkened, then he gave a casual shrug. "It was a long time ago. Why?"

"You have powdered sugar on it. Kind of a mess."

"Ah." Touching his cheek, he looked at the sugar, then back at her. He lifted a dark eyebrow. "Don't mock. You have maple syrup on your chin."

"I do not!" she said indignantly, then licking her chin she discovered it was true. She heard the sudden catch of his breath.

"Let me help with that," he said huskily, and he leaned forward on the bed to lick it off her chin.

Seconds later, both breakfast trays crashed to the floor as he pushed her back against the bed, drizzling maple syrup all over her body, and she was smearing it on him, and they were licking and kissing every inch of each other. Afterward, they were seriously sticky and had to take a long, hot shower. Where they then discovered the sexy possibilities of having hot steamy water shooting all over their warm, wet, naked skin.

Laney couldn't get enough of him. And Kassius couldn't get enough of her.

After the shower, they toweled each other off and were tempted to get back into bed until they got a good look at the tangled sheets, sticky with syrup.

"Maid service," Kassius said breathlessly.

She brightened. "We'll go out!"

They let management know that maid service was required, then got dressed to venture out of the hotel. Laney was suddenly glad for the excuse. She was keen to show him her city—in a way, also his city—at the most thrilling time of the year. Mardi Gras.

Taking him by the hand, she led him out of the elegant formality of the hotel to the sheer madness that was Bourbon Street. It was barely noon, but crowds of people bedecked in over-the-top costumes or the Mardi Gras colors of purple, green and gold already filled the neon-lit bars and the sidewalks and streets. They walked around, gawking, then had lunch at a crowded courtyard restaurant, the best in the city. Since it didn't accept reservations, and Laney flatly refused to allow him to try to get bumped up the wait list by giving the hostess a thousand-dollar tip, they had to wait an hour to be seated. It was a novel experience for Kassius.

"I can't believe you want to wait for a table," he grumbled as they stood in the crowded outdoor bar. In the distance they could hear the music of a brass band over the noisy chatter of others waiting for a table.

"Anticipation is half the fun," Laney informed him.

Reaching out, he took her hand and tenderly kissed her palm, causing her to tremble. "Yes." His dark eyes smoldered as he straightened. "It is."

Laney stared at him, feeling hot and shivery all over. Even though they were having fun wandering around, and even though Kassius had made love to her so many times already, she knew he was already counting down the minutes until he could get her back to the hotel. To his bed. And suddenly, so was she.

"Get you something?" the bartender said brusquely, clearly having no clue who Kassius was, treating him like just another rowdy reveler.

Kassius started to order his usual martini, but Laney interrupted him. "He'll have a hurricane. A sweet tea for me, please."

"Hurricane?" Kassius said with a frown.

"You'll see."

A few moments later, he was looking down with dismay at a garishly colored red-and-orange cocktail of rum and fruit juice in a large curved glass. "It looks like something a tourist would drink."

She sipped her own sweet, nonalcoholic iced tea. "How convenient, since you're a tourist."

"I don't like sugary things."

"You sure?" Her grin widened. Her eyelashes fluttered a little as she picked the glass off the bar and held it out toward him, her breasts pressing against him as she whispered, "Try it. You'll like it."

Never taking his eyes off her, he grabbed the glass and put his mouth on the straw. He gulped the whole thing down. Then he gasped, "I'd rather have some tart with my sugar…"

Then he kissed her, and she tasted the sweet tang of the orange juice and grenadine and rum on his lips.

After a lunch of Cajun-style cooking that Kassius

raved about for hours, they ventured back outside. Bourbon Street had only gotten more crowded as the afternoon faded. A parade went down a nearby street and people went crazy as the floats went by, revelers waving in their sparkled costumes. Confetti and bead necklaces filled the air, along with noise and laughter and music.

As twilight fell, the French Quarter became so crowded it was almost impossible to walk through the streets. He held her hand tightly so as not to get separated.

"Let's have dinner back at the room," he growled, his palm pressing against hers, and she felt a zing of electricity through her body, an intense need that was overwhelming. Quivering, she nodded.

But as they hurried down a back alley, Laney heard shouting above them. She looked up to see three college boys on a covered wraparound wrought-iron balcony. They were hollering at her, shaking necklaces of beads. She blushed.

Kassius frowned and looked at them, then back at her. "What do they want?"

She said meekly, "If I lift up my shirt and flash them my breasts, they'll throw me down some bead necklaces."

"Those bastards," he growled, his hand tightening over hers. "I'll go up there and teach them some manners…"

"It's not an insult. They mean it as a compliment—it's tradition."

Kassius looked both speechless and enraged.

Laney tilted her head as if considering. She tapped her chin. "Honestly, I could use some new jewelry…"

So it was that a half hour later, she found herself at an exclusive jeweler's in the Vieux Carré, where he'd immediately dragged her and insisted on buying her a necklace of diamonds and sapphires that reminded her of that obscenely big sparkler in the movie *Titanic*.

"You can flash me later," he whispered in her ear, and she blushed and gave a laugh almost like a giggle.

She'd just been teasing him before, but as they walked the last blocks back to the hotel, Laney kept touching the cool platinum-set stones against her neck, thrilled that he was so determined to spoil her—in every way.

It was proof he cared. Wasn't it? And caring was almost like love. Wasn't that what such an irrational gift meant?

Then she remembered another diamond necklace, which he'd given to another woman in London. Her delight fled. The necklace suddenly felt like cold rock against her skin as she remembered her old boss Mimi, and Kassius's strange loans.

However it might seem right now, when they were married and taking such pleasure and joy in each other, Laney actually didn't know her husband at all. Yes, she knew where his mother had been born. But there was so much about him that was mysterious. She still had so many questions that now—with her promise—she couldn't even ask.

And how she wanted to know everything. She felt achingly close to him. Like she hadn't been a fool to picture him as noble and good. Like he might actually be that man.

If only he would share his past, share his secrets and heart with her!

But she feared he never would.

There are other ways to learn secrets. The poisonous thought crept into her mind. When they'd first met, Kassius had hired a private investigator to dig through her life. Before, she'd been furious at the invasion of her privacy. Now she shuddered with the temptation.

No, Laney told herself firmly. She wasn't going to sneak behind his back. She would just love him, be a good wife and pray that he would choose to open up to her.

If she just loved him, sooner or later he would tell her everything. Wouldn't he?

CHAPTER EIGHT

EXCEPT, OF COURSE, he didn't.

Six months later, Laney was trembling as she pressed her phone tighter to her ear. "What did you say?"

"Your husband's real name is Cash Kuznetsov," the investigator said.

Laney's heart was pounding as she sank into a chair in their new Monaco flat. With a deep breath, she rubbed her enormous belly. She'd hoped it wouldn't come to this. Hoped that over the course of their marriage, her husband would just reveal his secrets to her of his own free will.

But he hadn't. And as they'd traveled frequently around the world, in some ways—in spite of his generosity with his wealth, his care of her family and of her—he'd been more secretive than ever.

Last week, she'd discovered him out of bed in the middle of the night in their new Monaco home. Apparently, the villa on Cap Ferrat that he'd been hoping to buy for the last six months was still not on the market. So in a fit of pique, Kassius had purchased a bigger penthouse in a luxury high-rise, five bedrooms with a rooftop terrace and panoramic view of Fontvieille Harbor, the rocks and the sea. She was still in shock that he'd make a thirty-million-euro purchase on impulse. As a temporary replacement for the house he *really* wanted.

That villa on Cap Ferrat must really be something, she thought in awe.

That night, she'd discovered her husband pacing as he spoke quietly into the phone. When she'd confronted him, asking him whom he could be speaking with at two in the morning, he'd refused to explain. "If you don't want me to lie, you promised never to ask," was his terse response.

It had been the last straw.

The next morning, feeling hurt and anxious and twisted up with emotion, she'd contacted a private investigator recommended to her by Kassius's friend, the best man at his wedding, Ángel Velazquez. The Spaniard billionaire was the only person she knew who wouldn't be afraid to go against Kassius Black.

Ángel had been amused when he'd gotten her call. "You already wish to hire a detective, after just a few months?" he'd said sardonically. "How pleasant marriage must be."

She'd gone hot with embarrassment and tried to stammer out excuses before he'd mercifully cut her off. But at least he'd given her the name of a very good private investigator, who liked the idea of a challenge—of discovering the true background of the man whom no one else had ever been able to properly trace. He'd told her, "I just need a place to start."

Feeling like a traitor, Laney had given him the address of the Cash home on St. Charles Avenue—the address where Kassius had recently decided to build a brand-new house expressly for her grandmother and father, with a guest wing where she and Kassius could visit after the baby was born.

Just thinking of how she'd gone behind his back while he was building a house for her family made her feel ashamed.

And he'd done far more for the Henry family than just the house. Since the marriage, Laney's grandmother and father now considered Kassius family. So they were happy to let him spend money on them. They didn't see his generosity as charity, but merely as his way of showing love.

"Some men just aren't good with words, Laney May," her father had explained.

"Any man that's a man," her grandmother grumbled.

So they hadn't fought Kassius when he'd insisted on sending Clark to Atlanta on his private jet to see a highly regarded doctor who offered innovative medical treatments. Especially after Kassius had explained his anguish that he'd been unable to get the best care for his own mother when he was young.

Only a heart of stone could have refused him, and Clark Henry, beneath his gruff exterior, had no heart of stone. After months of treatment, her father was seeing improvements, with partial sight already restored in one eye.

"There's this nurse with a really sexy voice who's been taking care of me. I'm just trying to get a good look at her," he'd explained half-jokingly, but he'd sounded happier than Laney had heard him in years.

As if her father having hope and a new crush wasn't enough, her grandmother had been traveling the world. Yvonne started with a ten-day cruise of the eastern Caribbean, but the day she'd returned, she'd hopped on a new ship to see the western side. In the last six months, the longtime widow had cruised the whole world, meeting new friends and even a few new boyfriends.

"You've left a trail of broken hearts across the world," Laney liked to tease her.

Yvonne just said coyly, "I can't help it if men keep falling for me." Her grandmother had now branched out to even greater adventures, backpacking across Europe, staying at hostels, and most recently visiting Angkor Wat in Cambodia with a Norwegian man friend ten years younger.

Laney was incredibly touched and grateful for what Kassius had done for them—all of them. She'd tried to be satisfied. She'd reminded herself that Kassius was a good husband and would be a good father. She'd told herself that every man had secrets.

But she couldn't let it go. And now she understood why.

"What's his father's name?" she whispered now, but as

the investigator told her, she'd already known what it would be. By the time she hung up the phone, all the pieces were clicking into place. The loans he'd made to a man who was unlikely to ever repay. The secret gifts to Mimi du Plessis.

Laney thought of the hard light in his eyes the night of their wedding, when he'd shown her the empty land where his grandparents' elegant mansion used to be. *This precious house meant everything to them. After they died, I bought it. Had it demolished.* It was the only thing that made sense.

She knew why he kept coming back to Monaco and what he was after. And why.

Laney paced through the afternoon, waiting for Kassius to come home. When he finally did, it was hours later. She was sitting wearily by the wide windows overlooking the sparkling lights of the city in the dark night, and the dark sea beyond.

Kassius frowned at her, obviously shocked to find her awake so late, with a bottle of scotch on the table beside her.

"You're drinking scotch?" he said in disbelief.

Well might he be surprised—she hadn't had even a sip of champagne since she'd discovered she was pregnant. Opening the bottle, she poured some in a short crystal glass. "It's not for me." She held out the glass. "It's for you."

Setting down his laptop bag, he looked at her with a frown and slowly took the glass.

"I know who you are, Kassius," Laney said quietly, looking up at him from the sofa. "And I know who your father is."

He took a small sip of scotch, watching her. "Do you?"

Exhaling, she nodded. "All this time, I've wondered about your expensive gifts to Mimi du Plessis and your endless anonymous loans to her boss. Now I understand. You didn't want her to tell Boris Kuznetsov all those loans were from the same source—you. You didn't want him to get curious about you. Because if he looked at you too closely, he might recognize you as the eleven-year-old boy he abandoned in Istanbul. Cash Kuznetsov, the illegitimate son of Boris Kuznetsov and Emmaline Cash."

"How did you learn this?"

"An investigator. I got his name from Ángel Velazquez."

For a long moment, Kassius looked at her, then he barked a laugh. Lifting the glass, he drank all the scotch in a single gulp. He set the glass down with a clunk.

"Fine," he said abruptly. "You got me."

"What are you trying to do to him?" she whispered, hoping against hope she was wrong.

He poured himself another glass of scotch, then considered her. "Destroy him, of course."

"How?"

His sensual lips curved in a bitter smile. "Like I told you, Kuznetsov wasn't around much when I was growing up. He was a busy man, working in Moscow, and had to do lots of travel throughout the Soviet Union and beyond. That was how they'd met, when she was a stewardess based out of Istanbul." He took another sip of scotch. "After he abandoned us, after my mother got sick, I went through her papers and found his address in Moscow. I wrote letters. He never replied. When I was sixteen, I hopped a train to Moscow and found out why. *He was already married.*"

"Oh, no," she breathed.

He shrugged. "I saw him walking, arm in arm, with his beautiful blond wife in her fancy clothes, into a mansion, followed by three golden retrievers bounding at their heels. So cozy. So rich. So happy."

Laney sucked in her breath.

"I was so shocked I stumbled back. Straight into a metal fence. That's how I got this." He traced the raised white scar on his cheekbone. His lips twisted. "He'd strung my mother along for sixteen years, promising her he'd marry her someday and buy her a candy-pink villa in the South of France. I still remember how happy those dreams made her. She always believed he was coming back to her. I didn't have the heart to tell my mother what kind of man he really was."

Laney suddenly understood so much. "No wonder you hate the idea of love," she whispered brokenly. "To you, all it means is a lie."

His jaw clenched, and he looked away, toward the vast darkness of the sea.

"I didn't want you to know, Laney," he said heavily. "Because it's not your way. I wanted you to keep your ideals about love. About me," he added quietly.

She slowly rose from the sofa. At eight months pregnant, she had to push herself up with a little more force than in the past.

Grabbing his hand, she placed it over the spot on her belly, where she felt her baby kicking inside her.

"That's our son," she said in a low voice. His eyes went wide.

"Son?" he breathed.

She smiled bashfully. "I know we promised each other we would wait to find out, but well… I couldn't help myself from asking at my last appointment."

"A son." He blinked fast. "Perfect. I've already got my hands on what's left of his company. All he has left now is the villa. If he takes one more loan, I will have that, too."

Pain ripped through her. "Don't do this. Revenge won't make you happier. It won't. Please, just let it go!"

"Let it go?" He stared at her incredulously. "He has to be punished for what he did."

"Please," she whispered. "For my sake. For our baby's. Just talk to him. There might be extenuating circumstances. You don't know."

His eyes hardened. "I know enough."

"Listen…" Her voice cracked. "I was angry all the time

when I was a teenager, hating my mother for leaving us, blaming her for dumping everything on us so she could run off and be free. But I was so unhappy. So awfully unhappy. I didn't want to feel that way. So I decided to forgive her. To remember the good times. I chose love—which is what I feel for you, Kassius." She took a deep breath and lifted her gaze to his. "I love you."

His expression looked frozen. "You love me?" he said in a low voice. "After everything I told you?"

"You're a good man. I know it." She put her hand over his as their baby kicked again. "Don't hurt your father. Our child's grandfather."

He pulled back his hand, looking angry. "You care so much about the man?"

"I care about you. And our baby. And what this revenge will mean for us—all of us."

His sensual mouth curved. "You're part of it, Laney."

"Me?"

"It was always part of my plan. A beautiful family, a wife, a child. Kuznetsov's wife divorced him for another man long ago. He has no other children. After I take his villa and tell him who I am and why I've ruined him, he'll know he's lost every chance at happiness he might have had. Including his only family who might have loved him. His own grandchildren will never know his name."

Laney stared at him in shock.

"No wonder you wanted to marry me," she said numbly, feeling heartsick. "No wonder you were so determined from the first night to get me pregnant. I thought it was love at first sight. But for you, it was only revenge…"

Reaching down, he put his hand on her shoulder. "Not only that. Not anymore. I've come to trust you, Laney. That's why I'm telling you the truth."

Great, she thought bitterly. *Now* he was trusting her.

Her eyes narrowed as she shook her head. "If you're not going to try to talk to him, I will—"

Kassius's expression changed in an instant. He grasped her shoulders tightly, looking down at her with a ferocity she'd never imagined. "If you even think of telling Kuznetsov, you are dead to me, do you understand? I will never see you again. Neither you nor the baby."

Shocked, she searched his gaze.

"I don't believe you," she said slowly.

"Don't you?" His jaw set. "I think you do. If you betray me, I will divorce you, Laney. I will start new. Find another woman. Have a different child."

His grip tightened. "You're hurting me!"

He released her. She rubbed her arm, feeling hurt and bewildered by the savage change in him.

"I have to trust you, Laney." Kassius looked at her for a long moment, a mixture of emotions crossing his face. When she didn't answer, he grabbed his laptop bag and left the penthouse without another word. The front door closed with a bang.

But it wasn't her arm he had injured. It was her heart.

She stared after him, filled with despair. Walking around the enormous five-bedroom luxury flat, with its wide windows overlooking the sea and harbor, she felt alone, aimless and lost.

Laney stopped in the doorway of the cheerful nursery she'd decorated for their baby. She'd been so happy when she'd gotten Kassius to put up the goofy giraffe on the wall. She'd convinced herself that he was starting to open up to her. To care.

If you even think of telling Kuznetsov, you are dead to me, do you understand? I will never see you again. Neither you nor the baby. If you betray me, I will divorce you, Laney. I will start new. Find another woman. Have a different child.

He didn't love her. To him, she was interchangeable.

Any woman would do. Any child. All he needed was window dressing for his revenge.

Fury and despair coursed through her, and without thinking, she grabbed the giraffe decoration and ripped it half off the wall with a cry. Then she saw what she'd done, and she collapsed into sobs, covering her face with her hands as she fell on her knees to the brightly colored rug.

All a lie. All something she'd done to convince herself that Kassius could change.

He couldn't. He didn't even want to.

Kassius was destroying his own soul, and she was helpless to save him.

She cried herself to sleep. At dawn—sunrise came early in late August—she found Kassius's side of the bed hadn't been slept in. Hadn't he come home last night? She crept downstairs and saw his laptop bag outside his home office. She peeked in the open door and saw him sleeping fitfully on the black leather sofa. She exhaled.

She was starting to push open the door to talk to him, then stopped. What was the point? He was so lost in his childhood grief and rage that he'd spent a lifetime planning his revenge. He didn't see how destructive it was. Whether or not Boris Kuznetsov deserved punishment for what he'd done so long ago, Laney felt with all her heart that her own baby deserved a father who knew how to love. How to forgive.

But Kassius was so lost in his anger, telling him that was a waste of time.

Laney's eyes suddenly narrowed.

If only she could just get the two men to talk, face-to-face. That was the answer—it was always the answer. Maybe the problems wouldn't be solved, but it had to be more satisfying than all this sneaking around, grudge holding, revenge. They had to talk and get this in the open.

She recalled the stark look in Kassius's dark eyes as

he'd said, *I will never see you again. Neither you nor the baby.* For a moment, fear gripped her.

She looked down at her belly, putting her hand protectively over her baby. She was only three and a half weeks from her due date. She thought of the risk she would take, trembling between love and fear.

But her life had taught her to choose love. Wasn't that worth the risk? She had to try to save him as she hadn't been able to save her mother. She was the only one who could. She told herself that his words had been spoken in anger, to try to control her actions. Kassius was too good a man to actually desert her, and especially not their baby.

As Mrs. Beresford—who had volunteered to come here from London to look after them—made breakfast, Laney took a long shower and then got dressed in a simple cotton sundress and sandals. As she ate scrambled eggs, croissants and fruit at the dining table, her stomach fluttered with nerves as she looked up Boris Kuznetsov's address.

By late morning, when Kassius still hadn't left his home office to talk to her, she realized he was probably on the phone wrapping up the final loan right now and preparing with his accountants and attorneys to move in for the kill. It was now or never. She made her decision.

Going down to the garage, she discovered Benito conversing with the driver as he waxed the limo. They both snapped to attention when they saw her.

"Do you need me to drive you somewhere, madame?" he asked respectfully. She backed away.

"Um, no…" She saw the key to the sports car hanging in the open wall safe and snatched it up. "I'm just running a quick errand."

"Monsieur Black prefers that I drive you…"

There was no way she was going to risk him finding out where she was going. Not before this silly business was settled and smoothed over. "Thank you, but it's not necessary," she stammered. "It's just a little thing, and I want to surprise my husband."

She thought of how surprised he'd be. But first, she had to get into the sports car. With her big belly, the low-slung seat was a tight squeeze, and very low to the ground. Once in, she wondered if she'd ever be able to get out again.

"All right, madame?"

"Absolutely." Swallowing, trying not to be nervous, Laney started the engine, automatically turning the air-conditioning on full blast. Even with the coast's cooling sea breezes, August in Monaco felt uncomfortably hot to her at her advanced state of pregnancy. She'd gained thirty pounds, plus the growing baby felt like her own personal furnace. The blast of cool air was welcome as she also rolled down the windows and drove the tight, curvy coastal road west, over the border into France.

Her hands were shaking as a half hour later, she turned onto Cap Ferrat, the famously beautiful green peninsula jutting out into the shining blue Mediterranean, one of the most expensive residential areas in the world. It was filled with gated villas owned by famous people, from tech billionaires to rock royalty. She passed a few guarded gates before she reached the right one. She stopped at the gatehouse.

"Madame?" the guard said respectfully.

Laney licked her lips awkwardly. "I'd like to see Mr. Kuznetsov," she blurted out. "He's not expecting me. Please tell me that I'm the wife of Kassius Black, and I bring news of his son."

The guard turned back into his guardhouse, and made a quick call. He returned looking stern. "He says he has no son, madame."

"I'm speaking of the son he abandoned in Istanbul."

The guard spoke quietly again, and when he turned back to face her, his expression was wide-eyed. "You're to go in at once, if you please."

Laney drove through the gate, passing overgrown gardens before entering a courtyard. Behind the big stone fountain was the entryway to the villa, which was big, pink and gaudy, with an amazing view of the sea behind it.

She parked the black sports car in the courtyard, next to a shiny red convertible with a Monaco license plate. She turned off the engine. The flowering trees and brilliant bougainvillea were a riot of color, but she noticed the garden seemed strangely overgrown, almost entirely wild, as if no gardeners had touched it for months.

She was doing the right thing, wasn't she? Laney's hands tightened on the steering wheel as she took a deep breath. Right or wrong, it was too late to turn back. She had to take courage for what lay ahead.

She felt ungainly as an elephant climbing out of the low-slung sports car. Especially when she saw the slender, well-dressed blonde who'd just come out of the mansion. Her lips parted in shock.

It was Mimi du Plessis, her old boss, the American-born Comtesse de Fourcil.

When she saw Laney, her red lips curled.

"If it isn't my former employee. Now the glamorous Madame Black." Coming closer, Mimi looked her over contemptuously. "You really think you've won it all, don't you, Laney? You think he will love you. He won't. You're nothing but a broodmare." She patted the glossy red convertible. "Do you like it?" She smiled viciously. "Your husband had it delivered for me this morning."

That explained the midnight call Kassius hadn't wanted to explain. Laney blessed her investigator. Otherwise, she'd have believed her husband to be unfaithful and been devastated. As it was, she lifted her chin defiantly.

"I know all about it," Laney said. She tilted her head as she faced her old boss. "So what was he paying you for this time? Was it the final payoff for facilitating his very last loan to your boss?"

Mimi looked disappointed. Tossing her blond mane, she said spitefully, "Much good it will do him now. I brought all the paperwork for the loan, but Mr. Kuznetsov was suspicious about why anyone would lend him money now, when his company is bankrupt, or why I would choose to help him when he's had to let all his employees go. The game is up. Nothing left for me now but to find some wrinkled old rich man to marry." She sighed. "But I told him what he wanted to know. All the loans he's taken over the last two years have secretly been from the same man— Kassius Black." Her smile widened. "So all the gifts your husband gave me were for *nothing*. He's still busted."

Laney stared at her old boss, this beautiful, empty woman, divorced four times, who cared about nothing and no one. "I feel sorry for you," she said quietly.

Mimi's eyes blazed, then she gave a brittle laugh. "Sorry for me? Don't be ridiculous. Everyone wants to be me."

Climbing into her gorgeous red convertible, the comtesse adjusted the mirrors and drove away from the pink villa with a squeal of tires and a cloud of dust that left Laney coughing.

"Madame Black."

Looking up, she saw an older man, trim and well dressed, with salt-and-pepper hair, waiting anxiously by the front door. Recognizing him, she came toward him, smiling, and extended her hand. "Thank you for seeing me."

He shook her hand, then motioned for her to follow him inside.

Laney walked through the villa, which was oddly sparse of furniture. She saw rectangles on the walls where the wallpaper was suspiciously bright. He saw her glance, and gave a rueful smile.

"I've had to sell off a few unnecessary things. Like

paintings." He looked at her, and added kindly, "And turn off the air-conditioning, I'm afraid." That explained why the villa felt so uncomfortably hot.

He escorted her into a large sitting room, empty except for a few antique cushioned chairs and a table. A breeze came from the open windows overlooking the sea. "Would you care for some tea, Mrs. Black?"

"Thank you."

"I hope it's not too strong." He poured her a cup of tea from a small electric samovar. "I'm out of practice at this. I used to have servants, but I've had to let them go. Along with all my other employees."

"That must have been hard."

His expression sagged. "My company just couldn't compete with all the cheaper supplies flooding the market. Other than my security guard who keeps thieves and reporters away, I have only my housekeeper left, but she's too old and frail to work. She just has nowhere else to go. Kind of like me." He looked wistfully around the elegant, half-empty salon. "I have just this villa left, but soon this, too, will go."

He paused, sitting in the chair across from her. Then he leaned forward, his dark eyes burning through her, reminding her so much of Kassius's. She thought he would ask her about Kassius's loans. But he didn't.

"Now. You said you have news of my son?" he said anxiously. "My Cash? He's alive?"

Laney took a deep breath.

"Yes," she whispered. "Very alive. And close."

Emotions crossed the man's face painfully. "How do you know this?"

Laney looked at him, her heart pounding in her throat. She prayed she was doing the right thing that would save their family, not destroy it.

Setting down her tea, she said quietly, "Because I'm married to him."

* * *

"Mrs. Black is on the house phone for you, sir."

Kassius looked up from his laptop with a frown to see Mrs. Beresford in his doorway. Sitting at his dark lacquered desk in his home office, with its view of the sea, he was simultaneously going through the numbers for the potential development of a ten-story residential building in London and holding his cell phone with his shoulder as he spoke with his head contractor on the new stadium being built in Singapore. He covered his phone with one hand. "She's calling me from the bedroom?"

"No, sir. From your father's house. She said you weren't answering your mobile."

It took two seconds for that to sink in. He said tersely into the phone, "I'll call you back." Pressing his hands against the desk, he rose furiously and took the cordless receiver from his housekeeper's hand. Electricity was making his nerve endings vibrate and hum with something he hadn't felt in a long time—fear. "Laney?"

"Kassius, don't hate me," her sweet voice pleaded. "I had to do this. For you. I'm with Boris Kuznetsov and I've told him everything. Who you are, the loans, how you got your scar in Moscow. Everything. We're drinking tea in his parlor."

It was like being punched in the gut. Harder than he'd ever been punched in his life. His knees went weak as he felt the work of a lifetime undone by a woman's betrayal.

Not just any woman. His wife.

Not just any wife. The mother of his soon-to-be-born son.

If you even think of telling Kuznetsov, you are dead to me, do you understand? I will never see you again. Neither you nor the baby.

He'd told her what would happen. He'd *told* her.

"I'll be there as soon as I can," Kassius said tightly and

hung up. But for a moment, he continued to grip the phone, so tight that the plastic receiver started to crack beneath his fingers. His eyes stung as he realized what Laney's naive, reckless action had just cost them all.

He closed his eyes, leaning his head against the receiver. He hadn't cried in years, but when he opened his eyes again, they were watery.

He'd just lost everything.

The dream of his past—of getting his revenge.

The dream of his future with her—of their family.

Laney had thought she knew better. Thought she could cure him with her ridiculous beliefs about love. Her foolish idealism had just cost him everything he cared about.

He'd trusted her.

And this was the result.

If someone ever shows you the truth of who they are, if they lie or cheat or betray you, promise me you'll believe them the first time! Don't destroy your life, or your child's, wishing and hoping and pretending they'll change.

Kassius felt the phone crack beneath his grip. Tossing it down across his lacquered desk, he looked for his car keys. He went down to the garage and saw the sports car was gone. Laney, with her laughable driving skills, had taken his favorite car on her way to betray him. Of course she had.

"Benito," he called tightly to his bodyguard. "Have Lamont pull the limo around."

Perhaps it was better this way. Better for him to bring his bodyguard and driver so his wife could immediately face the price of her betrayal.

Kassius looked out bleakly at the sunlit Mediterranean as the driver, with his bodyguard in the front seat beside him, twisted the tight curves of the slender cliff road. The driver pounded on the brakes when a car wove briefly into their lane, and loud French curses came from the front seat. Kassius barely noticed as he took a phone call from his business manager.

Hanging up a few moments later, Kassius looked out the window. He felt weary. He felt dead. His hand tightened. The damage was done.

The car drove up to the guardhouse at Kuznetsov's gate and was almost instantly waved through.

"Stay here," he ordered his men after the limo was parked. "You know what to do."

The driver nodded and reached for something in his jacket that looked like a flask. "Just juice," he said in response to Kassius's frown.

"Benito?" he demanded.

"Got it." His bodyguard looked mutinous, but then, he'd come to respect and admire his boss's wife. Everyone had.

Kassius's soul felt hollow as he looked up at the ostentatious pink villa, the villa that he'd intended to take for his own and throw the former owner into the gutter to starve, as he'd left Kassius and his mother so long ago. A lump rose in his throat.

He'd already heard from his business manager that his father had canceled the last pending loan. Kassius could take possession of all the other homes Boris Kuznetsov had signed over as collateral. But who cared about those? This—he looked up with a sharp pain in his throat—this pink mansion, made of spun sugar and fairy-tale dreams, was the only one that mattered. And he'd failed, through no fault of his own.

That was a lie. It was *entirely* his fault, for trusting Laney. For letting himself be vulnerable to her. If he hadn't taken her to his mother's childhood home the night of their wedding, it was unlikely any private investigator could have made the connection. He'd covered his tracks too well. He'd been careful.

Until Laney had gotten under his skin and left him open for attack.

He walked up to the front door, which opened before he could knock. A tiny elderly woman, nearly bent over with osteoporosis, motioned to the right hall. "They're in the salon, monsieur," she said grandly in French. "I'll show you the way…"

But seeing how she hobbled painfully in front of him, he said hastily, "No, *merci*, I can easily find my own way, madame."

Tossing him a grateful look, she gave a nod. Kassius walked down the empty hallway to a high-ceilinged, elegant room in cream and pale blue, with sparse antique furniture and walls devoid of decoration. And at the center of it all, his traitorous dark-haired wife sat at a small table with the man who'd destroyed Kassius's childhood and driven his mother into an early grave, the two of them cozily drinking tea from an electric samovar.

"Kassius!" his wife exclaimed, rising to her feet and coming forward, holding out her hands to him as if she expected an embrace, as if she expected him to thank her for destroying his life. It was cruel, he thought, that she'd never looked more beautiful than now, even dressed in a plain sundress and sandals. With her lush breasts and belly, and the sparkle in her brown eyes and bounce in her dark hair, she was loving and warm. Laney Henry Black was everything he'd ever wanted in a wife.

Everything he should have known would ultimately destroy him.

"Laney," he responded coldly, not touching her. He turned his attention to the older man who'd risen from the chair beside her. His face was haggard and pale, and he was staring at Kassius with stricken dark eyes exactly like his own.

"Is it true?" Boris Kuznetsov whispered, looking at him

searchingly. "You're my son?" He choked out, "My little Cash? Can it really be?"

Cash. A blast of memory went through Kassius like the heat of a fiery explosion. No one had called him that in a long, long time.

All his years as a child, he'd yearned for his father's acknowledgment, his acceptance. Just his presence. And now, at last, they were in the same room, but now Kassius no longer wanted anything from him—but justice.

"It's true, old man." Turning to Laney, Kassius said blandly, "Why don't you wait outside?"

"Really?" Her forehead crinkled uncertainly.

"My father and I have much to discuss."

Laney bit her lip. "If you're sure—"

"I'm sure."

She looked up at him anxiously. "Please don't be mad at me for this," she said. "I know you didn't want me to tell him, but it was the only way to save you from making a horrible mistake."

"I understand." And he did. Laney being who she was, she'd actually believed she could change him. That she could save him. That he could become like her—someone who believed in love. "You couldn't have done any differently."

"Exactly." Laney looked at him with a tearful smile. "I love you," she whispered, reaching up a hand to caress his cheek. "So much."

Kassius shuddered beneath her touch. He felt choked by competing emotions of fury, regret, agonizing desire and loss—such deep loss!

Looking down at her, he savored the beauty of her lovely face, the curve of her cheek, her full lips. Her warm, loving brown eyes, deep enough for a man to drown in. He took a picture of memory. He knew this would be the very last time he'd ever look upon Laney's face.

"Benito is outside. You can wait in the car." He forced himself to give her an encouraging smile. "There's air-conditioning."

"Ooh," she said happily, as he'd known she would. "All right, I'll wait outside." She squeezed his hand. "Just let him explain. Give him a chance!"

He gave a single nod. It was hard to speak over the lump in his throat. "Goodbye, Laney."

Patting him on the shoulder, she left. Going to the far window, Kassius drew back the curtain and watched her go out into the courtyard. He saw Benito come up and talk to her.

Dropping the curtain, Kassius turned away. He couldn't watch what would happen next.

"Cash?"

He turned sharply to his father.

"What happened to you?" the man whispered. He was staring at Kassius as if looking at a ghost he was afraid to touch. "When I finally got your letters, I rushed to Istanbul, but no one knew where you were…"

"Oh, did you finally come looking?" he replied coldly. "I sent letters for five years."

"My wife hid them from me. She only gave them to me at our divorce—"

"Yes," Kassius ground out. "Your wife." His lip curled. "Mama always defended you, did you know that? In spite of the way you seduced her with promises of love and marriage, when you knew you were capable of neither."

The older man took a single staggering step back.

"You're—right," he said finally, running his hand over his forehead. "When I fell in love with Emmaline, I was already trapped in a loveless marriage. I hid it from Emmaline, because I knew she never would have looked at me…"

"You're right about that," he said scornfully. "She would

have told you to go to hell. But unlike you, my mother had a soul."

"I wanted to marry her," Boris whispered. "I wanted it desperately. But my wife refused to divorce me."

"Liar."

"It's true." The older man's voice trembled. "I begged her. But even though Tania already had taken many lovers of her own, she wouldn't let me go. She knew that with my position I had the opportunity to make a lot of money in the breakup of the Soviet Union. She told me I'd have to pay her millions of rubles to agree to divorce me." He took a shuddering breath. "I tried to make money as fast as I could. But it wasn't fast enough."

Kassius looked contemptuously around the front room, with its faded wallpaper, its missing furniture, its dust. "All the while talking to my mother of the fantastical villa you would someday buy her."

The man swallowed. "I wanted to buy Emmaline her villa. I wanted to live with you, be your father. Your hero." He gave a weak smile. "Do you remember, when you were young, how we used to pretend to be Roman gladiators, fighting with wooden swords? We sometimes knocked over the furniture. You loved it when I told you stories about the Roman Empire, far past your bedtime, until your mother was furious at both of us…"

A memory floated back to Kassius. It had been his father who'd told him stories of the Romans? Pain went through him. The pain of a boy who'd loved his father, only to be rejected by him, abandoned. It was pain he'd thought he was past feeling, and fury filled him that he was not.

"And you left us," he said hoarsely. "You left my mother to die without help. For five years, you could have come back to help us—could have phoned, sent a letter—"

"She wouldn't let me," his father cried. "When you were eleven, your mother found out I'd been married to another woman since before we'd even met. It didn't matter to her that we'd been estranged for fifteen years, or that my wife had a lover but wouldn't divorce me until I had made a fortune to pay her off. After Emmaline found out, nothing I could say or do would persuade her to let me visit again—or even send her money! She told me to get out and never come back, never try to contact either of you again until I was free to love you both. So I went back to Moscow, determined to finally get the divorce Tania had denied me." His voice broke. "I never imagined it would take me five years to earn enough, because each time my business grew, she only became greedier for more. The only reason she finally agreed to the divorce was that she fell pregnant by her longtime lover. And by then, it was too late." His voice was hollow. "Your mother had already died."

Kassius wouldn't show mercy. "Because of you."

He clawed his hand through his gray hair. "I never knew Emmaline was ill," he whispered. "Not until it was too late."

Kassius reminded himself of the pain he'd felt when he'd seen Boris with his wife in Moscow, living in a mansion, apparently without a care in the world—while his own mother lay dying in poverty in Istanbul. He said tightly, "You still deserve to be punished."

His father looked at him.

"I have been," he said in a low voice. "I spent all those lonely years desperately missing you. When I finally rushed to Istanbul, you both were gone. All I found was your mother's grave. I've spent all these years looking for you. I thought you were dead."

"You destroyed her life."

Tears filled the old man's eyes. Blinking fast, he looked away, staring blindly out the windows. "I thought we'd grow old together. She was the only woman I ever loved.

I always meant to go back to her. I just thought we'd have more time—"

His voice choked off.

Kassius stared at him, refusing to feel sympathy.

"Forgive me, Cash," he whispered. His knees collapsed beneath him, and he fell back on the chair. "I never loved anyone again after I lost her—and you. I never wanted another wife, another child. You were both everything I ever wanted, but it was based on a lie, so I lost it all. I tried to keep the business going for the sake of my employees, but to tell you the truth, I never had the heart for business. All I have left—" he looked around the half-empty room "—is this villa. It's all I had left of her. Keeping that promise I'd made to her..."

His voice broke, and he covered his face with his hands. Kassius stared down at the weeping old man.

It was his moment of vengeance, just as he'd dreamed about. He should have felt a sense of triumph.

Instead, all he felt was empty. Boris Kuznetsov was old now. He'd committed the crime of falling in love with a young, idealistic stewardess and pretending he was free to marry her, when he was not. For that, he'd lost everything.

So much had been lost, by everyone.

Kassius had the faint memory he hadn't let himself think of in a long time. His father teaching him in the Istanbul street, when he was a young boy, how to play fight with a sword. How to be a gladiator. How all the other kids who lived on the street had been jealous and fought to be included. How happy he'd been. How proud of his father. His hero.

I was so unhappy. So awfully unhappy. I didn't want to feel that way. So I decided to forgive her. To remember the good times. I chose love...

No. His stomach clenched. He couldn't think about Laney now, on top of everything else.

His phone buzzed in his pocket. He saw Laney's number. Repressing his churning emotions, he lifted it to his ear. "Yes?"

"What's going on?" Laney sounded frightened. "Benito pushed me into the car. He says they're taking me to the airport then sending me back to New Orleans. I don't understand."

Kassius set his jaw. He made his heart very small.

"It's over," he said coldly. "As I told you. I will pay money for your support and nothing more. My lawyer is drawing up the paperwork for our divorce."

In the room, he heard his father's intake of breath at the same time as Laney's.

"Divorce?" she whispered.

"I told you what would happen if you betrayed me. I will never see you again, or the baby."

She gave a long, brittle, anguished gasp. It rattled and echoed across the line. "I don't believe it," she choked out. "You wouldn't be so…so heartless."

"You did this, Laney. *You did this.*"

"Kassius—"

Then her voice cut off with a scream. He heard a squeal of tires, a scream, a crack. And then nothing. A moment of silence, and then a busy signal. Frowning, he stared down at the phone in his hand. Was it a trick? He had to suppress the intense desire to call her back. It had to be a trick. But he couldn't be manipulated so easily.

"You are wrong to treat her so badly," his father said behind him. "All she's done is love you and try to bring us together."

Kassius put his phone in his pocket and faced him with a cold sneer. "*Love?* What do you know about that?"

"I know how it feels to lose it." His father looked at him with tears in his eyes. "I know how it feels to make one bad choice that ruins everything. When Emmaline told me to leave and not come back until I was free, I tried so hard to do it. I told myself I could make up for all the lost years. But the truth is that time is all we possess. Time and love. Choose carefully." His voice broke. "Before you throw it away."

Kassius shook his head coldly.

"My business manager informed me you already canceled the loan you were going to take on this villa. You might have managed to keep this place for now, but I have taken over your bankrupt company and I'll be selling it off for parts. Along with everything else I've taken from you. This villa will be small comfort to you when…"

"It's yours."

Kassius's eyes widened. "What?"

"I give it to you freely," his father said quietly. "The last thing I possess. I built it for your mother, after she died. You are all that we have left. The last memory of our love. Cash, this villa is yours."

For a moment, Kassius couldn't find a voice to answer. Kuznetsov simply giving him the villa was the last thing he'd expected. The last thing he'd wanted.

"Keep it while you can," Kassius bit out, turning away. "My lawyers will be in touch."

Outside the villa, dark clouds had covered the sun. From far away, he heard a low rumble of rolling thunder as a cold wind rose from the sea. He turned his face up to the first drops of rain, relishing the feel of it on his hot skin.

As ordered, his men had taken his wife away in the limo and he was left with the sports car, the key beside it. He was grateful to be the one driving the two-seater, since with the rear-wheel drive and performance tires, it could be a little dodgy on slick, wet roads. He wouldn't want Laney to be taking any risks—

Then he remembered Laney was no longer his problem, since he was never going to see her again. He'd never even see his son born. A pang ripped through his heart. He was leaving her and the baby.

Just like her mother had done to her.

Just like his father had done to him.

Kassius took his phone out of his pocket, testing himself against the savage temptation. He couldn't call her. He *couldn't*. That would be breaking his vow. Revealing his own weakness. He couldn't be weak. He couldn't break his word.

Like a miracle, his phone suddenly rang in his palm. He saw his bodyguard's number and snatched it up. "Yes?"

"Boss, we've had an accident," Benito said hoarsely. "A truck collided into us on the road. Police and ambulance just got here. Lamont's dead…that flask smelled of alcohol. I think it slowed his reflexes…"

Kassius gripped the phone. "Let me talk to Laney."

There was a long silence. "I can't."

"What do you mean?"

"The truck plowed into her side. I wasn't touched. She and Lamont got the worst of it." The man's voice was a whisper. "They're loading her into a helicopter to take her to the Hôpital Princesse Florestine. They're not sure…" His voice broke. "I'm sorry, boss. They're not sure if she and the baby will make it."

Not sure she and the baby will make it…

A haze went over Kassius's eyes. A memory of everything Laney had tried to do for him…trying to love him, to convince him to love her, to even love himself. Trying to make him a better man.

And for that he'd ripped out her heart and sent her and his child away, unknowingly to their deaths…

He staggered against his car. He dimly noticed that his father had followed him out of the villa and now stood beside him in the rain, staring at him with wide eyes.

"Boss?" His bodyguard sounded panic-stricken.

"The main hospital in Monaco?" Kassius whispered.

"Take the north road. Get here as fast as you can."

Turning from his father, Kassius flung himself into the car. Starting the engine, he drove as fast as he could, focusing with hellish intensity on the drive beneath the rain, pushing the sports car to the limit. He crossed the border into Monaco and then roared up to the hospital, parking beneath the portico, leaving his car helter-skelter in front with the door still open.

He ran inside, and his shout carried up and down the hallway. "Where is she? Where is my wife?" he cried. "Where is my son?"

"Monsieur, calm down!"

"Please, monsieur, this is a hospital! Show some respect!" the nurses tried to hush him.

"Where is she?"

"If you don't stop yelling, we'll have you thrown out of this hospital!"

Kassius saw the nearest nurse motion to a hospital security guard, who came forward. He gritted his teeth. Where was Benito when he needed him? Where was Laney?

He took a deep breath, trying to force himself to remain calm when he felt like screaming and grabbing the nurse by her scrawny neck and forcing her to cough up the information he needed. Wiping his eyes hard, he spoke over the jagged razor blade in his throat. "Please," he said tightly. "My wife was in a car accident on the coast. She is thirty-six weeks pregnant. I was told she was brought here via helicopter…"

"Ah… Her." The nurse looked up at him with pity in her eyes. "I'm sorry, monsieur," she said quietly. "You're too late."

CHAPTER NINE

"Too late?" A man's voice roared suddenly behind Kassius in French. "You tell him this in the hallway?"

Kassius whirled around and saw his father, who must have broken speed records to follow him to the hospital, standing furiously beside him.

The nurse stiffened. "Monsieur?"

Boris had fury in his dark eyes. "Are my daughter-in-law and grandson dead?"

"Lower your voice, this isn't—"

"They were brought here. You either let my son see his wife or get a doctor out here to explain—now!"

Scowling, the nurse retreated to the desk and checked her computer. Kassius waited, breathless with hope that she'd say it had all been a mistake. She'd tell him that Laney was absolutely fine, and the baby doing perfectly well, and Benito had simply made a mistake...

But the woman's eyes only clouded as she saw something on her computer that made her give a brisk nod. "It is just as I thought." Looking at them, she hesitated, biting her lip. "If you please, messieurs, go wait in the waiting room, and I will get a doctor to discuss—"

If Kassius had to wait another second to hear if Laney and his child lived or died, he thought he would collapse. He already felt like he was on a thin margin. To his surprise, he felt his father's hand on his shoulder, giving him strength.

"We're not moving until we know where she is," Boris said forcefully.

The nurse glanced around as if she wished desperately there was someone else they could speak to. Then she sighed. "Your wife is in surgery," she said reluctantly. "That is why I told you it was too late. They are performing a caesarean in an attempt to save the baby…"

An attempt? Just an attempt? "Then she is—"

"That is all I can tell you. Now go—" She pointed firmly toward the large nearby room filled with plain white plastic chairs and televisions blaring the news from Paris. "I will send the doctor to speak with you."

Waiting in the Princess Florestine Hospital waiting room, waiting to hear if his wife and child would live or die, felt like the most agonizing hell of Kassius's life. As he sat down heavily in a flimsy plastic chair, questions pounded through his head.

How badly had Laney and his son been injured? Were they dying? Could his wife already be dead?

They are performing a caesarean in an attempt to save the baby.

In an attempt.

Leaning forward in his chair, Kassius put his elbows on his knees. He folded forward in his grief and fear, covering his face with his hands.

"She's a fighter, son." He felt his father's hand rest comfortingly on his shoulder. "She loves you with all her heart. She'll fight to stay with you."

"Why would she?" Pain gripped Kassius's heart. "I told her I never wanted to see her again. I was so angry with her for talking to you. I saw it as a betrayal. I told her I was divorcing her and sending them away." He looked at Boris bleakly. "You heard me."

He heard his father's ragged intake of breath. "You were angry. She knew you didn't mean it."

"She knew I did." Misery swamped through him, shame and anguished grief. He'd threatened to abandon her and the baby and start a new family. *Oh, my God!* He clawed back his dark hair. In this moment, he would have given every penny of his fortune to know they were safe. He would have given his life to be able to hold her in his arms and tell her he loved her!

He...

He loved her.

Kassius's lips parted silently. His heart was beating so fast it felt like it was rattling inside his rib cage. He loved her. And it was only now, when he was so close to losing her, that he realized it. He loved her...

His father's hand tightened on his shoulder. "We all make mistakes we regret. She will forgive, and you can spend the rest of your life making it up to her..."

If she lives. It was the unspoken thought that hung over everything. If she lived. If his baby lived. And Kassius had so casually thrown them away! After she'd disobeyed him, he'd thought he had no choice—as if holding firm to prideful, petulant promises were the true mark of a man!

Loving his wife. Loving his child. Those values were the true mark of a man.

But the realization might have come too late. His relationship with Laney had begun with a car accident. Now, it seemed, a car accident would end it. He'd thought he had eternity to play with. He'd never imagined eternity would end so soon. A memory of his father's voice came back to him.

She was the only woman I ever loved. I always meant to go back to her. I just thought I would have more time...

Kassius looked at his father, whom he'd judged so harshly. He'd spent over half of his life determined to destroy him, but instead of punishing Boris for his crimes, maybe he should have taken a hard look at his own.

"Thank you," Kassius said thickly. "For being here."

"Oh, my boy," his father choked out, "there's nowhere else on earth I could be."

"Monsieur Black?"

The doctor had come in. They both rose to their feet. Kassius felt the floor trembling beneath his shoes. The verdict he was about to get from the doctor would determine if he would live or die. Because his family was his life now.

"Your wife..." The doctor suddenly smiled. "She is out of danger. She's stabilized, but still under anesthesia. She broke multiple bones, including ribs. She couldn't breathe well and lost so much blood. It was touch and go. If the impact had been a little to the right, or it had taken longer for the paramedics to arrive, we might have lost them both."

Grateful tears rose to Kassius's eyes. His heart was in his throat. Wiping his eyes hard, he said hoarsely, "And my son? Is he all right?"

The doctor's smile widened. "Would you like to see him?"

Laney's eyelids fluttered. She woke in a dream.

Golden sunshine was shimmering through tall windows. She was stretched out in a comfortable bed. And there, like a miracle, sleeping in a hard chair beside her, she saw Kassius. His handsome face looked weary, as if he'd had very little rest that night.

"Kassius," she croaked out through dry lips.

His eyes flew open. Leaning forward, he gently took her hand. In spite of the dark circles beneath his eyes and the scruff on his jawline, his handsome face glowed with joyful tenderness she'd never seen there before.

"You're awake," he whispered, gently brushing back a tendril of her hair. "Thank God." He gave a rueful laugh. "It was quite a night."

For a moment, she wondered what he was talking about. She just felt happy to see him. Then realization slowly crept in that she was in a hospital room, wearing a plain hospital gown. Wires were hooked onto her arms. She heard the slow beep of machines nearby. Parts of her body had been immobilized, other parts covered in bandages. Her brain felt strangely fuzzy.

"What happened?" she said slowly.

His dark eyes searched hers. "Don't you remember?"

Laney started to shake her head, but it hurt too much, made the whole room twirl.

"You're still on a lot of painkillers."

Laney licked her lips. "I…"

She suddenly had a dim, chaotic memory of seeing a semitruck skidding across the road, coming straight toward their car. She remembered seeing it bounce off another car and head straight for her side of the limo, where she was carefully buckled in. She remembered the loud squeal of brakes and the angry blare of a horn. She remembered dropping her cell phone and wrapping her arms protectively around her belly, turning away with her eyes squeezed shut as she heard the sickening crunch of metal on metal and felt the impact.

After that, her memory was jumbled. She remembered crying her mother's name, and Kassius's, begging them to help her. She had a strange memory of the *thwup-thwup* noise of a helicopter and paramedics shouting in French and loading her onto a stretcher before the pain was too great. The last thing she remembered was putting her hands on her belly and whimpering, "Please, you have to save my baby…"

With a gasp, Laney put her hands on her belly now. She looked up at Kassius in horror.

"Where's my baby?" she cried.

"Shh…it's all right." Rising from the chair, he went to the bassinet across the room and lifted out a tiny swaddled form. "He's here. Right here."

Returning to the bed, Kassius placed the bundle gently in her arms, on the side of her body that wasn't broken. He kept his hand on the other side of the baby, supporting his weight, protecting them both.

Laney looked down in awe at her sleeping newborn son, swaddled and wearing a little cap to keep his head warm. Tears rose in her eyes as she marveled at his precious little face. "He's all right?"

"Six pounds, four ounces—almost three kilograms," Kassius said proudly. His dark eyes were tender as he gently stroked his sleeping son's cheek. "For a preemie, he's a bruiser."

"Preemie." She looked up in a panic. "He came too early!"

"He's fine," he said soothingly. "His lungs are developed enough he doesn't need any extra medical care. The nurses and doctors were amazed. But I wasn't. He has his mother's spirit." He looked at her, and his eyes glistened suspiciously as he glanced at her injured body in the hospital bed. "I know even this won't keep you down for long. We were lucky." Lowering his head, he softly kissed the top of Laney's head, and whispered, "*I* was lucky. To get another chance."

She looked up at him, her heart in her throat. "So you— forgive me? For what I did?"

"What *you* did?" Kassius repeated. For a moment, fear gripped her heart.

Then, keeping one hand on the baby, he fell to his knees next to the hospital bed in front of her astonished eyes. His handsome face was anguished.

"You were right about everything, Laney," he said in a low voice. "Everything. And the way I treated you for trying so hard to save my useless soul…" Reaching for her hand, he kissed it, then pressed his forehead against it fervently, like a prayer. "Forgive me. I almost threw you

and the baby away for the sake of my own foolish pride..."
He took a shuddering breath, and his voice was ragged,
barely above a whisper. "When I said I would get a new
wife, a new child..."

"You were angry," she said in a small voice. "I betrayed you."

"You, betray me? Never. You saved me. You were right
about my father. I spent a long time talking to him last
night, in the waiting room..."

"He's here?"

"He didn't want me to suffer alone," Kassius said. "All
these years, he hated himself for lying to my mother. He
was haunted, wondering what happened to me."

"Do you forgive him?"

"I would have once thought it impossible." He looked
up at her, his dark eyes shining with tears. "But now...
how can I not? He made a ghastly, unforgivable mistake.
But so did I. Treating you so badly... Can you ever forgive me? Will you?"

"Oh, my love," she whispered. She tugged weakly on
his hand. "Yes."

He rose to his feet, then leaned forward over the bed,
supporting their sleeping baby with one hand, cupping her
face with the other.

"I love you, Laney. I never knew what those words
meant before, but now I do. I love you."

Her heart skittered as she heard him speak the words
she'd feared he would never say.

Straightening, he stood tall and powerful and proud
beside the bed.

"And I make you a promise. One I will never break.
When I thought I'd lost you, I wanted to die. I knew then
that I'd gladly die for you, and our baby. But now I know
you're alive..." He put one hand gently on her shoulder as

the other rested on the downy head of his sleeping son. He said softly, "For the rest of my life, I will live for you."

"I love you," she whispered, tears in her eyes, turning her face toward his. And he kissed her.

EPILOGUE

FOUR MONTHS LATER, Christmas had come to the French Riviera with a burst of sunlight and color. And family, Laney thought. Family above all.

They were all there, celebrating the holiday at Boris's redecorated pink villa on Cap Ferrat. Even Laney's grandmother had interrupted her world tour for a weeklong holiday visit, with her current boyfriend in tow. For much of the last year, Yvonne had traveled the world with a backpack, a floppy hat and a total fearlessness that still left Laney in awe.

"My boyfriend is great, isn't he?" her grandmother said archly as the two of them cooked in the huge, bright kitchen.

"Very," Laney agreed. "Everyone likes Ove."

"Handsome. Athletic, too. Energetic. I had to beat back the other ladies on the ship with a stick. But I got him," Yvonne crowed as she stirred the gumbo.

When her grandmother had visited here last month, the Henry women had announced that both Kassius and Boris must give their household staff Christmas off, as Laney and Yvonne would be making Christmas dinner personally.

Kassius had looked overjoyed, then doubtful. "Are you sure you want to take the trouble, Laney? It's a holiday. You've only just fully recovered. A month ago you were walking with a cane. You should just relax and let someone else work."

"I'm fine now," Laney had protested.

"Let someone else cook for Christmas!" Yvonne said indignantly. "Are you crazy? What kind of fool idea is that?"

So Kassius hadn't tried to put up any more of a fight.

He'd just wiped tears of joy from his eyes. He'd been looking forward to Christmas ever since, as eagerly as any child counting down the days until the magical morning.

Thinking about it, Laney gave a low laugh. Her husband appreciated their cooking, that was for sure. Only a few hours now till Christmas dinner, and he still anxiously stuck his head into the kitchen every few minutes, as if that would make the time fly by faster. She'd finally had to banish him from the kitchen when she'd discovered him sneaking in surreptitiously with a spoon.

"What?" he protested as she pointed firmly at the door. "Just trying to help with quality control!"

Still smiling, Laney checked on the cinnamon swirl king cake now in the oven. It was baking nicely. She also had the tiny plastic baby figurine ready to stick into the cake after it cooled, for one of the guests to find over dessert. That person would then be allowed the privilege of choosing where they hosted family Christmas next year. That had been her father's idea.

"It's really the only way to be fair about it," he'd explained, glancing at his girlfriend, who lived in Atlanta. That was true, since their family now lived all over the world.

Hearing her four-month-old baby coo, Laney lifted him from his baby seat and twirled him around the kitchen until he giggled and squealed, the best sound in the world. He was a brilliant baby, and very good at grabbing his own feet. Clearly, she thought proudly, a baby genius.

"And how is Henry Clark?" her grandmother said fondly.

"He loves Christmas. Don't you, Henry," she cooed, and he giggled back at her.

"Can't believe that husband of yours bought him a puppy for Christmas. A puppy for a baby!"

"I'm suspicious about who the puppy is really for."

Laney grinned. "Kassius can't wait until he's delivered tomorrow. Says this is the best Christmas ever!"

"Wait until he experiences Christmas in New Orleans." Yvonne sighed. "It's been lovely to travel, but after all these months, I've seen enough of the world. I'm ready to go home."

The grand new house on St. Charles Avenue had just been finished and was ready for Yvonne and Clark to move in, with a dedicated guest wing for Kassius, Laney and baby Henry to visit. Although there was still some question if Clark ever meant to return.

After months spent at the top medical clinic in Atlanta, cutting-edge medical treatments had partially restored his vision. Laney had wept openly when she'd first tucked her baby into her father's arms and he'd been able to see the color of his grandson's hair, the boy named in part after him. There was some hope he'd eventually gain complete vision in his left eye. He'd never looked better, Laney had thought. He'd looked positively muscular as he rolled his new wheelchair around the Christmas tree that morning, a gift from his daughter and son-in-law, which had made him exclaim over the "kick-ass rims."

Clark had brought his new girlfriend, Jeanie, a nurse from the clinic, for Christmas, too. The plump and pretty divorcée, with two grown children and a grandchild of her own—all of whom were spending the holiday with her ex this year—kissed him affectionately as they finally sat down to Christmas dinner.

Laney looked at her family around the big table spread with Cajun Christmas cheer, mixed with some French breads and wine and even some Russian borscht and vodka, thanks to Boris, and felt tears in her eyes. After so many years of despair, they were all happy. They were together. A Christmas miracle.

Even Kassius's father looked fifteen years younger. His

son had insisted he continue to keep this as his home, and all the sold-off furniture had been replaced and, except for Mimi, all his laid-off employees rehired. His oil company had been folded into Kassius's worldwide portfolio as a loosely held subsidiary, and with the influx of new investment and technological innovations, there was hope for the company's future.

But Boris was happy for his son to run it now. All he wanted, all he'd ever wanted, it seemed, was his son, and to be part of his family.

"Aha!" Yvonne said, holding something up triumphantly. It was the tiny baby figurine. "Next year, Christmas in New Orleans!"

Everyone looked at her suspiciously.

She widened her eyes, the picture of innocence. "What?"

"Sabotage!" Boris cried, waving a jar of hot-pepper sauce. "That's what!"

"It was pure luck!" she protested.

No one believed her, but they just laughed. Everyone was happy, and it was impossible to hide it.

Life had once felt so dark for all of them, Laney thought as they shared Christmas dinner around the table. Each of them had lived through a different kind of pain. But for each of them, love had melted it away.

Kassius had done it, Laney thought suddenly. He'd changed their lives. He'd been the miracle.

But when Laney told him as much, when they'd all risen from the dinner table to take a family walk through the villa's beautiful, well-kept gardens, Kassius snorted and shook his head.

"If there was a miracle, it all came from you, Laney," he said as a cool breeze whirled around them from the sparkling blue sea. He glanced back at his father, who was smiling tenderly at his baby grandson harnessed to his chest in a baby carrier, walking with Yvonne and Ove and Clark and Jeanie. Turning back, Kassius tucked a tendril of her long dark hair behind her ear and said seriously, "It all started with you. Your courage, and wisdom, and grace. From the moment we met..."

She tilted her head teasingly. "You mean when you hit me with your car?"

He grinned, then sobered. "I'm just sorry I made you go through far worse pain than that." He looked down at her, his dark eyes deep with emotion. "But you didn't give up on me. You loved me, even when I didn't deserve it. You always knew I could be the man you deserve. The man who loves you. The man who always will."

She swallowed over the lump in her throat. She felt so happy, it brought tears to her eyes. "Kassius..."

"Wait." Abruptly, he pulled her away from the rest of the family, into a small copse of oak trees behind the box hedge. Looking up at the oak tree, he said innocently, "Oh, look...mistletoe."

Astonished, Laney looked up at the evergreen leaves and white berries growing on the oak tree. Then she narrowed her eyes.

"You lured me to this spot on purpose," she said accusingly.

He lifted a dark eyebrow. "Would I do that?"

"Totally."

Kassius grinned. "You know me well." He ran his hand slowly down her back. "So you might as well know, I intend to lure you into bed later. Maybe more than once."

Eyes shining, Laney reached up to caress her husband's rough cheek.

"You don't need to lure me," she whispered. "Just kiss me. And never let me go."

So lowering his head, that's exactly what he did.

* * * * *

'Miss Jameson.'

It wasn't a request. It was an order couched in a pseudo-reasonable tone.

Keep walking. She took another step.

'Elise.'

She froze, the sound of her given name so unbelievably sensual coming from his deep, slightly accented tones that she couldn't suppress a gasp. She slowly turned around.

'One last thing. My company isn't the place to find your next boyfriend or a husband. As long as you're contracted to work for me you'll practise a zero-fraternisation policy. I find that petty lawsuits are best avoided that way.'

'Are you speaking from personal experience?' she asked.

Alejandro's face tightened into a rigid, forbidding mask. Hell, she'd struck another nerve. God, what was *wrong* with her?

'That is *not* your concern. Just be sure to let Grandma know you'll be disappointing her for a while longer where potential wedding bells are concerned, would you?'

Just keep walking.

Rival Brothers

When rivalry is thicker than blood…

Estranged brothers Alejandro and Gael Aguilar are titans of technology and each other's biggest rivals.

It will take two special women to help these sexy Spaniards put the past behind them and join forces to become more powerful than they ever dreamed!

Battle commences in…

A Deal with Alejandro

And find who will be victorious in…

One Night with Gael

Available November 2016

A DEAL WITH ALEJANDRO

BY
MAYA BLAKE

First Published in Great Britain 2016
By Mills & Boon, an imprint of HarperCollins*Publishers*
1 London Bridge Street, London, SE1 9GF

© 2016 Maya Blake

ISBN: 978-0-263-92133-5

Maya Blake's hopes of becoming a writer were born when she picked up her first romance at thirteen. Little did she know her dream would come true! Does she still pinch herself every now and then to make sure it's not a dream? Yes, she does! Feel free to pinch her, too, via Twitter, Facebook or Goodreads! Happy reading!

Books by Maya Blake

Mills & Boon Modern Romance

Signed Over to Santino
A Diamond Deal with the Greek
A Marriage Fit for a Sinner
Married for the Prince's Convenience
Innocent in His Diamonds
His Ultimate Prize
Marriage Made of Secrets
The Sinful Art of Revenge
The Price of Success

The Billionaire's Legacy

The Di Sione Secret Baby

Secret Heirs of Billionaires

Brunetti's Secret Son

The Untameable Greeks

What the Greek's Money Can't Buy
What the Greek Can't Resist
What the Greek Wants Most

The 21st Century Gentleman's Club

The Ultimate Playboy

Visit the Author Profile page
at millsandboon.co.uk for more titles.

CHAPTER ONE

ALEJANDRO AGUILAR STEPPED out of a bracing, ice-cold shower
to the sound of a ringing phone. At 4:00 a.m. such an occurrence would have alarmed most people. He already had a fair
idea of why his early-morning routine was being disturbed.

Crossing the master bedroom suite of his Chicago penthouse, he draped the towel round his neck and picked up
the phone.

'Is it done?'

A muted sigh from his chief strategist, Wendell Grant,
greeted him. 'I'm sorry, sir, but they wouldn't be swayed.
We've thrown everything at them, including my firstborn
son.'

The attempt at humour fell flat, causing the weary-sound-
ing man to clear his throat uncomfortably.

Alejandro's grip tightened on the handset, the inkling
he'd harboured for several weeks expanding to nape-tingling
certainty. There were far too many indicators to ignore the
suspicion any longer.

'Frankly, I'm at a loss as to why they've suddenly become
so intransigent,' Wendell continued. 'The Ishikawa brothers' team refuses to even discuss what the problem is beyond
stating that they need more time.'

Alejandro knew what the problem was. The heads of the
Japanese e-commerce conglomerate were protracting the
deal, which should've been finalised a month ago, in order
to accommodate a third party's interest.

'How did you leave things?' he asked.

'They've asked for a few more days. We tried to get an
earlier date but they wouldn't budge. We've agreed to a
videoconference on Friday.'

'That's unacceptable. I'm not waiting another five days.

Call them back. Tell them I want the Ishikawa brothers in conference tomorrow.'

'Yes, sir.'

About to hang up, Alejandro sensed his executive's reticence. 'Is there something else?'

'Well…I got the feeling they think they have the upper hand. The dynamic has definitely shifted…'

Hearing his suspicions voiced by another brought a clench of anger to Alejandro's gut. If his executives had sniffed out the same issue, it was time to take over the helm again.

'Sir? Is there something we should know?'

Alejandro squashed his ire. 'I'll take it from here. Extend my gratitude to the team and tell everyone to take the day off. You've earned it.'

'You still want me to make the call?' Wendell asked.

'No. I'll take care of it.' Now that he knew with whom he was dealing, it was time the gloves came off.

'If you're sure, then I better get home to my wife before she serves me with divorce papers.' Another weary laugh, which fizzled away, the other man sensing Alejandro's tense mood. 'Oh, one last thing. I had my assistant compile the shortlist of PR firms for you. Jameson PR has the most extensive experience in Asia. I think at this stage we need all the help we can get.'

Alejandro finished the call and hung up. Snatching the towel from around his neck, he dropped it and padded naked to his dressing room. His signature grey suits, black shirts and bespoke pinstripe ties were within easy reach. Selecting a charcoal suit, he dressed with military efficiency, and was heading out of the door fifteen minutes later.

The drive to the Loop, the financial heart of Chicago, took less than ten minutes. The early hour meant very little traffic and Alejandro gained marginal satisfaction from letting the engine of his Bugatti Veyron roar along the quiet streets.

But nothing could ease the iron-hard fist of unwelcome knowledge trapped in his gut. Nor the accompanying rage that mounted with each passing second.

He'd moved from Spain, the country of his birth, to California at the age of twenty-one, and then relocated to Chicago a year after that because he'd wanted nothing to do with his family. The move from Spain had been to remove himself as soon as it was legally possible from the volatile quagmire that was his parents' sham of a marriage. Alejandro had put several thousand miles between himself and the two individuals biology had used to create him, and never looked back. Little did he know he'd been placing himself within touching distance of another powder keg in the form of his half-brother.

Gael Aguilar.

He was half of the equation that had worsened the acrimony in Alejandro's life over two decades ago. Gael and his mother had put faces on the hitherto faceless monsters that were his father's indiscretions. Those monsters had grown until Alejandro had had no choice but to leave the only home he'd known.

But the nightmare hadn't been ready to let him be.

Gael had arrived in California shortly after him. And Silicon Valley hadn't been large enough to contain the two of them. Especially when his younger half-brother had started making himself a nuisance by going after the same deals Alejandro showed interest in. Wiping out Gael's burgeoning e-commerce start-up would've been an easy accomplishment for Alejandro. But that would've indicated he cared one iota about the life he'd put behind him. It would've given the impression that the countless instances of infidelity, rancour and falsehood that had peppered his childhood still had the power to matter.

So he'd walked away.

He might be an Aguilar, but he was so in name only. Nothing about it was worthy of being lauded. He'd cut all ties. As far as he was concerned, he existed in this world alone.

Except his half-brother hadn't got the memo. A decade after meeting for the second and final time, it appeared Gael was determined to insert himself into Alejandro's business once again. Or at the very least, scurry away with the deal Alejandro had worked tirelessly to pull together.

Turning off his engine, he launched himself from the car and crossed the underground car park of his company's building. Entering the lift that would take him to the top-floor offices of SNV International, he recalled that last exchange with his brother when Gael had found out he was leaving California.

'I hear you're relocating your business. Why? You scared I'm going to show you up?' Gael's white smile, cocksure, taunting and tinged with bravado, had reminded Alejandro too much of their father's, eliciting nothing but cold indifference.

'Don't kid yourself. My company is successful enough to thrive anywhere in the world. But perhaps you should count your lucky stars that I'm leaving and removing myself from the temptation to crush you into the dirt. This way you at least have a hope of making something of yourself.'

His brother's smile had evaporated like mist in sunshine. A look Alejandro had ironically recognised in himself— one of implacable will and determination—had passed over Gael's features.

'I look forward to the day when I make you swallow those words, *hermano.*'

Alejandro had shrugged and walked away. He hadn't bothered to tell Gael they would never be true brothers because they'd never meet again. Crossing paths once when they were teenagers had been bad enough. A second time, in their twenties, was overkill.

He'd thought there wouldn't be a third.

Except, walking away hadn't ended it. Foolishly, it seemed Gael had taken offence at his words at their last meeting. And like a damn virus he was determined to corrupt as many of Alejandro's dealings as he could.

He strode into his office as the April sun rose over Lake Michigan. Normally, he stopped to admire the view as he enjoyed his morning espresso. This Monday, however, he tossed his car keys on his desk, tugged off his jacket and went to work.

By 9:00 a.m. he had definite confirmation that it was indeed Gael meddling with the Japanese deal.

He sat back in his chair, fingers tented together as he forced down the acid bite of distaste. Gael's company, Toredo Inc., had grown into an e-commerce powerhouse second only to Alejandro's own company. Not for a single moment had that reality fazed him. His company was worth billions, and more than held its own in the industry. At times when he felt generous, he even welcomed Toredo's competition.

Not this time. Bagging this deal would launch SNV into an echelon of its own. It would be the culmination of the success he'd striven for since walking away from the tatters of what the common man termed a family. Others might accommodate such failures. He didn't. He'd cut his losses on an irredeemable life because nothing he did could fix what was permanently broken. Instead he'd concentrated on what he was successful at. He'd made his first million at twenty-four, just before he left California. In the ten years since, he'd risen to the top.

The Ishikawa deal would be his crowning glory. He'd worked too long and hard to see it dismantled by Gael.

His strategy team had suggested hiring a PR company experienced in dealing with Japanese companies to work alongside his in-house PR department. Alejandro had shelved the idea until negotiations had stalled. Although he still had his doubts as to the efficacy of employing an outside PR company, he opened the first file.

The headshot caught his attention immediately, although, staring at the picture critically, Alejandro couldn't pinpoint why. Her mouth was too wide and full, her nose a little too perfectly pointed. Her almond-shaped hazel-gold eyes held too many shadows, and, for his taste, she was wearing a little too much make-up; he preferred the natural look. The shadows and the make-up alone jarred him further into memories he didn't want to dwell on. Like the memories of his brother, they were reminiscent of a past he'd striven hard to forget.

Yet he couldn't drag his gaze away from Elise Jameson's picture. The almost absurd notion that if he stared for long enough the image would come to life gripped him. His gaze dropped past her jaw and neck and he experienced the tiniest stab of regret that there wasn't more to see.

Gritting his teeth, he perused her academic accomplishments, which were impressive enough to compel him to read on. The discovery that Jameson PR was a family company brought a twisted smile, but Alejandro suppressed the useless threat of emotion. Not every family was as dysfunctional as the one he'd left behind.

Suficiente!

He needed his head screwed on straight to see this merger through, not spend time dwelling on the past. He moved on to the other two files. Within minutes he'd dismissed the other candidates.

When he found himself staring at the headshot again, he reached for the phone.

'Margo, set up an interview with the Jameson PR people for this afternoon, would you?'

'Umm, one of their executives is already here. Shall I send her in? Your diary is free since you've cleared most of your appointments already.'

He frowned. 'They came here on the off chance I'd want to see them?' Alejandro wasn't sure whether to applaud them for their brazenness or condemn them for wasting valuable man hours on the likelihood of being hired by SNV.

'Wendell thought it might be prudent in case you wanted to move quickly on the PR front.'

Alejandro made a mental note to increase his team leader's bonus. His gaze dropped to the headshot. 'Which representative from Jameson is here?'

'It's a junior executive—Elise Jameson. I can arrange for a senior member to come in if you pref—'

'No, it's fine. Send her in.' He would glean as much from

the younger Jameson as he would from her parents. Besides, he didn't have time to waste. 'I'd like some fresh coffee, too. *Gracias.*'

A brisk knock on the door a few minutes later brought his head up.

Margo entered first, wheeling in a tray of coffee. Alejandro's gaze swung past her, his attention almost compelled to focus on the dark-haired woman who followed. A part of him disliked the fizz of compulsion almost as much as it anticipated his first glimpse of her.

True, his wholehearted immersion in this potential merger had left little time for physical dalliances for the better part of a year now. The occasions when he'd been tempted to indulge in carnal pleasures, the chase had surprisingly grown boring. Enough to abandon his date at the after-dinner-coffee stage on more than one occasion. Nevertheless, he was a red-blooded male, as the momentary tightening in his groin informed him now when Elise Jameson stepped into the office.

The early morning sun struck her face as she paused on the threshold, bringing every feature in her photo to vivid life. Her face was impeccably made-up, just like in her headshot, but where he'd been healthily captivated before by the glossy two-dimensional version, he was paralysingly riveted by the flesh and blood reality.

She advanced farther into the room. Her stride was confident but minimised by the navy pencil skirt whose matching jacket was secured by a single button beneath a full chest. The cut of her clothes immediately drew Alejandro's gaze to her Venus-like body and shapely legs. Attractive. Alluring. But nothing extraordinary.

And then she smiled at a departing Margo, and realisation struck.

Elise bore an unsettling resemblance to a painting he'd once seen hanging in his father's study when he was fourteen years old. The woman had been standing before a window with the sun shining on her arresting features. Her dark hair had been caught at the back of her head, her eyes shut and her face lifted in sun worship. The artist had captured her image from the point of view of a lover staring down at his paramour.

Their differences in height once Elise Jameson reached his desk were strikingly similar.

Except that woman had been nude.

And that painting had also caused prolonged rows between his mother and father, with one vowing to burn the painting and the other mocking the jealous fit. The painting had lasted six days before it'd disappeared. And even though he'd snuck into his father's study to stare at it, Alejandro had been glad once it was gone.

All he'd cared about was that the rowing had ceased. Albeit, inevitably, temporarily.

He blinked the memory away, irritated with his ongoing traipse down memory lane, to find a manicured hand proffered.

'Thank you for seeing me, Mr Aguilar. I'm Elise Jameson.'

He took her hand, noted the soft but firm grip, the smoothness of her skin, the spark that travelled along his palm, and released her.

'I'm aware one of my employees suggested we may be interested in your services, but don't you think it was a touch foolish to just present yourself here? You could've wasted the entire day,' he stated in a voice he knew was clipped.

Her eyes, which were more tilted and vivid in real life, widened a touch, before she blinked back her composure. 'You say foolish, I say impeccably timed,' she replied coolly.

He lifted a brow. 'Are we to disagree so soon? You think that bodes well for our potential working relationship?'

Her shoulders tensed infinitesimally. 'Pardon me for being forward, but if you require a yes-man or -woman who'll jump at your every suggestion, then perhaps Jameson isn't the right fit for you. Sycophancy isn't in our remit.'

He noted then that, although her accent was American, her

features bore a hint of an Asian heritage, making her beauty even more enthralling. He also noted his own faint amusement with irritation. Rounding the desk, he approached the tray laden with coffee and bagels and poured his fifth cup of espresso. 'Coffee?'

'No, thank you. I've had my daily allotment. Any more and you'd have to prise me off the ceiling.' One corner of her crimson-painted mouth twitched and Alejandro found his gaze tracing the full curve.

Striding back to his desk, he gulped down half of his beverage. 'In that case, sit down, Miss Jameson, and tell me what *is* in your remit.'

She took the time to unbutton her jacket, giving him a glimpse of the jade-coloured silk top beneath and a shadowed cleavage before she sat down.

'Normally, it works the other way round. You tell me what you need PR-wise and we advise you how to achieve it, sycophancy not included, of course.' Another smile that didn't quite reach her eyes.

Over the scent of ground coffee beans, he caught the faintest hint of her perfume. Crushed berries mixed with an elusive spice. Unique. Captivating. He caught himself inhaling deeper to chase the scent and gritted his teeth.

'We seem to have skipped a step or two in the traditional interview process, so perhaps we should go with the flow here.'

She blinked. 'I *could* go with the flow. Except I'm not even sure where the river starts, Mr Aguilar. Wendell Grant was equally cryptic when he called and asked me to come here. Sadly, cryptic won't cut it if you need my help.'

'Since I haven't decided whether I do or not, I'm not going to go into the specifics of a highly confidential deal.'

Her mouth tightened a touch before she smiled her insincere smile. 'If you're worried about confidentiality, our impeccable record speaks for itself.'

'Be that as it may, until you're officially hired, I prefer to practise a little…restraint.'

Her gaze locked with his for a long moment. Then she nodded. 'As you wish. So let's talk hypotheticals. What can I do for you?'

A frown tugged at Alejandro's brow. She was intelligent. And she was saying all the right things. But he couldn't shake the feeling something else was going on beneath the surface.

'How old are you?' he asked.

Her eyes widened. 'Why is that relevant?'

Alejandro folded his arms, mildly disturbed by his own question. 'Is it a state secret?'

'Of course not.' Her gaze dropped to his desk. 'But you have my file right there in front of you. You've read it so you know my age. If I wanted to lie to you about anything—which I don't, by the way—lying about my age would be the stupidest one to start with, don't you think? And other than to catch me out in a lie, I'm not sure why—'

'Do you always answer a simple question with a diatribe?'

Beneath the make-up, heat flushed her cheeks. Her nostrils flared a touch before she blinked back her composure.

'I'm twenty-five. As it says in my file,' she returned acerbically.

'How long have you worked for your parents?' Again a question he hadn't anticipated asking.

Her mouth compressed. 'Since I graduated university at twenty-one.'

Alejandro studied her silently. To her credit, she didn't fidget.

Unfolding his arms, he rested his elbows on his desk. 'I don't think this is going to work out, Miss Jameson. Thank you for coming.'

First came a look that closely resembled relief. Followed by surprise. Then her lips parted as shock set in. *'Excuse me?'*

'If you can't see your way through answering a few simple questions without getting emotional, I don't see how you can deal with the hard stuff. Margo will see you out.'

She started to get up. Halfway through the act, she dropped back down. 'This is some sort of trick, isn't it?'

It was Alejandro's turn to be surprised. He regained his senses quickly. 'I've been working on a deal that is determined to fall apart at the last minute. Trust me, wasting time with tricks is the very last thing on my mind. Goodbye, Miss Jameson.'

Shadows and questions swirled through her hazel-gold eyes. Her lower lip twisted, as if she was gnawing it from the inside. Eventually she rose, her fingers clamped around her briefcase, her jaw angled with stubborn pride.

Without a word, she turned away from his desk. In that moment, Alejandro wished he'd also turned away. The sight of her trim waist and voluptuous backside triggered another onset of libido-tugging.

He gritted his teeth.

The timing and circumstance of this attraction to her were abhorrent enough to send him to his feet. He'd vowed a very long time ago never to mix business with pleasure when another deal had disintegrated because of a fleeting liaison with a competitor. He'd been young and foolish enough to imagine one would not affect the other. Although the incident had only temporarily slowed down his meteoric rise, Alejandro had learned the lesson well enough to keep his affairs private and brief.

Dragging his gaze from the shapely legs heading for the door, he strode to the window and stared at the view. Lake Michigan didn't offer much solace. Like a lead domino falling over, Elise's image, the feel of their palms touching, the silkiness of her skin, tumbled through his mind. Even the sound of the door shutting barely created a ripple in the sizzling *awareness* gripping him.

What the hell was wrong with him today? First he'd cracked open the vault of memories he'd vowed never to revisit. Now he was getting hot under the collar because of a woman who should barely register on his radar?

He shoved a hand through his hair and turned around.

Elise Jameson was standing before his desk, her eyes square on his.

'Unless I've grown senile in the last five minutes, I'm sure I told you to leave.'

She exhaled slow and steady. Alejandro was certain it was a composure-gaining technique. He had a feeling he'd need one of those before the day ended.

'You did. But I'm still here. The way I see it, you're either going to hire me or we'll never see each other again. So I need to say this. I wasn't being *emotional*. I just didn't see the point of wasting time with questions to which you already had answers. And yes, my...irritation could've been kept on a tighter leash. Give me another chance and you have my word it won't happen again.'

'What *it* are we talking about, just to be certain? The irritation or the emotion?'

The whitening of her knuckles on her briefcase was the only sign that his question had further irked. 'Either. *Both*. Whichever you wish.'

He leaned back in his chair. 'Because I'm the boss?'

'Because you're the boss. Once you hire me. But allow me to say one last thing before you make up your mind.'

'Yes?'

'I'm good at my job. You'll get nothing but the best from me. I promise.'

He shrugged. 'That's a good speech. But it's *just* a speech. I also don't deal in promises.' Promises were easy to make and easier to break. He'd learnt that lesson with shocking frequency as a child.

Her gaze swept down for an instant before rising again. 'Finish the interview. Whichever way you want. Then make up your mind.'

The urge to dismiss her was strong. The urge to have her stay was stronger. Alejandro stepped back from examining why. This whole day had been askew from the start.

'Very well. Sit down, Miss Jameson. But let me make one thing clear.'

She sat back down. 'Yes?'

'I never play tricks. I abhor subterfuge of any kind. Remember that before we go any further.'

She nodded and folded her hands in her lap. 'Understood.'

CHAPTER TWO

WHAT THE HELL just happened?

Elise reeled as if she'd just been dragged upside down through an earthquake. Only she wasn't sure whether she'd survived it or whether what felt like aftershocks were, in fact, another larger quake poised on the horizon, ready to flatten her.

She took another slow, steadying breath.

It was clear the man across the desk from her—the intensely masculine man, whose green eyes tracked her every movement like a spotlight searching for a flaw—was intent on rattling her. Why, she wasn't exactly sure. She was here to help, after all.

Perhaps it was the air of mistrust fairly vibrating off him. Or her own blaring instincts about being in a predator's presence that had produced his thunderous frown when she'd walked in.

Whatever it was, it'd ruffled her calm, which had in turn reminded her of the hell letting her guard down with a client had created just one short year ago.

Her palms grew clammy.

Reeling herself back in, she pushed the disquieting memories away.

Unlike last year, she'd chosen this commission herself. Alejandro Aguilar the man was an unknown quantity, but as CEO his reputation was stellar. She needed to bring her A-game because she couldn't lose this commission.

Earning SNV's contract would mean freedom from Jameson and her parents' clutches. It was the visceral need for freedom that had eroded the temporary relief to be free of this man's disturbing aura when he'd asked her to leave.

It was what had halted her flight when every instinct had screamed at her to accept his cold, terse dismissal. And run.

The instinct still clamoured. But then so did the burning need to fulfil her duties to her parents and finally, *finally* walk away.

'I understand completely,' she reiterated, projecting a firmer voice.

'Good. Now answer me this. Hypothetically, if a deal you were working on for a year suddenly started to fall apart, what would you attribute it to?' he asked in that smooth, deep voice that transmitted right through to the soles of her feet.

'That depends on who the other party is, although most eleventh-hour setbacks usually involve money.'

'This one isn't money related. I'm sure of it.' A grim smile fleeted over his lips before his face hardened into a beautifully arresting sculpture she had a hard time dragging her eyes from.

In truth, everything about Alejandro Aguilar was insanely absorbing. From the square-cut jaw to the cheekbones that belonged on a Roman statue, to the broad shoulders, tapered torso and neat backside she'd glimpsed when she'd turned around mid-flight, his looks and aura were overwhelming enough to cause another shaky exhalation.

Silently, intensely, she repeated her warning mantra to herself.

Looks *were* deceiving; power and arrogant charm were stepping stones dangerous men used on their prey. Quite apart from her parents wielding those assets with almost lethal force, her own harrowing experience had taught her to be extremely wary of those qualities.

Marsha and Ralph Jameson had taken turns drilling into their only child that exploiting those elements were what would get her ahead in life. They hadn't accommodated the notion that she wanted to live a different life. Had gone as far as to push her into a situation she'd barely been able to escape from unscathed, then derided her ordeal.

That, above everything her parents had subjected her to, still had the power to burn her raw.

Elise pushed the traumatic memory away and redoubled her efforts to focus. 'If it's not money, then it's a competitor.' He regarded her steadily. 'But then you know that, too.'

He nodded. 'Yes.'

'So, the question is, what's your competitor offering them that you're not?'

'Nothing,' came the immediate, rigid reply.

'Are you sure?'

One sculpted eyebrow rose. 'Are you questioning the veracity of my due diligence?'

He was touchy. Extremely. Men like Alejandro Aguilar didn't rise to lofty CEO positions of extremely successful corporations by being touchy. Men like him usually had rhinoceros-thick skins. Had she adversely demonstrated her wariness about being in the presence of another powerful man? Was she being overly sensitive?

The tense conversation she'd had with her mother before coming here had put her on edge. Marsha Jameson had wanted to spearhead the SNV commission herself, despite Elise having cultivated the initial contact with SNV's PR department. Elise had stood her ground, a fact that hadn't pleased her mother. It was another reason Elise had stopped herself from walking out of the door just now.

She wouldn't...*couldn't* blow it.

Inhaling slowly, she picked her way through the mine-infested landscape. 'Of course not. But there's nothing wrong with an extra pair of eyes.' For some reason her statement brought an even deeper scrutiny of her face, his gaze holding hers with fierce control. She hastened to continue. 'It *is* why you're looking to hire an outside PR firm, isn't it?'

He remained silent for a brief spell, his fingertips pressed together. 'Your file says you specialise in US–Japanese commissions.'

'Yes.'

'This merger involves a Japanese company.' He paused. 'The Ishikawa Corporation.'

Elise's heart missed a beat. The reason behind it was puzzling. It'd come sooner than expected, but he would've needed to trust her with *some* details in order to secure her help. That he'd done so mere minutes into the interview shouldn't trigger such a response from her.

Yet the tiniest sliver of warmth curled through her.

To counteract it, she nodded briskly. 'Give me an hour to do a little research... I mean a more *personal* research, and I'll see if I can come up with something.'

His eyes narrowed. 'You think an hour is all it'll take to fix my problem?' he taunted.

'I won't know until I try whether or not I can help you, Mr Aguilar. Let me try.'

'You have half an hour.' He nodded to the far side of his office, where two stylish studded leather sofas faced each other across a smoked-glass coffee table. 'I'll have Margo set you up with a laptop—'

'There's no need. I brought my own.' Elise held up her briefcase and attempted a cool smile.

His scowl deepened. 'I'd prefer it if those confidential details we spoke about don't leave my building. Pass the test, and we'll see about redressing your security access.'

The warmth evaporated. 'Oh, right.' She was irritated with herself for feeling stung by the implication that she wasn't trustworthy. But then hadn't she experienced a similar feeling towards him moments ago? Wasn't she even now kicking herself for continuing to be mesmerised by the sheer depths of raw sensuality oozing from him?

'Is that going to be a problem?' he enquired.

Realising she'd been staring at him for a fistful of heartbeats, she pinned on another smile and rose. 'Of course not. I'm ready when you are.' She headed for the sofa to the sound of Margo being summoned, but the tingle between her shoulder blades and down her back indicated he was watching her. Keeping her movements fluid, she set her case down and removed her jacket before choosing the seat farthest from his desk.

Only then did she risk another glance in his direction.

His head was bent over a document, two fingers tracing the words downward as he speed-read. As with everything she'd noticed about him so far, the action was unmistakably absorbing. To the point where she was in danger of appearing like a hormone-engorged groupie at a rock concert!

She exhaled in relief when Margo knocked and entered. The laptop she set before Elise looked custom-made and top of the line.

After she departed, Elise opened it and stared down at the wallpaper that depicted the majestic Sierra Nevada mountain range in Spain. In the middle of the screen, the SNV logo blinked its request.

'Is there a problem?' Alejandro asked coolly.

'Yes. This requires a password.'

He rose with smooth animal grace, document in one hand and his tiny espresso cup in the other. Pausing at the tray, he refilled his cup, then crossed the room to her.

The notion that she'd unwittingly invited him closer sent equal amounts of chagrin and wariness coursing through her. Her senses jumped as he reached for the laptop. Elegant fingers flew over the keyboard and then he handed it back.

Expecting him to return to his desk, she stared dry-mouthed as he picked up the document and cup, relaxed against the sofa, and crossed one leg over the other.

Elise had always thought that men who sat that way were a little too in touch with their feminine side, but there was nothing even remotely feminine about Alejandro Aguilar as he lounged with almost predatory indolence and flicked through the papers in his hand.

'Unless you intend to prise your answers from my subconscious, I suggest you get on with it, Miss Jameson.'

Heat flared into her cheeks for the third time in less than

an hour, eliciting a thorough self-loathing for her inability to curb her jumpy reactions.

Dragging her focus back to the laptop, she settled it on her lap and went to work. Her initial searches produced run-of-the-mill information about the Ishikawa Corporation Alejandro most likely already possessed. She sent three quick emails to trusted sources in Kyoto and Osaka, delved deeper into the company history, then traced the genealogy of the founders.

Fifteen minutes later, a tiny spurt of excitement lanced her.

'Found something you want to share?'

She looked up and found laser eyes trained on her. 'What?'

'You just made the universal feminine sound of excitement,' he drawled, lifting his cup and draining it.

She tried to look away, but found herself unable to. 'I'm not sure what that is, but yes, I may have found something.'

'And?' he pressed impatiently.

With effort, she refocused on the screen. 'And I have another thirteen minutes until my time is up. So if you don't mind?'

He made a sound beneath his breath, a cross between a growl and a huff, as he stood to refill his cup yet again. The sound rumbled along her nerve endings, causing her fingers to stumble over the keys.

God. What on earth was wrong with her?

Even before the incident that still had the power to make her stomach turn in sick horror, she'd never reacted this strongly to another man. Ever. She hadn't allowed herself to even indulge in thoughts of the opposite sex since the incident. Sure, there hadn't been a shortage of male attention despite her often blatant lack of interest. From those who wanted to date the boss's daughter to further their own ends, to those who thought she would be accommodating with her affections because of the rumours surrounding her parents' marriage. Each and every one of them had been firmly rebuffed.

Alejandro Aguilar hadn't so much as flicked an interested

eyelash in her direction. Yet her senses seemed poised on the edge of an unknown precipice, anticipating a sensation she couldn't quite name.

The ping of an incoming email brought blessed refocusing. She read it quickly, then reached for her phone. 'I need to make a quick phone call.'

'Why?' he asked without lifting his gaze from his document.

'I want to confirm a few things before I present my findings. I still have five minutes left.'

He nodded to the state-of-the-art gadget crouched in the middle of the coffee table. 'Use that phone.'

The bite of distaste stung deeper, prompting her to utter words she would've been better off stemming. 'Are your trust issues as big as your caffeine problem?'

Glacial green eyes sliced into her. 'You call them problems, I think of them as necessary tools that keep me at the top of my game. Your time is almost up. Use the phone or cut your losses and leave.'

Her hand tightened around her phone. 'You'd toss me out before you hear what I've found out? Just because I state a few home truths?'

'We met an hour ago. Are you naive enough to demand that I trust you in so short a time?'

'Of course not. Nevertheless, I don't appreciate being treated as if I've committed a crime or I'm about to commit one when all I'm trying to do is to help you.'

'You take pleasure in debating non-issues when the only thing that should be important here is your service to me. Learning to give me what I want will go a long way to improving your chances of earning this contract.'

Her breath hitched as another voice surged into her head.

Stop playing so hard to get. Give me what I want and I'll reward you...

The distaste of bitter memories made her snap, 'I told you, if you're looking for someone to lie down for you to walk all over, then I'm the wrong person for the job.'

He strolled the last few steps to the coffee table and dropped his papers on the gleaming surface. Regarding her with cold detachment, he drawled, 'Lying down, in any shape or form, won't be necessary. But once again we're at an impasse, it seems. The next move is yours.'

Every atom in her body screamed at Elise to slam shut the laptop, get her things, and leave. She stayed put. Tried to get herself under control.

Yes, Alejandro Aguilar had done nothing but make demands that chafed, but they weren't uncommon.

Sucking in a breath that didn't quite rebalance her equilibrium, she set her phone on the table and, using Alejandro's conference set, dialled the number she knew by rote.

When the familiar voice filled the room, Elise wondered for a moment whether she'd done the right thing.

'Hi, Grandma.'

A furtive glance at Alejandro showed both eyebrows lifted in cold mockery.

'Elise, my dear, what a pleasant surprise. I hope you're calling to tell me you've finally found a young man worthy of your affections? I know half of them are dim-witted and the other half focused on the almighty dollar, but a beautiful, intelligent girl like you is capable of landing the right man. You're not being too picky, are—?'

'No, Grandma, I'm not… I'm calling about something *else*.' Cringing and red-faced, Elise switched to Japanese, her chin lowered to avoid Alejandro's drilling stare. 'Something *work* related.'

'Oh. Okay…'

Elise asked the questions she needed to, then a few more to verify she was on the right track, then quickly ended the call, unwilling to invite her beloved grandmother's laser probing into her non-existent love life.

In the seething silence, she cleared her throat, momentarily gripped by embarrassment.

'In the interest of getting this surreal hour over and done with, can we attempt to get past the fact that you blithely dropped your work to make a *personal* phone call?' Alejandro snapped.

'It...umm...wasn't a personal call. At least not from my end...anyway.' Elise stopped, smoothed her damp palms over her skirt, and tried to form coherent words. 'My grandmother is Japanese. She lives in Hawaii now but she still owns several businesses in Kyoto. I thought she might have insights as to what's stalling your merger.'

Alejandro returned her gaze, narrow-eyed, then took the seat opposite her. Wordlessly, he waited, his powerful arms braced on his knees.

Elise cleared her throat. 'Kenzo Ishikawa, Jason and Nathan's grandfather, started the company.'

'I'm aware of that.'

Elise barely managed to keep her lips from pursing. 'He's old school. Traditional.'

'I know what old school means. Explain yourself better.'

'Kenzo has taken a back seat, but he's still on the board.' At his darker glare, she hurried on. 'The company's been based in Kyoto since it was created. Were you planning on moving any of their factories from Kyoto?'

Alejandro nodded. 'Seventy per cent of them, yes. It'll save millions of dollars in revenue and deliver a faster service if we relocate the factories and warehouses to Europe and the US.'

'That probably doesn't matter to him. Since this is a merger and not a buyout, they'll still be associated with it. Kenzo won't want to see everything he's worked for moved to another continent.'

'So your opinion is that this deal is stalling because of *nostalgia*?'

'Sentimentality can be a strong motivator.'

'I don't have time for sentimentality. Or protracted delays. Sitting back while they grapple with their touchy-feely emotions isn't cost-effective for me.'

'Perhaps it hadn't been a card they felt they could play and win,' she ventured. 'But now they do?'

His jaw clenched. One fist wrapped around the other, then he surged to his feet.

'You know, don't you?' she queried.

'Why the Ishikawas have suddenly gone dewy-eyed? *Sí*, I do,' he breathed.

Elise was certain fire would shoot from his nostrils, so devastating was the rage simmering from him.

But he simply returned to his desk. Slightly dazed, she heard him order Margo to summon his strategy team. Once the instructions were snapped out, he jammed his hands into his pockets and turned to the window. Although his gaze remained fixed on the view of Lake Michigan, Elise sensed his thoughts were very much turned inward.

To the source of the problem she'd just helped him uncover.

She sat, hands in her lap, as minutes crawled by. Finally, irritation snapping at her fraught nerves, she stood and shrugged on her jacket. Buttoning it, she approached him.

'Pardon my interruption of your non-Zen rumination, but does the light bulb I just handed you mean that I'm hired?'

His shoulders stiffened. Slowly he turned and leaned against the window, his ankles crossed. Elise forced her gaze to remain on his face, not glance down to the thighs bunched against the taut fabric of his trousers.

'*Sí*, I'm inclined to give you the commission.'

She tamped down the absurd fizz of excitement. 'I hear a busload of *buts* in there.'

His eyes gleamed a dangerous, hypnotic green. '*But*…we need to establish a few ground rules.'

'I can live with a few *reasonable* rules.'

His mouth twisted with a parody of a smile. 'I assure you, it'll be in your interest to do so.'

She attempted a smile of her own. 'I'll be the judge of that. So shoot.'

'First, there will be instances when if I say jump, you *will* ask me how high.'

'I don't think—'

'Like now, for instance, when I say if you want to be hired, you'll let me finish speaking before you give in to the urge to interrupt.'

She swallowed hard against the urge to tell him to go to hell and reminded herself why she needed this commission. Practising a woefully inadequate restorative breathing exercise, she forced out a nod.

'Second, are we agreed on the extreme confidentiality of this deal?'

'Yes.'

'So, no more phone calls to Grandma.'

Heat rushed up her neck. 'No more phone calls to Grandma.'

'Good. You'll work from here in my office, full time, until this deal is done.'

'I thought I'd be working alongside your own PR team.'

'They'll be brought in when extra support is needed. Don't worry, you'll be adequately compensated.'

Not seeing any way around that bar refusing, she pressed her lips together and nodded.

'Was that a yes, Miss Jameson? If so, I prefer to hear the word, so there's no misunderstanding.'

She gritted her teeth. 'Yes. It was a *yes*.'

'Perfect. You'll start today. Right now. Margo will escort you to HR and you'll sign the requisite confidentiality papers. If you need lunch, let her know and she'll organise something for you.'

'I'm quite capable of getting my own lunch.'

'This is one of those instances where wasting time on a matter will be considered a breach of your work rules.'

Shock widened her eyes. 'I beg your pardon?'

'Lunch, unless you have specific dietary requirements, is lunch, Miss Jameson. Wasting time arguing about who gets you lunch is counterproductive.'

'I... Are you serious?' she asked, unsure whether to be grossly offended or mildly hysterical.

He jerked his head to a connecting door at the far side

of the room. 'There's a Michelin-starred chef employed to prepare and serve whatever dish you desire to my personal dining room. All you need to do is ask.'

Elise was aware the scenario he'd just described would be most professionals' idea of a dream perk. Certainly, her parents would relish the chance to laud such a privilege over their competitors and brag about it to clients.

'I have simple tastes, Mr Aguilar. A sandwich from a bistro is perfectly adequate for me. Besides, taking a few minutes away from the office to walk to said bistro helps my cogitative process.' She took a breath. 'But I concede that you're under time pressures. If the chef isn't offended by making me a sandwich, then I'll be happy to eat in your dining room.'

Another hard non-smile twitched his sculpted lips. 'I do believe you've just jumped again, Miss Jameson. Although in a puzzlingly overcomplicated way.' He nodded at his door. 'Don't keep Margo waiting.'

Elise forced fists that had unconsciously curled to loosen. She stared at him as he resumed his seat...his *throne*...and carried on ruling his kingdom as if he hadn't just swatted her away like an annoying fly.

'Is there something about me that rubs you the wrong way, Mr Aguilar?' she asked, suppressing the part of her that questioned her compulsive need to go head to head with him. She reassured herself it was because she didn't want to be caught by a horribly unpleasant surprise further down the line, the way she had last year. If something swirled beneath Alejandro's forbidding mask, she preferred to uncover it sooner rather than later.

He scrutinised her from head to toe, then back again. Slower. More intensely. Until her whole body tingled from the penetrative stare.

'Are you about to start another argument with me?' he enquired silkily.

She shook her head but stood her ground. 'No. But if there happens to be something bothering you about me, I think we need to address it now, before…' She stopped, unwilling to bring the ugly past to this discussion.

One brow lifted. 'Before?'

She shook her head. 'I don't like surprises, Mr Aguilar. I like working in a fraught environment even less.'

His jaw clenched for an infinitesimal moment, then he did something unexpected. He pressed two fingers against each temple and rubbed. The sigh he emitted was filled with thick weariness.

'This deal should've been done months ago. I don't mind the challenge of a difficult deal if it's warranted,' he murmured, surprising her further by admitting to being anything other than omnipotent. 'But I'm bored by the games the Ishikawas have suddenly decided they want to play.'

'I don't think—'

Cool green eyes met hers. 'Yes, I know what you think. But I'm bored nevertheless. Boredom makes me…unpredictable.'

He was skimming the real issue behind his acerbic attitude. What she wasn't sure of was whether the real reason, somehow, involved her. Just as she was certain he wouldn't answer if she probed further.

She needed to leave this office. Go find Margo and get the HR papers signed. The earlier she got to work, the quicker her last ever commission for Jameson would be done. Then she could truly put the past behind her.

So why was she picking up a sleek bottle of mineral water from the coffee tray and holding it out to him?

Alejandro looked from the bottle to her face. A face she willed with everything inside her not to redden *again*.

When he didn't take it, she set it down in front of him. 'Try drinking some of this instead of guzzling down gallons of caffeine. It might ease that tension headache you've got going on.'

He ignored the bottle. 'I don't anticipate adding nursemaid to your list of duties. The ones I have in mind for you will be quite involved. Let's concentrate on those, shall we?'

'Duly noted. You can be assured that if I happen to be around when you're struck by lightning or a murder of crows decide to use you for pecking practice, I'll continue on my merry way.'

The smile that twitched his mouth was a shade warmer than the last one. Elise found herself wondering what a genuine smile from him would look like and abruptly stepped back.

Turn around. Go.

She headed for the door.

'Miss Jameson.'

It wasn't a request. It was an order couched in psuedo-reasonable, even tones.

Keep walking. She took another step.

'Elise.'

She froze, the sound of her given name so unbelievably sensual coming from his deep, slightly accented tones, that she couldn't suppress a gasp. She slowly turned around.

He was no longer massaging his temples. But he'd wrenched the top off the water bottle, the tip of it poised an inch from his lips.

'One last thing. My company isn't the place to find your next boyfriend or a husband. As long as you're contracted to work for me, you'll practise a zero-fraternisation policy. I find that petty lawsuits are best avoided that way.'

'Are you speaking from personal experience?' she asked before she could stop herself.

His face tightened into a rigid, forbidding mask. Hell, she'd struck another nerve. God, what was wrong with her?

'That is *not* your concern. Just be sure to let Grandma know you'll be disappointing her for a while longer where potential wedding bells are concerned, would you?'

Elise turned back around, too filled with roiling emotions to trust herself to speak.

Keep walking.

CHAPTER THREE

IS THERE SOMETHING about me that rubs you the wrong way?

Of all the words she could've chosen.

Alejandro snorted, inwardly grimacing at the sexual bent he'd afforded the words. But they wouldn't fade away. Like the headache pounding his temples, each heartbeat flashed an image of Elise Jameson onto his retinas, each one more vivid than the last.

Madre de Dios.

He didn't need to waste time on an attraction his principles wouldn't allow him to act upon.

Now he knew the cause of the stalled merger, he could simply pay Jameson PR for services rendered, plus a generous bonus. He had no doubt that Gael had arrived at the same realisation as he had, but, since negotiations hadn't yet been severed with SNV in favour of Toredo, it was most likely Gael hadn't found a satisfactory way to appease the Ishikawas, either.

With that last puzzle unravelled, he didn't need Elise Jameson.

Except she'd rooted out his problem with a single, albeit unorthodox, phone call, whereas his strategy team had spent weeks trying to unravel the mystery of the stalled negotiations.

Sending her away would save the irritating prickling of his senses whenever she was near. Or he could keep her around as the extra pair of eyes she'd advocated until this deal was in the bag.

He stemmed the need to call HR and retract the contract. He never set rules for his staff he didn't follow himself. Regardless of how looking at Elise Jameson's face and body made certain parts of him stir, his only focus in dealing with her would be this merger.

A pep talk. He was giving himself *a pep talk. Por el amor—*

He tossed the curiously empty water bottle on the tray, having no recollection of drinking it. He refused to believe his easing headache was because of his water intake. Or the unknotting of his muscles because Elise had helped him finally unravel the mystery of his failing deal.

He eyed his phone, the temptation to call Gael out on the games he was playing surging high. But no. First he would see what strategy Elise came up with. Every employee had their uses. He'd found hers. No reason not to see how she fared for a few more days.

Resolutely, he got back to work. Only to find his gaze straying with annoying frequency to the clock on his desk. An hour later, he snatched up the phone.

'Margo, do I not recall paying for an efficient time management seminar recently?'

'Umm…yes. Two months ago.'

'Great. So is there any reason the HR team are taking over an hour to send Miss Jameson back up?'

'Oh, yes, sorry. She called to say Mr Michaels was ordering lunch for the department and that he would be adding her order in so she could eat and get the papers signed at the same time. That's super-efficient, don't you think?'

Alejandro gritted his teeth. *'Exceedingly.'*

'Shall I order your lunch now, sir?' Margo asked.

'No.' He started to lower the phone. *'Gracias,'* he tossed in before slamming down the handset.

He told himself he was irritated because he wanted her working ASAP. Time was of the essence.

So why was he eyeing the door, listening out for the click of high heels?

With a vicious curse, he refocused on the extensive list of products his marketing team needed his approval on before offering it through SNV in the next quarter. He was halfway down it when her laughter echoed through the door.

He knew it was her because the charge through his blood was hauntingly familiar. And thoroughly unwelcome. His PA joined in the laughter, as did a male voice.

Alejandro continued reading. More laughter filtered in. He didn't recall moving. Or turning the door handle.

'So lunch was great, then?' Margo asked.

'Gosh, yes,' Elise enthused. 'The club sandwich was *amazing*! Thanks for recommending it, Oliver.'

Alejandro watched, unobserved, as Oliver Michaels, his head of HR, delivered a smile that made Alejandro's hackles rise.

'My pleasure. Although it's wickedly sinful, it's more than worth the extra hour at the gym.' He patted his abs.

Elise smiled. The act was slow, measured. A revelation. As if she didn't do it often, so was taking time to draw her companions' attention to the extraordinary gift she was bestowing on them. Alejandro's breath strangled in his throat. He watched Michaels and Margo stare as her smile transformed her face from visually stunning to exquisitely entrancing. 'I call that a win, then.'

Oliver Michaels was the first to recover. 'Uh...yeah. I like to think—'

Alejandro stepped into Margo's office, achieving instant silence. 'If you've quite finished rhapsodising about culinary delights, perhaps we can *all* get back to work?'

Margo's eyes widened; no doubt she was realising what Alejandro's chilled voice represented. With a quick nod, she refocused on her keyboard.

Elise met his gaze, her smile now non-existent, tension in her body as her nostrils flared slightly. Alejandro's gaze dropped to her lips. She'd lost some of her scarlet lipstick since she'd left his office. The result was a softer look that made him imagine what she'd look like after being thoroughly kissed. Those lips would be much plumper than

they were now, of course. And she would have more natural
colour in her cheeks—

Suficiente!

He redirected his attention to Michaels, who was holding out a folder. 'I brought Elise's contract down for you to
countersign—'

'Leave it with Margo.' He glanced pointedly at Elise.

She took a few steps forward, then paused. Looking over
her shoulder, she let loose a smaller smile. 'Thanks, Oliver.
See you around.'

Michaels jerked out a nervous nod.

Alejandro waited until she stepped into his office, and
slammed the door. 'See you around?' he repeated.

She stiffened. 'What?'

'I didn't stammer.'

'No, you didn't.' She sighed. 'You're clearly having a bad
day. I get that. But do you really need to drag everyone down
just because you're in a mood?'

'Excuse me?' Alejandro bristled.

'On second thought, don't answer that. I'm here. I'm ready
to work.' She walked away from him, taking the subtle scent
of her perfume with her. After retrieving her briefcase, she
stopped in the middle of the room. 'Margo said you haven't
assigned a desk for me to use yet?'

'No,' he answered shortly, his mind still fixed on the fact
that she hadn't answered his question to his satisfaction.

'Is there one I can use?' she pressed.

He inhaled deeply, dismissing the smile, the exchange.
Everything that had happened in the last few hours.

Going to his desk, he grabbed the substantial file that was
always within reach. 'Come with me.'

He led her to a side door across the room from where she'd
done her work that morning. Throwing it open, he walked to
the desk directly opposite from the door. Unlike his office,
it was sparsely furnished, the only thing besides the desk
and chair was a floor lamp set against the single glass wall.
He set the file down.

'You'll work in here. I use this office when I don't want to be disturbed. Margo is excellent at keeping physical intrusions away when I need it, but even I can't resist checking my emails when I'm in the middle of a deal.'

Her smile was tight and false. Alejandro willed himself not to wish for the genuine one he'd caught a brief glimpse of. 'It'll do great, thanks.' She pulled the file towards her. 'Anything in particular you want me to watch out for?'

Alejandro shrugged. 'Read up on the merger. I have a conference call with the Ishikawa brothers tomorrow. You'll sit in on it with me. You wanted to be my extra pair of eyes. My Japanese is adequate but not expert. You can be my eyes *and* ears.'

'Okay.'

She dropped her case on the desk and removed her jacket. The second button of her blouse had come undone. Alejandro shoved his hands into his pockets, irritatingly caught between the need to point it out or ogle the creamy silkiness of her skin.

Several seconds passed.

Elise sat down, opened the file and glanced up. 'Was there something else, Mr Aguilar?'

'Leave the door open. There's no phone or intercom in here. It'll save you having to get up and come to me if you have any questions.'

Her gaze flicked past him to his office. Her eyes widened a touch.

'Yes, I can see you from my desk,' he confirmed.

A whisper of a smile touched her lips. 'I'll resist the urge to chew on my nails or burp loudly, then.'

'That would be very considerate of you, *gracias*.'

Her eyes widened further and Alejandro suppressed a rare smile. He'd lived so long in the States that most people forgot he was of Spanish origin. And more than one past conquest had been enthralled by his occasional lapses into his mother tongue.

'I…I didn't actually mean that, Mr Aguilar. That was just a—'

'Joke? It may not seem that way to you, but I do know what those are. I've occasionally been known to make one or two of them myself.'

One shapely eyebrow lifted. 'But not recently?'

The reminder of why this deal was going sour darkened his mood. 'No, Elise. Not recently.'

'Okay. How's the headache?' she asked, then her forehead twitched, as if she hadn't meant to blurt out the question. Alejandro felt an odd sense of kinship as his own unnerving need for something that had no place in this office threatened to return.

'No longer an issue. Perhaps we can work towards keeping it that way by getting this merger back on track?' he said brusquely.

'Umm…sure,' she murmured, still looking mildly puzzled.

Alejandro returned to his desk, satisfied that control had been established. Not that it'd been too far from his grasp. Granted, this morning's revelations had unsettled him.

But he'd never shied away from a challenge. He wasn't about to start now.

CHAPTER FOUR

ELISE RESISTED THE URGE to glance into the outer office. She'd already done that far too many times. Thankfully, not once had Alejandro looked her way. His focus on his work was absolute enough to induce envy. He'd taken a few phone calls, one of which he'd conducted at the far end of his office in front of the bank of floor-to-ceiling windows.

For one absurd second, Elise had wondered whether the low murmured conversation involved a lover. She'd jumped away from the thought as if physically scalded. It was beyond none of her business, and straying into dangerous territory she knew better than to approach.

Refocusing on her work between those times hadn't been a hardship. The intricacies of the merger were staggering and fascinating. But more importantly, the deal Alejandro was chasing would *create* thousands of jobs. Granted, the merger would also elevate him to top five on the World's Richest list, but he would be helping thousands along the way.

The other thing she'd noted was the mind-bending scale of philanthropy attached to each year's estimated earnings. For each year Alejandro achieved the target he'd set his company, he planned to donate a share of the company's profit to humanitarian projects.

Elise frowned as she finished the charities section. Nothing she'd read so far should make the Ishikawa Corporation want to do anything other than bite Alejandro's hand off in their haste to secure the merger. If nothing else, they stood to become instant billionaires.

'You're frowning.'

She stumbled to a halt, realising she'd entered his office. He was bathed in the mid-afternoon sun, the contrast of olive skin against the rolled-up sleeves of his black shirt striking enough to command her stare. 'Oh… I'm almost done reading the file.'

'And?'

'And the deal…the charity benefits… It's all amazing.'

'*Amazing* directly contradicts that frown.'

She looked away from him, anxiously noting her elevated pulse rate, and crossed over to the drinks tray. 'Well, I expected to find a thread of dissatisfaction right from the beginning. Something that would indicate they were unhappy. There's nothing. I'm just wondering why they chose *now* to throw a wrench in what was from the very start a once-in-a-lifetime opportunity.'

'My guess is another party is dangling promises they may not be able to keep.'

Elise picked up a bottle of water and traced her finger across the top. 'You guess? Sorry, but you don't strike me as the kind of man who guesses.'

'And have you known many men like me?' he drawled.

She flushed, then cursed herself for being flustered at the deliberate taunt. 'You know what I mean, Mr Aguilar.'

Contemplative eyes probed hers for several seconds. When he held out an imperious hand for water, she picked up another bottle and passed it to him, curbing the urge to roll her eyes.

'You're right. I don't guess.'

Surprise spiked through her. 'So you know who's trying to jinx the deal?'

'*Sí*, I do,' he murmured in a tone that sent a shiver down her spine. When he didn't elaborate, she frowned.

'Are you going to tell me who it is?'

'Have you finished reading the report?'

'Not yet.'

He uncapped the bottle and drained half of it in greedy gulps. Elise stopped herself from staring at the solid column of his throat. Or at the dark stubble that had crept over his jaw in the last few hours.

'Go finish it. The "who" doesn't really matter. What I

need is a PR strategy on how we can resolve this problem if they remain intransigent.'

She returned to her office, fully aware there was no point pressing him for more information.

When she next raised her head, the view at her window had changed from day to evening, with lights from the adjacent skyscrapers illuminating the night sky. Her senses jumped when Alejandro filled the doorway.

'You done?' he asked, leaning against the jamb.

Elise nodded, wishing there was something else she could refocus her attention on besides the sleek musculature of Alejandro Aguilar's body.

There's the file. Her work. The reason she was here. She'd signed a contract mere hours ago that had drawn clear lines of boss and employee. While her past experience had borne witness that clients could violate contracts, she had a feeling Alejandro would stick rigidly to his.

But that didn't mean she could drop her guard...or ogle his breathtakingly gorgeous body whenever she was in his presence.

She dragged her focus to the file. 'My opinion hasn't changed. They would have to have been offered something over and above what you're offering. And that's...'

'That's what?' he encouraged.

'That's bordering on financial suicide, unless the other party has unlimited funds. Or are willing to go all out to steal this deal from you.'

His gaze swept downward, veiling his expression. Her senses twitched. She used to think she was a good reader of people. A horrific violation of her trust had robbed her of that last year.

Even so, she knew she'd struck somewhere in the vicinity of a nail.

Alejandro turned around without answering.

Elise rose. 'Am I right? Mr Aguilar, is someone going to extraordinary lengths to see you fail?'

'Alejandro,' he murmured.

'What?'

'If we're to work together, you'll have to call me Alejandro.'

Elise wasn't sure why the thought of repeating his name, even minus that sensual Spanish intonation she had no hope of mimicking, sent a shiver of awareness through her. 'I… Okay.'

'The chef has prepared dinner for us. Come. We'll talk some more while we eat.'

She followed him out of his office to a set of smoked-glass doors, which swung open to reveal a small twelve-seater dining room. At the head of the table and directly adjacent, two places had been set, complete with silver tableware and glasses that indicated this was a multi-course meal.

They sat, and the chef walked in bearing two platters. Elise chose the chicken ravioli starter and almost groaned with pleasure as the delicate tastes melted on her tongue.

'Okay, I take it back. Given the choice of going outside for fresh air and a sandwich or this, I'll choose this every time.'

The chef, who was almost at the door, grinned at her compliment. Smiling in return, she turned back to her place and noticed Alejandro's scowl.

Her smile dimmed. 'Um, in case you missed it, I'm conceding that I was wrong before. No need to give me the evil eye.'

His eyes narrowed on the shutting door before returning to hers. 'Do you make a habit of flirting with every man you come into contact with?'

Elise froze in the act of lifting her fork. 'I *don't* flirt,' she bit out, her insides congealing at the accusation that struck a direct hit and dredged up haunting memories. No matter how many times she'd told herself the assault hadn't been her fault, a part of her always wondered if she'd emitted the very vibes she'd striven to avoid her whole life.

Her parents might have chosen to use their God-given looks and charm as weapons, and Marsha Jameson might have advised Elise to exploit her sexuality to her advantage, but Elise had vowed never to follow in their footsteps.

Unfortunately, that rigid belief had proven to be an irresistible challenge for Brian Grey...

Hastily shoving aside bitter memories, she pushed the chair back and surged to her feet.

Her wrist was captured before she'd taken a single step. 'What do you think you're doing?'

'I don't like the tone of this conversation. Perhaps I was too hasty in taking back the benefits of getting my own meal. *I don't flirt,*' she reiterated, the need to reassure herself that what had happened a year ago hadn't been her fault pumping through her blood. 'But I have manners. And if someone does something nice for me, I *thank* them.'

He regarded her intensely for far too long. 'Sit down, Elise. We're not done.'

She shook her head. 'I've lost my appetite. Besides, it's seven in the evening. I didn't sign up to work all hours.'

'But you committed yourself to working reasonable work hours. Are you calling this an unreasonable hour?'

'I'll re-evaluate if I'm not subjected to unfounded allegations,' she challenged. She looked pointedly at the hand manacling her wrist.

He waited a beat, then released her. 'You were enjoying your food a few minutes ago. I'll refrain from ruining our meal with...touchy subjects.'

Elise eyed her plate, then the door. She knew her outburst had flared brightly on Alejandro's radar, but walking out at this stage would be counterproductive. She sat back down.

'While you're doing that, perhaps you'd like to remember that I haven't flirted with *you*. Unless you count yourself *above* men?' It was a cheap shot, regretted the moment she uttered the words.

One corner of his mouth quirked. 'We'll leave that debate alone, shall we?'

Her face reddened slightly, and for the rest of the first course they didn't speak.

Once the second course of roast beef and vegetable med-
ley had been served, he held up the bottle of expensive red.
'Wine?'

About to refuse, she sprung for a little Dutch courage to
see her through and nodded. 'I'm not much of a wine drinker,
or a drinker at all, so don't hold it against me if I don't appreciate the vintage.'

He filled her glass, then his. 'I prefer honesty to a preten-
tious diatribe on non-existent flavours and bouquets.'

Despite the residual sting of his earlier accusation, a smile
tugged at her lips. 'Score one for me.'

Sharp eyes met hers. 'Remain straight with me in all
things, and you'll score a lot more.'

For some reason the statement produced equal amounts
of dread and anticipation. Anticipation of what, she had no
idea. They were halfway through their main course before
he spoke again.

'So, in light of what you've discovered, what would Jameson PR advise?'

She knew her parents would advise him to go for the
usurper's jugular. Setting a bloodhound on the trail of sala-
cious gossip and secrets to discredit was a favourite tactic
her father relished.

'A charm offensive. And a reminder of everything they
have to gain by merging with you.'

'Not a declaration of war on my competitor?'

Her mouth soured. 'You can take that route if you want
to, I guess.'

'Which route would you take?'

'Not that. Blood and gore turn my stomach.'

'Perhaps you need a stronger disposition,' he mocked.

Choosing not to take the bait, she sipped her wine, a little
surprised when it slipped down smoothly. 'The looking-into-
the-whites-of-their-eyes approach works, Alejandro. Nothing beats a personal touch. How many times have you met
the Ishikawa brothers face to face since deciding to pursue
this merger?'

He swirled his wine glass. 'Twice.'

'After you had your team investigate their viability and profit margins?'

'Of course.'

'I'm guessing both times were here in the States where you wined and dined them at the best restaurant in town?'

'Their every wish was catered to. They left happy.'

'In your opinion.'

His gaze probed hers. 'What's your point?'

'I'm willing to bet my sizeable manga collection that you didn't divulge a single personal detail about yourself.'

'At the risk of repeating myself, I don't do—'

'Touchy-feely. Yes, I'm aware. But letting them see you as remotely...*human* may have prevented this from happening.'

'That might work for the average Mom and Pop ice-cream-parlour business. If they can't see their way past those...*feelings* to a multibillion-dollar merger, then perhaps I'm dealing with the wrong business.'

She sent him a droll look. 'We both know this isn't a mistake. The Ishikawa Corporation's business record is outstanding. So is SNV's. A successful merger would be the stuff of breaking news headlines and serious accolades. All you'll need to do is...bend a little.'

'Is that what you'd do in my shoes? Bare your life to strangers in order to secure a deal?'

She lifted her glass and took a healthy gulp, relishing the warmth that blanketed her insides. 'We're not talking about me here.'

'You're fond of hypotheticals. So let's have it. Would you give yourself the same advice, were you in my position?'

'Maybe.' She bore his intense scrutiny for a minute before she sighed. 'Yes, I would.'

'And what would you tell them about yourself?'

Elise shook her head. 'That's too broad a question.'

'Let's streamline, then. You attended a university on the west coast when your family is based in a state with excellent universities. Why?'

Nerves began to eat into the warmth. She took another sip, despite the faint warning that this form of Dutch courage hadn't been her best idea. 'The need to broaden my horizons?'

'If you had such a need, why did you return to work with your parents?'

She stiffened at the other raw subject that grated her nerves. 'Is there a law against that?'

'Is that the answer you'd give a prospective business partner?'

'No...' She paused, aware she had skidded towards a chasm of her own making. 'I agreed to work at Jameson in return for my parents paying for my university tuition.'

A slow frown gathered on his brow. 'They expected you to pay for the education they gave you?'

Elise chose to blame the Malbec for loosening the tight leash she normally had on her emotions. 'They expect a lot of things. Including not giving free rides to anyone, including their daughter.'

The enlightened gleam in his eyes further unnerved her. 'Things aren't cordial between you and your parents?'

A harsh laugh escaped before she could stop it. 'You could say that.'

'Then why do you work with them?' he queried.

'Because jobs don't automatically fall from the heavens the moment you graduate from college. And if, by some divine grace, you make it to a second or third interview and your prospective boss finds out that you're the daughter of Marsha and Ralph Jameson, they question why you'd snub the chance to work for the exalted Jamesons. Half of them won't touch you because they don't believe you'll be committed to your job. The other half have certain...preconceived notions about you and won't even give you a chance. Seven months of polite rejections and my parents demanding repayment of their loan left me little choice.'

Elise took another sip of wine to drown the sinking knowledge that she'd divulged far more than she'd intended to.

Silence seething with questions filled the room. Alejandro levelled a gaze at her, speculation swirling in his shrewd eyes. 'And is that debt paid off?'

She swallowed. 'No. But I'm almost there.'

He raised his brow. 'Almost?'

'Yep. With your help, of course.'

'My help?' he enquired thinly.

'Helping you nail this deal would be great for you, of course, and it'll boost my résumé, too, but, more importantly, it'll see me freed from the shackles of Mum and Dad. So really, it's a trifecta of pure *winning*.'

Alejandro slowly swirled his glass. 'I see.'

Shame nibbled at her. As he continued to stare at her, heat that had nothing to do with the great food and wine swarmed up her neck. 'I'm sorry, you didn't ask for my life history.' Setting the nearly empty glass down, she stood. And swayed. Alejandro surged up and grasped her waist. She averted her gaze from eyes that saw way too much. 'I told you I wasn't much of a drinker.'

'*Sí*, you did, but you're not drunk. Trust me, I know the difference.' His voice was faintly self-mocking.

'All the same, this isn't going to look good in the morning, is it?' she muttered.

'You barely finished your glass. I'm not going to hold it against you.'

Her eyes flicked to his. And stayed, absorbed by the faint gold flecks splaying from his pupils. 'Thanks,' she whispered.

'*De nada,*' he murmured.

They remained like that, their breaths close enough to mingle. Elise knew it was unsafe to let those dark-rimmed eyes bore right into her soul. 'I didn't mean to carry on. I just...'

His eyebrow lifted. 'You just...?'

'I don't like talking about my parents.'

'Why?'

'It...it just hurts too much, you know?'

A curiously bleak smile quirked his lips. 'No. I don't know.'

Elise frowned. 'Of course not. I'm guessing you had a brilliant childhood, filled with nauseatingly blissful memories.'

The hands curled at her waist tightened imperceptibly. 'Nauseating more often than not, yes. Blissful, no.'

Her brain suddenly locked onto the fact that his hands were on her body. Elise couldn't think beyond the electric heat seeping into her skin. Or the need to feel it glide elsewhere.

'Well, I'm sorry.'

'For what?'

She attempted a shrug. 'For both of us.'

'I don't need your pity.' His voice was edgy, filled with a thousand barbs.

She shivered. Immediately, his hands slid up her arms, warming her. Elise struggled to focus. 'I wasn't offering it. I was just…'

His gaze dropped to her mouth and her thoughts momentarily scattered. Dragging her eyes from his face restored temporary sanity. A question that had been probing the back of her mind surged forward, but his hands on her body wreaked havoc with her thought processes.

'Alejandro?'

'*Sí?*' he breathed.

Her insides shook at the sultry, exotic word. 'You can let me go now. I promise I won't fall over.'

His hands tightened on her for a heated second, then he freed her. 'Good to know. Would you like some coffee or shall we put an end to this *work*day?'

She gripped her arms where his had been a moment ago, absurdly aware she wasn't ready for the evening to end. 'You were going to tell me who was behind the stalled merger.'

Several emotions curled through his eyes, most of them forbidding enough to send a chill through her.

'It's my brother,' he finally offered. Contrary to the expression in his eyes, his voice was bled of every emotion.

'Your *brother*?'

'Yes.'

'But…why?'

He took a step back, then another. Striding to the ever-present coffee cart, he poured a shot of espresso. 'Because like you, for me, *family* isn't a word that conjures hearts and flowers.'

Elise wished she didn't understand what he meant. All the same… 'That's still a little extreme, isn't it? Your brother wants to hurt you that much?'

His mouth twisted. 'You assume I'm capable of being *hurt*. At the worst, he'll make a nuisance of himself. No more.'

The staggering confidence behind the words further chilled her. And yet, she felt an affinity with Alejandro, sensed an underlying emotion that she couldn't quite pinpoint.

She was twisting the puzzle in her mind when he drained his cup and set it down. 'I think I've used up my reasonable workday quota where you're concerned. Come.'

He walked out of the dining room. She followed at a slower pace, and entered his office to find him returning from hers with her jacket and briefcase.

He held out her jacket for her, and Elise murmured her thanks. About to bid him goodnight and beat a hasty retreat, she froze as he caught up his own jacket and came towards her. 'You're leaving, too?'

'I'm taking you home.'

She shook her head. 'There's no need to do that. The subway will get me home in twenty minutes.'

He took her elbow and steered her towards the door. 'It's late. Letting you brave the subway at this time of night is out of the question. If nothing else, I wish to see you return to work tomorrow in one piece.'

'It's really not—'

'You haven't already forgotten our agreement to dispense with unnecessary arguments, have you?'

She firmed her mouth and followed him into what looked like a private lift. Enclosed in the small space, she couldn't think of one thing to say to the man whose presence loomed powerful and vibrant beside her. In contrast, she felt small and shamefully inept, so she turned her face away from him. To the mirror that reflected his image in perfect detail.

Even in profile, Alejandro was unforgivingly captivating. In the harsh light, his skin glowed a vibrant olive, his thick dark hair gleaming invitingly. Elise had never felt the urge to touch a man's face, let alone his hair. Pursuing a double major had been time-consuming enough, and the casual dates she'd occasionally accepted in college ended when she discovered sex was the subtext behind each date.

That reality had followed her into her working life, but she'd become an expert at holding male interest at bay.

But staring at Alejandro, she felt an alien need to do the opposite, to give in to the subtext of sex pulsing through her right to the tips of her fingers.

As if he sensed her unvarnished scrutiny, Alejandro's head snapped up. Their eyes met in the mirror. His gaze held hers easily, compelling her completely, so she couldn't look away. The whine of the descending lift the only sound, they stared at each other as silence seethed, thickened into something else. Something that had intense heat dredging low in her belly, and flaring tingles all over her body.

His gaze probed, darkened with each jagged second. It dropped to her lips, and Elise, as if she were under a spell, parted them.

Someone made a sound. A tiny fracture of breath. The beginning of a curse. Or a prayer. She never got the chance to guess.

The lift arrived with a slight bump and the doors glided open.

And the spell was broken.

CHAPTER FIVE

ELISE HAD RIDDEN in her fair share of supercars, her father being a firm believer that a show of power and success bred even more of the same. Each time she'd ridden with her father, she'd prayed for the ride to be over as quickly as possible, silently enduring the 'life lesson' speeches that came with those trips, while Ralph Jameson had walked away congratulating himself for showing his daughter what material benefits could be plucked like fruit from the nearest low-hanging tree, should she play her cards right.

Tonight, she was far from uninterested. Her gaze strayed frequently to the man behind the wheel of the Bugatti, a tiny part of her not minding the traffic that slowed their progress through downtown Chicago.

Even the silence, although charged with residual awareness from the lift, was welcome. It gave her a chance to breathe, and evaluate just what it was about Alejandro Aguilar that threatened the careful foundations of the walls she'd built around her emotions and sexuality.

When it came right down to it, he'd done nothing presumptive or offensive to make her believe she had anything to fear from him. His comment about her flirting had stung, of course, but he'd dropped the subject at her challenge. Which was far more than a few of the men she'd interacted with professionally and privately had done in the past.

But that tiny consideration still didn't account for why she felt this unsettling excitement just by being next to Alejandro Aguilar.

Whatever it was, she needed to get it under control quickly.

He changed lanes as they neared her South Shore apartment. In an effort not to stare at his hands or the taut thighs centimetres from hers, or even breathe in the aftershave-mingled maleness of him, she cleared her throat.

'So…are you going to go after your brother?'

His jaw clenched as he pulled to a stop at a traffic light. One hand rested on the top of the steering wheel, the other scrubbing restively over his stubble. 'No. For now, I'm choosing to resist that impulse.'

A breath freed itself from her chest. 'I'm glad.'

He glanced at her before he eased away at the green light. 'Do you advocate the "make love, not war" route with all your clients?'

'My commissions so far have involved damage limitation or using the best PR approach that makes the client look good. I won't be helping you if I advocate an approach that makes you look bad to investors in the long run.'

He slid another glance at her. 'What do you care? This is your last commission. What happens after this shouldn't concern you.'

Elise bit her lip as a mildly hollow sensation washed over her. 'No, I guess it shouldn't. Maybe I don't want my swan song to leave a bad taste in my mouth,' she replied. She looked out of her window and saw her apartment block slide into view. She indicated the quieter side street. 'If you pull over here, I'll jump out.'

He ignored her and the no-parking zone in front of her building and stopped before the double glass doors. Stepping out, he came round and opened her door.

Elise took a gulp of restorative fresh air. 'Thanks for the ride.'

He took her arm and started towards the double doors. 'You can thank me by letting me see you to your door. You can also tell me why your building doesn't have a doorman. Or adequate security.' He eyed the hippy-looking couple who breezed out, then transferred his scathing gaze to the doors that didn't quite shut behind them.

To counteract what the thought of being enclosed with

him in another lift was doing to her insides, she waved his terse demand away. 'I have a super. Does that satisfy you?'

'No, it does not.'

Her mouth twisted. 'Not everyone can afford a Barrington Hills mansion, Alejandro.'

He pressed the lift button. When it didn't arrive quickly enough, he pressed it again, several times. 'I don't live in Barrington Hills.'

'My parents do.'

He stared at her. 'And you choose to live here?'

'Yes,' she answered simply.

He didn't probe further, leaving Elise with the feeling that the subject of family was as unwelcome to him as it was to her. What he did probe was the lift button, uttering a skin-flaying Latin curse when the lift made no move to arrive.

Relief and disappointment spun through her. 'I'll take the stairs. I'm only on the third floor.'

He whirled with fluid grace and indicated for her to precede him. Battling to suppress her self-consciousness, she hurried up the stairs, and arrived at her door two minutes later, struggling not to pant. Alejandro, on the other hand, had barely broken a sweat.

She unlocked her door. Almost reluctantly her eyes drifted up only to find his waiting for her. 'Since conventional working hours are out the window, what time do you need me tomorrow?'

'To avoid another argument, you can arrive at seven.'

Her eyes widened. 'As opposed to what? *Five a.m.?*'

He shrugged. 'That's when my work day starts.'

'Dare I ask when it ends?'

'When the coffee machine threatens to quit. Which it does on a daily basis.'

She laughed. His lips twitched. Then his gaze dropped to her mouth.

The laughter died. She scrambled backwards, bumping her backside into the door. 'I'll see you in the morning?'

Penetrating eyes collided with hers. '*Sí*. You will. *Buenas noches.*'

He departed with the quiet strength and power of a jungle predator. And even though his footsteps barely echoed down the stairs, she found herself listening for them.

Catching herself, she stepped back and shut her door.

Twenty minutes later she was showered and dressed in her favourite sleeping shirt. Sitting in bed, she tugged her laptop close and powered it on. Her buzz disappeared beneath the volume of emails from her mother earlier in the day, then her father demanding responses to her mother's emails.

She'd muted her phone for her interview with Alejandro and then neglected to turn it back on. She activated the sound and wasn't at all surprised when the handset rang almost instantly.

The buzz now replaced with cold trepidation, she braced herself and answered the call.

'Finally! Your father and I were beginning to wonder whether you'd been abducted by aliens,' her mother snapped, her voice containing a bite that always raised Elise's hackles.

'I turned the sound on my phone off when I met with Mr Aguilar. Things got out of hand after that.' She immediately cringed at the poor choice of words.

She didn't bother retracting them, because her mother was already enquiring sharply, 'Out of hand? Are you saying we didn't get it? Damn, I should've handled it myself. But we're the number one PR firm in Chicago. People beg to come to us, not the other way round. All the same, this commission could've been huge for us. You should've called us when things started going bad. Ralph! Come here. We have a problem.'

Elise's grip tightened on the phone, all too familiar anger and hurt welling inside her. 'Mom—'

'Your father and I will have to see if there's any way to salvage it—'

'Mom!'

'What?'

'I signed the agreement with SNV this afternoon.'

Stunned silence followed. Elise tried to breathe through the hurt clogging in her chest.

'Well, that's…commendable?'

The question mark hooked like a rusty claw into her. It was the same question mark with which they'd greeted her devastation after being nearly assaulted by a client they'd pushed her into dealing with.

'Are you sure it wasn't a harmless pass, Elise?'

'You're mistaken. Brian Grey doesn't normally go for girls like you…'

She breathed through the anguish. 'Thanks for your rousing belief in me,' she replied, but the murmur of voices in the background told her they were engaged in a side conversation about her.

Her father took over a minute later. 'I hear congratulations are in order?'

Again the insidious disbelief that she'd been able to land SNV's business. 'Is that a question, Dad?' she asked stiltedly.

'You can take that tone all you want, but you've made it perfectly clear you're just passing through the business that kept you in clothes, ponies, and round-the-world vacations, not to mention college tuition fees.'

'Some of those things were your responsibility to me as my parents. The others I never asked for. And I'm paying you back for my education. Let's not forget that.'

'You wouldn't have had to if you hadn't misled us about your true intentions. We didn't pay hundreds of thousands of dollars to send you to college to study *art*. Any fool can draw. You were supposed to make marketing and PR your main focus.'

'I'm not a fool, Dad. And I graduated with *double* majors. You just choose to ignore that fact because it suits your argument. I'm sorry I disappointed you and Mom by not wanting what you want, but my life is my own. If you can't respect that—'

'Elise—'

Her father was cut off abruptly as her mother took control. 'Enough of this. These arguments give me migraines and I can't afford one tonight. We're entertaining the Greenhills. They're not as prestigious as Alejandro Aguilar, of course, but both your father and I need to be on top of our games. A commission from them will guarantee us a significant mention in the *Tribune*. I know you'd rather be doing other things than talking to us, so just forward me a copy of the contract so Accounts can set up a payment schedule with SNV.'

Elise exhaled shakily. She'd tried to bury the futile wish for affection from them, but their cold-hearted indifference to her and everything except climbing the social and financial ladders, despite the shockingly harrowing events of last year, still caused anguish. 'Mom—'

'Goodbye, Elise.'

Her mother hung up, leaving her no choice but to swallow the words that never quite managed to pave the way for a non-confrontational conversation.

She blinked rapidly when she realised tears were forming. Dashing her hand across her face, she forwarded the contract to her mother.

Powering down her laptop, she slid properly into bed and pulled up the sheets to her chin, firmly refusing to dwell on the past.

Instead, she analysed her day.

In some ways, today could've gone better. She could've summoned more control over her errant emotions around Alejandro, for instance. Been less absorbed by his raw magnetism, that hint of bleakness that echoed the knot trapped inside her.

But she'd secured and held on to the SNV commission.

Tomorrow would be better.

She groaned out loud when her alarm sounded at six. Rolling over, she debated the wisdom of making middle-of-the-night decisions like running to SNV's offices as a perfect start to the new day.

Eyeing the backpack she'd readied with her work clothes and everything she needed for the day, Elise groaned again, wondering what she'd been thinking.

You need a clear head to deal with Alejandro Aguilar. Running does that for you.

Grudgingly accepting the voice of reason, she rose and donned her running gear. Tying her hair into a ponytail, she caught up the backpack and headed out.

Twenty-five sweaty minutes later, she arrived at SNV. She was gulping thirstily from the water fountain when she sensed she was being watched. Her heart leapt into her throat, but when she raised her head it wasn't Alejandro, but a sandy-haired man who approached with a smile and an outstretched hand.

'I'm Wendell Grant. I'm with the strategy team on the Japanese merger. Alejandro mentioned he'd gone with my recommendation and hired you.'

Wondering when Alejandro would've had a chance to do that since it was only six thirty, she plastered a smile on her face. 'Oh, I see. I guess I owe you big for that.'

His smile widened. 'I accept payment in caffeine-related beverages.' He fell into step beside her and held the lift door for her. 'Good thing is, in this place, it's *free*,' he whispered conspiratorially.

Elise laughed. 'Noted.'

He pressed the button for the same floor Alejandro's office was located, then sent a swift glance over her body. 'You better hustle. Alejandro might want a meeting. In my experience it's better to make yourself available and not be needed, than the other way around.'

She nodded brisk thanks, although her body developed a curious thrum at the mention of Alejandro's name as they exited the lift. Wendell turned right and she headed for the women's bathroom that held fully stocked shower cubicles.

'Oh, by the way…'

She paused and turned.

'I take my coffee black with two sugars,' Wendell said.

Acknowledging him with a quick wave, she darted into the bathroom.

She arrived at Margo's desk one minute before seven. The middle-aged PA looked up and rolled her eyes.

'Be warned. He's in a mood. There's a briefing in the conference room. You better head there, too. He'll join you when he's done with his phone call.'

Elise eyed the door, heard the growled imprecation from within, and exchanged a nervous smile with Margo before heading the other way.

She entered the conference room and greeted the three men and three women comprising the strategy team. After Wendell made introductions, Elise went to the coffee cart and prepared two coffees, and held one out to him.

'Black, two sugars.'

He took the coffee from her and took a sip. 'Perfect. You can stay.'

Exaggerated groans and ribbing sounded around the table.

Smiling, Elise started to raise her cup, and froze at the sight of Alejandro, silently observing her from the doorway.

She locked her knees, the bolt to her stomach just from the sight of him enough to knock the breath from her lungs. Tension emanated from him. The team lapsed into silence, furtive glances passing between them.

Alejandro prowled forward and stopped at the head of the table. 'You've all met my new PR guru. Good. This will be a short meeting.'

Bodies shifted. Throats cleared. The tension remained.

'Are you going to sit down, Elise?' Alejandro addressed her without looking her way.

'Uh, sure.'

About to take the seat farthest away, she froze again when Alejandro pointed to the chair adjacent to him. Again without looking her way.

Clutching her untouched coffee, she made her way round the table and slipped into the chair. A few heartbeats later, Alejandro sat down.

Like yesterday, he wore a black shirt and faintly pinstriped tailored trousers. If he'd worn a tie with the ensemble, he'd discarded it—the two top buttons opened to reveal his strong throat and the hint of silky curls. She quickly averted her gaze from the evocative sight and concentrated on the file in front of her. The thin file that, upon closer inspection, held everything she'd discovered yesterday.

Her eyes widened. Had he returned to the office last night to put this together? The man was superhuman.

'Yesterday, Elise confirmed what we've all suspected for the past few days. The Ishikawa Corporation is considering another player for the merger. What the report doesn't say is that player happens to be my brother.'

Elise tensed at the icy chill of his tone as shocked murmurs went around the table.

'Your brother?' Wendell echoed.

Alejandro's eyes hardened a touch. 'Yes. He's CEO of Toredo Inc. That fact shouldn't alter our strategy. At least not yet. Elise believes Kenzo Ishikawa and the proposed relocation of the factories is the bone of contention fuelling the sudden switch in their end goal. We'll concentrate on that instead.'

Wendell frowned and glanced at Elise. 'Their *grandfather*? Are you sure?'

She nodded. 'As sure as I can be without hearing it straight from his mouth.'

Alejandro levelled a hard stare at him. 'Do you have a problem with that assessment? If so, prove it wrong,' he bit out.

Wendell's eyes widened. 'Umm…no, I believe her.'

'Good. I want a preliminary report of what it'll cost to relocate fifty per cent of the factories and leave the remainder in Japan for the next five years. That will be all.'

He rose, signalling an end to the meeting. A few steps from the door, he looked over his shoulder. 'Elise?' Her name was a terse command.

She rose, aware of the speculative glances she drew.

Wordlessly, she followed him into his office, the door swinging shut behind them. The familiar-looking coffee cart stood beside the sofas. Alejandro strode to it and poured himself an espresso.

After taking a healthy gulp, he faced her.

'Are popularity contests your thing?' he enquired. His tone would have been cordial, but for the deadly bite threading it.

Elise frowned. 'What?'

'You walk into a room and instantly feel a burning need to make sure everyone *likes* you, is that it?'

A quiver of anger, and something else she couldn't define, shot through her. 'The only thing I'm sure of right now is that I have *no* clue what you're talking about. Wait, maybe I am sure of one thing. You definitely woke up on the wrong side of the bed.'

His mouth twisted. 'You're assuming I went to bed at all.'

'Well then, that's your problem right there. Grumpiness due to sleep deprivation is a common ailment. And I don't need you to fight my battles for me.'

'Excuse me?'

'I could've defended my findings to Wendell. You didn't need to lumber in.'

Green eyes narrowed. 'Watch it, Elise. You're in danger of forgetting who's boss.'

Another shiver passed through her, but it was in response to the sparks arcing through the air. And the fact that she wasn't shying away as she'd promised herself last night she would. In truth, the opposite seemed to be the case. Something inside her relished it. 'I haven't forgotten. But I appear to have done something specifically to annoy you between last night and right now. Something I have no clue about—'

'Unless I haven't been paying attention to my team, Wendell Grant hasn't lost the use of his limbs. Is there any reason you felt the need to fetch him coffee?'

Her snort escaped before she could stop it. 'You're annoyed about *that*?'

His brows clenched in a frown. 'I don't wish to set a precedent,' he snapped. 'Or breed an atmosphere of sexism at the workplace.'

Elise took a deep, bracing breath. 'So why didn't you just say that? Why go with the popularity angle? And yesterday it was about me *flirting* with Oliver.'

'You're making my point for me.'

'Am I? Or are you going out of your way to find fault with me because *you* have a problem with me?'

His jaw tightened. 'I assure you—'

'No. Let *me* assure you. I'm familiar with a work environment where it's believed that throwing your weight about and reminding those around you who's boss every minute of every day is the way forward. Both times you've bitten my head off, your employees have seemed surprised. Which tells me you don't normally do that. Your problem is with me specifically. So I'll explain myself in the hope we can start another day with a clean slate, shall I? I met Wendell on my way up. He told me he'd recommended you to use Jameson. We joked about what his reward would be. I got him the coffee as a *thank-you*. End of story.' Realising she'd delivered another diatribe, Elise heaved in a breath.

Alejandro stared at her for several beats without speaking. Eyes still fixed on her, he drained his espresso, set down the cup on his desk and prowled to where she stood.

'As I said…you want to be *liked*,' he taunted, her ramble clearly having had zero effect.

'Are you *serious*—?'

'So, what about me?' he inserted. 'Do you *like* me, Elise?'

'I… What?' She exhaled.

He shrugged, piercing green eyes examining her face in rapt detail before they locked on her mouth. 'Grant merely recommended you. There were two other candidates I could've gone for. I chose you. So, tell me? How will you thank *me*?'

Electricity stormed the air. Invisible sparks flew, crackling thick and volatile charges between them. Her mouth tingled, her throat growing dry as she tried to swallow and speak. The first few attempts, words failed her, her senses swimming as she tried to step back from the edge of the dangerous abyss that suddenly loomed before her.

She shook her head. The movement was jerky. Uncoordinated. 'I'm not falling for this,' she said, her voice a croak above a whisper.

'Falling for what, Elise?' he asked, his tone containing an unfamiliar pulse that sent more shivers chasing through her body.

'For whatever trap you're setting for me.'

'You're far too fixated on traps,' he drawled, his gaze still glued to her mouth.

'You're far too adept at laying them.'

'I'm waiting, Elise.'

She licked her lips. It was a quick lick, a desperate act to stop the insane tingling. But his eyes darkened dramatically, and he exhaled a breath that sounded pent-up. Aggravated.

What was happening—?

No. Whatever was happening here didn't require fathoming. She knew first-hand how quickly things could escalate from seemingly tranquil to potentially life-scarring. She'd been wary before Brian Grey had taught her a salutary lesson last year. But that incident had only tripled her efforts to stay away from emotional and sexual pitfalls.

Granted, Alejandro evoked an entirely different sort of apprehension from the sensations Brian Grey had produced in her. But they were all equally dangerous. Even more so this time, because her emotions weren't as non-receptive as they'd been with Brian.

The realisation troubled her enough to propel her one step back. Then another.

Do you like *me, Elise?*

This close, when his scent was sucking her into that sensual vortex, when his body was close enough to feel the heat pulsing off him, her senses screamed *yes*.

'I'm here to work, Mr Aguilar. There's nothing in my

contract that says I can't be *nice* to other people. So unless
you have another problem with me, or something specific
you wish me to work on, I'll be in my office.'

She turned and walked away, painfully aware of his gaze
tracking her every step.

Elise entered the room she'd used yesterday and stopped
in her tracks. The space had been transformed. A computer
had been set up, together with a phone, sleek stationery and
her own refreshment trolley. Two large ferns had been placed
at each end of the window, and a bouquet of fresh, expen-
sive-looking flowers stood on a pedestal beside her desk.

She looked over her shoulder to find him staring at her.
Elise's lips parted with the urge to say something, but, after
their terse exchange, appropriate words failed her.

Alejandro turned away from her and the moment passed.
Strolling with lean-hipped grace, he took a seat at his desk.

'Your brief today is to find me an in to Kenzo Ishikawa,'
he ordered.

Her eyes widened. 'You're going after the grandfather?'

He eyed her. 'Contrary to what you may think, I don't go
around annihilating every opponent who crosses my path,
Elise.'

She flushed. 'I'll see what I can do.'

'You'll do better than that. You insist on reminding me
of the terms of your contract, so let *me* remind *you* that your
contract holds as long as you remain useful to me. Find me
something I can use, or you'll cease to be useful.'

The warning gripped the back of her mind all morning
and afternoon, long after the video conference that proved
to be a colossal waste of time.

Ten minutes into the call, it was clear the Ishikawa brothers were merely spouting platitudes in order to buy themselves more time. She was surprised Alejandro went along
with it, giving them the further week they requested to iron
out what were clearly nonsensical minor issues.

Then he and the team spent the rest of the week digging
deeper into every aspect of the Ishikawa Corporation.

Elise felt a moment's unease when the words *hostile take-over* were thrown on the table. Alejandro's head lifted and he stared directly at her as he vetoed the idea. She wasn't sure why her heart tripped over. Nothing had changed between them. Their Tuesday morning conversation had set a precedent for their stilted relationship.

Each morning, Alejandro gave her a different brief. She clocked off late in the evening by presenting him with a carefully typed-out report.

He never invited her to dine with him in his private dining room. He never offered her a lift home.

She told herself she was glad about that. Very glad.

CHAPTER SIX

ALEJANDRO READ THE message on his phone for the fifth time as he stood before his window on Monday morning. For the umpteenth time, he wondered if he'd been right in contacting Gael in the first place. What had seemed like a sound idea—calling his brother to warn him he didn't intend to lose—in the early hours of Sunday morning coated his mouth with distaste a few short hours later.

He hadn't expected Gael's quick response, nor had he expected the request contained within his brother's email.

Gael wanted a meeting.

The stark request sounded more like an order. Clearly, his estranged brother hadn't lost his renowned arrogant swagger. As for the caveat that the meeting take no longer than fifteen minutes…

Pursing his lips, he dialled the number attached to the email. It was just after 6:30 a.m. on the east coast, which meant the middle of the night in California. With an unhealthy amount of relish, he pressed the phone to his ear.

It was answered on the fourth ring. 'Aguilar.'

His name on another's lips threatened an influx of memories. Memories that revolved around why his brother existed in the first place. Ruthlessly, he pushed them back.

'If I've disturbed your beauty sleep, just say the word and I'll call back at a more appropriate time,' he said.

He received a scoffing grunt in return. 'The only thing you've interrupted is a hearty breakfast, followed by a proper greeting of the woman currently warming my bed, both of which I intend to get back to in less than sixty seconds since I don't anticipate this call lasting any longer.'

'You make a habit of eating breakfast in the middle of the night?'

'The great thing about not having to answer to anyone is that I can do whatever the hell I want, when I want. But as it so happens, we're in the same time zone, *mi hermano*, so your concern about my digestive system is touching, but unwarranted.'

Alejandro gritted his teeth at the familial term, wondering why Gael insisted on taunting him with a past he was sure they both wanted to forget. He'd never bothered to confirm the rumours behind Gael also leaving his childhood home in Spain the moment he'd reached adulthood, but they'd involved their father.

And yet, Gael never missed the chance to remind him they were related.

Dismissing the baited response, he carried on. 'About this meeting tomorrow—'

'I'll stretch it to half an hour if you wish. But no longer than that. I have back-to-back meetings in New York in the afternoon that I need to fly straight back for.'

Alejandro's mouth twisted. 'A face-to-face meeting needn't take place at all if you see reason and back off. Now.'

Terse silence greeted him. He knew the line hadn't dropped because he could hear Gael's steady breathing.

'Need I remind you that *you* contacted *me*?' his brother eventually snapped, a throb of annoyance in his voice.

Alejandro started to shrug, then stopped at the futile action. Unbidden, Elise's voice sliced across his mind.

The looking-into-the-whites-of-their-eyes approach...

It annoyed him greatly that snippets of their conversation darted into his thoughts when he least expected it. Even greater was the despised thought that perhaps one of those snippets was what had fed his desire to contact Gael. A decision he regretted with each passing second. 'I was mistaken to think you would pay better attention if we were face to face. But that would be disrespecting you. You can hear me just as succinctly over the phone. This has gone on for long enough.'

'And it will keep going until I win the merger. I'll be at your offices tomorrow as scheduled. I advise you to be there.'

'You'll do well not to issue threats, Gael.'

'Or what? You'll up sticks and relocate again?' There was a gruff note in his brother's voice that made Alejandro's brow twinge in a brief frown.

'I have no intention of going anywhere. What I'll do is pull out all the stops to end this if you don't back off.'

Gael laughed. 'I look forward to hearing all about it when I arrive in Chicago tomorrow. And don't bother sending your jet for me. I have one of my own.'

Alejandro braced one hand on the window, welcoming the cold glass's fractional calming of his turbulent emotions. Slowly he breathed out. 'Gael, I don't wish to go to war with you.'

Another pulse of silence ensued. 'This only ends one way, brother. With one of us walking away. And I don't intend it to be me.'

Alejandro closed his eyes against the morning sun's glare. Behind him he heard the door open. He didn't need to turn around to know Elise had arrived, at precisely 6:45, as she'd done all last week. He also knew that he'd spend the day with his senses attuned to her every movement in her office, although his interactions with her would be clinically brief because those charged ten minutes last Tuesday morning had deeply unsettled him. To the point where he had still remained perplexed at his own behaviour hours later. To the point where he'd questioned his own sanity.

He'd almost kissed her.

Had almost dared her to kiss him in payment for obtaining her services. Even more deplorable, for those insane minutes, he hadn't cared about the potential damage he risked with his actions. Hadn't cared about the 'once bitten, twice shy' warning that had been the dogma of his professional relationships for a decade.

The need to taste her had been unrelenting. Consuming.

He remained disconcerted that just beneath the surface of his interactions with her, the need still fiercely burned.

'Do you wish me to repeat that in Spanish, *hermano*?' Gael's voice brought him back to earth. To the room. To the click of heels drawing closer.

'*Muy bien*, if this is the route you wish to take, then so be it.'

He ended the call and turned around.

Elise eyed him from her position before his desk. 'Good morning.'

He nodded tersely, then made a concerted effort to shake off the barrage of unwanted sensations evoked by his brother and Elise. '*Buenos días*. I trust you had a good weekend?'

Her eyes widened, no doubt because his cordial tone was unexpected. 'It was okay, nothing life-changing.'

'How unfortunate. Weekends that aren't life-changing ought to be stripped of their title and renamed Pointless Days.'

Her head tilted to one side. 'Is that your attempt at a joke, Alejandro?'

'Since you're not laughing, I must respond firmly in the negative,' he replied, his tone bone-dry.

Her mouth twitched, then she smiled. It was transformative enough to deliver a punch to his solar plexus, causing his breath to snag and the hairs on his arms to rise in near alarm.

Alejandro had dated women who could command the covers of fashion magazines with a snap of their fingers. And yet he was certain none of them could hold a candle to Elise's smile.

All the same, he shouldn't be this enthralled.

And yet…

'Are you okay?'

'Of course. Why should I not be?' he quipped.

Her smile dimmed. 'No reason. I just…overheard a little of your conversation. Something about not wishing to go to war?'

Any trace of mirth disappeared. 'Eavesdropping, Elise?'

'Not intentionally.' She glanced at his phone. 'Was that your brother?'

Her lack of fear when it came to him should've aggravated him. Sure, he tolerated the underlings who challenged him, but it was what he paid them to do.

Elise challenged him because she couldn't help herself. When she wasn't irritating him, Alejandro had found himself almost…refreshed by her.

But not right now.

'Yes,' he replied, paradoxically going against his better judgment of telling himself he owed her no answers.

A soft look entered her eyes. 'And?'

His mouth twisted. 'As predicted, he refuses to listen to reason.'

'So he's just like you, then?'

Alejandro stiffened. 'Excuse me?'

She shrugged. 'You're both determined to win.'

'You say that as if there's something wrong with winning.'

'What's wrong is you gripping that phone as if you're about to crush it. You want to win, yes, but I'm guessing not if it's costing you this much.'

He glanced down and visibly unclenched his fingers from the handset. 'You guess wrong. Pain and the cost of winning only affect you if you give them the power to,' he replied, then froze at the words that had left his lips without permission.

Elise's eyes rounded. 'Unless there's a mind trick you picked up along the way to dull it, no one is immune from pain.'

A note in her voice tweaked his flaring senses. 'When have you known pain?' he asked, then realised he was holding his breath for her answer.

Her gaze flicked away from him. 'I'm human. I feel pain.'

The thought that she'd been hurt shouldn't have abraded his equilibrium. And yet it did.

'You seek specifics from me, yet generalise about yourself.'

'I was just pointing out you're not the only one with issues, professionally or personally.' She jerked towards the
drinks trolley and picked up a bottle of water.

Alejandro frowned. 'You have a professional issue with
me?'

She looked up from toying with the lid. 'What? No. I
mean…I like to think our differences have been aired suc-
cessfully.'

The slow drag in his groin as his gaze landed on her lips
informed him his success in that department was distinctly
lacking.

'Then what do you mean?'

Nerves clearly fuelled her sudden twitchiness. 'I don't
want to talk about it.'

An answer that birthed further burning questions. 'Did
something happen to you?'

Her cheeks lost a little colour, but her face closed mu-
tinously. 'Nothing I want to reprise. What's on the agenda
today?' she hurriedly asked.

It took a huge dose of the willpower he was renowned for
to step back from demanding answers from her. Even then,
he needed a minute before he tracked properly.

'Since we're biding our time till our next call with the
Ishikawa brothers, I'd like your help on another matter. Are
you free this evening to accompany me to a client dinner?'

She blinked. 'Uh…yes.'

'Good. Reservations are for seven. Feel free to leave early
today if you need to. I'll pick you up from your apartment
just before seven.'

'Okay. Will the purpose of the dinner be damage limitation or image enhancement?'

'A little bit of both. I'm meeting a client and his wife for
dinner. She's taken to overt displays of affection whenever
I'm in her company. He's chosen to encourage it in the hope
that I'll do business with him. My patience is wearing thin
but I'd like to put a stop to both without jeopardising our
business relationship. You think you can handle that?'

Her relief at the changed subject turned to shock, but she rallied after a few seconds. 'Sure. Of course.'

Alejandro nodded briskly, despite his continued mental state of flux. He needed to emulate her, and regroup quickly. Gael's imminent arrival should be what commanded his entire focus, not the banked anguish still shadowing Elise's eyes.

Heading for his desk, he provided her with the client names and watched her walk away. The suit she wore today was feminine and stylish. Beneath the edge of her jacket, the trousers cradled her pert backside and emphasised her curvy hips. When she shed the jacket upon reaching her desk, he caught a glimpse of her trim waist and the full swell of her breasts.

A sound, rough and unwelcome, punched up from his throat.

She started to look his way.

He dragged his gaze away and focused on the pile of work on his desk. She was off limits. And even outside the scope of their professional relationship were he to consider her for an affair, he would still reject the idea.

Because Elise Jameson exhibited signs he'd hitherto not encountered in a woman before—she had the potential to get under his skin.

He reminded himself of that fact as his chauffeured limo pulled up to her apartment building that evening, an irritably large proportion of him anticipating her presence.

Her smile…

He shook himself free of the low sizzle in his stomach and stepped out. Seeing the unlatched main doors, a different type of irritation surged. He pressed her buzzer none too gently.

'I'll be right down.'

Since he wasn't sure whether the lift functioned with any efficiency tonight, he kept his attention between it and the stairs, flatly refusing to acknowledge the rising thrum in his blood.

Heels on the stairs alerted him to her mode of descent. She arrived at the top of the last flight of stairs and his heart rate increased.

She wasn't smiling.

In fact she appeared distinctly nervous.

Yet, she was captivatingly breathtaking.

Her chocolate-brown hair was swept to one side of her face and pinned at the back in a loose style that left several tresses falling free to caress her neck. Her knee-length dress, made of dark green material, skimmed her hips but hugged her breasts and left her shoulders bare. A simple necklace drew attention to her slim neck. In one hand she held a wrap and purse, her other hand clinging to the rail as she came down. He wasn't aware he'd moved until she paused on the stairs. Her gaze met his as she slid her hand into the one he held out.

'Thank you,' she murmured.

'*De nada.* Breaking your neck before the first course is served would be extremely bad form.'

A hint of a smile appeared. 'Wow. Two jokes in one day. Do we need to notify record keepers in some obscure office?'

He found his mouth curving. 'Best not. We wouldn't want to incite any unnatural disasters.'

A full-blown smile appeared. Something vibrated in the region of his chest. Keeping her hand in his, he led her to his car, choosing not to mention the state of her lobby security. Or lack thereof.

And if a part of him suddenly wished their dinner involved two less people, he brushed it away under the guise of it being a temporary aberration.

They arrived at Millennia, one of Chicago's most lauded restaurants, ahead of Jeff and Mindy Stoneley, for which Elise was just a tiny bit grateful. It gave her a chance to gather herself. To deliver a much-needed pep talk that involved *not* getting carried away with what was happening tonight.

This *wasn't* a date.

It was *business*.

She was doing work for which she was being *paid*.

PR work held many facets. Fact. When she was a newly employed member of Jameson, her parents had inundated her at all hours with absurd requests before she'd finally put her foot down.

'You're frowning. Is the venue not to your liking?'

'What? Oh, no. It's not that. This is great!' She noted the gushiness in her voice and dialled it down. 'I'm sure your clients will appreciate it.'

Alejandro's narrow-eyed speculation didn't abate. 'But something disturbed you just then.'

She tried to wave it away. 'I was just remembering some of the things I had to do when I started working at Jameson.'

'Are you referring to the incident you didn't wish to speak of before?' he asked, still narrow-eyed.

Her heart missed a beat, the thought that she'd nearly spilled her guts to Alejandro earlier today stabbing discomfort through her. Determinedly, she pushed it away. 'No. I meant something else,' she murmured, fervently hoping he'd let the matter drop.

'Something that doesn't compare favourably to this?'

'Are you kidding? Dining in a Michelin-starred restaurant beats getting up at two a.m. to go rescue a client's dog from the airport because our paparazzi-fleeing client had left it behind.'

He frowned. 'You're serious.'

'As frostbite.'

'Isn't that more of a minder's job?'

She shrugged. 'It is. I found out later.'

'How?' he asked.

Her mood dimmed further at the recollection. 'My parents were trying to teach me a lesson.'

'A lesson? Or punishment?' He cut through the excuse.

'Does it matter?'

'*Sí*. It does. And I'm guessing this wasn't a one-off event?'

She shook her head.

'Why did they do that?'

'They found out that I had graduated with two degrees, not one.'

'Surely that's a cause for celebration?'

Her heart lurched. 'You'd think so, wouldn't you?' she muttered. Realising they'd arrived at another subject she didn't relish probing too deeply, she cleared her throat, intending to steer him away from the testy issue of her parents, but Alejandro beat her to the punch.

'You only list one degree on your résumé.'

'Because it's the only one that's relevant to my present job.'

'Or it's the one that invites the least scrutiny?'

Her gaze rose from where she'd feigned interest in the place setting and met shrewd green eyes. 'You're digging, Alejandro. I may be tempted to dig back.'

'Will you be divulging anything that isn't already public knowledge?'

'No...but that's not what I meant.'

One shoulder lifted. 'You can tell me or I can unearth the truth myself.'

'Okay, it was an art degree.' Elise wasn't sure why admitting that stirred a deeply buried hurt. Probably because a once-precious dream had been desiccated while she'd been scrambling to be done with her current reality.

'Impressive. And do you use it—'

'There you are. Apologies for being late, *bello*! Please say you'll forgive me? The car service was atrocious. I'm never using that firm again. Oh... I didn't realise this would be a *foursome*.'

Alejandro rose, albeit with minimal enthusiasm, as Mindy Stoneley paused dramatically at the table, her wide grey eyes assessing Elise.

Behind her, her husband, a giant of a man with thinning hair and a face that leant towards excess, cracked out a forced laugh.

'Careful, Mindy. You might give the impression we live a risqué lifestyle.'

Mindy ignored him and held out both hands to Alejandro. When he bent towards her, she pressed her lips to his.

The sharp dart of disquiet that went through Elise held her in place for several paralysing heartbeats, only easing when Alejandro stepped back from Mindy's embrace.

'Jeff, Mindy, allow me to introduce you to Elise Jameson.'

Mindy sniffed, the skintight sequinned dress that stopped a good foot above her knees rising even further as she leaned over and offered her hand to Elise. 'And what exactly is your connection to *Alejandro*?'

Elise cringed at the forced eroticism of Alejandro's name. 'I'm afraid that's confidential. But I hope you don't mind me joining you tonight. I've been dying to try the food here and Alejandro kindly offered to bring me along.'

'The offer wasn't generated by kindness, *querida*,' Alejandro drawled, his gaze lingering suggestively on her as he sat back down.

Her pulse leapt wildly, despite the clear evidence that his words were only for show.

Mindy's gaze swung to Alejandro as she and Jeff took their seats across from them. 'Alejandro *is* generous like that, isn't he? He's personally opened so many doors for us. I don't know how on earth we'll ever be able to thank him.' Her hand found Alejandro's on the table, her 'gratitude' lingering a touch too long before Alejandro removed his own hand.

The knot in his jaw equalled that in Elise's throat. She looked up in relief as the head waiter approached.

The first course of Cajun fusion food arrived. Alejandro directed the conversation towards business as often as Mindy tried to direct it to the personal.

Jeff drank more and the atmosphere grew tense.

Cognisant of the extent of Alejandro's temper, Elise racked her brain for something to alleviate the tension. When Mindy invited Alejandro to come and inspect her newly built steam room for the third time, Elise shifted her seat closer and placed her hand on Alejandro's arm, his earlier statement lending her the bravery to risk the move.

Gleaming green eyes darted to her. Mindy stopped speaking. Jeff rushed in to fill the taut silence.

Elise leaned in, her mouth a whisper from his ear. 'I'm sorry. I'm doing my best to steer her away from you,' she murmured, 'but short of crawling into your lap and performing a lewd act on you, this is the only way I can think of to get her to back off. Do me a favour and pretend you're enjoying the sweet nothings I'm whispering in your ear?'

He didn't move. Or respond. Horror dredged through her, colour surging up her cheeks as seconds stretched.

Beneath her hold, his muscles flexed. Then he turned and aligned his face with hers. His breath washed over her neck as his neat stubble brushed her cheek. Strong fingers found hers on his arm, strangling her breath as he murmured, 'Crawling into my lap isn't the worst idea I've heard, but perhaps the timing isn't quite right for that. And these aren't sweet nothings. They're extremely useful *somethings* that could do the trick.'

Her breath caught. She started to move away. He held her still.

'No. Stay. And don't look now, *guapa*. You'll ruin the effect.' Slowly, his mouth drifted light kisses along her jaw to the corner of her mouth, then returned along the same trail to the pulse beating beneath her ear.

Elise, not having taken a breath in almost a minute, felt her heart hammering against her ribs as she held still and let him deliver his message. The drugging excitement that launched through her veins was a mere by-product of this act, she assured herself. Once Alejandro was done, sanity would be restored.

After an interminable age, where Mindy cleared her throat more than a few times, Alejandro finally pulled back.

'I didn't realise you two were a *thing*,' Mindy said after a brief moment of sullen silence.

Alejandro, his hand still locking hers into place, replied,

'We aren't just a *thing*, Mindy. We're exclusive.' He sent Elise a heat-filled glance.

The Stoneleys departed shortly after that. When Elise refused coffee, Alejandro requested the bill. Elise excused herself to visit the ladies' room and was returning when a shadow fell across her path.

'I see you're practising your moves on another chump.' The statement was delivered with a sinister laugh she'd hoped to never hear again. 'I'm surprised, though. I credited Aguilar with more sense.'

Ice filled her veins as her gaze snapped up to meet Brian Grey's. A part of her urged a swift retreat back into the ladies' room. Or a quick dive past the heavyset man back to the safety of the restaurant and Alejandro.

But she'd stood up to him once, had fought tooth and nail to prevent a life-altering assault. And though her insides shook alarmingly, Elise didn't back down.

'Your self-esteem must be at an all-time low if you're referring to yourself as a chump. Just proves money can't buy you everything, huh, Brian?'

Arctic-blue eyes that gleamed a little too brightly snapped pure hatred at her. 'I see you still haven't learnt your lesson. Maybe I should've put more effort into teaching it to you last year.'

Anger and pain fought for supremacy within her. Cold anger won. 'And I should've delivered *two* knee-to-groin responses instead of one?'

His face reddened. His shadow loomed larger as he reached for her.

Fighting panic, she stepped back. Into strong, solid arms.

'Everything okay, Elise?' Alejandro drawled.

Relief punched through her despite the latent danger she heard in his voice. Whirling, she looked up into his rigid face. 'Can we go now?'

He didn't answer. His gaze remained pinned on Brian, his eyes coldly assessing.

'Alejandro, please?'

His glance shifted to her. Elise knew her emotions were displayed clearly for him to see, but she just wanted to leave Brian's unpleasant presence.

After a beat, Alejandro nodded and settled his hand in the small of her back.

The walk through the restaurant and into the back of the limo was conducted in silence. As were the first ten minutes of the journey.

But tacit questions churned through the air. When he finally turned to her, her stomach dipped.

'Grey was the professional issue you spoke of.'

It was a question disguised as a statement. But she didn't want to answer. 'Please, can you let it be?'

'No.' He caught her chin between his fingers. 'Answer me, *por favor.*'

She grimaced at the politely couched command. When she shook her head, his face hardened. 'You can tell me or we can return to the restaurant and I can ask him myself.'

'Alejandro…' She stopped at the intractable expression on his face.

'Now, Elise.'

She sucked in a steadying breath. 'You mentioned him by name so you know who he is and what he does?'

He nodded. 'He runs nightclubs but recently added a clothes line to his business, is that correct?'

She nodded. 'Mostly lingerie. He contracted Jameson to help launch his lingerie line last year.'

He released her chin, but his gaze didn't waver from her face. 'And?'

'My father and I worked on the campaign for the first month. Then Brian requested that I take over. I didn't think anything of it.'

Alejandro's jaw clenched. 'Go on.'

She stopped when she realised they'd pulled up in front of her building. Alejandro noticed, too, and made a rough sound of impatience.

'We'll continue this inside,' he snapped.

The walk to her apartment was rushed and silent. He requested her keys and unlocked her door. 'Invite me in,' he muttered, his low voice tight.

Tension gripped Elise, but, because she didn't want to conduct the rest of the traumatic tale on her doorstep, she cleared her throat and stepped into her apartment. 'Come in.'

He followed, kicking the door shut.

Her one-bedroom apartment was compact, decorated with whatever money she could spare after rent and loan payments. The living room held a single faux-velvet sofa, matching armchair and floor rugs. The pale walls were brightened with cheap landscapes, and floor and table lamps softened the starkness of the battered cabinet on which perched her TV and MP3 player.

Alejandro didn't spare the room a single glance. His gaze remained fixed on her, tweaking her already frazzled nerves.

'Would you…umm…like a drink?'

'No.' He came forward, took her wrap and purse from her nerveless fingers. 'Sit down, Elise.'

He was ordering her around in her own home. Part of her wanted to stomp on his autocracy. A greater part wanted this over with.

She sat. He shrugged off his coat, draped it over the armchair, leaving on the bespoke dinner suit. She dragged her gaze from his intrinsically masculine form as he sat down next to her. 'Finish.'

A knot twisted inside her as unpleasant memories flooded her. 'He wanted to hold the launch at one of his nightclubs. I went there to take pictures for the press packets. He suggested I'd get a better sense of his style if I tried on some of his lingerie. I refused.'

She ventured a glance at Alejandro.

His face was a rigid mask of fury. 'And?'

'He…insisted.'

'How?' he rasped.

Elise shivered. 'He…restrained me. Said he wouldn't let me leave until I gave him what he wanted.'

Alejandro surged to his feet. *'Madre de Dios!'* He paced her living room in a tight circle, one hand slashing through his hair. Mid-pace, he jolted to a stop. 'Did he...?'

Elise shook her head. 'I... It didn't get that far.'

'Did you report him to the authorities?' he jerked out.

Pain lanced her. 'Yes. But he wasn't charged.'

Darkness clouded his eyes. 'Why the *hell* not?'

'He had cameras in his nightclub, but he knew how to position himself so his actions seemed benign. And the parts where I fought back were out of shot. Also...' She stopped.

'What?'

'He *encouraged* my parents it would be in Jameson's interest if they convinced me to drop the allegations.'

'Your parents? And did they?'

'They didn't have to. The case fell apart on its own.'

'Dios mio,' he breathed.

Elise had no idea tears had slipped free until he sat back down and cradled her face in his hands.

His thumbs dried her tears as he regarded her. 'You're strong and intelligent. You will *not* let this damage you,' he declared.

She sniffed. 'Aren't we all damaged in some way?'

A solemn look entered his eyes. *'Sí,* we are. But yours shouldn't centre on this. The bastard shouldn't even cross your thoughts, never mind reduce you to tears.'

She blinked rapidly, unwilling to show how his words affected her. 'I told you I didn't want to talk about it,' she murmured.

A hint of regret washed over his face. *'Lo siento,* but you intrigue me in many ways, Elise. I couldn't help myself.'

She didn't have a response for that because his expression was changing, morphing from anger into something equally powerful. Something that caused her breath to shorten, then hitch in her throat.

His hand slid to her nape.

'Elise.' Her name was a deep intonation that drew a shudder from her.

She met his fiery green gaze. Her mouth parted on a needy little whimper. His eyes latched on her lips and the air thickened with sensual promise.

He was going to kiss her. She wasn't going to stop him. Because...because...

Reason dissolved into mist the moment his mouth seared hers. Firm, chiselled and lush. His kiss went from exploratory to demanding in a flash. He groaned when her head fell back and she let him in.

One hand captured her waist, pulled her in closer, until she was plastered against him.

The elevated beat of his heart echoed against her chest.

Elise squirmed as she drowned in the power and magic of Alejandro's kiss. She wriggled closer, moaning when his tongue stroked hers with an urgent expertise that arrowed pleasure straight between her thighs. Growing more desperate by the minute for an unattainable pleasure, she slipped her hands beneath his jacket. His warm cotton-covered flesh was hers to explore.

And explore she did, until the need for air forced them apart.

Alejandro stared down at her with drugged, fierce eyes. '*Dios*, you taste incredible.'

Another blush, hotter and faster, surged into her cheeks.

He laughed low and deep, passing his thumbs over her cheeks. 'And you blush like an innocent. A seriously lethal innocent.'

Before she could respond, he was kissing her again, bearing her back on the seat. She gave herself over, happily swapping unwanted memories in favour of *this*. Kissing Alejandro brought no pain. Touching him filled her with excitement. Joy.

Her hands slid up to his broad shoulders. His hair. Spiking her fingers through it, she let out a little cry as his hand cupped her breast. Somewhere along the line, her dress had shifted, her strapless bra exposed to his clever fingers. Alejandro's mouth left hers, and she stared, dazed and engrossed, as he slowly moved back one lace cup to expose a budded pink nipple.

Her breath strangled as he caught the peak between his fingers. Need arrowed straight to the apex of her thighs. Then he lowered his head and, eyes riveted on hers, took her nipple in his mouth.

Sensation exploded through her, arching her in a tight bow, and feeding him more of herself.

Alejandro uttered a pained groan as he suckled her. One hand slid beneath her to hold her to his rapt attention, while the other wandered feverishly down her body. His fingers trailed fire over her bare thighs as his mouth drifted across the slope of one breast to capture the peak of the other.

Desire throbbed at her core, drowning her in rabid need.

From one frantic heartbeat to the next, his fingers slipped beneath her panties to graze her damp flesh.

Elise cried out, a fever like she'd never known flooding her.

'*Dios mio, bella dama*, you intoxicate me.'

One finger breached her core. Elise tensed, a different sensation racing down her spine. She wanted to block it out, but the flashing sign in her brain wouldn't let her.

...*you blush like an innocent*...

Except she wasn't *like* one. Her virginity was something she'd guarded with almost zealous care before the incident with Brian. Not because she was hung up on giving it to the right man, but because it was the one thing, besides her art, that affirmed to her that she was nothing like her parents. After Brian, she was even more wary about her sexuality. She would never succumb to casual pleasures.

Not even with the most charismatic man she'd ever met.

She pushed at his shoulders. 'No. Stop!' When he stared at her with a puzzled frown, she shook her head. 'I can't do this.'

His eyes slowly cleared. When his fingers left her core and he sat back in the seat, Elise bit her lip to stop from protesting.

'*Sí*, I know. I'm breaking my own rules.'

He believed she'd called a halt because of her contract with SNV.

Elise shakily exhaled. 'You misunderstand. I wouldn't sleep with you even without your rules. This shouldn't have happened. And it won't happen again…ever.'

Every last trace of lust left his face and with each passing second, a greater part of her mourned. He stood, shoved his hands deep in his pockets and stared down at her as she scrambled up and righted her clothes.

'Explain.'

'Do I need to? You caught me at a low moment—'

Tension clamped his frame. '*Perdón?* Are you suggesting I took advantage of you?' His voice was clipped with ice. 'If so, let me remind you that you were with me every step of the way, *guapa*.'

A hint of shame slammed her. 'I think it's time we brought the evening to an end. I've gone above and beyond my duties for one day, I believe.'

'If this is a taster of what your *duties* could be, perhaps we should renegotiate your contract. I'm sure we can agree to a mutually benefitting addendum.'

She gasped, ice dredging through her insides. 'You didn't just say that to me.'

His eyes gleamed, an unfathomable emotion flickering in his eyes. 'We're laying our cards on the table. I want you. I believe the feeling is mutual. We can wait until the merger is over. Or we can agree to terms now.'

'I don't want to agree to any further terms with you. And I'm sorry if your ego doesn't like hearing no from a nobody like me.'

Impossibly, he stiffened further. 'You wouldn't be making the mistake of likening me to that bastard, would you, Elise?' he murmured with deathly calm.

The smooth lethality of it froze her vocal cords for a few seconds too long. His face lost a shade of colour and his jaw clenched tight.

'Alejandro, I'm—'

'Save your breath. You can deny it all you want, but you took as much as you gave tonight. And you knew the precise moment to call a halt to achieve maximum effect.' His mouth twisted in a cruel smile. 'That skill has to come from somewhere, right?'

She hadn't thought hearing the words she'd dreaded most and had heard whispered about her would hurt coming from Alejandro. But it stung deeper than it ever had.

She rose, willing her legs not to give way, and walked to the door. Turning the handle, she threw it open. 'And here I thought you were enlightened enough to realise that sometimes the apple *does* fall far from the tree. How disappointing. I'm glad I could be of extra-curricular service to you tonight. Do me a favour and let's keep things strictly business from now on, shall we?'

He didn't deign to utter a response. Cold eyes raked her from head to toe. Then he strode out with arrogant indifference.

Elise slammed the door hard. And even before she turned the key, she was cursing the hot scald of tears choking her.

CHAPTER SEVEN

ELISE SLEPT THROUGH her alarm and woke up at seven-thirty. The ominous start to the day thankfully didn't earn her Alejandro's scorn because he wasn't in the office when she hurried in just after quarter past eight. She breathed a sigh of relief when Margo informed her he would be out of the office all morning.

She got on with putting finishing touches to the work she'd left unfinished yesterday. As she recalled the unfortunate end to the evening, her heart dipped with disappointment and hurt.

Enough! Knowing she would always be in some way tarred with the same brush when it came to her parents, she'd learned to toughen up at an early age. Alejandro had merely lucked out and cornered her in a weak moment after coercing her to spill her guts about Brian.

Nothing more.

When the words continued to echo hollowly at the back of her mind, Elise decided to use her free time for the head-clearing run she hadn't managed that morning. She struck out for nearby Millennium Park, the exertion and the light April breeze doing an effective job of clearing her tension and lending a little perspective.

Last night, she'd got carried away. She'd glimpsed sympathy that had been sorely lacking on all fronts following Brian's assault and had grasped it with both hands. Then she'd followed it by falling into a web of sexual attraction while ignoring the accompanying pitfalls.

But she had put on the brakes. There was nothing to feel guilty about. If anything, Alejandro's attitude was what should be causing her grief. And yet, all through the night of tossing and turning, that fleeting expression on his face

had haunted her. Continued to haunt her. For a single moment, just before he'd accused her of comparing him to
Brian, she'd glimpsed a sharp pain, felt an alignment of her
own hurt. As much as she wanted to dismiss it, the notion
wouldn't die. Nor could she deny his sympathy and comfort
had been genuine.

But afterwards…

Was she attributing more humanity to him than was warranted? Accepting her thoughts were going around in futile
circles, she completed her run, performed her stretches, and
returned to SNV.

She walked through the doors and was crossing the foyer
to the drink fountain when she saw Alejandro.

Except it wasn't Alejandro.

The hair, stature and innate confidence that were imprinted on him were almost identical. But apart from the
visual confirmation when the man turned from calling for
the lift, her stomach didn't quite dive and clench the same
way it did in Alejandro's presence.

This was Alejandro's brother. The resemblance was un-
canny. All the way down to his lifted eyebrow when he realised he was the object of scrutiny.

Her very blatant scrutiny.

A very male, very confident smile curved his lips as he
abandoned the lift and sauntered towards her. His return
scrutiny didn't make her skin prickle the way Alejandro's
did, but nevertheless Elise grew conscious of the cling of
Lycra and sheen of sweat coating her skin.

'A beautiful woman who shows dedication in taking care
of herself is a sexy thing to behold.'

His voice, so much like Alejandro's, but also so different, made her smile emerge a little weaker than usual. 'You
don't know me from a lamp post, so what makes you think
I'm in any way dedicated? For all you know this could be
the start of a very late New Year's resolution.'

His gaze drifted from her head to the tips of her trainers and back again. 'Then I commend you for the excellent, decidedly non-lamp-post-like framework you're building on.' His words held the same Spanish intonation that curled around Alejandro's.

Laughter bubbled up, easy and unexpected, providing a touch of relief from her roiling thoughts. 'I'm not sure whether to thank you for the compliment or roll my eyes at that smooth line.'

'Gael Aguilar.' He held out his hand. 'And you wound me.'

She shook his hand. 'You're Alejandro's brother,' she confirmed.

A shadow crossed Gael's features. 'For my sins, yes.'

A sixth sense warned her his words were meant literally. The lift arrived and she stepped into the small space beside him. She couldn't help but notice with every floor that passed, his tension escalated.

This brother wasn't anticipating an amicable meeting.

And with Alejandro, was there any other kind?

Elise cleared her throat. 'I hope you can sort things out with the Japanese deal.'

His eyes hardened for a moment, before he smiled. 'That outcome would depend entirely on my brother.'

She frowned.

'You look shocked. What has my brother been telling you about me?'

'Nothing, save that he expects the same thing from you.'

A smile, icy but tinged with a hint of bleakness, tweaked his lips. 'What can I say? We're not known for giving quarter,' he rasped.

The doors opened and they stepped into the hallway. 'It was—'

'Elise!'

They both turned at the thunderous summons. Heat and ice invaded her body, both bringing equally painful awareness, as Alejandro's incandescent gaze slashed over her, dashed to his brother, and then remained fixed on Gael.

* * *

Alejandro had never experienced possessiveness about anyone or anything in his life. Sure, he was attached to the success he'd worked hard for, but he possessed nothing in life that would cause him physical pain to part with. He'd learned at a very early age that affection or material things given one day could be taken away the next with no rhyme or reason. Every occurrence in his life as a child had revolved around whether his mother had decided to be happy, or whether she was locked into playing the wronged wife, visiting her misery and pain on everyone around her. And that had solely depended on whether his father was in the mood to reprise his role of philanderer or not.

Everything in his life had been coated with a transience that had forced him to create a bubble around himself. Because if he get didn't attached in the first place, he wouldn't feel the loss. The logic was absurdly simple.

But for some reason, right from the very beginning, he'd detested the interest Elise garnered from every single person she came into contact with. Acknowledging the curious problem privately to himself hadn't seen it diminish. Getting a taste of her last night and then being forced to walk away, after realising just how transient *she* was, had done something to him. He couldn't place his finger on what it was, save for the knowledge that she'd stirred something so powerful and turbulent within him, he hadn't been able to concentrate worth a damn all day.

Seeing her standing next to his brother, Gael's barely disguised interest in her visible even across the space between them, Alejandro wanted to breach the distance, claim her by branding his name on the skin she didn't have any qualms about exposing, in the most blatant way possible. That bubble of self-denial he'd existed in was gone, leaving a stone labelled *Need* in his gut, which seemed to grow heavier with each second.

Dios. This was beyond unacceptable.

'Did you want something, Alejandro?' Elise said, her chin lifted in challenge.

'Other than to request that you be at your desk where you're *supposed* to be?'

Her eyes darkened, her gaze flickering to Gael with a touch of embarrassment. A second later, her lips pursed. 'Sorry, my bad. I thought the shackles attached to my desk were for decorative purposes only. Let me change out of my running gear and I'll get back on the workhorse.'

He caught Gael's low chuckle, but he couldn't look at his brother. Not when the sight of Elise approaching ripped his senses wide open with voracious hunger, reminding him of her scent, her responsiveness beneath his touch.

He dragged his gaze from her hips, forced his scrutiny up past her luscious breasts, her slender neck, to her face, and locked his knees to remain upright.

Every day since her first day at SNV, she'd arrived fully but impeccably made-up. Today, her face held the barest hint of artificial colour. Her skin glowed with a natural beauty, her eyes even more vivid without the added frills.

Gael had seen her like this first...

Irrational, primitive jealousy threatened to shame him, but it was shoved aside by other emotions rippling through him.

Emotions that involved his brother.

His eyes finally shifted to Gael. Lingered against his will. A tug pulled at him deep inside. In the decade since they'd last seen each other, his brother had grown in resemblance to the man Alejandro himself saw every day when he looked in the mirror.

A carbon copy of their father. The man who'd betrayed his family over and over again.

He admitted to himself that the resemblance made it hard for him to look at Gael. Alejandro also admitted it might have contributed to him leaving California all those years ago. Acceptance of that flaw made him swallow. And wish he'd never sent that email suggesting a meeting.

'I'm here, Andro,' Gael stated when they were six feet

from each other. 'Are we going to waste the day imitating a Mexican standoff or are you going to make me an offer I can't refuse?'

Alejandro thrust his clenched fists into his pockets, willing his gaze not to stray to Elise as she walked past and headed for the changing room. When the door swung shut behind her, he narrowed his eyes at his brother. 'We'll take the meeting in my office. And don't call me that.'

Gael's lips pursed as he fell into step beside him. 'Still as touchy as ever, I see. It's surprising you've managed to pull off a few impressive deals over the years while wearing your emotions on your sleeve.'

Alejandro slammed his office door and faced Gael. 'What the hell are you talking about?' he snapped.

'It's obvious you have a thing for that gorgeous creature out there, and don't bother denying it. For a second there, you looked ready to drop kick me. I'm guessing the rumours about you being a shark in the boardroom are false, then?' Gael taunted.

Alejandro forced his shoulders to relax. Going to the drinks cabinet, he poured two shots of single malt whisky and held one out to Gael. His brother accepted his with one raised eyebrow, but didn't drink it.

Alejandro downed his in one go, memories of last night almost pushing him into slamming the glass down. 'There's nothing going on between Elise and I. She's here to do a specific job. Once her usefulness is expended, she'll be duly compensated and disposed of. End of story.'

Gael gave a low whistle as he strolled confidently to the window. 'Consider my concerns about your softness revised.' He appreciated the view for a long minute, then turned. 'I don't intend to back down on the Japanese deal. Toredo needs this deal—'

'Your company specialises in offering streaming media and cloud-based services. It's not an e-commerce outfit like mine *or* Ishikawa Corp. There are a dozen companies you can merge with that better suit your business—'

'But none with a similar foothold in Asia,' Gael countered. 'This has the potential to be the perfect merger for me to combine e-commerce with streaming media.' He shrugged. 'I'm yet to be convinced there's a downside to it.'

Alejandro pursed his lips. 'I'll repeat what I said to you yesterday.' The bite of further frustration made him slash a hand through his hair, uncaring whether the sign made him appear anything other than in total control. 'There will be other deals. I'll help you secure the next one, if you need it. Walk away from this one.'

Gael's lips curled and his fingers tightened around the glass. 'I haven't asked for or needed your aid for a long time, not since I came to you for help in finding my mother when I was thirteen and you turned me down flat.'

Another tug in his chest, this time one he recognised as guilt, made him tense, even while his frustration grew. 'You accuse me of being soft, and yet you can't seem to let go of the past. I didn't want to get involved in your mess then, and I want to even less now.'

Gael's jaw clenched. 'You knew where she was, Andro. Despite our father lying through his teeth that he wasn't with her, you knew they were shacked up in that godforsaken apartment he kept on the side for his mistresses. For three weeks, I had to live with not knowing whether she was alive or dead.'

Alejandro's face stiffened, his whole body numb as he held himself rigidly in the present. 'You found her in the end, did you not?' he bit out.

'No thanks to you. You made it clear then that I was nothing to you. That you didn't even want the whiff of this bastard brother anywhere near you. I got the message loud and clear.'

Alejandro gritted his teeth. 'Regardless of what your imagination conjured up, I had my hands full with other matters.' Like keeping his mother from going off the deep end when she realised once again that her husband's promises of fidelity meant nothing.

Gael's mouth twisted as he set the glass down without

drinking the whisky. '*Si*, ensuring your popularity as the school's soccer star was firmly in place so you could continue dating the hottest girls was much more important than helping me out when I needed it. If your best offer is to tell me to walk away, then this meeting has been a colossal waste of my time.' He flicked a glance at his watch. 'I guess I'll be on my way. Thanks for the drink.'

Quick strides saw him at the door before Alejandro exhaled. 'What will it take?'

Gael froze. '*Que?*'

'For you to drop this deal. What will it take?'

His brother's hazel eyes turned a dark, dangerous green. 'We're blood, Andro. There's no bribe on earth that will remove that fact. And no amount of money that will appease my need to see you lose. Just once. *Hasta luego*,' he threw in sarcastically, before the door slammed behind him.

Alejandro braced his hands on top of the desk, his chest expanding and contracting for a full minute, before he dropped into his chair.

He'd expected it to go better. And of all the reminders of Gael he'd wanted to avoid, the reference to those hellish weeks was at the top of his list. Because that was the time when he'd finally accepted his father was beyond redemption. That his mother cared more about steeping herself in the frenzied, dysfunctional state of her marriage than she did about her son.

Bitterness, awakened and rancid, dredged through him. His fist curled on top of the file on his desk as he fought it back down. He wasn't sure how long he stayed that way, his gaze turned inward in memory.

The sound of the door opening and shutting, followed by the click of heels, finally dragged him from his unwanted musings.

She'd changed into a dress. Some sort of grey wool blend, high-necked thing that ended just above her knee and left her slender arms exposed. On her wrist a delicate bracelet drew his attention to her soft skin. He'd touched that skin last night. Tasted it.

Still hungered for it.

Reining in his unwanted craving, he watched her cross to her office. Alejandro found himself upright and following her before he'd fully computed the move. She was leaning over her desk, stretching for a file when he reached the doorway. Leaning against the frame, he questioned for the umpteenth time what it was about her that drove this unchecked compulsion within him.

She turned, and jumped. 'Uh… I didn't see you there.' She thrust the file she held at him. 'This is what I was working on this morning. I wouldn't like you to think I was idling away the time while you were out of the office.'

He took the file. 'I owe you an apology. Last night…I shouldn't have reacted quite so—'

'Ogre-tastically?'

Despite himself, a smile attempted to lift his mood. 'I was going to say "unprofessionally". My apologies.'

Her strikingly long lashes swept down for a moment. 'And I would've been better advised to keep things from getting too…personal.'

The reminder that there was something he needed to do had him striding forward to her desk to press the intercom.

'Sir?'

'Draft a memo to the marketing department. I want all contracts with Brian Grey's company terminated immediately.'

Elise gasped.

'Umm…yes, sir.'

He hung up. She stared at him, her parted lips trembling for a second before her gaze dropped. 'I don't need you to fight my battles for me, Alejandro.'

'And yet, it is done,' he stated, the rage that burned in his gut threatening to erupt all over again. His emotions when he'd left Elise last night had skittered close to the edge. Returning to the restaurant to confront the bastard had been high on his list but he accepted that satisfaction from violence would be fleeting. But *this*…this was a good start. And he intended to pay the piece of scum back in many varied ways. As for what she'd said about her parents… His gut clenched harder. Parents were a subject he wasn't yet willing to touch.

Her stunning eyes rose to his once more. 'I…don't know what to say.'

'Then let's move on.'

She nodded after a moment. 'How did things go with your brother?'

His laugh was a touch self-deprecating. 'As badly as I suspected they would.'

She smoothed back her fringe, a nervous tic of hers he'd noticed. 'I'm guessing from that tight-jawed look you're wearing that you couldn't find any middle ground?'

'You sound disappointed, *guapa*. Perhaps you expect too much for a first meeting in ten years.'

Her eyes widened. 'That's how long it's been since you saw each other?'

Alejandro felt that twinge again. 'Yes.'

'Why?'

'He reminded me of a past I wanted to leave behind.'

'*Reminded?* As in the past tense?'

He frowned, caught off guard by the slip. Shaking his head, he changed the subject. 'Did you find me anything I can use?'

A look, almost of disappointment, crossed her face. 'Nothing that would aid your war, but there's something else. Before you use it though, can I just suggest that SNV and Toredo could be different arms of the same company? Is a three-way merger out of the question?'

'It's low on my list of ideal outcomes.'

Her gaze dropped, her smile as tight as her nod.

He traced her face for a minute, noting that, apart from lip gloss, she hadn't applied any more make-up when she'd changed. He curbed the urge to trace his fingers over her skin as he had last night.

She'd made her feelings more than clear. She wasn't interested in blurring the professional lines of their relationship. And he needed to relocate his little black book.

Opening the file, he speed-read through the half-dozen pages and paused when he reached the most interesting morsel of information. 'Grandma to the rescue again?'

A light blush washed her cheeks. 'I didn't see the harm in tapping a useful source.'

He closed the file. 'I'll take it under advisement. The conference call with the Ishikawas is in fifteen minutes. I want you there.' Not that he held out much hope that it'd be any more progressive than the last one.

Gael had drawn battle lines and he would be going all out to sink his claws deeper into the deal.

As expected, Alejandro was met with platitudes and empty promises. He played along for half an hour, then changed tactics.

'How is your grandfather?'

Jason and Nathan Ishikawa exchanged quick glances. 'He's very well. Thank you for asking.'

Alejandro nodded, ignoring the fact that Jason's gaze slid once again to Elise. 'Send him my congratulations on his upcoming seventy-fifth birthday celebrations.'

Nathan cleared his throat. 'We will.' Alejandro waited. The brothers exchanged another glance. 'Until next time, then, Mr Aguilar. *Sayōnara.*' They bowed their heads.

'I look forward to meeting him when I'm in Kyoto soon.'

'You're coming to Japan?' Jason asked.

Alejandro smiled. 'Yours isn't the only deal I'm interested in. I'll have my PA liaise with yours about dates. *Buenos días.*'

He disconnected the call to apprehensive faces.

'I didn't know you had other business interests in Kyoto,' Elise said.

'I don't, but I will by the end of the day. Specifically with Kenzo Ishikawa. Is your passport up to date?'

She frowned. 'Yes, it is. Why?'

'It's time to put your theory to the test. We leave for Kyoto tomorrow morning.'

Elise recognised the luxury town car the moment she stepped out of the similar car Alejandro had sent her home in. They'd worked late into the evening, then he'd spent an hour grilling her on Japanese custom. She was exhausted, but in a good way.

But she'd yet to pack for the trip to Japan and Alejandro was picking her up at 7:00 a.m.

Seeing her mother's lithe, seven-days-a-week-at-the-gym honed body unfold from the back of the car caused her stomach to dip.

And not in a good way.

'You're ignoring my phone calls again.' Marsha Jameson couldn't be accused of beating about the bush. She was dressed to kill in top-to-toe designer clothes and accessories, and not a hair or eyelash deigned to be out of place.

Elise sighed, her grip tightening on her briefcase. 'I'm not. I've been swamped all day. I texted you back to say so.'

Her mother sniffed. 'You know how I feel about texts. If I wanted a text conversation with you, I would've initiated one.'

'I intended to call you when I got home.'

Marsha eyed the apartment block with mild distaste. 'Well, I'm here now.'

Elise raised her eyebrows. 'Would you like to come in?' she invited, torn as to whether she wanted the answer to be yes or no.

'For a minute. I have a pressing engagement in forty-five minutes.'

Ironically, the lifts were downstairs and waiting when they walked in. Elise stepped in, conscious of her mother's gaze, which held its usual disdain as it drifted over her. 'Really, Elise. That grey does nothing for you. And why aren't you wearing any make-up?'

'I am.' She refused to continue applying the unnecessary amount of make-up her mother had insisted she wear in the workplace.

Her mother's eyes narrowed on her face. Thankfully, before she could respond, the lift arrived.

Elise led the way to her door, praying the visit would be quick. But when her mother refused a drink, that pang of hurt made itself very much known.

She sat down on her two-seater while her mother perched on the armchair across from her. Her Realtor had described her apartment as *cute*. Elise knew her parents would have other, far more unsavoury, terms for it.

'I spoke to your grandmother today.'

Elise's stomach dipped further. This house call wasn't about business. 'Right.'

'She told me about the help she's been giving you.'

'Is that a problem?'

'That my mother is helping my daughter do her job? Of course not.' She sniffed. 'I just wanted to make sure you understood that if any help she provides you with doesn't reap the results the client wants, *you're* the one who'll be held responsible.'

Her heart twisted on a fresh wave of pain. 'You don't need to spell it out to me, Mom.'

Hazel-gold eyes the same shade as hers snapped irritation. 'Before you act affronted, I also wanted to say I hope it works out for what you need for SNV.'

Elise's mouth parted in surprise, but her mother wasn't finished. 'I was also alerted by the travel department that you'd requested details of your travel insurance.'

Her mouth snapped shut, the real reason for her mother's visit slowly unfurling. 'Yes. I'm accompanying Al—Mr Aguilar to Kyoto tomorrow.'

The flash of interest in her mother's eyes mildly sickened Elise. 'I thought so. This is excellent news. He obviously thinks very highly of you.'

'Obviously.'

Marsha's gaze hardened. 'Watch your tone, young lady.'

'Prove to me that you didn't drive all the way downtown to dispense the *motherly* advice I think is coming my way, and I will.'

Her mother stared at her for a moment before she shook her head. 'I don't understand you. You've had so many opportunities *handed* to you. And every single time you've turned your nose up at it.'

'Say what you came to say, Mom. Or prove me wrong.'

Her mother's jaw tightened. 'What is so wrong with telling you to make the most of *this* opportunity?'

Pain pierced her. 'The same way you pushed Brian Grey's "opportunity" on me?'

'Don't be ridiculous. That was different.'

'*How*, Mom? How was it different?' she demanded.

'For starters, Alejandro Aguilar is one of the world's most eligible bachelors. He already sees you as a worthy businesswoman, thanks to your association with Jameson. Capitalise on that and you could become one of the most powerful and iconic women in the world. Of course, I would recommend a trip to a stylist and more care with your hair, but these things can be achieved with a single phone call. Think of what that could mean for Jameson PR. Think of what it could mean for you!'

Blind, foolish tears rushed into Elise's eyes. 'Stop, Mom. Please, just stop.'

'Why? Where's the harm—'

'The *harm* is that I'm not *that* kind of woman! I won't sleep with a man just to get ahead. Alejandro already suspects I'm tarred with the famous Jameson brush!'

Fury surged into her mother's face. But Elise wasn't afraid. Marsha Jameson's fury was the quiet, lethal type. She wasn't prone to ranting or raving. She merely exuded icy rage until the other party deigned to grovel in apology.

But Elise wasn't in the mood to apologise. That need had diminished significantly over the years. Which was not to say the pain that ravaged her insides had abated one iota. In direct contrast to her mother's silent condemnation, her pain howled, long and vicious and deep.

So deep, she barely acknowledged her mother's icy exit.

Elise only rose when she realised her front door had been left wide open. Evidently, Marsha Jameson's anger had no room to accommodate thoughts of her daughter's safety.

After locking the door, Elise went into her bedroom and pulled out her suitcase. The effort not to succumb to tears for the second night in a row nearly failed as she packed. She'd shed enough tears, thanks to fate's decision over her parentage. She was in grave danger of becoming pathetic.

Straightening her spine, she glanced down at the contents of her suitcase. Seeing the greys and blacks tucked inside, she firmed her lips, determinedly zipped the case shut, and tugged it to the front door.

On impulse she pulled out an old, slightly battered flat case. Then immediately swallowed a sob. Adding it to her suitcase, she showered and went to bed. When a tear slipped free, she reassured herself it was for the dream she'd pushed to the back of her life.

A dream that perhaps wouldn't remain a dream for long.

CHAPTER EIGHT

THE RIDE TO Midway International Airport at what felt like the crack of dawn was non-eventful. Unlike the thumping of her heart as the limo Alejandro had sent for her stopped alongside a huge gleaming white private jet with the SNV logo displayed discreetly on the tail.

'Mr Aguilar's already on board, ma'am. Your luggage will be taken care of.' The impeccably uniformed driver doffed his cap after he helped her out.

As she crossed the Tarmac and mounted the steps, her mother's words filtered, unbidden, into her mind. Alejandro indeed commanded a powerful top step on the world stage. Thus far, she'd only experienced him in the environs of his company and very briefly at a dinner that only lasted a few hours.

The swiftness with which he'd secured an audience with Kenzo Ishikawa and started a different set of balls rolling in Kyoto had amazed her yesterday. Stepping into the plane and seeing Alejandro seated at a large conference table, a pile of documents at his elbow, while the crew buzzed around in preparation for the flight, she was suddenly struck by the sheer power he wielded.

Power her mother wanted Elise to whore herself to achieve a slice of.

The brightness of the morning dimmed as despair and desolation threatened to sink deeper into her.

'The quicker you find a seat, the quicker we can take off, Elise.'

She started at the deep drawl. Unwilling to admit what the tenor of that tone did to her see-sawing emotions, she smiled at a crew member who passed her, and made her way across the shockingly spacious midsection to where Alejandro sat. 'Good morning to you, too.'

He lifted a mocking brow at her, and indicated the seat opposite him. '*Buenos días.* If that sour look is because of the early hour, rest assured, you won't be required to work the whole thirteen hours of the flight. There are bedrooms on board. Take a nap, if you feel so inclined.'

Elise shook her head. 'I don't need a nap,' she replied, then promptly yawned.

He sent her a speaking glance. '*Sí*, you're fresh as the proverbial daisy.'

'I slept badly. So sue me.'

He frowned. 'Litigation won't be necessary. We've all suffered sleepless nights at one point or other.'

'I didn't meant that literally—oh, never mind.'

Tossing his pen onto the table, he sat back and observed her for a full minute before, raising a hand, he summoned an attendant and ordered coffee to be delivered after take-off.

'I'm surprised I didn't realise this before,' he murmured. 'Realise what?'

'You're not a morning person,' he supplied.

Her attempt at a laugh emerged more like a snort. 'Compared to what your idea of morning is, *no one* is a morning person.'

He pressed his fingers into a steeple against his lips, the silky-haired forearms bared by his rolled sleeves flexing in the morning light.

Studiously, Elise averted her gaze from that shockingly sexy display of brawn as the doors were locked and the plane taxied to the runway. She might have condemned her mother for her deplorable suggestions last night, but it didn't mean her insane attraction for Alejandro had dimmed. In fact, his less formal dress and slightly dishevelled hair only added to his intense appeal.

Once they reached cruising altitude, the attendant arrived with a platter of coffee, bagels and croissants. Seizing at the excuse to occupy herself, she grabbed a bagel, then poured and sugared her coffee, before passing Alejandro a cup of espresso.

'*Gracias.*'

When she'd devoured half of the bagel, she glanced at his documents. 'So what do you need me to do?'

'I meant what I said. You don't need to work during the flight.'

She frowned. 'I'm supposed to twiddle my thumbs for thirteen hours?'

'I'm attempting to be less…ogre-tastic, Elise. Take advantage of it.'

The words were too similar to those she'd heard a few short hours ago. As absurd as it was, they struck a chord of disquiet. She didn't want to take advantage of anything or anyone. 'I'd rather not,' she bit out.

'Why do I get the feeling I've misstepped?'

A quick investigative glance showed his incisive gaze on her. Elise shook her head, hoping to dispel his interest, but he carried on looking at her.

'It's not important. Seriously,' she stressed when his eyes narrowed.

After a moment he nodded, and returned his attention to his documents. A full hour passed before she lost the battle to stay still. With nothing for her to do but leaf through mindless magazines, her attention continued to stray to Alejandro. The pen he twirled through his fingers became a source of fascination. As did the drift of his fingers down the surface of his tablet.

Enough already.

Looking around, she smiled at the attendant who caught her eye. When he started towards her, she rose from her seat.

And gasped when Alejandro's hand closed over her wrist. 'Need something?'

She attempted to speak, despite the heat travelling up her arm. 'I…yes. I'm not sure how the luggage thing works on private jets. I'm wondering whether I can get access to my stuff. No problem if not…'

Without letting go of her, Alejandro rose to tower over her. 'Your things were stowed in one of the bedrooms. I'll show you.' A jerk of his head dismissed the attendant. Heading to the back of the plane, he indicated a short flight of stairs.

She'd erred on the side of not too casual but with travel comfort in mind when she chose the navy flared skirt and white short-sleeved shirt she was wearing. But now as she went up the stairs she wondered whether her skirt was too short, her shirt a little too clingy.

Hating herself for letting her mother's views seep into her confidence, she headed towards the single door at the top level and opened it. The bedroom was larger than her apartment's, with a king-size bed draped in cotton sheets and a blood-red coverlet. On the opposite wall, a high-tech entertainment and drinks centre stood beneath a wide-screen TV, with a dove-grey velvet-covered chaise longue set against one wall. Next to the chaise, she spotted an open closet where her suitcase and art bag had been stashed next to another set of suitcases.

The space was undoubtedly designed for relaxation, but it was the *sort* of relaxation that had Elise's breath snagging in her chest and her pulse racing at a frenetic pace.

She heard the door shut behind her and turned. 'I'll just grab my stuff and go back down.'

He walked towards her, his pace predatorily graceful in a way that made her want to watch him for a very long time. 'Why?' he asked, as if her question was absurd in the extreme.

'I get the feeling… Is this your bedroom?' she blurted.

'*Sí*. It's the quietest place on the airplane, thanks to great soundproofing. You won't be disturbed here.'

But *he* was disturbing her with his scent, his body and the banked heat emanating from his eyes.

'I really just want to grab one thing—'

'You have shadows under your eyes, Elise. Shadows that weren't there last night despite the events of the past couple of days. I need you on top of your game by the time we land. So rest. I insist.' He went to the bed and pulled down the covers. Grasping one pillow, he fluffed it.

The sight of his manly bronze fingers against the white sheet was so shockingly erotic, Elise felt a clenching between her thighs. Locking her knees, she held her breath as he strolled back to her. His forefinger traced the skin beneath her eyes for several heartbeats before he dropped his hand.

'There's a buzzer next to the bed that summons an attendant. Use it when you wake up if you need anything. Lunch will be delivered to you if you wish, or you can come downstairs.'

'Okay. Thanks.'

He was gone in quick, silent strides. The breath expelled from her lungs in a rush, her heart hammering as if she'd run a marathon.

Walking to the chaise, she sat and dragged a hand down her face. Heaven help her, whatever this fevered sensation was that came over her whenever Alejandro was near, she needed to find a solution to it, and quickly, before she made a fool of herself. Or worse, confirmed his 'like mother, like daughter' indictment.

The thought sent a cold shiver through her, dispelling a little of the hot tingles shooting through her body.

Rising, she went to the closet and picked up the extra bag she'd packed last night.

She hadn't touched her art supplies in years. Elise wasn't exactly sure why she'd packed it, or why she imagined she'd find solace in her art now when her every attempt in the last few years had felt forced and stilted. But ever since divulging the existence of her art degree to Alejandro, she'd felt a growing need to revisit her discarded dream. To see if, *this* time, it would speak to her.

Kicking off her shoes, she settled on the bed and set up the collapsible easel before her.

Her heart leapt into her throat as she scrolled through the pages of her sketchbook, revisiting abandoned stories. What if she could never reclaim this lifeline? Her manga creations were what had sustained her through her teenage years. Would they sustain her now? She turned the pages back and read through old sketches, trying to pull herself back into the story.

Half an hour later, her fingers were still poised over a blank sheet. A thread of fear feathered her nape. Had she lost her muse for ever?

Elise forced herself to breathe. Eyes shut, she traced the pencil over the blank sheet. She knew the subject of her sketch the moment her fingers began to move.

Almost trancelike, she sketched Alejandro's profile. Proud and regal, the image of him staring out of his office window at the view of Lake Michigan felt so real, her fingers trembled as she traced the fine lines, lingering with almost sinful delight over the curve of his lips. He was out of bounds to her for many reasons. But there was no reason she couldn't have this.

Except *this* was a dangerous pastime, one she couldn't afford to indulge in unless she wanted to invite a whole new set of problems for herself. She finished Alejandro's sketch and returned to her manga story. The first image appeared within minutes.

Relief punched through her as the next image unfolded, followed by another.

Elise worked until her muscles grew stiff and her eyes began to droop. Setting aside the papers and easel with a deep sense of awe and accomplishment, she released the clip from her hair, and slid down into the comfortable bed. The ironic thought that the man she was so desperate to keep her guard up around was the same one who'd turned out to be her creative muse was the last she had as the hum of the plane lulled her into a floating sleep.

Only to be awaked by a wildly jarring movement.

Blinking, she sat up. The shades on the windows had been pulled halfway down, and a soft lamp turned low, leaving the room in a golden glow.

In the chaise, Alejandro sat nursing a cognac.

'Uh…hi,' she murmured.

Intense eyes drifted to her as he took a sip. 'I left the light on so you wouldn't think I'm sitting here in the dark watching you sleep like some sort of creep,' he drawled.

His presence was inducing a myriad of feelings, but creepiness wasn't one of them.

She licked her lower lip and surreptitiously smoothed her hair. 'How long have I been asleep?'

'Five hours. I imagine you would've slept for longer had we not flown into turbulence. The pilot tells me it'll go on for a while. I thought you might appreciate a friendly face in case you're a timid flyer,' he mocked gently.

Her gaze darted to the windows, although there wasn't much to see. She shrugged. 'I'm the no-point-in-panicking-until-there's-something-to-*really*-panic-about type of flyer.'

He smiled into his drink. 'How fatalistic of you.' Rising, he crossed to the bar and poured a mineral water. Elise tried to avert her gaze as he headed for her, but her eyes refused to cooperate. Breathless once more, she watched him advance with a lithe, powerful prowl.

As he held out the water the plane bounced again, spilling it onto her outstretched hand. Alejandro placed the glass on the bedside table, grabbed a tissue and dabbed drops from her hand, his eyes on her face the whole time.

'Not as many shadows. I trust you slept better than you did last night?'

The deep timbre of his voice vibrated through her. 'Yes. Thanks for offering me your bed.'

Nice, Elise. Fighting not to cringe or blush, she started to reach for the water.

The plane bounced again.

Glancing at the distance between the top of Alejandro's head and the low ceiling, she smirked. 'Maybe you should sit down before your head makes a hole in the ceiling and you doom us all?'

His mouth twitched as he perched at the foot of the bed. 'You seem in a better mood, too.' His gaze flicked to the zipped-up portfolio case that held her drawings. 'Does this have something to do with it?'

She tensed slightly, unable to stem the ingrained wariness about her art. When his eyes reflected nothing but genuine interest, she nodded. 'It hasn't for a while but it helped today, yes.'

He nodded, his gaze resting speculatively on the case. When it flicked back to her, her heart tripped.

'Are you going to make me beg to see them, Elise?' he murmured.

Her fingers toyed with a corner of the sheet, her nerves jumping in time to the turbulence. 'I don't know...maybe?'

Eyes gleaming with intent traced her face before reconnecting with hers. '*Por favor.* I would be honoured to see your art.'

She grimaced. 'Damn. You don't play fair.'

A ghost of a smile curved his mouth. 'No. I don't.'

She reached for the case to extract her sketchbook, an absurd part of her acknowledging she would be totally crushed if he didn't like it. Calling herself all kinds of a fool, she held it out to him.

Alejandro opened it. Surprise flickered in his eyes, then both eyebrows gradually spiked with each page he perused. Finally, when she didn't think she would be able to stand the tension, he raised his head. '*Que están más allá de magnifica,*' he rasped.

'Translation, please,' she whispered.

'Magnificent.'

Pleasure shot through her, her smile powered by a thousand bulbs of happiness. 'Thank you.'

He stared at her for a beat before returning his attention to the pages. 'This is what you intend to do when you're done with Jameson?'

'It's what I've wanted to do for a long time, but...'

'But?'

'I was afraid I'd lost...something. My work has felt stilted for a long time now.'

He regarded her steadily. 'You had other things on your mind.'

Slowly she nodded. 'Yes.'

Deft fingers leafed through the pages with escalating speed. 'And your parents have a problem with *this*?'

Her fist knotted on the sheet. 'My parents have a problem with most things I do. Or more accurately, what I *don't*—' She bit her tongue to stop words she didn't want to spill.

His head lifted from the pages, green eyes narrowed. 'What do they want?'

She shook her head. 'I'd prefer not to—'

'Your talent is undeniable. So tell me why they'd choose not to support you,' he pressed.

'Do your parents support you in everything you do?'

His face froze, a darkly forbidding look blanketing his features. 'We're not talking about me.'

'Answer my question and I'll answer yours.'

For a long minute, she thought he wouldn't respond. 'I haven't sought my parents' approval and they haven't been in a position to give it because I haven't spoken to them in almost fifteen years,' he clipped out. 'Now you.'

Elise closed the mouth that had dropped open and tried to stem the rising dread. 'I don't like talking about them.'

His jaw tensed for a second. 'Because I erroneously likened you to them?'

The plane jarred her stomach into free fall for a second but her gaze didn't leave his face. 'Maybe. You have me as your captive audience at thirty-four thousand feet. Tell me what you'd have said differently.'

'I wouldn't have thrown your parents' reputation in your face, for a start. I, more than anyone, should know that genetically we're formed from their blueprints, but we're not the sum total of our parents' beliefs and actions.'

A sudden lump in her throat made it hard to breathe or speak. She tried anyway. 'I... Thanks.' She swallowed. Then realised he was waiting for more. 'They think I'm not making the most of my...assets.'

He tensed. 'Your assets,' he breathed.

'You want to know why I smile at everyone I meet?'

His eyes gleamed dangerously. 'Not particularly, but go on.'

'Because at seventeen, my mother told me that *not* smiling would make me more mysterious and attractive to men. That I would have them falling at my feet if I maintained a certain…aloofness. I've been getting advice like that since I hit puberty. After what happened with Brian, I wondered for a while if they'd been right.' She laughed bitterly. 'I even wondered whether I'd invited the assault.'

He captured her nape so fast, her breath stalled. *'You did not,'* he said through clenched teeth. 'That was all him. Never think otherwise.'

She nodded jerkily, her chest tightening with the intensity of him.

After a moment, he relaxed and released her. Lounging back on the bed, he regarded her. 'So you decided to smile because you didn't wish to have men falling at your feet?'

She grimaced. 'That sounds ludicrous, I know. They can fall all they want. I'd just prefer they wait two seconds and engage my intellect before they decide I'm worth falling for. Besides, all those potentially falling bodies to navigate? If I wanted that, I'd have trained as a stuntwoman.'

His low laugh dispelled the knot in her midriff, and promptly replaced it with a glow. 'That would be a sight to behold.'

She smiled. 'Thankfully, you'll never have to see it. I'm not built for that profession, either.'

His gaze lingered for a heartbeat, before raking down her body. 'At the risk of being called a chauvinist, I won't divulge my thoughts on what you're built for.'

She pressed her lips together to stop herself from demanding he tell her. Because the heat swirling in his eyes wasn't dangerous enough!

But he looked down. Started to turn the page.

'Wait!' Elise lunged forward.

His breath audibly caught.

The plane lurched, throwing her into an awkward sprawl

next to him. He caught and steadied her with one hand, his other holding the page open. The page that held his image. Silence, thick and heavy, hung in the room.

Elise tried to move. He held her still, his gaze rising to hers.

'This is how you see me?' he rasped after an interminable age. His voice was completely devoid of emotion, depriving her of any insight as to how he felt about the drawing.

She swallowed hard. 'I... Yes.'

Unreadable eyes dropped to the image again, prompting hers to follow. 'I look...'

'Angry. Sad. Lonely. Invincible.'

'*Dios.* Why did you draw it?' he demanded roughly.

'I don't know.'

'Yes, you do. Why?' he pressed.

'I couldn't concentrate...because you were on my mind?'

'Is that a question? Either I was or I wasn't.'

She was aware she was skirting that edge of danger she'd craved mere minutes ago. Her blood thrummed wildly in her ears. 'You were. Very much.'

He roughly shoved the case aside and pulled her fully into his body.

His fingers speared into her hair, his grip firm as he leaned down and stared, narrow-eyed, at her.

'You know why I'm angry.'

'The deal. Your brother. Yes.'

His nostrils flared. 'I'm not sad.'

'Maybe not right this minute.'

He made a rough sound of disagreement. 'I'm *not* lonely,' he rasped.

Her heart lurched, because the evidence to the contrary was right there in his voice. 'Okay.'

'My invincibility would be debated by some.'

'But only if they're blind?'

He shrugged. His head dropped another fraction. 'This picture... You see too much, Elise. I don't like it.'

'You see me, too, when you want to, but you don't see me throwing a tantrum about it.'

His eyes darkened. The fingers in her hair shifted, caressed. *'Madre de Dios.'*

Desire dripped into her veins, commencing a slow languor that held her captive and yearning.

She needed to pull back, retreat to her side of the bed. Or better still, out of the room completely. 'Alejandro…'

'Shut up. I've had quite enough words from you for now.'

His mouth slanted over hers, mastered her, showed her the depth of feeling moving through him. She didn't need words to know her drawing had affected him. The way he kissed, with hunger and a little anger, need and a touch of gentleness, told its own story.

Drugging enough to make her momentarily excuse herself from what shouldn't be happening; she explored him with the same hunger. Beneath her fingers, his warm muscles shifted, the hair at his nape curled into her touch, his whole body shuddering when her nails dug in.

'Elise.'

He lifted his head for a moment and she glimpsed the powerful hunger stamped on his face. It was enough to remind her that she was playing with fire. That she was stoking an inferno she might not be able to survive if it flamed much higher.

Before she could attempt to push him away, he was kissing her again, bearing her back so she was flat on the bed.

One hand traced her jaw, then stroked down to linger at the pulse beating at her throat. When he was satisfied she was sufficiently fired up, he trailed lower, and cupped one breast.

Elise moaned at the expert kneading, the clever teasing of her nipple. Liquid sensation sparked through her, singeing her between the legs until she was twisting beneath him. He uttered something guttural in Spanish, intensely erotic.

The plane lurched, separating them for a second.

They stared at each other. Awareness slowly crawled back. They'd been here before.

And yet here she was, thousands of feet in the air, on the edge of being initiated into an exclusive club with a man who would sign her paycheque when her business with him was over and walk away without a backward glance.

He started to lower his head.

She pulled away. 'No.'

He exhaled harshly. 'We've been here before. I misjudged you then. I'm not doing it now.'

She forced her hands to drop from his shoulders. 'Thank you, but nothing has changed. I can't do this.' Her lips were stiff, as if they didn't want to speak the words.

A frown formed. 'I've spent more than two seconds with you. I've engaged your intelligence.'

'So now you're ready to fall at my feet?' she parried.

His features slid into neutral. 'I don't fall, Elise. Ever.'

Something jarred hard and cold inside her. 'And I don't sleep with people I work with.'

'Who *do* you sleep with?' he queried tersely.

'Not that it's any of your business, but I haven't. Ever.'

One mocking eyebrow lifted. 'You expect me to believe you're a virgin?'

Heat stormed up her face in evidence before she could utter a word. Something akin to shock paled his face.

'Elise—'

'I'm not having this conversation with you. Believe what you will, but do it while you're not lying on top of me.'

He released her immediately, his movements jerky as he retreated.

She averted her gaze from him, slid off the bed, stood, and attempted to straighten her embarrassingly wrinkled clothes.

They both startled when the intercom buzzed and the pilot announced they would be free of the turbulence in a few minutes.

Elise almost snorted. The turbulence in her life had taken the form of a powerful and enigmatic man whose compulsive power drew her inexorably in as every instinct screamed for her to run in the other direction. She might have succeeded in stopping her emotions from unravelling completely a few moments ago, but Elise feared she wouldn't be as strong should any further turmoil be hurled her way.

Until she could finish her job and walk away, her only option was to distance herself as much as possible from Alejandro.

CHAPTER NINE

Of course that was easier said than done.

From the moment they landed, she found herself in the very close and personal position of being Alejandro's interpreter.

In between a whirlwind tour of Kyoto with her, he shamelessly courted Ishikawa Corporation's rivals.

He accepted a meeting with the Ishikawa brothers two days after landing, which he then cancelled at the last minute with profuse apologies.

'You're taunting them,' Elise observed as they stood beneath one of hundreds of red arches that lined the pathway to Fushimi Inari-taisha Shrine. They'd paused halfway on the two-hour trek to the top, and, beneath them, Kyoto glistened resplendently in the evening light.

Elise breathed in deep, her heart lifting with a serenity she hadn't felt for a long time.

Each morning since their arrival three days ago, Alejandro had instructed her to pick a place to visit. Their first visit had been to the Kiyomizu-dera temple close to where her grandmother lived. Her grandmother might have been absent but she'd arranged a private visit of the holy temple renowned for bestowing good fortune and love. As they'd strolled through the hallowed room, Elise had told herself the latter hadn't been why she'd chosen the temple as her first port of call. Her heart had twanged with disbelief, but she'd shoved the feeling aside. Alejandro had strolled beside her with ease, pointing out scrolls he needed translating, then looking at her with blatant heat as she read them out to him in Japanese, then translated.

In those moments, she'd asked herself whether she was taking her reticence a little too far. Whether she wasn't risking throwing away a spell of ecstasy for a lifetime of the unknown.

She glanced at him now as he traced his fingers down the scrolls on the arch. He turned, and one of the incisive gazes he'd taken to levelling on her since their turbulent and very eye-opening conversation on the plane bore into her.

She'd told herself she preferred things this way—looks without touching or any hint of the emotional and physical intimacy they'd shared on the plane. But slowly those feelings were changing.

'Giving them a taste of their own medicine,' Alejandro responded to her question.

She walked from one scroll to the next, her breath catching when he followed. 'You know your brother's here in Kyoto. What if they decide to go with him?'

He shrugged. 'Then I would've lost.'

Elise frowned. 'After all the effort you put in?'

A distant look entered his eyes. 'This is a battle I never wished to be drawn into in the first place. Winning at all costs may appear romantic on the big screen, but I've never been a fan of pyrrhic victories.'

She gazed up at him. 'What about compromises? Are you a fan of those?'

Narrowed green eyes speared hers. 'Explain.'

'Have you thought about sitting down with your brother and hashing this out?'

His mouth firmed. 'It won't work.'

'Why not? Because you tried before?'

'No.'

'Alejandro—'

'Leave it alone, Elise.'

Her gaze dropped for a second. 'You both want the same thing. Has it occurred to you that you can have it if you relent a little bit?'

His jaw clenched. 'I don't do well with family. I never have. I never will.'

She knew she ought to let it go, but the words poured out

nevertheless. 'You didn't do well *in the past*. But now you've met Gael again—'

'For a handful of minutes in my office.'

'Bite my head off if you want, but I've seen you two together. You can salvage this if you would just—'

'*Basta!* Enough.' He linked his hand through hers and started up the slope of the shrine. Elise fell silent, partly because their surroundings were too beautiful to spoil with an argument. And partly because she liked him holding her hand. A little too much.

Later that afternoon, he stood looking out onto the lotus-flowered landscape beyond the window.

The resort was situated north of Kyoto, built beside a meandering river and extending from a central villa said to have once been the private residence of an emperor. Its natural beauty was stunning and the contemporary design blended with traditional floor-level seats and indigenous decorations.

But she didn't see any of that beauty now, her attention absorbed wholly by Alejandro.

He sensed her behind him and turned. Her heart lurched at the contemplative look on his face.

'About our earlier conversation. I don't know why you think you know enough about me to present these opinions,' he drawled, his tone gruff. 'But let me give you a brief background about us before you think playing happy families is in any way an option for us.'

'I didn't say that—'

'Gael is a product of an affair my father had with his mother when I was three years old. When I was old enough, I found out there'd been affairs before I was born, and my father had no intention of stopping after I came along. But Gael's mother was the most…turbulent of all, probably because she was the only woman who managed to convince my father to leave my mother. And he did. For a short time, at least. He went to play happy families with Gael's mother. Gael was born, and then suddenly my father was back home. My mother hated herself for taking him back. To her, his previous affairs had been meaningless and easily overlooked.

'But it was different with Gael's mother. Perversely, she felt as if he'd broken her trust. They fought day and night. You know what it's like living with a parent who falls apart every time my father is five minutes late coming home? You know how many times she dragged me from my bed and into the car so she could go in search of him to make sure he wasn't in another woman's bed? Gael's mother did that to my family.' He turned from the window, prowling across the floor until he stood before her. 'Do you think, coming from *that*, that there can be any peace between us?'

'I'm sure Gael didn't exactly escape unscathed, either.'

'I *know*,' he breathed, shaking his head. 'But when you're caught in this…*powder keg*, rationality goes out of the window.'

Let it go, Elise. Your own family situation is far from a bundle of laughs. Let it—

'That was then, Alejandro. What about now?'

He shook his head. 'It's too late.'

'I don't think so.'

His expression underwent a subtle transformation. Elise was willing to bet he didn't know how vulnerable he'd looked for just a second before his features hardened. 'Don't presume to know how to fix me, Elise.'

'I wouldn't dare. I'm only stating the obvious. I can shut up if you want me to?'

He stared at her, narrow-eyed, for a second. 'I don't want you to shut up. But this subject bores me. So change it, if you please.'

She grimaced. 'Well, we've done the tourist thing, the business thing. We've made a mockery of family. What shall we do next?'

His gaze dropped to her mouth, but he didn't speak. He didn't need to. The look on his face told its own unfolding story, morphing from chillingly forbidding to stark raving hunger.

One hand snagged her waist. The heat in his eyes was back, full force. 'Sex, Elise. Let's do sex. And don't give me the excuse about our working relationship or you not wanting me. We can make this work. The day after we first kissed, you walked back into my office and carried on working even though my behaviour was less than exemplary. You didn't throw a tantrum or give me the cold shoulder like most women I know would've done. I have no doubt that whatever happens between us in the bedroom, it will not get in the way of your job.'

She tried to speak past the sudden clamouring of her senses. Tried to *think*. 'Wow. I sound like a robot.'

His mouth quirked, but his gaze didn't lose one ounce of intensity. 'If you were, you'd be the sexiest one ever created.'

Laughter barked from her, which he joined in with for a few seconds, before the sexual gravity of the moment rendered them both silent.

'I want you, Elise. You might not wish to reciprocate the statement right now, but let's agree to table it for discussion after Kenzo Ishikawa's birthday party tomorrow, *si*?'

The past few days had been leading to this. Somewhere along the line, she'd decided to take the chance. But now he was laying out terms so starkly, her senses shrieked a primal warning. 'Alejandro, I don't know...'

'Come on now, we've tried to pretend this isn't happening, but it is. You can't keep running from it and I don't intend to fail the challenge and pleasure of getting you into my bed. You have twenty-four hours to yield to me. And, Elise?'

'Yes?' she murmured despite her spinning thoughts.

'I don't intend to lose this one.'

A hard kiss preceded his exit.

Elise dropped into the chair, her stunned senses trying to grapple with what had just happened.

Alejandro had dropped a giant morsel of his past in her lap. Then segued into a demand for sex. She stared at the door through which he'd disappeared. Was the instigation of the subject of sex a way to distract her from his emotional revelations?

If so, it'd worked a treat.

Skirting past the momentous subject of sex with Alejandro, she replayed his childhood story instead.

She'd thought her childhood had been horrendous with the early realisation that her parents had what amounted to an open marriage, their vows shoved into the background in the interest of accumulating financial gain. For the greater part, Elise had been handed over to the care of nannies and housekeepers while her parents pursued their single-minded interests. It hadn't been until she hit puberty that things had changed for the worse.

Alejandro's experiences had been worse, because the infidelity had come from one side, with pain heaped on his mother while he'd been caught in the middle.

. She might not have heard Gael's side, or know the full story, but what little she knew explained the brief glimpses of bleakness and loneliness she sometimes saw in Alejandro's eyes.

Her heart squeezed in sympathy and despite telling herself that softening her feelings for him might be a dangerous path to take, she still found herself mourning long into the evening and into the night for the harrowing childhood he must have suffered.

As for the subject of sex, she continued to push it to the back of her mind whenever it sparked its heady temptation. She knew not confronting it wouldn't make it go away—she'd seen a determined Alejandro in action, after all—but all the same, she held it at bay, in the hope that morning would bring the clarity she needed.

CHAPTER TEN

SHE WAS STILL set on resisting him.

Alejandro knew this from the small frown knotting her brow. She wouldn't succeed. Having Elise Jameson in his bed had swept beyond a lustful, persistent want, into a primeval need. One he didn't intend to deny himself.

The subject of her virginity—if it was true—unsettled him somewhat. Then again, everything about Elise was turning out to be uncharted territory for him.

She got under his skin in the most disturbing way, but not enough for him to step back from the clamouring desire raging through his blood. Perhaps, once he'd had her, she would cease to have this peculiar power over him.

He *would* have her.

But for now he had other matters to deal with.

'My grandmother received your flowers,' Elise said. Her frown momentarily disappeared, a hint of the smile that toyed with his breathing when in full bloom curving her lightly glossed lips. 'She called when I was getting dressed. She wanted to thank you. She says to tell you they're the most beautiful flowers she's ever received.'

His own mouth curved. 'She was the perfect absent hostess and she ensured our invitation to Kenzo Ishikawa's birthday party. It was the least I could do.'

Her smile widened. 'She did say you owe her big, though. And that she might call in her chips when you least expect it.'

'I look forwarding to meeting her one day. She sounds formidable.'

Pride propelled her nod. 'She's one of the strongest people I know. She's the product of a Pearl Harbour love story that almost didn't happen.' Her smile slipped a little. 'Her childhood was rough. When it was her turn to become a mother, she tried to shield my mother as much as possible. She believes she overcompensated by spoiling my mother, which is why...' She shook her head and stopped.

Alejandro reached for her hand. It was an unfamiliar offer of comfort, and yet it felt right. 'You reminded me that the apple sometimes *does* fall far enough from the tree to seek its own roots and light. Your mother may have been spoilt as a child, but I doubt the grandmother who encouraged you to follow your dreams also encouraged your mother to take the particular path she's taken. I bet they disagree on a few things?'

'They disagree on everything! They fought constantly about the way she was bringing me up. My grandmother couldn't bear it any longer, which is why she moved back to Hawaii. Surprisingly, they have a better relationship now they're thousands of miles apart.'

'Distance provides clarity. Sometimes.'

She eyed him, and Alejandro knew what was coming. 'Did it do that for you?' she asked.

Surprisingly, her question didn't grate on him. Although the chafing layer of disquiet closely resembling guilt and regret that had manifested when Gael visited him in his office intensified.

He shifted in his seat. 'It taught me that I never wanted to be in that situation. I've seen the wedding pictures. I've heard the stories of how they met. My parents married believing they were happy. For some reason, that changed very soon afterwards. They took pleasure in hurting one another until they were locked so fully into their macabre roles they couldn't see anything or anyone else, not even their son. I knew very early, I wanted nothing to do with that level of emotional turbulence.'

She looked pensive. 'True compatibility in any relationship is hard to find, I know, but just because that happened to them doesn't mean it'll happen to you.'

'It didn't just happen to me. It happened to Gael. It happened to his mother. It happened to everyone my parents came into contact with. The Aguilar brain may be good for business, but there's no heart there to sustain meaningful relationships. I accepted that a long time ago.'

Her eyes shadowed, her face losing colour.

'What's wrong?' he asked.

She averted her face sharply towards the window. 'Nothing. I'm fine.'

Alejandro let it go, but he wondered if his declaration had been too harsh.

But the truth often was. Realising his parents had no room in their life for him had hurt for a long time. Time and distance had dulled the pain. Increasingly fleeting liaisons, which proved he wasn't built for relationships, had only confirmed his suspicions.

He was more than content to accept the status quo.

Except the regret continues to chafe...

The hand within his grip moved. He gripped it tighter. As he stared down at their entwined hands something moved through him. Something numinous that had nothing to do with the electric heat of their touching palms.

The emotion further unsettled him. So much so, when the limo driving them to Ishikawa's party drew to a stop at the top of a small hill, relief poured through him. Alighting, he took a deep, sustaining gulp of the cool evening air.

All around cherry blossoms flowered in pinks, reds and whites. Spring in Kyoto was breathtaking. But nothing surpassed the beauty of the woman who stepped out beside him a second later.

His gaze moved over her, quiet satisfaction eroding some of the tumult.

He'd called in a stylist when she'd asked for time off to go shopping. Her clear embarrassment and distress had made him probe deeper, which had led to the discovery that she hadn't packed adequately due to a visit from her mother.

She hadn't needed to go into great detail for him to know

her mother was the reason she'd boarded his plane with shadows under her eyes. Those shadows were gone now. He paused to appreciate her feminine form in a red gown that bared her shoulders and warmed her complexion, the lightly made-up face and elegantly styled hair.

Alejandro decided then and there that he would encourage her to wear more red. Especially in bed. Drawing back from anticipatory carnal pleasures before he succumbed to the urge to hustle her back into the car and to their hotel room, he offered his arm.

She readily accepted it, a fact that pleased him greatly.

Kenzo Ishikawa's birthday party was being held in a converted Japanese temple on the grounds of the Ishikawa private estate. The structure was a replica of the world-renowned Golden Pavilion, and, like its namesake, golden light poured from wide windows and spilled onto the man-made lake surrounding the structure.

Alejandro escorted Elise across a wooden bridge and they were met with barefooted geishas, serving champagne and canapés. He handed her a glass and took one for himself, but Alejandro wasn't interested in drinking.

He spotted his brother from across the room and acknowledged Gael's stiff greeting with one of his own. Then a well-dressed old man with a walking stick heading their way drew his attention.

Setting his glass down, he held out his hand. 'Mr Ishikawa-san, thank you for inviting us to your party,' Alejandro said. 'Allow me to introduce you—'

'No introduction needed, Mr Aguilar. Elise's grandmother is a good friend of mine, and is quite adept at twisting my arm when it suits her,' Kenzo replied dryly, his shrewd eyes lingering on Elise for a moment before returning to Alejandro.

'We're honoured to be here,' Elise replied, her smile warm as she gave a small bow. She handed over the oblong ribbon-tied present. 'A gift from my grandmother.'

The old man's snowy brows lifted. 'More gifts? I received yours this afternoon, Mr Aguilar. Along with your note.'

Alejandro nodded. 'Twenty minutes of your time later, if you would be so kind.'

Kenzo's dark eyes regarded him steadily. 'That is twice longer than your brother requested.'

Alejandro's kept his expression neutral. 'Then between us we won't take up too much of your time.'

The old man watched him with eyes that saw too much. 'Did you not consider it expedient to speak to me *together*?' he replied.

The chafing reasserted itself, rubbing harsh and relentless. 'The timing isn't quite right.'

Kenzo nodded, his expression holding an understanding that jarred Alejandro. 'Of course. Timing. The one thing we all wish we were experts at.' Before Alejandro could respond, he turned to Elise. 'Would you accompany me to my seat, my dear? I'd love to hear what you've been up to since I last spoke to your grandmother.'

Elise sent Alejandro a wary glance. He didn't want to let her go. The realisation wasn't surprising. After all, hadn't the days since the incident on his plane been revelatory in many ways? He desired her. But he was drawn to her in other ways besides sexually. He wasn't quite ready yet to explore those other emotions. But somewhere along the way an acceptance of his suddenly possessive disposition had settled in.

'Alejandro?'

He focused on her stunning face, realised he was still holding on to her and released her. '*Sí*. Of course. I'll see you later.'

Her wariness didn't abate, but she nodded. Vowing to address it at the first opportunity, he watched her walk away, her revived smile luminescent enough to draw glances as she made her way through the crowded room.

'*Madre de Dios*. If beauty like hers could be bottled, I'd be a hell of a lot richer than I am right now,' Gael drawled from beside him. 'Things are still platonic between you two, right? So you won't mind if I ask her out—'

'She's off limits to you, Gael,' Alejandro snarled. The icy fury that scoured through him at the very thought of Gael with Elise was shocking in the extreme. 'For your own sake, don't make me repeat myself on this subject. Ever.'

Gael held up his hands in mock surrender, a low laugh accompanying the gesture. 'Okay, okay. *Basta de charla!*' Enough said.

Alejandro exhaled, unclenching fists he hadn't realised he'd balled. When another champagne server approached, he grabbed a glass, just for something to do with his hands.

'Are you always this wound up? It can't be good for your health,' Gael muttered, sipping his own drink.

'My health is none of your concern,' he snapped.

Gael's face closed up. 'Of course. Trust me, you made that pretty clear in Chicago.'

The emotions eating at him suddenly multiplied, sapping his control. 'This may be a party, but I'm here for business only. If you're seeking me out under the misapprehension that it would be anything else, you're about to be sorely disappointed.'

A grim smile touched Gael's lips. 'And does that statement apply to everyone here, or just me?'

'What are you talking about?' he demanded, yearning for something, *anything* to help end this conversation. With an unstoppable compulsion, he sought out Elise.

She was at Kenzo's table, with the old man and his grandsons surrounding her. Alejandro watched as Jason Ishikawa leaned over and whispered in her ear. She laughed, her face so beautiful. His breath caught.

'Nothing. Forget it,' Gael murmured.

Alejandro barely heard him leave. Jealousy pounded, strong and hot through him as he watched her interact with the younger Ishikawa brother.

As if sensing his regard, she lifted her head. Her expression dimmed, escalating his suspicion that something was wrong.

Something he'd said to her in the car had upset her. But what?

Go to her. Find out. Claim her.

No. She needed to be handled with care. If she was as innocent as he was beginning to believe she was, the way he was feeling right now would cause more harm than good. She wasn't a fragile creature by any means, but neither was she equipped to handle the riotous emotions surging through his veins. She'd already borne the brunt of his jealousy on more than one occasion.

He needed to calm down a little...*or a lot*, before he tackled anything further with her.

He mingled. He sipped vintage champagne. He forced himself not to react each time Jason whispered in her ear.

Alejandro turned away, knowing he was one heartbeat from ripping Jason Ishikawa from her side. He swallowed his ire, torturously reined in his fraying control, and mingled for an hour until the traditional dinner gong sounded.

'Alejandro?'

Her voice lanced through him, touched him places he couldn't quite name. Turning from the female acquaintance who'd sought him out under the pretext of discussing business only to shoot him interest-filled looks the moment they were alone, he glanced at Elise.

'Are you ready to be seated?' she asked.

'*Sí*. Are you?' he enquired, refusing to glance in Jason Ishikawa's direction.

Her eyes skated away from him, but her smile stayed in place. 'Yes.'

'Then come.' Dismissing the acquaintance with a stiff smile, he held out his arm.

She hesitated. Dread snapped up his spine.

'Something wrong?' he asked as they neared their table.

'Is there any reason it should be?' she tossed back.

'You're answering my questions with questions. Is this a prelude to an argument, *guapa*?'

She swallowed. 'I don't know what you're talking—'

'Mr Aguilar, my grandfather would be honoured if you and Elise would consider joining us at our table.'

Alejandro faced Jason Ishikawa, every nerve in his body yearning to refuse the invitation. In fact, right then, he wanted to call a halt to everything: the merger that had dominated his life up to only a handful of days ago but was now a load he wanted to shed. The brother whose weighted gaze he could even now feel upon him... Everything, just so he could walk out of the party with Elise.

But leaving would be a gross insult not just to her and her grandmother, but also to their hosts. So he gritted his teeth and nodded his acceptance.

A few feet from the table, he noticed Gael had also been relocated. And Elise was placed beside Kenzo, with his grandsons on either side of them.

The old man had an agenda of his own, one Alejandro wasn't certain of yet. But he would play along. For now.

He'd come to Kyoto with the intention of saving the merger, but no deal was worth mind games or further interminable delays if they meant not having Elise in his bed. He would leave here tonight with the merger agreed. Or he would not.

It was that simple.

Decision made, he allowed himself to enjoy the food, the drink, and his immediate companions. For his own state of mind, he chose to ignore the overt gestures Jason made towards Elise. She would be leaving here with him, not Jason. And after tonight, there would be no doubt in her mind that she was his. He would make sure she understood that attention from other men wouldn't be tolerated.

Once dinner was over, he sat back as Gael invited a female guest to the dance floor. Elise excused herself to the bathroom and the Ishikawa brothers went off to fulfil their hosting duties.

He wasn't surprised when Kenzo stood and gestured for Alejandro to walk with him.

They stepped out into the balmy late-April evening, Kenzo's steps slow but steady as they took a meandering path that led to a smaller, well-lit pagoda surrounded by stone statues.

Inside, the old man selected a seat, indicating the one opposite him. Once Alejandro sat, he said, 'Speak, son.'

'You know why I'm here.'

'You think I'm the one getting in the way of the merger?'

'I just want straight answers.'

Kenzo nodded. 'Very well. You're a lone wolf, Mr Aguilar. Your brother—' he looked to where Gael was swaying on the dance floor, smiling down at the woman in his arms '—he has his issues, but he has a better understanding of what the term *family* means. You, on the other hand, do not. My grandsons may very well override my wishes—they have the majority vote, after all. But I mean to sway them to my way of thinking.'

'Which is what exactly?' He was only mildly curious, the decision to walk away solidifying with each passing minute.

'That selling what I've spent my lifetime building to a man who is so determined to reject his blood and his past won't end well. Ishikawa Corporation is about family. I won't go to my grave without ensuring my legacy remains intact.'

'And that's your final word on the matter?' Alejandro asked.

'You'll do one of two things. You'll either walk away from this deal, or you'll reassess your priorities and do what is necessary for your own soul. Either way, I wish you the best. But I urge you to do the latter.'

The old man's parting words struck him hard. Alejandro sat, frozen in place, as Kenzo rose and shuffled off. He wasn't aware how long he sat there, staring at the water. It might have been three minutes. Or three hours.

But words he'd pushed away for a long time suddenly surged back, pounding through his brain.

Family. Compromise. Brother. Legacy.

When he sensed a presence behind him, Alejandro didn't need to look to know it was his brother. Gael took the seat Kenzo had vacated, his elbows braced on his knees. He looked as if he needed a drink.

'You met with the old man?'

Alejandro nodded.

'Did he give you the *family* spiel, too?'

'*Si*, he did.'

Gael sighed. 'I guess you win this round. Kudos to you.'

Alejandro frowned. 'What?'

Gael spread his hands. 'I have to give it to you, it was a good move. Although, I thought…' He shook his head. 'Forget what I thought.'

'Gael, what are you talking about?'

His brother froze. 'I don't think I've ever heard you use my name.'

The pang in Alejandro's chest was deep and painful. 'Well. Perhaps…' He paused, not quite sure how to proceed. 'When this is done, we need to talk.'

Gael's smile was grim and unwelcoming. 'So I can listen to you gloat? No, thanks. Your neat trick paid off. You bagged this one. Accept the congrats and let's retreat to our respective kingdoms, *si*?'

'I don't play tricks.' He spiked his fingers through his hair. 'Look, things didn't happen the way you thought they did…those three weeks when your mother went missing.'

Gael frowned. 'I was *there*, I know what happened.'

'You thought I was too busy chasing girls to help you. I wasn't. I was dealing with my own mother and the breakdown she was having over the whole thing.'

Gael's mouth twisted. 'Right.'

Alejandro sighed. 'You found her in the end, didn't you?'

'No thanks to you.'

Alejandro's smile felt as stiff and grim as his soul. 'You found her thanks to a note shoved under your door at half-past eight on a Saturday night. I can repeat the exact words on the note if you want?'

His brother's face went slack. *'You?'*

Alejandro nodded. 'The time when I wasn't trying to talk my mother down from full-blown depression, I was trying to get my father to come home. I attended soccer practice because my coach warned me he'd throw me off the team if I missed any more games.'

Gael shook his head. 'You...' he breathed again.

'It wasn't as easy for me as you think. Trust me on that.'

His brother stared at him for an age, before he nodded. 'Okay.'

Alejandro stared off at the reflective lake for a minute before he turned around. 'The deal is yours if you want it.'

Gael looked puzzled. 'Why would you hand me a deal that's already yours? I wouldn't have gone that way myself, but you played your ace and you won. There's no need to be coy about it.'

'*Santa Maria*, I have zero idea what you're talking about,' he growled.

'I'm talking about Elise.' Gael shook his head. 'Bringing an exquisitely beautiful woman with Japanese ancestry to pave the path for you? She's playing the part to perfection, I have to give her that. The old man is eating out of her hand. And if my eyesight is still twenty-twenty, Jason's set on getting lucky before the night is out.'

Cold dread tightened Alejandro's nape. He lunged for Gael's lapels. *'What did you say?'*

'I said—'

'Where is she?'

Gael drew back sharply. 'Hey—'

'Where?'

His brother pointed to the gardens at the side of the pavilion.

He barely felt the ground beneath his feet as he sprinted towards the cluster of cherry-blossom trees. The few guests who'd drifted out to enjoy the evening air hurried out of his way. His frenzied gaze darted over them, searching for her.

She wasn't there.

A quick three-sixty turn and he wondered whether Gael had got it wrong. But then he spotted an archway into another garden. The typical Japanese garden was designed around a pond of lotus flowers, water lilies and rock steps.

Alejandro appreciated none of that as he stepped over a short bridge and arrived at a shallow waterfall that fed the lake. To one side of it pooled a larger pond, with a love seat at the end of it, complete with mood lighting.

He froze at the sight before him, shock and disbelief colluding to tell him he was hallucinating. But then a more urgent sensation took hold. The ever-tightening vice around his heart forced him to breathe through the shock, to blink away the disbelief.

To acknowledge that Elise was indeed in Jason's arms.

Kissing him.

'Elise.' His voice was a ragged croak. She didn't hear him. Her eyes were shut, her face concentrated…hand on his chest…lost in the kiss.

His dead feet stumbled closer, every atom in his body hoping he'd mistaken her for someone else. But it was her. The red dress. The hair. The *body*.

'Dios mio. Elise!'

They parted unhurriedly, as if he were a nuisance they were reluctant to deal with.

Jason raised his head, speared him with a triumphant look. 'Mr Aguilar, you're intruding on a—'

'Do not speak!' he snarled, his gaze fixed on Elise's back, which remained rigidly turned to him. 'Turn around, Elise. *Now.*'

She turned slowly. Her face was coolly indifferent. But her eyes blinked sultrily as if she was drunk. *Drunk on another man's kiss.*

'Explain this to me,' he rasped.

One shoulder lifted. 'I would've thought it was obvious?'

The loud clanging in his head wouldn't stop. *'Why?'*

'I don't owe you any explanations, Alejandro. Not when

it comes to my personal life. Just as you don't owe me any about yours.'

Alejandro stared at her, heard the cool words. Still his mind refused to compute.

'Was there something else you needed?'

Shaky fingers spiked his hair. '*Madre de Dios*, I thought you were *different*.'

An expression crossed her face, but he was too far gone to read it accurately. But then her features settled once more into serene, *treacherous* perfection. 'I *am* different, Alejandro. Shame you're too blind to see it.'

CHAPTER ELEVEN

Six months later

ALEJANDRO STARED AT his flashing phone. Margo wouldn't put the call through if it weren't essential. She'd borne the consequence of not heeding his *do not disturb* edict the single time she'd taken her eye off that particular ball.

A fleeting twinge in some remote corner of his being was the only sign that he regretted his scathing reaction to her mishap. To her credit, she hadn't cried. Or thrown a tantrum. She'd sucked it up and made sure it didn't happen again.

He admired that. Her ability to be what he wanted her to be. If he was brutally honest with himself, Margo was the only constant in his life.

Now that everything had changed.

Which made him certain this call was probably important.

He started to reach for it. It stopped ringing. He exhaled in relief and turned in his seat. About to rise and head to his window, he paused as his mobile began to ring.

He recognised Gael's number. This twinge was a different sort. A hint of apprehension. Anticipation. His brother had called only once since Japan. The conversation had been tense, the past tentatively broached. It had by no means been a reconciliatory call, and Alejandro wasn't certain if they'd ever get there.

But somewhere in his heart a tiny sprouting of hope lingered. He hadn't decided whether to feed it yet...

He picked up the phone and slid his thumb across the surface. 'Alejandro.'

'Good to know you're alive. Now I don't have to badger your PA into listening at your door for signs of life,' Gael drawled.

'Anything in particular I can help you with?' he demanded gruffly.

Gael paused a tense beat. 'Your diary is clear for the next two hours. And no, Margo didn't divulge that information. I graduated first in my class from MIT. I know my way around computer code.'

Alejandro gritted his teeth. 'Please tell me you did not just admit to hacking my company's system?'

'Of course not. Your appointment is with me.'

Discomfort moved through him, but then so did a certain level of acceptance. For better or worse, Gael was his brother. The question now remained how to move forward with this. 'Then why are you calling me beforehand?'

'You have a private chef. I'm proposing a lunch meeting to discuss new developments.'

Alejandro exhaled. 'The food will be taken care of. Explain the second part.'

Gael paused for a moment. 'The Ishikawa deal may be back on the table.'

'I'm not interested.'

His brother made an impatient sound. 'I'll be there in ten. We'll discuss this further.' He hung up before Alejandro could draw breath.

After relaying instructions to Margo, he tossed the phone down and jerked to his feet. He started to head for his window, but changed course at the last moment.

This was something else she'd ruined. He couldn't enjoy the view now without remembering her sketch of him standing at this very window, staring out. She'd seen inside him. Uncovered what he'd spent over a decade trying to hide.

She'd made him believe there was a connection between them.

But it'd been a lie.

She'd changed everything.

His world had been an acceptable regiment of clinical routine before her. SNV was his number one priority. Nothing else mattered.

Elise Jameson had thrown a grenade into that existence. She'd made him feel. Worse, she'd made him...*hope*. To think he'd actually been considering making adjustments in his life that included family and compromise. That he'd spent that hour in Kenzo's garden, seeking ways to accommodate the new and uncharted into his life.

When all the while she'd been pursuing another agenda. So far he'd stopped himself from dissecting which part of her history had been a lie. Her claimed innocence? The fact that landing one of the Ishikawa brothers had been an addendum to her job or her goal from the beginning, probably orchestrated by her grandmother? Because when Alejandro thought about it, he noticed that she'd resisted any discussion about *them*. Any pursuit of a sexual nature had come from Alejandro. Because she hadn't been interested?

No. She had been. He wasn't insane enough to have misread their chemistry.

But she still fell into another man's arms.

Balling his fists, he shoved them into his pockets and turned his back on the view, just as the door opened and his brother entered.

Gael was dressed for an early start to the weekend, if his jeans, T-shirt and leather biker jacket were any indication. The mid-October temperatures were balmy enough not to require further covering, which suited his west coast resident brother.

They exchanged a less stiff nod, then Gael crossed to the drinks cabinet and pour two cognacs. He handed one to Alejandro.

'You don't think this is premature? Celebrating a dead deal before a conversation has even taken place?'

Gael shrugged as he sat down on the sofa, his focus slightly pensive. 'Prematurity means there's something to *mature* into.'

Alejandro downed the drink, revelling for a single mindless moment in the warmth that flowed through him because he knew it wouldn't last. 'You're pushy.'

'I'm relentless. And ruthless.' Gael sipped his drink. 'And you're the man I keep hearing all these formidable stories about. From this side of the room, I'm not seeing much evidence of it,' he mocked.

'You flew all the way here from California with this feeble tactic? To reverse-psych me into entering into this deal with you?'

Gael raised a brow. 'Tell me if it's working and I'll tailor my answer accordingly.'

'It's not working.'

The knock on the door halted a response. Margo entered. 'Your food is ready. Shall I set it up in here or the dining room?'

Alejandro pried himself from the wall. 'In here. And take the rest of the afternoon off, Margo.'

Her eyes widened. 'Really?'

He nodded. 'Enjoy your weekend.'

The food was delivered. Gael devoured half of the club sandwich before he sat back and wiped his mouth on a napkin. Alejandro lost his appetite after one bite.

'The Ishikawas are prepared to go forward with the merger. With *both* of us.'

Alejandro opened his mouth to dismiss the offer outright, but paused. 'Why?'

'Why not? It's the best of all worlds. You bring the e-commerce arm, I deliver the digital streaming and cloud-based services. They provide the infrastructure. Together we'll be unstoppable.'

Just as Elise had suggested.

He watched Gael pick up his remaining sandwich and bite into it, and tried to swallow past the ashes in his own mouth.

Pushing his plate away, he shook his head. 'There are no guarantees they won't start getting us to jump through hoops again. It doesn't work for me.'

Gael's unforgiving gaze connected with his. 'Is that the real reason? Or it is something—or someone—else? Someone like Elise, perhaps?'

He froze. 'Watch it,' he warned.

Of course, his brother didn't heed him. 'Six months later and you're still hung up about her?'

'*Suficiente!*'

Gael plucked a bottle of water off the table and gulped down several mouthfuls. 'Have you seen her since Kyoto?'

Alejandro's insides knotted. Icy fury and other emotions he didn't want to name wrestled within him. 'No. Why are you asking me this?'

'Because you're right. There's one tiny condition to this deal.'

A hot curse erupted from him before he could stop it. 'I'm overwhelmed with shock.'

Gael grimaced. 'The old man wants Elise back in on the deal.'

'*Ni hablar!* Hell, no.'

Gael's jaw clenched. 'We're both businessmen, Andro. There have been women in the past and there will be women in the future—hey, don't growl at me. If you intend to live like a monk, go right ahead. But you're letting her get in the way of a revolutionary deal. The longest she'll need to be involved in the negotiations is a couple of months. Are you telling me you can't handle that?'

'Don't test me, Gael,' he snarled, deeply unsettled by the raw sensations moving inside him.

His brother eyed him for a minute, then reached into his pocket. 'Your private life is your own. But this is business.' He pulled out a folded piece of paper and set it down on the table. 'You'll need this if you want the deal to go ahead. When you decide, call me.' Gael walked to the door. 'Thanks for lunch,' he tossed over his shoulder before he exited.

Alejandro stared at the paper for a full minute before he reached for it. The address was out of state. In fact it was several states away. But it wasn't the other side of the world. *It isn't Kyoto.*

The distant thrumming of his blood gathered speed. Grew louder.

The image of her in another man's arms tore through him. He'd walked away. He needed to let this be.

But...

I am different... Shame you're too blind to see it.

She'd dared to taunt him. And in the last six months, those words had flashed through his mind more times than he cared for.

I am different...

He stared at the address until the letters were burned into his retinas.

It looked as if he was going to Montana.

The sound of the vehicle thundering down the dirt road was different from the rattle of tractors or Steven's banged-up old truck. Elise was in the zone, so she didn't lift her head or move an inch from her position beneath the apple tree. She continued to sketch, sending a silent plea that her rare moment of concentration wouldn't be disturbed.

Peace had been so hard to come by. Ironically, the more breathtaking the landscape in Montana grew, the unhappier she became. Summer had been the worst. Sultry evenings that were handpicked for harvest and lovers had seen her curled up in bed, stifling her sobs with her fist. In those desolate weeks, she'd wished for the numbness of May and June, when her emotions had remained in suspended animation. Because with the thaw had come the stark truth that her feelings for Alejandro were in no way resolved. Another truth was knowing the way she'd handled that last night in Kyoto had hammered nails into a door she wished she could prise open just one last time.

The thaw had exposed the depth of her craving for him; how deep the hurt and pain that resided in her heart ran. It'd also reminded her why she'd had to end any hope of a connection with Alejandro.

There's no heart there to sustain meaningful relationships.

Elise hadn't known a handful of words could turn her world black until she'd heard them.

Then she'd known.

She'd been fooling herself by contemplating a dalliance with Alejandro. So she'd drawn a definite line through any possibility. She'd needed to, to preserve her own heart.

Except her heart had gone and broken all the same. On top of that, he'd taken her creativity away again. For four long months, she'd been unable to pick up her pencil. Even drawing him had been too much when all she could recall was his face that last time she'd seen him.

The urge to abandon her dream again had been strong, but the thought of losing both Alejandro *and* her art had been unbearable, so she'd soldiered on.

The first attempts had been shockingly abysmal. But she'd persisted, dredged pockets of time when Alejandro hadn't been dominating her thoughts. Pockets where she'd dreamed he was standing before her, a hint of a smile on his face even as those mesmeric eyes bore into her—

'Elise.'

Her head jerked up. The pencil dropped from her numb fingers. Vital air strangled in her lungs as she blinked hard, sure he was an apparition.

'Alejandro?'

He crested the hill and towered over her, his eyes inscrutable as he stared down at her.

'What—' She stopped, looked around. Nothing gave her a clue, so she attempted again. 'What are you doing here?'

His mouth firmed in a painfully familiar show of displeasure. 'Hunting you down, of course. What else?' His tone implied he wouldn't otherwise be caught dead in the rolling mountains of the mid-west.

'And why would you want to do that?' she queried, her heart still attempting to jackhammer out of her chest. To give herself something to do besides stare with fervid attention at his enthralling face, his hard-packed—albeit leaner—body, she started gathering up her art supplies.

'We have unfinished business.'

A gasp attempted to form. It died in her throat. 'No. I'm sure we don't.' That last night in Kyoto had been definitive in every way. The reminder was effective in reducing her pulse from light speed to mere jet propelled.

She stood, zipped up her sketch case and fiercely resisted the urge to smooth her unruly hair. She'd let it grow in the last six months, her inclination to groom it, or herself, non-existent. The result was a wavy mess that hung halfway down her back, framing the denim shorts and a seriously unsexy plain T-shirt she'd picked up on one of her rare trips into Portland.

When his silence thickened, she risked a glance at Alejandro. To find his rapier-sharp gaze scouring her from head to toe.

'You've lost weight.'

'You didn't come all this way to tell me that, I'm sure.' She started down the hill.

He caught her arm. 'We need to talk, Elise.'

'I can't imagine what you'd want to talk to me about.' She tried to pull away. Admittedly she didn't put much effort into it because the tingling warmth seeping into her felt embarrassingly good.

Alejandro's hold firmed nevertheless. 'The man I met down there. Who is he?' he scythed at her.

'Steven? He owns the ranch.'

'And?'

'And nothing.'

His nostrils flared. 'Elise.'

She tugged harder. He released her, but prowled closer when she stepped back. 'What gives you the right to come here and question me? We said all we had to say in Kyoto, remember? Our business is over and done with.'

Arctic green eyes snapped at her. 'Not quite.'

Dread found a foothold inside her. 'What are you talking about? You terminated the contract with Jameson. I saw the paperwork.'

'I *suspended* it because I had no interim work to make up for the unfinished commission, but I paid the full commission your parents demanded.'

Cold disbelief engulfed her. 'You can't possibly want me back. What do you need me for that your PR department can't handle?'

Emotion flicked in his eyes, but the slant of the mid-afternoon sun made it difficult for her to read it accurately. 'The Ishikawa deal is back on. Kenzo insists you be part of my team.'

Her heart lurched. Squashing the despondency that came from knowing Alejandro was truly only here for business, she shook her head. 'I can't just…leave.'

His face tightened. 'Why not?'

'Because I have responsibilities. Jobs I have to do around the ranch in order to pay my way.'

He frowned. 'You left Chicago to mess around with cows and horses? What about your art? Or pursuing your dream?'

Elise took a few more steps away from him, as if that would stop the probing questions. 'I'm not playing twenty questions with you, Alejandro. Especially about my personal life. What I would like to do is to work something out with you about how to pay off the rest of the commission—'

'You can pay it off by coming back to finish what you started. I'm afraid it's non-negotiable.'

She raised her head then, stared into his beautiful, implacable face. The thought of going back to work in close proximity with Alejandro, suffering his presence while knowing that there would never be a future for them together, slayed her. She couldn't do it.

'I can't.'

Restless energy charged from him. '*Sí*, you can. You speak about responsibilities and obligations. You have a responsibility to finish what you started with SNV.'

'Or what?' she flung at him, desperation fuelling the brazen demand.

He stared down at her for a handful of seconds, before he

shook his head. 'I won't threaten you, Elise.' His voice was low, a little ragged around the edges. 'You showed me your true colours in Kyoto. So I'll leave it entirely up to you as to whether you want to do the right thing or not.'

If only he'd threatened. Or tried to blackmail her. She would've stood a chance. But Alejandro hadn't achieved global success without knowing which buttons to press to achieve the results he wanted. And by striking at the heart of her integrity, he'd left her with nothing to fight back.

'So is that a yes?' he pressed. He'd moved closer. Enough for her to feel his body heat. She locked her knees to prevent herself from closing the gap between them, inhaling the scent she hadn't realised all those months ago that she would miss until it was gone.

'That depends.'

'On what?'

'On how long until you expect this merger to be finalised.'

His eyes narrowed. 'What's the hurry?'

'I have a life to get on with. I may be contractually obligated to finish what I started with you, but that doesn't mean I'm content to put my life on hold indefinitely.'

His mouth compressed. In the distance, a tractor droned on. 'Are you in such a hurry to get back here? To your lazy afternoons under the apple tree?' he sneered.

'If that's your roundabout way of asking if I miss the cut-throat world of high finance, then no, I don't miss it. I miss *nothing* at all about Chicago.'

Ripples of emotions ghosted over his face, and had she wanted to fool herself, she'd have imagined her words had wounded him somehow. But she was too busy convincing herself of the lies she told her heart to fathom his feelings.

Besides, she needed to remember that the only reason he was here was because of his precious merger. 'How long, Alejandro?' she asked briskly.

'One month. Six weeks at the most, to accommodate visits to the countries we settle on for the initial satellite bases of operation. Is that agreeable to you?' he asked.

Six weeks to draw a definite line under her association with Alejandro. To train her heart to live without him all over again.

She swallowed past the rock of anguish lodged in her midriff, and, with a single jerk of her head, sealed her fate. 'Yes.'

He took the case and waited, silent and powerful as she gathered the small picnic basket and blanket, then escorted her down the hill to the ranch house.

When she saw the sleek SUV parked in front of the ranch house, her heart jumped into her throat. 'When do you need me to come to Chicago? I'll look into flights tonight and email you tomorrow...'

She trailed off as he shook his head. 'I didn't come all this way to return without you, Elise. You'll pack what you need and we'll take my plane back tonight.'

She didn't see the point in arguing. Apart from the fruitlessness of it, going back with Alejandro would mean she wouldn't have to raid her meagre savings to pay for her flight.

Handing in her notice and turning her back on Jameson PR had been freeing, but it'd also left her without an income.

As for her parents, they had tried to guilt her into staying. There'd been accusations revolving around the loss of the SNV contract, but Elise had been too steeped in the fog of pain to pay them much attention. Her debt to her parents was paid. Her father had made a half-hearted attempt to stay in touch during her first weeks in Montana. Her mother had emailed.

Elise had answered dutifully, but her heart had been too heavy to make much of an attempt. It still was. But she'd accepted that the only way her parents would truly embrace her was if she shared their dreams. It hurt to know that would never happen, but she would learn to live with it.

Steven stepped out onto the porch. He nodded at her, then his gaze swung to Alejandro.

Her old college friend's offer of room and board in return for odd jobs around his ranch had saved Elise six months ago. Steven Bosworth had for the most part let her be, content to share the odd beer with her on his porch when his busy day was done.

She'd seen the concerned looks he'd sent her when he thought she wasn't aware, but thankfully he hadn't pushed her.

'Steven, this is—'

'There's no need to introduce us. We've already met,' Alejandro inserted, his voice tight.

'Everything all right, Elise?' Steven asked.

'Yes, I'm just—'

'I'm on a tight schedule, Elise. You have five minutes to pack,' Alejandro said, his deep voice thick with formidable authority.

'You're being rude. And I'll be more than five minutes. If you're in that much of a hurry, leave without me. I'll catch the next available flight,' Elise said firmly.

Eyes the colour of frozen moss glared at her. She glared right back, but, in some corner of her being, excitement leaped. She'd never thought she'd ever cross paths with Alejandro again, never mind lock horns with him. Now that she was, she wanted to argue with him for ever.

The thought was frightening enough to propel her back a step.

He shadowed her move. 'Ten minutes, Elise.'

'Twenty, *Alejandro.*'

He didn't respond, only made the short trip to his SUV, her sketch case still in his hand. Pressing on a fob, he tossed the case into the back and slammed the boot.

Returning to the front of the vehicle, he leaned against the bumper, arms crossed, eyes laser-fixed on her. 'You have nineteen minutes, and counting. One second over that and I'll drag you out.'

The sound she made was unladylike. Turning, she startled, having forgotten Steven's silent witnessing of their exchange from the porch. Heat rushed up her face as she grimaced.

'I guess from all that...*spiky* conversation that you're leaving?' he murmured.

She nodded as she climbed the porch. 'I'm sorry, Steven. I don't really have a choice.'

His eyes narrowed, but she waved him away. 'It's not as grim as that. I just have...unfinished business to attend to,' she said, repeating Alejandro's words.

'Okay. Will you be back?' he asked.

About to answer in the affirmative, Elise stopped. 'I don't know,' she murmured. Steven's ranch had been a much-needed sanctuary, but she couldn't hide out here for ever. Once Alejandro was well and truly behind her, it would be time to forge the path she'd always dreamed of.

She swallowed past the ragged pain still lodged in her midriff, and smiled at Steven. 'I'll let you know in a day or two, okay?'

He nodded, his sand-coloured hair gleaming gold in the late afternoon sun. 'You have a standing invitation to stay any time you want. Least I can do to repay you for the free PR and advice on how to get the stud farm up and running.' His glance slid past her to a bristling Alejandro. 'You better hop to it before something catches fire around here.'

She glanced over at Alejandro. His jaw was locked. His eyes mere slits as he observed them. Sucking in a breath, she darted into the century-old two-storey ranch house Steven had inherited along with the farm. Her room was at the top of the stairs.

As she packed her meagre belongings into the single suitcase, she accepted that her stay here had only ever been a stop-gap. She'd been marking time until she could come alive again.

But while she felt alive now, her heart dipped with wrenching anguish to also accept that in a few short weeks she would need to continue feeling alive, without Alejandro.

The man in question was stalking the porch when she opened the front door. And he kept right on coming. Once he had possession of her suitcase, he caught her arm and started to lead her away.

'Wait.' She ignored his growl, and crossed over to Steven, giving him a quick hug. 'Thanks for everything.'

'No problem. Seriously. Now go before he tears me limb from limb,' Steven muttered.

She went, her heart racing as she slid into the seat beside Alejandro. His exit from the ranch was aggressively fast and dusty. Hanging on, Elise fought the urge to roll her eyes. And failed.

'If I lived in an alternate universe, I'd say you were jealous.'

The SUV swerved to the side of the deserted road and screeched to a stop. Tension mounted until she was sure she could reach out and touch it. For the longest time, he stared at her and just breathed; heavy, chest-filling breaths that vibrated right through her.

'For the sake of my ability to function, Elise, tell me you haven't spent the last six months in his bed?'

Her mouth dropped open. Her body flushed with heat. Then cold. 'I... Why on earth should that matter to you?'

A harsh laugh wrenched through the vehicle. 'Because contrary to the laws of common sense and everything that should dictate otherwise, you continue to rage like a damn *fever* in my blood.' The delivery was intense. A lethal blade cutting through everything he'd said in the last hour. Striking the heart of his presence here. 'I want you. I crave you. Despite everything.'

Her low gasp dissolved before it'd even fully emerged. '*Despite* everything? You hate yourself for feeling the way you do about me, don't you?'

Another ragged exhalation. 'A lot of things have ceased to make sense to me. *Including* this.'

While she was trying to compute that, he lunged for her, buried his fingers in her loose hair and gripped her tight. '*Por el amor de Dios*, tell me!'

'Why should I?' she hissed, anger and hurt scything

through her despite the intoxicating proximity of him. When his breath feathered hot and decadent over her mouth, she almost lost her ability to think. 'There's nothing between you and I, Alejandro.'

His nostrils flared with towering rage, before he let out a harsh laugh. 'You made sure of that by falling into another man's arms!' he charged with a quiet fury that was no less volcanic for its rumble.

She pulled away, at once afraid of the depth of her feelings and the temptation of him. 'I was—'

'*Dios mio*, you were kissing another man, when I couldn't have made it clearer that I wanted you to be mine!' One hand spiked through his hair before it balled into a fist.

'Yes, *you* wanted! Did you ever stop to think about what *I* wanted?'

His features tautened. 'What are you talking about? Nothing excuses what I saw.'

'In that case why are we having this conversation?'

He seethed for tense seconds.

'Because I can't get you out of my head.'

The words were stark. Rough. Jagged.

Her heart lurched as they stared at each other across the console. 'Tell me you've gotten me out of yours.'

She shook her head, the words clogging her throat.

'I want to hear the words, Elise,' he stressed.

Her mouth parted, ready to issue lies. But they locked, strangled, morphed into other words. Words that she knew before she uttered them would doom her. She'd wished for the door she'd slammed shut to open one more time. She was getting her chance. 'I haven't been able to get you out of mine,' she murmured.

Alejandro's eyes glinted with a mixture of satisfaction and disillusionment, as if he'd found a prize that had turned out to be only semi-precious.

He threw the car into gear and accelerated down the dirt road.

She cleared her throat. 'Alejandro, I need to explain what happened with Jason—'

'No,' he cut in coldly. 'I don't wish to hear it. You've told me the only thing that matters. It may be six months longer than I anticipated, but I'll have you in my bed, Elise. You'll come to me. You will enjoy it. And when we're done, we'll walk away from each other. But I never want to hear you utter his name again. Is that clear?'

CHAPTER TWELVE

SHE WAS IN deep trouble. Elise had thought she'd sorted through her feelings in the six months Alejandro had been out of her life, but she found out very quickly that being around him was tantamount to living in emotional chaos. And a determined Alejandro only made things worse.

The first exhibition of the juggernaut that was Alejandro's sheer willpower came her way even before she'd stepped on his plane. The second she responded 'no' to having a place to stay, he nodded.

'We don't have time to find you an apartment. You'll stay with me.'

He'd taken the same dominating path to his discovery that her one suitcase only contained clothes fit for ranch work and work boots. Clothes had arrived in her suite in his multimillion-dollar penthouse displaying designer labels that made her gasp. Her hasty, 'I can't accept these!' had been met with an inflexible, 'You can and you will. If it eases your sensibilities, donate them to charity when you're done with them.'

Of course, the reminder that their time together was finite had robbed her of breath and an adequate response. She'd fallen back into the routine of being his eyes and ears. Only this time, Alejandro demanded her stronger participation with client liaisons; had taken to touching her hand or arm to gain her attention when her focus strayed for even a second; his trips into her small office were more frequent, and his gaze lingered long and hungrily on her body when they were alone. Most evenings they dined out, although conversation during their meals was stilted, with Alejandro barely eating more than a few mouthfuls while she wasn't allowed to leave a meal unfinished.

But there'd been no kisses, no attempt to take her to bed.

And more than once, she'd encountered his harsh, disillusioned stare that dragged icicles across her heart.

As she slipped her feet into four-inch heels and smoothed her hands down her black pinstriped dress in readiness to join Alejandro for breakfast before they headed in to work, her heart squeezed painfully, even as she admitted the wait was driving her slowly insane.

It had disturbed more than a few nights' sleep, which had in turn fuelled a frenzy of sketches. It hadn't surprised her when she'd noted that all the stories charted a tale of heartache and loss.

Pushing the state of her turbulent emotions aside, she caught up the matching jacket and her handbag and left her bedroom.

The scent of freshly ground coffee drew her to the dining room, and she smiled as she passed Alejandro's butler, Sergio.

'Buenos días, querida,' Alejandro drawled, his hard gaze skimming over her before returning to the paper in his hand.

Breathing through her escalated heartbeat, she returned the greeting, sat down and helped herself to a cream-cheese-spread bagel and coffee.

'Anything of interest in the paper?' she asked.

'Surprisingly, not even a whisper,' he replied, a hard smile doing nothing to soften his sculptured features.

Speculation had been rife for the past week, with financial pundits going wild with what the rumours of the SNV/Ishikawa/Toredo deal would mean if it went ahead.

Alejandro's in-house PR department, with her supervisory input, had kept a tight leash on all press releases. But by day's end, the Aguilar brothers would make history.

Because today, two weeks after dragging her back to Chicago, Alejandro and Gael would finalise the merger.

Her blood thrummed in anticipation of what tonight would bring, her excitement unable to be suppressed despite the quiet pride and awe she felt in being part of this financial-landscape-changing merger.

'Are you ready for the ride?' he asked.

Despite the casual nature of the question, there was an edge to his voice, one that made her hackles rise.

She knew what he was asking.

She'd sensed that Alejandro was waiting for the merger to be signed before making his move. Whereas she'd been ready to take the insane leap back on that dirt road in Montana.

She raised her head and locked eyes with his narrowed ones. 'Yes.'

He nodded once, stood and held out his hand. She slipped her hand into his and he pulled her up. His gaze dropped to her lips.

Unbearable need propelled her tongue into a quick swipe of her lower lip.

Alejandro made a rough sound in his throat, his eyes losing focus for a second. Then he stepped back, and straightened his faultless tie.

The ride to The Loop was fast, his Bugatti eating up the miles. Elise walked at his side as they entered his building, the tension between them growing thicker with each second.

At SNV the mood was one of muted excitement.

Gael's presence took a little bit of Alejandro's focus off her, but all through the excitement-tinged day she sensed his gaze tracking her, the ominous intensity leaving her in no doubt that, one way or the other, the subject of their own personal merger was about to be broached.

Kenzo Ishikawa arrived with his grandsons at two. By three o'clock the documents were signed. Alejandro gathered his employees in the largest conference room and broke the news to thunderous applause, then stood beside Gael as he did the same via video link with his employees in California.

After champagne toasts were given, the entourage headed to the ground floor where the press had gathered.

Elise spotted her parents the moment she stepped out of the lift. They were holding court with the rest of SNV's PR team in preparation to head into the conference.

They'd tried to inveigle their way, via her, into getting more commissions from SNV. When Elise had made it painfully clear she was only back to finish the work she'd started, they'd requested inclusion into the press conferences scheduled for when the merger was formally announced.

Her mother sent a dismissive glance that made her stiffen with hurt.

Alejandro glanced sharply at her. 'What's wrong?'

'Nothing I want to ruin your day with.'

His eyes narrowed. Then he scoured the room until he spotted her parents. 'If I'd known they would cause you this much distress, I would've had their invitation revoked.'

She shook her head. 'No. I'm serious. Don't concern yourself about this.'

'You need to remind yourself that falling in with them would've been so much easier than resisting. You chose a different path. A better path.' His hand lightly holding her wrist tightened, imbuing her with warmth. 'Give yourself credit for that at least.'

The unexpected accolade hit her square in the chest. Her breath shook as her eyes met his. 'Okay...I...umm, thanks.'

He gave a curt nod.

Gael approached, his own tension adding to the almost capricious excitement. 'We ready to do this?' he rasped.

Alejandro's glance lingered on her, his expression taut. '*Sí*. I'm ready.'

Four hours later, Elise stood in front of her mirror. This time her attire was far removed from office chic. The dinner party Alejandro had decided to host to celebrate the merger would start in fifteen minutes.

She'd opted for a 1920s-style cocktail dress in a deep green with a sequin-fringed hem and capped sleeves. The heavy chiffon skimmed her curves and ended a few inches above her knee. But while she loved the style, she was ashamed to admit that she'd chosen the colour because it matched Alejandro's eyes.

She drew a brush through her hair, her movements slowing as she recalled his words to her this afternoon. Her heart performed a worryingly familiar somersault, even though her more feet-on-the-ground mind told her she risked a whole lot more than a dizzy spell if she read more into Alejandro's words than the blatantly carnal.

But she couldn't deny his words had provided a much-needed balm. She'd been able to withstand her parents' preening and brazen spotlight seeking without feeling the urge to retreat into her own world. And her mother's narrow-eyed assessment of her dress and smug conclusion that Elise was finally taking her advice and getting what she could from her relationship with Alejandro had bounced off her for the first time in her life.

A knock on her door drew her from her musings. Alejandro stood tall and proud in her doorway, his customary black shirt and charcoal suit swapped for a black dinner jacket and snowy white shirt.

Dizzyingly overwhelmed by his presence, she stepped back. 'I'm just about—'

'*Dios mio*, you look breathtaking.'

Her blush should've embarrassed her. She should've wrung her hands and sought self-deprecating words. But something earthy and powerful in his eyes made her chin rise, her spine straightening as she drank in his compliment, for the first time, accepting and acknowledging her femininity without bitterness or shame.

'*Muchas gracias.*' She murmured the words she'd heard him use.

His eyes darkened and her pleasure escalated.

They stood like that, staring. Appreciating. Acknowledging *their* impending merger. And even when the trace of cynicism crossed his eyes, her excitement didn't dim.

He reached into his jacket pocket. 'I have something for you.'

'I… What?'

'A gift to remind you of a momentous day.' He held out the box.

'There's no risk that I'll forget it any time soon. You don't need to give me a gift.'

'I'm doing it all the same.'

'Alejandro—'

'We're arguing again,' he murmured, his jaw slightly clenched.

'You like our arguments.' She attempted to lighten the mood, unable to drag her eyes from the olive-skinned beauty of him, or her senses from the intoxicating scent of him.

'I do. They drive me half insane, but the victory is always worth it.'

Her eyes widened. 'The victory?'

'*Sí*, you always inevitably capitulate, but not before you make me jump through hoops.'

'I *don't*…' She stopped, her mind drifting back to realise that it was true. Somehow Alejandro got his way in the end.

'Take the gift, *querida*. My arm is about to fall off from the strain.'

She took it, partly out of curiosity and partly because she was still replaying his words. Reason took flight as she opened the box and saw the glittering gems.

'Alejandro! I can't take this. It's not… What would your team think?' she blurted.

'They'll think themselves incredibly lucky to be working for me since they all received bonuses of their own.'

'Oh…' The diamond bracelet was exquisite, the design simple but flawless.

He took the bracelet from its velvet bed and secured it around her wrist. Then taking her hand, he kissed the back of it. Elise didn't miss the hard triumphant light in his eyes as he placed her hand in the crook of his arm.

Mild dread shivered down her spine, but she pushed it away, attempting to lighten the tension once again. 'No need to look so smug.'

His mouth twitched in a tight smile. 'There's every need, *mi corazón*. I have you exactly where I want you.'

Alejandro kept ahold of her all through the party. And even though they drew more than a few speculative glances, Elise didn't care. Her decision was made and cemented in her heart. Besides, although it hadn't happened yet, Alejandro's constant attention in the form of little touches had already sparked enough rumours to snowball its own story.

She went with the flow, chatted to acquaintances and executives from all three companies, with the exception of Jason Ishikawa, whose name had been blatantly excluded from the guest list.

She was walking away from Jason's brother, Nathan, when a hand slid around her waist. 'You were right about one thing,' Alejandro drawled in her ear.

Her smile wasn't as full as she hoped. 'Just the one?' she teased.

She expected a quick comeback, and her steps faltered when he didn't answer immediately. Stopping in the hollowed-out space between reception rooms, she faced him, her heart thudding sickeningly.

'Alejandro… I think we need to talk. Clear the air?'

His mouth tightened. The look on his face was harsh. And yet vulnerable. Elise was stabbed with the visceral urge to comfort him, but she remained still.

'I'm not sure what *talking* will achieve, *querida*. And *sí*, you were right. I'm jealous of every man who looks at you. Of every man you smile at,' he breathed.

Her soft gasp landed between them. 'It's…I…'

'It's irrational. And deplorable, considering I know how detrimental such feelings can be.' His gaze flicked to hers as if he was gauging her reaction.

Elise gave in to her need and cupped his cheek. 'It's only deplorable if you deliberately use it to hurt or manipulate. As for the rationality of it…' She shrugged. 'Nathan Ishikawa's date was almost introduced to my irrational side when she flashed her cleavage at you for the third time at dinner. But I guess we all have our crosses to bear, don't we?'

One corner of his mouth lifted. The harshness dissipated. He laid his hand over hers and pressed her back until her shoulders touched the wall. His gaze scoured her face with an intensity that bordered on fanatic, before locking on her mouth. 'Smile for me, Elise *mio*. Just for me,' he ordered thickly.

Her breath shook out, and her mouth wobbled with her first attempt. But her smile shone through and stayed when she heard his strangled groan.

'You look nothing like her,' he mused roughly.

Elise tensed. 'Like who?'

'A painting that briefly hung in my father's study. The first time I saw you, you reminded me of that painting. But I see now it's only a passing resemblance. Your smile, your face, is so much more exceptional.'

Some of the tension seeped out of her. 'Was that why you reacted to me the way you did?'

He inclined his head. 'Yes. I was captivated. I still am.'

She blushed. To cover her embarrassment, she blurted, 'Tell me more about the painting.'

His face shadowed. 'Regrettably, as with all things my father paid attention to, it caused too much friction for it to last. But there is one detail I recall though.'

'Yes?'

Dark hunger scorched her. 'She was nude.'

Her gasp was swallowed, her hand caught in his and curled against his chest as he kissed her, deep and long and masterfully. Elise moaned, strained closer until his hard body was imprinted against hers. The sound of clinking glasses and drifting voices finally made them part.

Alejandro's face was stamped with the same naked hunger clawing through her.

'I have waited long enough, *querida*. Tonight you'll be mine,' he commanded thickly. 'Say the words, Elise.'

Her heart lurched, then sped up its beat. 'I'll be yours,' she whispered.

His breath shuddered out. Cradling her hands between his, he kissed her knuckles, then drew her out of the alcove. Wordlessly, he led her back to the party.

Elise spent the rest of the evening drifting in a haze of anticipation and trepidation.

She'd pledged her virginity to a powerful, virile man who knew his way around a female body, whereas the circumstances of her upbringing had made her shy away from even the mention of sex. She knew the technicalities of the act, but beyond that she would be operating blind.

A hysterical bubble rose in her throat. Quickly swallowing it down, she tried to breathe through her nerves. She was still battling her way through her anxiety when Gael approached where she stood with Alejandro saying goodbye to the first wave of departing guests.

The brothers shook hands, a look passing between them that was almost too intense to witness. 'Not bad for a good day's work, huh?' Gael joked, but his eyes shone with more than just triumph. They shone with pride, and yearning for acceptance, both of which Alejandro's lopsided smile reflected.

'You have my permission to pat yourself on the back now.'

Gael snorted. 'That's what the girlfriends are for.' His expression veiled for a moment, then returned to Alejandro. 'I'm heading to Spain in the morning. I'll be back in time to join you for the first site tours at the end of the week.'

Alejandro had stiffened at the mention of his homeland. Imagining the subject disturbing enough to be dropped, she was surprised when he nodded. 'Do you see her often? Your mother?'

Eyes a few shades lighter than his shadowed before Gael's expression cleared. Shrugging, he said, 'She visits me in California a couple of times a year. I've set her up in a villa outside Barcelona. I try to see her when I can.'

Mild shock lit Alejandro's eyes. 'She's no longer in Seville?'

Gael shook his head. 'She moved ten years ago.' He paused a beat. 'Reconnecting should be easier now...for all concerned.'

Alejandro's tension mounted. 'The past needs to stay where it belongs.'

His younger brother looked as if he wanted to debate the point, but eventually, he shrugged. *'Muy bien. Hasta luego, mi hermano.'*

This time their goodbye involved clasped hands and half-hugs.

Alejandro remained the attentive host to his remaining guests, but he got more brooding the later the evening grew. It didn't take a genius to guess Gael's words had penetrated to a vulnerable place. But the moment the last guest left, he strode across the living-room floor and seized Elise in his arms.

The kiss was ferocious, his need a living beast intent on devouring her. She met him in hunger and desire, her need just as potent. When hands framed her face, and his kiss deepened, something incredibly powerful jolted within her. She wanted to hang the sexual desire term on it, but Elise knew it was more. So much more.

For good or ill—and a dark painful place within her suspected it might be the latter—she had fallen in love with Alejandro Aguilar. Deeply, irrevocably in love.

The beauty, purity and hauntingly doomed nature of her feeling caused tears to prickle her eyes. Desperate to seek the pleasure and forget the impending pain, she tightened her grip in his hair, luxuriating in the brilliant vitality of him.

He swung her into his arms without breaking the kiss. She didn't need to know where he was taking her. Surrender was as inevitable as breathing.

In his room, he placed her on her feet and broke the kiss. Eyes turned a dark, gleaming moss, fired only by hunger, unrelenting and all-encompassing, blazed down at her. His hands found the side zip of her dress, and tugged. The heavy material dropped, leaving her in the new white lingerie set she'd let the stylist talk her into. White, the colour of innocence, the symbol of inexperience.

Nerves arrived, cold and urgent, to gnaw at the edges of her desire.

Sensing her sudden wavering, he closed his hands over her shoulders, his possessive touch warming her inside and out. 'You're breathtaking. I want you, *amante*, more than I've wanted anyone in a long time.'

She shivered at the intensity, the harsh purpose in his voice. She didn't doubt the veracity of his statement. Only her ability to reciprocate even an ounce of that purpose. And then there was that vein of disillusionment in his eyes. She knew it needed addressing.

'Alejandro, can we…clear the air?' she ventured.

Coldness momentarily washed over his features. 'No, *amante*. You're about to be mine. By the time I'm done with you, you'll forget every single thing about him. But until that happens, there will be no discussion, *entiendes*?' he bit out roughly.

She shook her head. 'Please—'

His thumb on her lower lip stilled her words. He took her hand, placed it on his chest, over his strong, *racing* heartbeat. 'Feel what you do to me, even before we're in bed together. You kiss me like you need me, like you're on fire for me—'

'I do,' she asserted, her voice clear and certain. 'I am.'

A deep shudder ran through him, transmitting through his thundering heartbeat. Dropping his head, he brushed his lips against hers. 'That, Elise, is all I need.'

She allowed relief to wash away the doubt, aware that she was also buying her heart a little time before it was totally devastated. Because once she explained her reasons for Kyoto, she would be laid bare.

Standing on her tiptoes, she deepened the kiss, which he allowed her for a few dizzying heartbeats. Then his primal dominance took over.

Turning her in his arms, he traced his hands down her side and over her waist to cradle her hips. When a soft, hot kiss landed at the base of her spine, she shivered, even while her skin tightened and tingled with the most delicious pleasure.

Sure fingers hooked into her panties and drew them down her legs, his fingers lingering in places she hadn't known were sensitive. Her shoes followed, and then she was naked. Naked and exposed to the man who held her heart in his hands without knowing it.

She sensed him rise behind her, felt the towering wall of his lust engulf her.

'Turn around, *mi corazón*,' he growled, his voice barely recognisable, but at the same time empowering her.

Slowly, she turned, met his bold, burning gaze. Something shifted in his eyes. She wanted to hope that it was an emotion akin to that which moved through her, but then his gaze swept down, possessing her, branding her.

'Tu es magnífico,' he grated roughly.

'And you…you have too many clothes on,' she whispered brokenly.

His rough laugh broke the spellbinding moment. But only for a second. In the next breath, the air thickened again, unspoken wishes and frenzied desire whipping around them even though he took his time to shrug off his jacket and step out of his shoes.

It was like her own personal striptease show; she watched, totally captivated as he undid the buttons of his shirt. Golden skin, a chiselled torso dusted with silky hair became her prize. Heat flooded her entire being, before centring hard and hot between her thighs. By the time he lowered his zip and tugged down his trousers and boxer briefs, Elise was certain she'd lost the ability to breathe. He was big and proud and utterly beautiful.

'Alejandro…'

He closed his eyes for a second, as if gathering in his control. When he opened them again and speared her with green fire, he was once again in command. He caught her hand and led her to the king-size bed, stretched her out on it, then reached into his bedside drawer. At the sight of the condoms, she blushed.

He laughed almost cruelly as he stretched out beside her, his fingers tracing her heated cheeks. 'Am I insane to still love your blushes?'

'Yes. I hate them.'

'As much as I'd love another battle of words with you, right now, *amante*, I crave your kiss even more. Kiss me, Elise.'

With a moan torn from the very soul of her, she wrapped her arms around his neck and satisfied their need. Within seconds the drugging kiss had set her on a course from which she didn't want to return. Alejandro's hands explored, gripping, demanding, lingering, and moulding until her moans threaded together in a continuous litany.

Then his fingers breached the heart of her. Her eyes flew open, her breath catching as pleasure arrowed, swift and lethal, between her thighs. Teasing the bundle of nerves, he dipped lower, one finger sliding inside.

He groaned, and swallowed hard. '*Dios, so wet*. So tight.'

She shuddered as he pulled out and slid back in. 'Oh!' A different set of emotions gathered, a promise of something transcendental on the horizon that shimmered just beyond her reach. Heart hammering, she strained for it, groaning in protest when Alejandro's finger left her.

His trailing mouth on her skin made up for it though, until she sensed his destination.

Her head jerked off the pillow. 'Alejandro, no...'

Molten eyes speared hers as his shoulders parted her thighs. 'Yes. Save your breath, *querida*. I intend to win this argument, too.'

He didn't ease her into pleasure. Alejandro dropped her hard and screaming into it. Emotion she came to recognise as bliss engulfed her seconds later as she climaxed, wild and free and shattered, against his open-mouthed kisses.

She floated down, vaguely aware of his hot, sweat-sheened skin beneath her hands. But slowly, her senses sparked once more, her body responding to the demands of his hands and the pressure of the body braced above hers.

He parted her thighs, positioned himself at her core. His eyes locked on her face. And she glimpsed the look again.

He started to lean down. She placed a hand on his chest. 'Wait.'

He froze, his breathing harsh, teeth clenched. 'Elise, *por favor*, now is not the time—'

'Yes, it *is*. I didn't... Nothing happened with... In Kyoto,' she stammered.

Shock built in his eyes, but there was also scepticism. 'You don't need to say that to appease me,' he bit out.

She shook her head. 'But it's the truth, Alejandro. I'm still a virgin.'

He stared deep into her eyes, his gaze piercingly raw. Whatever he saw in her face made his chest heave. 'Elise...' His voice rumbled away like distant thunder.

He didn't need her reassurance. She knew he saw the truth in her face. But she gave it anyway. Reaching up, she placed her hand on his cheek. 'I'm still untouched, Alejandro. Make me yours?'

The arms braced on either side of her trembled as the last trace of harshness trailed away from his face to leave fierce, ravenous hunger.

His kiss was deep and rough and intense, as if he meant to consume her completely.

When he lifted his head, her excitement was cresting a fever pitch.

She swallowed as his gaze latched on hers. '*Lo siento, querida.* I'm sorry. This cannot be helped.'

Biting her lips, she nodded.

'Hold on to me,' he rasped.

She complied, her hands finding purchase on his muscled shoulders and holding tight. Before she could take another breath he penetrated her, sliding in deep and sure.

Pain jerked through her, sharp and primal, ripping a scream from her.

Above her, Alejandro hissed and held himself still. '*Dios*, are you all right?'

She blinked through prickling tears and struggled to speak. 'Y…yes.'

He kissed her again, a gentle anointing and a promise of things to come. The pain receded, leaving behind the reality of the power and fullness of him inside her. He moved. Her nails dug deeper into his skin as a different sensation thrummed inside. His hips rolled again. Intoxicating pleasure lanced through her, dragging her eyelids down.

'No. Look at me,' he instructed. 'Feel me. *Feel what you do to me.*'

Her gaze reconnected with his. Exhaling, he increased the tempo, and she cried out. 'Oh…*yes!*'

The word seemed to breach a dam inside him. With a guttural groan, he sealed his mouth to hers, his tongue commencing a brazen mimicry of what his body was doing to hers. Elise could only attempt to keep up as he set her on a trajectory of pleasure so overwhelming her cries grew into a scream, right before sheer bliss catapulted her into a different dimension.

Alejandro watched her, unable to take his eyes off her radiant beauty as her pleasure overtook her. She was already proving to be a responsive lover; her eyes didn't once stray from his, a deed he found almost too much to bear when his pleasure surged high. Higher than he'd ever felt before. For one wild second he wondered if it was because she'd confessed her innocence at a crucial stage. He didn't deny the declaration had filled him with a primal emotion that had left him raw and exposed. That beast still prowled through him, urging him to possess, to stake his claim here and now.

But no. This feeling of heightened awareness and existing on a visceral realm had existed between them long before they'd stepped into his bedroom.

The sex had just brought it to the fore.

But now it was here? Now he'd had a taste of it? *Dios*, he wanted to die in it. Alejandro spiked his fingers into her hair, angled her head to receive his deeper kiss, the feeling of falling, losing himself in her tight heat a drug he never wanted to be freed from.

Her legs clamped tighter around his waist, urging him on, welcoming him home. A harsh groan ripped from his throat. And he allowed himself to fall.

CHAPTER THIRTEEN

ELISE WOKE UP some hours later to the feel of a warm towel drifting over her skin. Blinking awake, she blushed at the sight of Alejandro perched naked on the side of the bed, tending to her.

'You don't need to do that,' she blurted.

A slow, sexy smile lit his face, drawing her absorbed attention to the delicious stubble gracing his jaw. 'No, I don't. But doing it pleases me.'

He grasped her knee and spread her wider. Elise's hands flew up to cover her face, shaking her head wildly as a full body blush engulfed her.

Alejandro laughed. After a minute, he said, 'Open your eyes, *guapa*. The ordeal is over.'

She dragged her hand down her face to see him toss the washcloth away. 'That can't happen again. Ever.'

His smile was arrogantly confident and blatantly possessive. 'I have extensive and uninhibited plans for your body, *amante*. After-sex care should be the least of your worries.'

Prowling over her, he took her mouth in a long, mind-melting kiss. 'Do I have a say in these plans at all?'

His mouth drifted down her collarbone, planting kisses on her skin. 'Only when it comes to vocalising your pleasure.'

She cringed. 'I seriously doubt that will happen.'

He smiled against her skin. 'Is that a challenge?'

A sliver of ice cooled her desire. 'No. It's not.'

Alejandro's head jerked up. 'What's wrong?'

Elise shook her head. 'It's nothing… I don't want to ruin the…this.'

'Then tell me what's wrong.'

'What you said about being vocal…it was another of those

motherly pieces of advice I received when...' She pressed her lips together. 'Can we change the subject, please?'

'No.' Alejandro rose and planted his hands on either side of her head. 'It's time to end this.'

'Alejandro—'

'You have severe hang-ups about your sexuality. Which is understandable considering the less-than-stellar guidance you were given regarding your body. Your parents tried to turn what should be a natural expression of desire into a commodity to be peddled. You denied them the power to do that by choosing how you used your body. You're beautiful, *querida*.' He punctuated the compliment with a kiss. 'You have nothing to be ashamed or embarrassed about. When we made love, you held nothing back. You fell apart in my arms and that's how I want you, every time. Telling your lover what you want in bed doesn't demean you, especially if he wants it, too. *Sí?*'

Elise didn't realise tears had welled up until she blinked. When they rolled down her eyes, he brushed them away. 'Yes.'

'Good.'

He kissed her, soft and sweet. Then he rolled them over so she was poised above him. 'Now, to demonstrate, here comes your first instruction. Brace your hands on the headboard.'

She glanced up at the smooth, silk-lined board that extended halfway up the wall. 'I... What?'

His grin was pure wickedness. 'I didn't stutter.'

When she continued to stare in puzzlement and trepidation, he gripped her waist and pulled her up until her torso was suspended above him, her breasts a tantalising inch from his mouth.

With a deep groan, he parted his lips and closed them over one nipple. Elise gasped, her hands seeking the solid reassurance of the headboard as white-hot pleasure seared her.

After an age he freed her bud, and licked her areola. 'I've wanted to do this since the day you walked into my office.'

'Just this?' she asked, her voice a breathless mess.

A sexy smile formed around her aching nipple. 'Oh, no, *amante*. But this was what I had in mind for starters. Hours and *hours* of this.' His tongue flicked rapidly over her heated flesh, sending spears of need straight to her core. Fingers digging into the headboard, she gave in to the insane urge to look down, see what he was doing. The visual sensation was even more intense as he switched his attention to her neglected nipple.

'That sounds…dangerously mind-altering,' she whispered.

Merciless teeth nipped. 'You've had me in a state for a while. It's only fair that I reciprocate.' He nipped again.

'Alejandro!'

He groaned. '*Sí*, say my name like that.'

She repeated his name because she couldn't form any other words. And because beneath her, his flesh thickened against her thigh each time she said his name. Power, feminine and wicked, surged through her. For a moment, she was ashamed of it, certain it was similar to that which her mother had honed and wielded for as long as Elise could remember.

'I hope you're not trying to induce a different form of mind-alteration by thinking about anything else but what's happening in this bed right now?' Alejandro growled.

Elise shook herself free of the intrusive thoughts. 'No. I wouldn't dare.'

Alejandro lifted an eyebrow. 'You and I both know you would. You've been daring me since the day we met.'

'Okay, maybe I would, but I want you more than I want to risk you stopping what you're doing. So I surrender.'

His eyes flared for a single, gripping moment. Reaching across, he plucked a condom from the table. His gaze still trapping hers, he slid it on, positioned her in place and gripped her waist.

'Time for your next lesson. And, Elise?'

'Yes?' she gasped, her senses already on fire as his powerful erection probed her core.

He entered her in one smooth thrust, his teeth clenched

on a guttural groan. Only when he was fully seated inside her did he continue.

'You will not hold back.'

Those five words set the bar for the next few weeks as Alejandro and Gael took the financial world by storm. With a specially selected team, they crisscrossed the globe, setting up satellite offices and factories and vetting other conglomerates who vied to be affiliated with the newly formed Atlas Group that comprised SNV, Toredo and Ishikawa Corporation.

In her role as his PR consultant, Elise was never far from his side during the day. And Alejandro's inexhaustible demands ensured she was even closer to him at night.

The ride was undeniably thrilling, the sex even more so.

But in her rare quiet moments, she couldn't silence the hopeful voice that questioned whether this *could* ever be more than just sex.

Alejandro didn't show signs of tiring of it, which initially helped her to talk herself into believing that what they had was enough.

But with the slow passage of the weeks, and the stark realisation that their working relationship was winding down, fear had taken hold.

There had been no further mention of Kyoto, Alejandro finding effective ways of silencing her whenever she attempted to explain. And she…she'd taken the coward's way out, protecting her heart for a little longer whenever she let him kiss away the subject of why she'd kissed Jason.

His avoidance tactic had bled into the subject of his family. The few times Gael had mentioned Spain, Alejandro had tensed and changed the subject.

To say he was still aggressively opposed to tackling his past was an understatement.

Which was why she ground to a halt after entering the study of the Kensington mansion they'd rented for their week-long stay in London.

The brothers glared at each other across the large George V desk, the strewn papers indicating tempers had been fraying for a while.

'Umm...should I leave you two alone? I came to inform you that dinner with the Finance Minister is set for tonight, but I can go over the details later if you want?'

Alejandro's gaze locked on her for a studying minute. Rounding the desk, he shut the door and slid his arm around her waist.

His features remained pinched but his flashed smile was genuine. 'No, stay. My brother suffers from selective memory. Perhaps you should hear this, too, so I have a witness down the road the next time he feels like laying into me.'

Gael grimaced, but there was a whisper of apprehension in his expression as he eyed his brother. 'I'm just trying to get a picture of what it was like for you.'

'What good would it do to rehash everything?'

Gael shrugged. 'Maybe none. But if those three weeks I spent looking for my mother were anything like you claim yours were—'

'You think those three weeks were hell? I lived like that from the moment I was born until the day I walked away. Count yourself lucky you only got to spend a limited amount of time with our father, Gael. When he wasn't playing away, he taunted my mother with the possibility of it. When he did stray, she tortured herself and everyone around her with her desperate unhappiness.'

Elise's breath punched out in desperate sympathy.

Shock glinted in Gael's eyes. *'Madre de Dios.'*

Alejandro walked her over to the grouping of sofas set before a roaring fire in the oak-panelled room and pulled Elise down next to him. Gael joined them, settling on the opposite sofa.

November in London was picturesque and quintessentially autumnal, with a light drizzle hitting the giant Victorian windows. But as much as she wanted to stand at the window and absorb everything British, staying at Alejandro's side as he allowed his rigid facade to crack for a moment was the only place she wanted to be.

'If ever there were two people more unsuited to each other, it was them. I used to go to bed at night praying they would tell me in the morning that they were divorcing.' A rough laugh barked from his throat. The sound tore at Elise. Leaning closer, she placed a hand on his chest. After a moment, he absently covered hers with his.

'While children around the world wished upon stars that their parents would stay together through thick and thin, I yearned for the opposite. Both sets of my grandparents were dead, my remaining relatives were spread far and wide, but I didn't give a damn where I ended up. All I wanted was for the hell I lived in to be over.'

'Alejandro, you can't hate yourself for wishing for a better life. None of us can.'

He blinked, several emotions drifting through his eyes. 'What about hating one's own parents? Is that allowed?'

'*Sí*, it's allowed,' Gael uttered grimly.

Elise sensed he was going through his own issues regarding his parentage, but her only focus right then was Alejandro.

'The only person who can truly judge you is you. You're also the only one who can determine how the past influences you. You told me that, remember?'

He shook his head, his smile tinged with sadness. 'It's not the same, *amante*.'

She lifted her eyebrow. 'Isn't it?'

His eyes darkened. 'I won't be drawn into a debate, Elise. Not on this.' The warning was clear. His mind was made up about the subject. But he caught his brother's gaze from across the table. 'I admit, I made you into a villain, too, in that hellish reality, Gael. Back then, I believed you and your mother contributed to the problem.' He shook his head. 'But only one person is to blame for this. And it's not you.' His voice was solemn, his gaze as beseeching as an inherently proud and autocratic man could achieve.

Emotion rippled across Gael's face. He swallowed hard. Nodded silent acceptance. Then he surged to his feet and gathered up a sheaf of documents. 'I'll go through these before our meeting with the minister,' he said gruffly, then left the room.

'My father had wanted a son, someone he could pass on his well-honed cut-throat business skills to. Did I tell you that?' She spoke into the silence several minutes later.

Alejandro's chest rose and fell in a mildly frustrated manner. 'Elise...'

'My mother told me when I was twelve or thirteen and was refusing to wear some dress she'd bought me. I was a mistake my father convinced her to keep so he could pass on the family legacy. She'd refused to have any more children who would interrupt her career in prestige acquisition. They wanted a son and they got me instead. A daughter with ideals so far removed from theirs, I once heard them wonder out loud whether I was really their child.'

'Dios,' he swore under his breath.

'You're not the only one who wished for different parents. But what you feel in here—' she tapped his chest and the strong heart beating beneath it '—won't go away if you don't confront it.'

Green eyes pierced hers, probing. Suddenly afraid he would see too much, she dropped her gaze.

'Come here, Elise.'

Since she was already sitting pretty darn close, she wondered what he meant. He resolved her confusion by picking her up and settling her in his lap. His fingers removed the clasp in her hair and let the heavy tresses cascade around her face.

After pulling her into a long kiss, he set her back. *'Gracias,'* he murmured.

'What for?'

His expression grew brooding, introspective. 'I will know soon enough. But thank you,' he repeated.

Her heart lurched at the depth of emotion behind the

words. And even though she told herself it was futile to read anything into it, she found herself smiling.

'Okay.'

Emotion of a different, specific nature entered his eyes. His hand tightened at her waist as he devoured her smile. 'Feel like relocating upstairs for an hour or two before this meeting?' he rasped.

Her nod brought him to his feet. He didn't release her, instead walked out of the study and up to their bedroom with her locked in his arms.

And as he made love to her with a fevered, almost spiritual need, Elise wondered why she'd ever thought she could feel anything other than soul-searing love for this man.

Alejandro stilled in the act of securing his cufflink.

'Repeat that, if you please.'

Elise groaned and rolled her eyes, but it gratified him to see apprehension in her eyes. She was wise to be apprehensive. Because the words she'd just spoken threatened to rip a gaping hole somewhere in the region of his heart. He knew it couldn't be the actual organ that was affected, because that wasn't what they were dealing with here. Hearts and flowers and gentle words weren't part of their deal. Despite the decision he'd come to in the week since the study incident, those softer things would never feature in his life.

Nevertheless, a hole threatened. A deep black hole where emotions like desolation, despair, *pain* resided.

'Don't be upset, Alejandro. I made a promise. I have to keep it.'

He felt the ground beneath him shift. It was infinitesimal, but it registered. 'A promise?'

She sighed. 'Yes, you know those occasions where you pledge something and then you have to honour it?'

'I know the definition,' he murmured. 'I was very much aware of the existence of promises as a child but sadly I never got to experience anyone either making or keeping one.'

She paused in the act of tying the strings of a wraparound dress around her waist.

'I'm sorry, Alejandro.' Soft compassion blazed from her eyes and warmed him. Everything inside him strained to be closer to that sensation. To lose himself in it and let it wash away the cold loneliness that had been a part of him for so long he didn't remember a time when it hadn't existed.

'De nada,' he responded, aware his voice was gruff. Flicking his cuffs, he attempted to thread the links through again. Realising his hands shook, he slammed the studs on the dressing table. 'I'm still waiting for an explanation.'

'It's my grandmother's birthday this weekend. I always spend it with her. She expects me to be there.'

Alejandro noticed he was rubbing a precise spot on his chest where his heart thudded dully and transferred his fingers to the equally insistent throb at his temple. He had to tread carefully. He knew that. The last thing he wanted was to be drawn into an argument with Elise. But... 'She's in Hawaii, correct?'

She nodded warily.

'And I...' He searched for words that wouldn't make him feel so raw...so *exposed*. In the end the words poured out regardless. 'I need you here,' he rasped.

She crossed the dressing room and stopped in front of him. Her hand slid up his chest to curl around his nape. 'I'm sorry I can't come with you to Seville. But you were always going to make this final journey on your own anyway.'

His jaw clenched. *'Sí*, but not while you were on the other side of the world!'

'Alejandro—'

He whirled away from her, unable to stand having her in front of him and knowing it was only for a short time. Striding through the bedroom, he stepped out onto the warm terrace.

On the horizon, the sun was setting over the hills just outside Barcelona. During one of their recent and increasingly frequent talks, Gael had spoken of his estate outside

Barcelona and the neighbouring property that had just come on the market.

Alejandro had bought the fifty-thousand-acre estate, sight unseen. When Gael had thrown in the offer of his architect and interior designer, Alejandro had agreed.

His first visit to his property three days ago had been a pleasant surprise, especially when Elise had seemed to love the estate, too.

The whitewashed villa was vast, with staggered floors on three levels, each with a wraparound terrace that over-looked a private beach. It was a house that had a potential to be a home.

From a personal standpoint, it had been a place to pause and regroup before taking the final step back in time.

Because as Elise had counselled, he had to revisit the past in order to move on. Some aspects of his childhood had left scars he was certain would never heal, but he needed to find out if other building blocks he'd thought were eroded were in fact merely shrouded with bitterness.

Things like love and trust...

Alejandro knew he most likely wouldn't find those two components in his childhood home, but perhaps freeing him-self from other entanglements would open his eyes to new experiences.

New emotions?

But how could he see his way to finding answers when Elise was leaving? *Dios.* He rubbed at his chest when he sensed her behind him.

'We're going to be late to the dinner with the vintner.'

'We're not going.'

She sighed. 'Why not?'

He turned and leaned against the terrace wall, his back to the view. Right now the only view he was interested in was the one before him. 'Because he's another fat cat hoping to get fatter by riding on Atlas's coattails. He can wait one more day. Whereas you...' He stalked to where she stood, her stunning face glowing in the evening light.

'Yes…me?' she invited huskily.

He wrapped his hands loosely around her throat, sliding his thumbs under her chin to tilt her face up to his. 'You are making me *extremely* unhappy with your impending departure,' he said.

Her breath hitched and her arms slid around his waist. 'And you mean to punish me?' she asked.

Alejandro was marginally satisfied with the raw anticipation on her face. She wanted him with almost as much intensity as he craved her. It wasn't anywhere near enough, but that would have to sustain him in her absence.

'Yes, I do.' He pulled on the ties to her dress none too gently, and tugged the material from her body, leaving her clad in scraps of black lace. Alejandro wasn't worried about exposing her to unwelcome eyes. The position of the terrace guaranteed them complete privacy. As he stepped back his knees nearly buckled at her beauty. 'Your punishment will be very specific, *guapa*. And very, very thorough.'

He dispensed with foreplay, his need soul-wrenchingly acute. He left her only to locate a condom. When he returned, he placed her on her knees, dispensed of his clothes, and took her hard and fast. Groans turned to earthy demands, moans to cries of ecstasy. Somewhere in the middle of it all, Alejandro acknowledged that he would never get enough of her.

Hours later, he tucked her close, his fingers teasing through her hair as sweat cooled on their bodies.

She had given back as good as he dished out, but he knew the depth of his lovemaking tonight had worn her out. Her soft breathing told him she was almost asleep. A part of him wanted to keep the status quo. But a greater part of him felt the need to relax the reins of his control for her, even if it made him vulnerable.

'I'd never experienced jealousy before I met you. Now I'm jealous of every single moment you'll spend away from me.'

A soft gasp broke from her. 'Alejandro.'

'How long?' he grated. He kept his gaze fixed on the

ceiling, absurdly unwilling to risk looking into her eyes in that moment.

'Three days. Four at the most.'

He swallowed hard. 'Take my plane.'

'What? No, you need it—'

'Gael arrives tomorrow. He'll no doubt resume his efforts to remain a pain in my backside. He can fly me down to Seville on Saturday.'

'I—'

He captured a handful of silky hair. 'Say "thank you, Alejandro."'

'Thank you, *Oh, Bossy One.*'

He kissed her, because the time had long since passed when he could resist her. As passion whipped high and fierce again, Alejandro wondered if it was past time to stop trying to save his heart from bigger, riskier things, as well.

He ended up catching a commercial flight to Seville when Gael got caught up in an emergency. The mundane nature of it all helped keep his mind off the impending visit. And off the sheer intensity with which he missed Elise.

There were more satellite factories to set up and contracts to negotiate with new businesses, but from the start there'd been an unspoken agreement between them that this affair would only last for the duration of her contract with him.

Which meant that she would be gone in a few weeks. Or it had been that way. Until he'd woken this morning with a physical pain in his chest from missing her.

Alejandro didn't have anything to compare these emotions to, but whatever he felt for her, he knew he wasn't ready to walk away. And their goodbye in his plane two days ago had given him hope that she felt the same way.

All he had to do was lay a few ghosts to rest—

'Andro.'

He stopped in his tracks. The voice. The name. *Dios*, it dragged him back to a place he suddenly doubted he wanted to go.

Slowly he turned to his left. And exhaled at the sight of his father.

A tumult of emotions tore through him, cracking open places he'd thought were sealed for ever. *'Papá.'*

Tomas Aguilar held out his hand. Alejandro hesitated for a moment, then stepped forward and took it.

'We need to talk.'

The older man, who despite his greying hair and slightly stooped posture still turned female heads, nodded. *'Sí,* I don't imagine you came all this way just to sample the sangria.' He looked down at Alejandro's empty hand. 'No bags?'

'I'm not staying.'

Regret and sadness passed through his father's eyes. Although he steeled himself against it, Alejandro was buoyed by that show of emotion.

The sudden need to find *some* redeemable quality within himself didn't pass without ironic notice. He followed his father into the cool sunshine.

The ride to his childhood home was conducted mostly in silence. When his father drew up in front of the villa, Alejandro couldn't bring himself to step out.

The two-storey structure had been modernised over the years, a fresh coat of paint added recently. But it was still the same home where he'd witnessed and known despair and desolation. Where he'd lived in fear of flying missiles and broken trust.

'You won't find the answers you need sitting in the car, Andro. You may not even find answers inside, but at least make the attempt.'

His father got out and rounded the bonnet. Sucking in a breath, Alejandro followed suit. As they neared the front door it opened. A half-sob, half-gasp sounded from within a second before his mother appeared.

Evita Aguilar had aged with grace. And despite the similar sadness that lurked in her eyes, she carried herself with a quiet pride.

'Andro, *mi chico,'* she murmured. She held out her arms.

He stepped into the embrace, and felt another crack in his chest. He allowed himself to be drawn inside, bustled over and fed.

But eventually, his restlessness resurfaced. His father grabbed a bottle of wine, his mother brought glasses and they settled on the small terrace that abutted the garden.

As it happened, Alejandro didn't need to ask the questions burning in his heart.

'We made your life hell,' his father said gravely.

'Yes,' he responded.

Tomas glanced at his wife and the look they shared jarred something harder within Alejandro. 'We had access to marriage counsellors, and divorce courts. Perhaps you want to know why we never made use of them.'

Alejandro swallowed hard, the shame at admitting his secret wish profound. 'Yes.'

'That answer is simple. We stayed together because we love each other. Despite the tumult. Despite it not making sense to others, even sometimes to us.' Tomas reached for his wife's hand. 'No one has the right to judge us, or tell us how to love. Time and wisdom have helped us see the light in some ways, but in other ways we wouldn't change a thing. So if you came here seeking rationality, or a straightforward, risk-free way to love your woman—and I know all this is because of a woman; you're my son after all—we have no answers for you. You'll have to find your own way.'

Shock scythed through Alejandro, followed closely by an absurd understanding. He didn't know if what he felt for Elise was love, but it was certainly beyond his comprehension. And he'd been prepared to risk a business deal in order to hang on to it.

He didn't know what his next steps would be, but he was willing to take the leap. A knot in his gut eased and his next breath came easier.

'There are some things that we never forgave ourselves for, though,' his mother said, her hazel eyes pleading with his. 'We should've made sure you knew you were loved. I should've protected you more from my...insecurities. Losing you the way we did...' A sob caught in her throat and his father passed her a tissue.

'We probably have no right to ask you for forgiveness. But we would like you to consider it,' his father said.

Alejandro swallowed again to displace the rock in his throat. Rising, he bent down and kissed his mother's cheek. 'I'll consider it, *Mamá*. Goodbye.'

She caught and held on to his hand. 'Will...will I see you again?'

He'd taken Elise's advice. He'd confronted his past and had found a modicum of understanding.

The apple doesn't fall far from the tree. In some ways that was true.

Some apples fall far enough. In other ways that was also true.

'Yes, you'll see me again.'

CHAPTER FOURTEEN

ALEJANDRO RESISTED THE URGE to catch a flight to Hawaii and returned to Chicago instead.

Twenty-four hours. Elise would be back in his bed before nightfall tomorrow. It was a thought that kept him marginally sane, although Elise sending back his plane because she felt bad about it 'just sitting there doing nothing' irritated him in the extreme.

He looked up from the document he'd read for the last half-hour without taking a single word in, and accepted the espresso Sergio set before him.

'Do we know the weather forecast for Hawaii at this time of year? You haven't heard of any cyclones or tornados reported in that part of the world, have you?'

'No, *señor*. As far as I know the weather is copacetic over there.'

Alejandro tossed back the espresso. 'Good. She's been gone a week. I don't want anything interrupting her flight back.'

'Uh, she's been gone three days, *señor*.'

Alejandro glared at him and rose from the dining table. 'Don't you have something to be getting on with?'

He ignored his butler's sly smirk as he headed out to his car.

Three hours later he was reading the same document in his office, without success. He'd instituted a 'No calls bar Elise's' policy with Margo, but with each minute his phone remained silent, his irritation grew.

He abandoned reading when Margo knocked and offered to get his lunch. His *no* was a touch less than polite.

'Apologies, Margo. Thanks, but I'm not hungry,' he tried again. She nodded and turned to leave.

'Are you sure my phone is working?' he demanded.

She frowned. 'Um…yes, I think so.'

'You *think* so? Get the IT guys down here to take a look, would you?'

She cleared her throat. 'There's nothing wrong with your phone, sir. I'm *sure* of it.'

Alejandro picked up his cell phone and checked it. Full signal. He tossed it back.

'She's been gone for a week. Would it kill her to call at least *once* today?' he muttered.

'Sir…she's been gone three days.'

A tic throbbed at his temple. 'Why does everyone feel the need to keep correcting me?' he snapped.

Margo hid a grin and hurried out.

Alejandro's mood had in no way improved when he left his office to attend a meeting mid-afternoon. His half a dozen calls to Elise had gone straight to voicemail. And he'd realised that at no point had he thought it prudent to take her grandmother's number.

What use were all the introspection and realisations he'd come to if he couldn't share them with her immediately? And why wasn't she missing him enough to call him umpteen times the way his exes used to? A sludge of shame welled at the unkind thought.

He loved Elise because she was like no other.

Alejandro stilled on his way out of the business tower where his meeting had taken place and let the words sink in.

He loved her…

With every pump of his heart, the truth blazed brighter. Sheer, unadulterated emotion charged through him. For the first time in his life, he let it in and felt a rush so strong, so deep, he feared his heart would expire from the fullness.

He couldn't lie—it scared him. But on the flip side, it had the potential to fulfil him as nothing ever had in his life.

He just needed Elise back. Now. Reaching into his pocket, he pulled out his phone. He dialled, held the phone to his ear.

Someone bumped into him. 'Sorry, excuse me.'

Alejandro smiled, his newfound outlook on life allowing him to be accommodating. 'Elise, *Madre de Dios*, pick up—'

The words died in his throat as he stared across the vast, busy foyer to the trendy restaurant housed within the building.

It was Elise. Even on the extremely unlikely chance that his eyesight deceived him, her smile and accompanying laugh a second later reached inside him and touched the heart he'd discovered moments ago belonged to her.

Alejandro dragged his gaze from her face to stare down at his phone. It was ringing. It hadn't gone to voicemail like before. He looked back up in time to see her make the *one second* signal at her lunch companion. She reached into her bag, took out her phone. Saw his number, and dropped it back.

Ice drenched him from head to toe. In all his life, Alejandro had never felt the fear or desolation that struck his heart in that moment. He'd dared to take the risk, even before he knew he loved her. The knowledge of exactly what he felt for her made the heartache a million times worse. He stood there. He stared.

And he knew why his world had turned to ash.

She talked. She flipped her hair. Her smile was radiance itself.

Bile rose in his gut, threatened to choke him. Almost on automatic, he called again.

It went straight to voicemail.

Alejandro turned and walked out into the sunshine on numb legs.

He was sitting in the dark sitting room *two hours* later when he heard the click of the electronic lock. He'd given Sergio the night off to save the butler from the fallout of his impending devastation.

She sailed in and dropped her small suitcase on the floor.

'Honey, I'm home!' She giggled. She *giggled*. 'I've always wanted to say that ridiculous line.'

Her handbag followed and she hurried across the room to where he sat, an empty whisky glass clutched in his hand.

'Oh, Alejandro, I missed you so much!' She launched herself into his arms, knocking the glass to the floor. Her arms slid around his neck and her head slanted towards his. His breath snagged painfully, his insides going from ice-cold to furnace-hot just from the scent of her. 'Enough to change my flight to an earlier one. Enough to ignore why you're sitting here, drinking in the dark. I don't care why. I need to kiss you. Right now.'

Her mouth latched onto his. And in the second between killing himself to pull away and completing the act, he noted her confidence, her skill at kissing. The enticing way she moved her body over him. Just the way he'd taught her.

He wanted to latch on hard. He wanted to bind himself to her so she could never be free of him.

But he couldn't.

He ripped his head away from her, his arms holding her back.

'We need to talk, Elise.'

Her mouth went slack, her eyes widening into pools of shock before she composed herself and nodded. Climbing from his lap, she took a seat across from him. 'No good thing ever came from those words, but okay. Shoot.'

Alejandro had had enough time to run through several thousand scenarios of how this would go. For a thousand different reasons he'd discarded all of them.

'This isn't working for me.' False words. *Freeing* words.

Her breath audibly caught, and her hand rose to rest over her heart before she swallowed hard. 'Right. I… Okay. I… wish you'd emailed or texted me or something. I wouldn't have bothered you here…' Her chin dropped down, her hair momentarily shielding her face as she toyed with her fingers.

'Breaking up by text is uncouth.'

A sharp laugh barked from her. '*Uncouth?* Okay. Well, I wouldn't know. This is my first break-up.' She winced.

Alejandro grimaced, then got ahold of himself. He was doing this for *her*.

Then why did he feel as if he'd cut out his own heart?

Because he had.

She jumped up. 'Well, I guess that's it, then.'

He surged to his feet. *'That's it?'* His world was to end without so much as a thunderclap?

Eyes filled with hurt and the beginnings of anger finally met his. 'Why, what do you expect? Funeral bagpipes? Sorry, you'll have to be disappointed—'

'I saw you today,' he flung at her. 'At the Woodbine Building.'

She frowned for a second, then her face cleared. 'And?'

'And? You expect an addendum to that?'

Her eyes misted, but she blinked quickly. 'Only if you think I'm owed one. This is your show after all. But maybe you'll allow me three guesses? I saw you at the Woodbine Building having lunch, *and* you have spinach in your teeth so maybe you should go brush? Or, *and* I love the dress you're wearing but I've missed you like crazy and I'm dying to make love to you so I'm going to rip it off right now? Or is it more like, *and* I don't trust you, not even for one hot little second, so *sayonara* and have a nice life?'

Alejandro opened his mouth to give voice to the terrible pain tearing at his insides, but it was as if his vocal cords were suddenly paralysed.

'No answer? Fine, have it your way.' She stormed out of the living room towards the bedroom they'd shared for the last six weeks.

Alejandro charged after her. Only to stop when he found her frozen in the doorway. She whirled around when she sensed him. 'I...I can't go in there. I know this is absurd, but this is my first break-up. I'm not handling it well. If it isn't too much trouble, have my things put into storage...somewhere. I'll text you a forwarding address once I have one.'

She headed for him, making sure to keep a distance between them.

The words tore from his throat. 'I trust you.'

She froze. 'What?'

'You think this is about my lack of trust. But that's just

it. I trust you with my life. But I don't know if you can trust me with yours.'

'What on earth are you talking about?'

'I barely noticed who you were having lunch with. But I saw you look at your phone. And ignore my call. It may be irrational to you, but the thought that I might never be enough for you… You know why I never asked you about Jason?'

Numbly, she shook her head.

'I was terrified you'd say you'd compared us and decided he was a better bet,' he divulged. 'I don't want to know what happened with him after I left. All I know is that I had to come and find you. I dragged you back to Chicago with the knowledge that for whatever reason, you chose him. And then I found out you were back, in Montana, and that you *stayed away* after coming back.'

'Alejandro—!'

'I can't do that to you any more. I'm obsessed with you, Elise. I know what that kind of obsession can do. I saw it with my parents. Their love may not make much sense to me, but it's the version they're happy with. I've been sitting in the dark, trying to imagine what our version would be. And in each one, I can't help but see me hurting you. With my jealousy. With my possessiveness. Hell, I want you all the time! I tried to find answers from my parents. The best I got was that love doesn't make sense. That's not good enough. I can't risk you like that. So I thought I'd spare us both the messiness that would come later.'

She absorbed his words, then nodded. 'Okay. I get it. It makes sense.' She started to walk away again.

Naked fear gripped him. 'Elise!'

'Yes, Alejandro?'

'I… *Por favor*…say something.'

'Sorry, I have nothing. You make a sound case. I can't compete with all the bad things that might happen to us in the future.'

He frowned. 'But…you came back from Hawaii early.'

'Yes.'

'Because you missed me?'

'Like crazy.'

He slashed a frustrated hand through his hair. 'Then why didn't you call?'

'I turned my phone to flight mode, then forgot to turn it back on until I was on the subway. Before I could call you, I got a message from one of the five manga publishers I'd sent my sketches to. They'd been trying to reach me. I called them back. They were interested and wanted to meet me right away. I agreed to a meet. He wanted to go through each story with me. I was in the middle of begging him to reschedule our meeting for another time when you called. I ignored your call because I was already being rude and I couldn't tell whether he would accommodate me or not. After an hour and a half, I came clean and told him I missed the man I love and wanted to get back to him. This guy got engaged two weeks ago, so he's all about true love. Of course, I hightailed it here only for you to break up with me. You want to know the real reason I kissed Jason?'

His heart stuttered, the vice around his chest so painful with the glaring loss he'd brought on himself that he couldn't breathe. 'No, but go on.'

'I kissed him because it was the only way I could think of to stop myself from falling deeper in love with you. You said your heart wasn't made to love. I believed you. But I knew it wouldn't stop me from loving you. I was trying to think of how to stop my heart from breaking when Jason found me. The kiss was stupid. I hated every second of it. But seeing you walk away…that was the worst moment of my life. Until Montana. I didn't have to come back with you. I could've let you sue me. But I loved you. I still love you. So tell me, Alejandro, what am I supposed to do with all this love I have bursting in my heart for you, when you're so ready to throw us away?' she whispered, her voice a ragged caricature of its normal strength.

'Elise… *Dios mio*… Elise. What have I done?' He'd blown it. He knew it in the depths of his soul. He reached for her.

She jerked out of his way, her flared hands holding him at bay. 'No. You want to protect *yourself*. That's fine. Believe it or not, I understand.' This time she didn't turn. She walked backwards, righting herself when she bumped into the console table or a wall.

He followed, because not following would be the same as dying. 'Elise, please listen to me. I wanted to protect *you*. From a love that already feels too much.'

Her backward retreat halted, and the blood drained from her face. 'What?'

'I love you, *dulce mia*. So much. *Too much*. That's the problem!'

Her brow furrowed. 'How can love ever be too much?'

'It can, Elise. I've seen it.' He shook his head, unwilling to risk anything that would make her retreat farther. But how could he not state his deepest fear? 'It can turn ugly. It would kill me if I did that to you.'

She shook her head. 'You won't,' she said, and her voice held a core of steel that made him want to believe her. Almost.

He dragged a hand down his face, trying desperately to calm the panicked pants heaving from him.

'Alejandro.'

He stilled. *'Sí?'*

'The version you're talking about is nothing more than a twisted obsession. If your parents are okay with that, then all you can do is give them your blessing. But the love I want, the one I want to *give* you, is about offering you the best of myself, letting you be the best of *yourself*. Does that include going out of your way to hurt me?'

'No. *Never*,' he breathed.

'Are you willing to give us a chance?'

His heart tripped, the possibilities making him dizzy. 'I want nothing more than to treasure you, *amante*. Every second of every day. I know I handled this all wrong, but if you think we can do this... *Dios*, I'll *do* it. But I admit, I'm terrified. I realised how much I loved you seconds before I saw you. It was no excuse, but from the moment we met I felt as if I stood on a ledge, the sensation of losing my footing a credible threat. But today I realised I'd been looking down, making myself dizzy with distractions when I should've been focusing on what was right in front of me. On you, and on the heights we could achieve together...I'm sorry, *mi amor*. So very sorry.'

Her face crumpled for a fleeting second, and she swallowed. 'God, Alejandro, you ripped my heart out,' she cried.

He lunged for her, dropped to his knees and gripped her hips. 'Forgive me. Please, *Dios mio*, I'm the world's biggest fool. I love you. Please give me another chance?'

Her hand slowly reached out. Touched his brow. His hair. When she traced his cheek, he captured it and kissed her palm. 'I forgive you.'

His groan of relief was hoarse with unshed emotion.

'And, Alejandro?'

'Yes?'

'I love you, too.'

Elise dropped to join him on the floor, her pounding heart now, thankfully, beating from love and bliss, and not the terrifying pain of losing the love of her life. Their kiss held relief, joy, passion, and above all, love. After a lifetime of kissing, he stood and carried her to their bedroom, where he showed her with word and deed how much he loved and cherished her.

As they were drifting into blissful sleep a thought popped into her head.

'Umm, Alejandro?'

'*Si, mi amor?*' His voice was a lazy, sexy drawl that heated her blood and flooded her with pleasure in all the right places.

'I quit as your PR consultant. As of Thursday morning, I hope to have a new and shiny career.'

'Damn.' His fingers drifted over her skin, his caresses gentle and loving. 'Can I tempt you with another offer?'

She raised her head, stared into mossy green eyes burning with pure, everlasting love. 'That depends. Does it come with perks to die for?'

'No, it comes with perks to *live* for. Perks to love and cherish, in sickness and in health, until the heavens grant us eternal life amongst the stars.'

Tears stormed her eyes. For the longest time she couldn't breathe. Or speak. 'Alejandro,' she whispered.

His hands framed her face, and he stared deep into her heart. 'Marry me, Elise.'

'Yes. Until eternity.'

* * * * *

Maya Blake's RIVAL BROTHERS
duet continues with
ONE NIGHT WITH GAEL
Available November 2016

If you enjoyed this story,
check out these other great reads
from Maya Blake:
THE DI SIONE SECRET BABY
SIGNED OVER TO SANTINO
A DIAMOND DEAL WITH THE GREEK
BRUNETTI'S SECRET SON
Available now!

MILLS & BOON®

MODERN™

POWER, PASSION AND IRRESISTIBLE TEMPTATION

A sneak peek at next month's titles...

In stores from 20th October 2016:

- **Di Sione's Virgin Mistress** – Sharon Kendrick *and*
  A Diamond for Del Rio's Housekeeper –
  Susan Stephens
- **The Italian's Christmas Child** – Lynne Graham *and*
  Snowbound with His Innocent Temptation –
  Cathy Williams

In stores from 3rd November 2016:

- **Claiming His Christmas Consequence** – Michelle Smart
  and **Married for the Italian's Heir** – Rachael Thomas
- **One Night with Gael** – Maya Blake *and*
  Unwrapping His Convenient Fiancée – Melanie Milburne

Just can't wait?
Buy our books online a month before they hit the shops!
www.millsandboon.co.uk

Also available as eBooks.

MILLS & BOON®

EXCLUSIVE EXCERPT

Dante Di Sione can't believe the beautiful blonde
who 'accidentally' stole his family's tiara is blackmailing him – for a date to her sister's wedding!
If Willow wants to be his fake fiancée, she'll
have to play the part to the full. Only Willow's
confidence is fake…and she's a virgin!

Read on for a sneak preview of
DI SIONE'S VIRGIN MISTRESS
the fifth in the unmissable new eight book Modern series
THE BILLIONAIRE'S LEGACY

"I'm sorry. I'm out of here."

"Dante…"

"No. Listen to me, Willow." There was a pause while
he seemed to be composing himself, and when he
started speaking, his words sounded very controlled.
"For what it's worth, I think you're lovely. Very lovely.
A beautiful butterfly of a woman. But I'm not going
to have sex with you."

She swallowed. "Because you don't want me?"

His voice grew rough. "You know damned well I
want you."

She lifted her eyes to his. "Then why?"

He seemed to hesitate and Willow got the distinct
feeling that he was going to say something dismissive,
or tell her that he didn't owe her any kind of explanation.

But to her surprise, he didn't. His expression took on that almost gentle look again and she found herself wanting to hurl something at him…preferably herself. To tell him not to wrap her up in cotton wool the way everyone else did. To treat her like she was made of flesh and blood instead of something fragile and break-able. To make her feel like that passionate woman he'd brought to life in his arms.

"Because I'm the kind of man who brings women pain, and you've probably had enough of that in your life. Don't make yourself the willing recipient of any more." He met the question in her eyes. "I'm incapable of giving women what they want and I'm not talking about sex. I don't do emotion, or love, or commitment, because I don't really know how those things work. When people tell me that I'm cold and unfeeling, I don't get offended—because I know it's true. There's nothing deep about me, Willow—and there never will be."

Don't miss
DI SIONE'S VIRGIN MISTRESS
by Sharon Kendrick

Available November 2016

www.millsandboon.co.uk

MILLS & BOON®

Why shop at millsandboon.co.uk?

Each year, thousands of romance readers find their perfect read at millsandboon.co.uk. That's because we're passionate about bringing you the very best romantic fiction. Here are some of the advantages of shopping at www.millsandboon.co.uk:

* **Get new books first**—you'll be able to buy your favourite books one month before they hit the shops

* **Get exclusive discounts**—you'll also be able to buy our specially created monthly collections, with up to 50% off the RRP

* **Find your favourite authors**—latest news, interviews and new releases for all your favourite authors and series on our website, plus ideas for what to try next

* **Join in**—once you've bought your favourite books, don't forget to register with us to rate, review and join in the discussions

Visit **www.millsandboon.co.uk**
for all this and more today!